DROWNED WORLDS

Tales from the Anthropocene and Beyond

– Edited by Jonathan Strahan –

ALSO EDITED BY JONATHAN STRAHAN

DROWNED WORLDS

Tales from the Anthropocene and Beyond

– Edited by Jonathan Strahan –

First published 2016 by Solaris
an imprint of Rebellion Publishing Ltd,
Riverside House, Osney Mead,
Oxford, OX2 0ES, UK

www.solarisbooks.com

US ISBN 978-1-78108-451-9
UK ISBN 978-1-78108-450-2

10 9 8 7 6 5 4 3 2 1

A CIP catalogue record for this book is available from the
British Library.

Designed & typeset by Rebellion Publishing

Printed in Denmark by Nørhaven

ACKNOWLEDGEMENTS

THIS IS THE tenth book I've done with Jonathan Oliver, Ben Smith and the team at Solaris Books. It's been a pleasure and a privilege. I'd like to thank them for taking the risks they have with the books we've done, and for giving me the freedom to do the books I've wanted to do. I will always be grateful to them for stepping in and for believing in the books and in me. Special thanks to my agent Howard Morhaim who for over a decade now has had my back and helped make good things happen. Finally, most special thanks of all to Marianne, Jessica, and Sophie. I always say that every moment spent working on these books is stolen from them, but it's true, and I'm forever grateful to them for their love, support and generosity.

CONTENTS

INTRODUCTION
– Jonathan Strahan –

IN EARLY JANUARY of 2014 I read J.G. Ballard's landmark disaster novel, *The Drowned World*, for the first time. The book had just been published in a beautiful collector's edition and for some reason reading about it prompted me to buy a copy online. It's a lush, powerful book that tells of a post-apocalyptic world where rising levels of solar radiation cause the polar ice-caps to melt and worldwide temperatures to soar, leaving northern Europe and America cities submerged in beautiful and haunting tropical lagoons. It's one of the great British disaster novels, with more than a taste of the work of Graham Greene to it, all seen through a romantic haze that hangs over the flooded, inundated ruins of a world laid waste by raising oceans.

A few years earlier I'd been charmed, which is probably the wrong word but it comes close enough, by Paul McAuley's "The Choice", a powerful and beautifully written novella set in a flooded Norfolk, England, which has been inundated by rising sea levels. In the story a young boy sails a small boat across the flooded countryside in search of rumours of an alien vessel landed nearby. Reading *The Drowned World* reminded me of "The Choice", which in turn led me for no particular reason back to Kim Stanley Robinson's *The Wild Shore*. In no time, after finishing *The Drowned World* and re-reading "The Choice", I found myself pulling Robinson's debut novel off the shelf for the first time in nearly thirty years and getting lost in the story of a young boy growing up in a post-apocalyptic United States, though in this case an apocalypse caused by nuclear war.

Reading of these post-apocalyptic worlds, something that has always been close to the heart of science fiction, and in particular reading of these drowned and inundated futures, made me think. I'd just finished compiling my annual best of the year anthology and, as I always complain, I was stuck in the middle of Western Australia's long hot summer. There was a book in here, a set of tales to be told. A book, I said to my editor, which could explore, or at least discuss, how we sit poised on the precipice of one of the greatest ecological disasters to face humanity. As Ballard saw so presciently in the pages of *The Drowned World*, our world *is* warming and the seas *are* rising. While small islands are threatened now, one day soon London could be a submerged sargasso, Manhattan could be besieged by storms, and Australia be nothing more than a distant dusty memory of climatological loss. We are, it has become clear, living in the Anthropocene, that time when human actions start to have significant impact on the Earth's geology and ecosystems. It is a time of darkness and disaster, and it's a time we have to face, to confront, and to combat. There will be triumphs among the disasters, humanity among the apocalypse, and those are the stories that could appear in the right book. And my editor agreed, and so the book you are now holding was born.

I did what I usually do when that happens, and asked some wonderful writers to create stories set in drowned and inundated futures, in the possibly shattered worlds of the later Anthropocene, or in any drowned world they could imagine. As the agreements to write came in, Australia's Commonwealth Scientific and Industrial Research Organization published a report that said that the city I live in, Perth, was likely to be become the first Australian city to be abandoned due to climate change. Population levels are climbing dramatically, the environment is heating every year, ultraviolet radiation levels are typically extreme in the summer, rainfall levels are falling so quickly that more water currently evaporates from dams than runs off into them, we survive on desalinated ocean water, and are forced to pump water from underground aquifers back into the ocean to stop them from becoming poisoned by rising sea waters. They gave us until 2050, which seems frighteningly close.

It made it even clearer to me that this is one of the single biggest issues facing our world, and facing writers who want to discuss the future. What is happening to our world? How will we survive? Will we survive? And how will we remain human through it all? Will we turn into the desperate and debased people of a penny dreadful zombie apocalypse, or will we find better ways to cope? The fifteen writers who answered my call have, as you will soon see, answered those questions in different ways. Some have looked into the abyss and seen the worst in us; some have found clean, technological solutions to the problems we face; and some have jumped hundreds of years into the future, moving past the terrible times of transition to show us new worlds that are hotter, wetter and less populous that the one we know now. Some of these stories are serious, some are not. One looks at a parched future in a desert land, one of global warming's worst gifts. None of them are the way forward. Each of them, though, is part of asking the question of how we move forward from here, and show that, for all that the challenges of the Anthropocene are terrifying and overwhelming, they are challenges we will have to face together.

As always, I hope you'll find these stories as rewarding and enjoyable as I have. I hope they'll entertain you, make you think a little, and perhaps move you to action.

Jonathan Strahan
Perth, Western Australia
March 2016 (34 years before the Abandonment)

ELVES OF ANTARCTICA
– PAUL MCAULEY –

MIKE TORRES SAW his first elf stone three weeks after he moved to the Antarctic Peninsula. He was flying helos on supply runs from Square Bay on the Falliéres Coast to kelp farms in the fjords to the north, and in his free time had taken to hiking along the shore or into the bare hills beneath Mount Diamond's pyramidal peak. Up there, he had terrific views of the rugged islands standing in the cold blue sea under the high summer sun, Mount Wilson and Mount Metcalfe rising beyond the south side of the bay, and the entirety of the town stretched along the shore below. Its industrial sprawl and grids of trailer homes, the rake of its docks, the plantations of bladeless wind turbines, and the airfield with helos coming and going like bees, two or three blimps squatting in front of their hangars, and the runway where a cargo plane, an old Airbus Beluga maybe, or a Globemaster V with its six engines and tail tall as a five-storey building, might be preparing to make its lumbering run towards the sky. All of it ugly, intrusive and necessary: the industrial underbelly of a project that was attempting to prevent the collapse of Antarctica's western ice sheet. It was serious business. It was saving the world. And Mike Torres was part of it.

He was a second-generation climate change refugee, born into the Marshall Islands diaspora community in Auckland. A big, quiet guy who'd survived a tough childhood – his father drinking himself to death, his mother taking two jobs to raise him and his sisters in their tiny central city apartment. Age sixteen, Mike had been part of a small all-city crew spraying tags everywhere on Auckland's transport system; after his third conviction for criminal damage (a big throwie at Remuera Railway Station), a sympathetic magistrate had offered him a spell of workfare on a city farm instead of juvenile prison. He discovered that he loved the outdoor life, earned his helicopter pilot's licence at one of the sheep stations on the high pastures of North Island, where little Robinson R33s were used to muster sheep, and five years later went to work for Big Green, one of the transnational ecological remediation companies, at the Lake Eyre Basin project in Australia.

Desalinated seawater had been pumped into the desert basin to create an inland sea, greening the land around it and removing a small fraction of the excess water that had swollen the world's oceans; Big Green had a contract to establish shelter-belt forests to stabilise and protect the edge of the new farmland. Mike loved watching the machines at work: dozers, dumper trucks and 360° excavators that levelled the ground and spread topsoil; mechanical planters that set out rows of tree seedlings at machine-gun speed, and truck spades that transplanted semi-mature fishtail, atherton and curly palms, acacia, eucalyptus and sheoak trees. In one direction, stony scrub and fleets of sand dunes stretched towards dry mountains floating in heat shimmer; in the other, green checkerboards of rice paddies and date and oil palm plantations descended stepwise towards the shore of the sea. The white chip of a ferry ploughing a wake in blue water. A string of cargo blimps crossing the sky. Fleets of clouds strung at the horizon, generated by climate stations on artificial islands. Everything clean and fresh. A new world in the making.

Mike hauled supplies to the crews who ran the big machines and the gangers who managed the underplanting of shrubs and grasses, brought in engineers and replacement parts, flew key personnel and VIPs to and fro. He sent most of his pay packet home, part of it squirrelled into a savings account, part supporting his mother and his sisters, part tithed to the Marshallese Reclamation Movement, which planned to rebuild the nation by raising artificial islands above the drowned atoll of Majuro. A group of reclaimers had established a settlement there, occupying the top floors of the President's house and a couple of office buildings they had storm-proofed. Mike religiously watched their podcasts, and liked to trawl through archives that documented life before the flood, rifling through clips of beach parties, weddings, birthdays and fishing trips from old family videos, freezing and enlarging glimpses of the bustle of ordinary life. A farmer's market, a KFC, a one-dollar store, a shoal of red taxis on Majuro's main drag, kids playing football on a green field at the edge of the blue sea. Moments repossessed from the gone world.

He watched short films about exploration of the drowned ruins, feeds from web cams showing bright fish patrolling the reefs of sunken condos and shops. The reclaimers were attempting to construct a breakwater with fast-growing edited corals, and posted plans for the village of floating houses that was the next stage of the project. Mike dreamed of moving there one day, of making a new life in a new land, but places in the reclaimer community were fiercely contested. He'd had to dig into his savings to get his mother the stem cell therapy she needed for a heart problem, and one of his sisters became engaged, soon there would be a wedding to pay for... So when the contract at Lake Eyre finished, Mike signed up for a new project in the Antarctic Peninsula.

Lake Eyre had created a place where refugees from the drowning coasts could start afresh. The engineering projects run out of the Antarctic Peninsula were part of an attempt to preserve the continent's last big ice sheet and prevent another catastrophic rise in ocean levels, the loss of half-drowned cities and land reclaimed from previous floods, and the displacement of more than sixty per cent of the world's population. Factories and industrial plants on the peninsula supported a variety of massive geoengineering projects, from manufacturing fleets of autonomous high-albedo rafts that would cool ocean currents by reflecting sunlight, to creating a thin layer of dust in the lower stratosphere that would reflect a significant percentage of the sun's light and heat back into space. One project was attempting to cool ice sheets by growing networks of superconducting threads that would syphon away geothermal heat. Another was attempting to protect glaciers from the heat of the sun by covering them in huge sheets of thermally reflective material.

Square Bay's factories used biomass supplied by the kelp farms to manufacture the tough thin material used in the thermal blanket project. As a bonus, the fast-growing edited strains of kelp sequestered carbon dioxide from the atmosphere, contributing to attempts to reverse the rise in levels that had driven the warming in the first place. It was good work, no doubt, the sharp end of a massive effort to ameliorate the effects of two centuries of unchecked industrialisation and fossil carbon burning, but many thought that it was too little, too late. Damage caused by the great warming was visible everywhere on the Antarctic Peninsula. Old shorelines drowned by rising sea levels, bare bones of mountains exposed by melting snow and ice, mines and factories, port cities and settlements spreading along the coast... There were traces of human influence everywhere Mike walked. Hiking trails with their blue markers and pyramidal cairns, scraps of litter, the mummified corpse of an albatross with a cache of plastic scraps in its belly, clumps of tough grasses growing between rocks, fell field meadows of mosses and sedge – even a few battered stands of dwarf alder and willow. Ecopoets licensed by the Antarctic Authority were spreading little polders and gardens everywhere as the ice and snow retreated. They had introduced arctic hares, arctic foxes and herds of reindeer and musk oxen further south. Resurrected dwarf mammoths, derived from elephant stock, grazing tussock tundra in steep valleys snaking between the mountains.

Change everywhere.

One day, Mike followed a long rimrock trail to a triangulation point at a place called Pulpit Peak, fifteen kilometres south of the town. The pulpit of Pulpit Peak was a tall rock that stood at the edge of a cliff like the last tooth in a jaw, high above the blue eye of a meltwater lake. There was the usual trample of footprints in the apron of sandy gravel around it, the usual cairn of stones at the trail head, and something Mike hadn't seen before, a line of angular characters incised into one face of the rock, strange letters or mathematical symbols with long tails or loops or little crowns that reminded him of something he couldn't quite recall. And the triangulation point, a brass plate set in the polished face of a granite plinth, stated that it was thirty metres due north of its stated location 'out of respect to local religious custom.'

"I checked it with my phone's GPS," Mike told his friend Oscar Manu that evening. They were at the Faraday Bar 'n' Barbeque after a six-a-side soccer match, sitting on the terrace with their teammates under an awning that cracked like a whip in the chill breeze. "Sure enough, it was exactly thirty metres north of where it was supposed to be. And that writing? It's elvish. A guy I knew back home, old roustabout there, had a tattoo in the same kind of script. Back in the day, he was an extra in those old fantasy movies, had it done as a memento."

Mike's phone had translated the inscription. *The Place of the Meeting of Ice and Water.* A reference, maybe, to the vanished glaciers that had flowed into Square Bay.

"One of the sacred elf stones is what it is," Oscar said.

Oscar was from Tahiti, which had had its own share of troubles during the warming, but was in better shape than most Pacific Islands nations. One of its biotech firms had engineered the fast-growing, temperature-tolerant strain of staghorn coral the reclaimers were using to rebuild the reefs of Majuro. He was drinking Pangaea beer; Mike, who knew all too well that he was his father's son, was on his usual Lemon & Paeroa, saying, "You're telling me there are people here who believe in elves?"

"Let's put it this way: the road between Esperanza and O'Higgins has a kink where it swings around one of those stones," Oscar said.

"You're kidding," Mike said, because Oscar was famous for his patented wind-ups.

"Go see for yourself the next time you're up north," Oscar said. "It's just past the twenty kilometre marker."

Adi Mara chipped in, saying that a couple of Icelanders she knew took that kind of shit very seriously. "They have elves back home. The Huldufólk—the hidden people."

"Elf elves?" Oscar said. "Pointy ears, bad dress sense, the whole bit?"

"They look like ordinary people who just happen to be invisible most of the time," Adi said. "They live under rocks, and if you piss them off they can give you bad frostbite or sunburn, or cause accidents. Icelanders reckon some big rocks are actually disguised elvish churches or chapels. Building work and road construction can be held up if someone discovers that a place sacred to elves is right in the way."

"They don't sound that scary," Oscar said.

"Scary isn't the point," Adi said. She was their goalie, smaller than Mike, Oscar and the other guys, but fearless in the goal mouth. She punted every save way down the field, regardless of the positions of her teammates, and would tear you a new one if you didn't make good use of her passes. "The point is, Iceland is pretty bleak and tough, so it's only natural that Icelanders believe in forces stronger than they are, try to humanise the landscape with stories about folk who own it. And it's the same here."

Mike said that maybe it was the other way around. "Maybe the stones are reminders that Antarctica isn't really a place where ordinary people should be living."

"Back in the day that might have been true," Oscar said. "But look around you, Torres. We have Starbucks and McDonald's.

We have people who are bringing up kids here. And we have beer," he said, draining his glass and reaching for the communal jug. "Any place with beer, how can you call it inhospitable?"

The talk turned to rumours of feral ecopoets who were supposed to be living off the land and waging a campaign of sabotage against construction work. Roads and radio masts and other infrastructure damaged, trucks and boats hijacked, sightings of people where no people should be. Freddie Aata said he knew someone who'd seen a string of mammoths skylighted on a ridge with a man riding the lead animal, said that the Authority police had found several huts made of reindeer bones and antlers on the shore of Sjögren Inlet, on the east coast.

"Maybe they're your elves," Freddie told Mike. "Bunch of saboteurs who want to smack us back into the Stone Age, chiselling rocks with runes to mark their territory."

Mike still hadn't seen much of the peninsula. After arriving at O'Higgins International Airport he'd been flown directly to Square Bay in the hold of a cargo plane, catching only a few glimpses of snowy mountains rising straight up from the sea. There were vast undiscovered territories beyond the little town and the short strip of coast where he tooled up and down on service runs. Places as yet untouched by human mess and clutter. He found a web site with a map and a list of GPS coordinates of elf stones, realised that it gave him a shape and purpose to exploration, and started hitching helo and boat rides out into the back country to find them. There really was a stone, *The Church of the Flat Land*, on the road between Esperanza and O'Higgins, the two big settlements at the northern end of the peninsula. There was a stone at the site of an abandoned Chilean research station on Adelaide Island. *The Embassy of the Sea*

Swimmers. There were stones standing stark on hilltops or scree slopes. A boulder in a swift meltwater river. A boulder balanced on another boulder on a remote stony shore on the Black Coast. *The Land Dances*. A stone on a flat-topped nunatak in an ice field in the Werner Mountains, the most southerly location known. *The Gate to the Empty Country*.

They were all found pieces, incised with their names but otherwise unaltered. Markers that emphasised the emptiness of the land in which they stood, touching something inside Mike that he couldn't explain, even to himself. It was a little like the feeling he had when he paged through old images of the Marshall Islands. A plangent longing, deeper than nostalgia, for a past he'd never known. As if amongst the stones he might one day find a way back to a time not yet despoiled by the long catalogue of Anthropocene calamities, a Golden Age that existed only in the rearview mirror.

He had quickly discovered that visiting elf stones was a thing some people did, like birders ticking off species or climbers nailing every hard XS route. They posted photos, poems, diaries of the treks they had made, and fiercely squabbled about the origin of the stones and their meaning. No one seemed to know how old the stones were or who had made them, if it was a single person or a crew, if they were still being made. Most stoners agreed that the oldest was a tilted sandstone slab just a short steep hike from a weather station on the Wilkins Coast. *The House of Air and Ice*. It was spattered with lichens whose growth, according to some, dated it to around a century years ago, long before the peninsula had been opened to permanent settlement. But others disputed the dating, pointing out that climate change meant that lichen growth could no longer be considered a reliable clock, and that in any case establishment of lichen colonies could be accelerated by something as simple as a yoghurt wash.

There were any number of arguments about the authenticity of other stones, too. Some were definitely imitations, with crudely carved runes that translated into mostly unfunny jokes. *Gandalf's Hat. Keep Out: Alien Zone. Trespassers Will Be Shot.* There was a stone with a small wooden doorway fitted into a crack in its base. There was a stone painted with the tree-framed doorway to the Mines of Moria. There was a miniature replica of Stonehenge. There were miniature replicas of elf stones hidden on roofs of buildings in O'Higgins and Esperanza.

And even stones that most stoners considered to be the real deal were disputed by the hardcore black-helicopter conspiracy freaks who squabbled over the precise dimensions of runes, or looked for patterns in the distribution of the stones, or believed that they were actually way points for a planned invasion by one of the governments that still claimed sovereignty over parts of Antarctica, or some kind of secret project to blanket the peninsula with mind-controlling low-frequency microwaves, and so forth.

Oscar Manu found a website run by some guy in O'Higgins who looked a bit like a pantomime elf, with a Santa Claus beard and a green sweater, sitting at a desk littered with books and papers, a poster-sized photo of *The Gate to the Empty Country* on the wall behind him. Apparently he gave a course in elven mythology that included a visit to the stone set on the shoulder of a pebble bar north of the town's harbour, and awarded certificates to his pupils.

"Maybe he knows who made the things," Oscar said. "Maybe, even, *he* made them. You should go talk to him, Torres. You know you could ace that test and get yourself certified."

But as far as Mike was concerned, it wasn't really about elves, the whole fake history of aboriginal inhabitants. It was the idea that the essence of the land had survived human occupation and climate change, ready to re-emerge when the warming was reversed. The stones were an assertion of primacy, like the pylons set by the reclaimers around the perimeter of Majuro, marking the atoll's shape in the rolling waves that had drowned it. One of those pylons had Mike's name engraved on it, near the top of a list of sponsors and donors.

Despite their isolation and the stark splendour of the stones' settings, people couldn't help despoiling them. 'Robbo' had carved his tag at the base of *The Church of the Flat Land*. When Mike visited Deception Island, a three-day trip that included a stopover in O'Higgins (he ticked off the stone north of the harbour, but didn't visit the elf university), there was a cruise ship at anchor in the natural harbour of the island's flooded caldera, and he had to wait until a tourist group had finished taking selfies and groupies in front of a gnarled chimney of lava carved with a vertical line of runes, *Here We Made With Fire*, before he could have a few minutes alone with it. Someone had planted a little garden of snow buttercup and roseroot around *The Embassy of the Sea Swimmers*. There'd been some kind of party or gathering at *The Land Dances*, leaving a litter of nitrous oxide capsules and actual tobacco cigarette butts, illegal on three continents. And people had tucked folded slips of paper, prayers or petitions, amongst the small pyramid of stones, each marked with a single rune, of *Our High Haven*, on an icy setback high in the Gutenko Mountains.

Mike had made a short detour to find that last site after dropping off a party of geologists. It was a beautiful day. The blue dome of the sky unmarked except for the trail of a jet plane crawling silently northeast. Hardly any wind. In the absolute stillness he could hear the tide of blood in his ears, the faint sigh of air in his nostrils. Looking out across the pure white expanse of the Dyer Plateau towards mountain peaks sawtoothing the horizon he could imagine that the view was exactly as it had been before anyone had set foot on the continent. Ice and rock and snow and sky. Except that he remembered something one of the geologists had said as they'd unloaded their gear—that in the permanent dark of winter people heloed up to the plateau for wild skiing under the Antarctic moon and stars, using GPS to navigate from ice lodge to ice lodge. The snow here was fantastic, the geologist had said, a lot more of it than there used to be because the warmer air transported more moisture and caused more precipitation. Part of the expedition's work was measuring erosion caused by increased rainfall and snowmelt.

Change everywhere.

By now, it was long past midsummer. Christmas had come and gone. The weeks of 24-hour sunlight were over. Nights were lengthening inexorably. The first snow had fallen at Square Bay. As the research season ended, Mike and the other helo pilots were kept busy retrieving people from far-flung science camps, and Mike had a brief fling with one of the scientists. Sarah Conway, an English palaeontologist eight years older than him, part of a team which had been working on a rich seam of fossils in a sedimentary layer high in the Eternity Range. They met at one of the social nights in the town's two-lane bowling alley, where the pins were painted to resemble penguins and an ancient jukebox played K-pop from the last century. Sarah was a good-looking big-boned blonde with the kind of unassailable confidence and ambition, founded on good old-fashioned middle-class privilege, that Mike knew he should resent, but she was smart, funny and vivid, and when he saw how other men looked at her he felt a fierce pride that she had chosen him instead of any of them.

"She's a fine woman," Oscar said, "but you do know she's only into you for just the one thing."

"We're just having a little fun before she goes back to the World," Mike said.

"I have plenty of experience of short-term romances is all I'm saying," Oscar said. "Have fun, sure, but don't let her go breaking your heart."

Mike knew that Oscar was right, knew that he should keep it cool, fool around but keep a certain distance, but one day he told Sarah about the elf stones, and when she expressed an interest he took her up into the hills to show her the one at Pulpit Peak.

At first, she seemed to get it, saying that she understood why he hadn't documented the stones in any way. "It's about the moment. The connection you make through the stones. The journey you make to find them changes you. And when you actually see them, you're changed again. It makes you see their context afresh," she said, her broad smile showing the gap between her front teeth that Mike found terrifically attractive.

But then he tried to explain his idea that the stones had been sited in places that reminded people of what had been lost, the ice and the snow, the empty quiet of unpopulated Nature that would one day come again, and everything went north.

"This was all forest ten million years ago," Sarah said. "And a hundred million years before that, in the Cretaceous, it was even warmer. Covered by rainforest, inhabited by dinosaurs and amphibians and early mammals. Some big non-flying dinosaurs survived here after the asteroid impact wiped them out everywhere else. We found a nest with ankylosaur eggs this season that we think definitely post-dates the extinction event. And last season we found a partial hypsilophodont skull with enlarged eye sockets that confirms the dinosaurs lived here all year around, and had acute night vision that helped them to hunt during the polar night. The point being, choosing one state over another, ice over forest, is completely subjective."

"But this time the change isn't natural. Antarctica should be covered in ice and snow," Mike said, "and we fucked it up."

"I'm just taking the long view. Nothing lasts for ever. But that doesn't mean that when the Anthropocene passes it will be replaced by a replica of the immediate past. As my grandfather used to like saying, you can't unring a bell. There'll be something else here. Something different."

"It will come back if we help it," Mike said.

"Are we talking about Antarctica or your lost island home?"

"That doesn't have anything to do with the stones," Mike said, although of course it did. He was angry, but mostly with himself. He shouldn't have told her about the reclaimers. He shouldn't have shared his stupid ideas about the stones. He'd said too much, he'd opened his heart, and she was repaying his trust with a lecture.

"Antarctica could freeze over again, but it won't ever be what it once was," Sarah said. "And you can build new islands, but it won't bring back what you've lost. It will be something new. You can't hate change. It's like hating life."

"I can hate the wrong kind of change, can't I?" Mike said, but he could see that it was no good. She was a scientist. She had all the answers, and he was just a dumb helo pilot.

So they broke up on a sour note. A few days later, while Mike was out on a supply run to one of the kelp farms, Sarah caught a plane to New Zealand, leaving him with the feeling that he'd somehow fucked up.

"You definitely fucked up a perfectly good lay with that obsession of yours," Oscar said.

"I'm not obsessed."

Oscar laid a finger alongside his broad flat nose, pulling down his lower eyelid and staring straight at Mike. "I've been watching you, Torres. The time you spend chasing those stones. The time you spend talking about chasing them, or what you found when you ran one down. You think it's more important than anything else. And anyway, she's right."

"What do you mean, she's right?"

"She's right about bringing back the past. You can't. You drop a glass, it breaks on the floor. No way the pieces are going to leap up and fit themselves back again."

"You could glue them back together," Mike said, trying to turn it into a joke.

"You can't beat time, dude," Oscar said. "It only runs in one direction, and there's only one way out of world."

"I didn't realise that you are a nihilist."

"I'm a realist. Instead of trying to go against the current, I go with the flow. Don't fuck it up with ideas about rewinding clocks, Torres. Don't hang your hopes on some dream," Oscar said, half-singing that last sentence, having fun. "Don't, in a nutshell, be so fucking *serious* about what you can't get back."

Mike wondered unhappily if Sarah was right. If Oscar was right. If he'd become obsessed about bringing back what had been lost. Yearning for something he'd never known, something he could never have. Obsessing, yeah, over his romantic ideas about the stones. Because who knew what they really meant? What they meant to the person who had chosen and named them, and carved them with runes?

But he was too stubborn to give all that up so easily. Rootless and unsettled, he hitched a helo ride north to the Danco Coast, landing at the end of a fjord pinched between steep ridges and hiking up a shallow winding river towards the site of a stone, one of the last on his list. If he got back into his groove, he told himself, maybe everything would be okay. Maybe everything would become clear, and he'd think of the things he should have said to Sarah and the things that he needed to say to Oscar, to himself.

And as he picked his way between boulders alongside the river, cold clean air blowing through him and clear water chattering over and around rocks and dropping in little waterfalls, with the steep sides of the U-shaped valley rising on either side to bare ridges stark against the empty blue sky and snow-capped mountains standing ahead, he did feel lifted out of himself, the slough of his merely human problems.

There was change here, like everywhere else—the river fed by melting ice, with kerbs of pillow moss along its stony banks, stretches of sedges and cotton grass, some kind of bird, a kite or hawk, rising in lazy circles on a thermal above a scree slope starred with yellow flowers, amazing to see a land-based predator in a place where a century ago every animal species had depended on the ocean for food – but the land was empty and its silence profound, and he was part of it, absorbed in it, in the rhythm of walking, with a goal ahead of him and everything else dwindling into insignificance.

The river grew shallower and slower, breaking up into still pools and streams trickling between shoals and banks of pebbles, and there was the elf stone, an oval ice-smoothed boulder three metres high bedded in black gravel, with runes carved around its waist. *The Navel of Our Kingdom Under the Ice.*

Once upon a time, not so long ago, a glacier had flowed through the valley, debouching onto the ice shelf that had filled the fjord. But warm sea currents had undercut and broken up the ice, and the glacier had retreated to the 300-metre contour. The elf stone was one of many erratics deposited by its retreat, standing more than a kilometre in front of a tumble of ice chunks sculpted into fantastic shapes and a pitted cliff of dirty ice, the edge of a frozen river of tumbled ice blocks and crevasses curving away between snow-capped ridges.

After pitching his tent on a shoulder of sandy gravel, Mike lay awake a long time, listening to the whisper of water over stone and the distant retorts and groans of the glacier. When he woke, the air had turned to freezing milk. An ice fog had descended, whiting everything out. The sun was a diffuse glow low in the east; there was a rime of ice on tufts of moss and grass; every sound was muffled.

Mike brewed coffee on his efficient little Tesla stove, ate two granola bars and a cup of porridge with honey and a chopped banana stirred into it, and broke camp and started the hike back along the river, taking it slowly in the thick chill fog. He wasn't especially worried. Either the fog would lift and the helo would return and pick him up, or it wouldn't, and he'd be stuck here for a day or two until a bigger helo with Instrumental Flight Rules equipment could be diverted. No big deal. He had enough supplies to wait it out, told himself that it was a kind of adventure, even though he could call for help on his phone at any time, and GPS meant that he couldn't really get lost. Actually, he didn't even need GPS. All he had to do was follow the river.

He had been hiking for a couple of hours when he heard movement behind and above him. A soft heavy tread, a sudden sough of breath. He stood still, listening intently. The tread grew closer, shadows loomed out of the fog, bigger than any man, and Mike felt a spike of unreasoning fear. Then the wind shifted, the fog swirled aside, and he saw the first of them.

The high forehead and small brown eyes, the tear-drop ears with their elongated hair-rimmed lobes. The questing trunk. The shaggy pelt blended from shades of auburn and chocolate. Sturdy legs footing carefully on loose stones.

One by one, the SUV-sized mammoths trod past, five, seven, ten of them. At the end of the procession came a female with her young calf trotting beside her, trunk curled like a question mark, dissolving like the rest into the mist, leaving behind a musky scent and dinnerplate-sized footprints slowly filling with water in the gravel along the edge of the river.

And now another figure materialised out of the thinning fog, and a man's voice said, "Are you lost, friend?"

"I know exactly where I am," Mike said, resenting the implication that he was somehow in the wrong place. Trespassing. "What about you?"

"At the moment, I'm following the mammoths." The figure resolved into a slight man in his sixties, dressed in a red parka with a fur-trimmed hood, wind-proof trousers, boots. He had some kind of British accent, a neat salt-and-pepper beard, skin darkened by sun exposure but still pale at the roots of his widow's peak.

"You're in charge of them?" Mike said, wondering if the man was an ecopoet, wondering if there were others like him nearby.

"Oh, hardly," the man said, and introduced himself: Will Colgate. "May we walk on? My friends are getting away."

As they walked alongside the river, Will Colgate explained that he was studying the mammoths' behaviour, what they ate, where they went, and so on. "They need to eat a lot, so they cover a lot of territory. Yesterday they were ten kilometres south of here. Tomorrow they'll be ten kilometres north. Or more."

"So you're a scientist," Mike said. He hadn't been scared, not exactly, but he felt a little knot in his chest relax.

"Oh, no. No, I'm just an amateur. A naturalist, in the old tradition. Back in O'Higgins I'm a plumber," Will Colgate said. Adding: "I think I know why you're here."

"You do?"

"Only one reason why people would come here. To such an out-of-the-way place. You're a stoner."

"I'm interested in them," Mike admitted. "Why they are where they are. What they mean."

"Figured that out yet?"

Will Colgate had a sharp edge to his grandfatherly air.

"I think maybe they're memorials," Mike said. "Markers commemorating what was, and what will come again."

"Interesting. I once met someone, you know, who claimed she'd made them. She was a member of one of the seed-bombing crews. They take balls of clay and nutrients and seeds, so-called green bullets, and scatter them as they walk. Most of the seeds never germinate, of course, and most of the ones that do soon die. But enough thrive... Some of those willows might be theirs," Will Colgate said, pointing to a ghostly little island of shrubs standing knee-high in the river's flow.

"This woman you met—she really made the stones?"

"That's what she said. But she isn't the only one to lay claim to them, so who knows?"

Mike said shyly, "I think he or she may have been a helo pilot."

Will Colgate seemed to like the idea. "Of course, an awful lot of people use helicopters here. They're like taxis. When I was a geologist, back in the day, working for Rio Tinto, I was flown everywhere to check out likely lodes. Gave that up and went native, and here I still am. Place can get under your skin, can't it?"

"Yeah, it can."

They walked on for a while in companionable silence. Mike could hear, faintly, the tread of the mammoths up ahead. More a vibration coming up through the soles of his boots than actual sound.

Will Colgate said, "If you were going to mark up one of those stones with runes, all you'd need is an automatic cutter. Neat little thing, fits into a rucksack. Programme it, tack it in place, it would do the job in twenty minutes. Chap I know in O'Higgins uses one to carve gravestones."

"You'd also need to know which places to choose, which stones," Mike said. "How each relates to the other."

"Mmm. But perhaps it started as a joke that slowly became serious. That gained its meaning in the making. The land will do that to you."

The river broadened, running over a pavement of rock deeply scored by the ice. Mike smelt the sea on the fog, heard a splashing of water and a distant hoarse bugling that raised hairs on the back of his neck. And then he and Will Colgate arrived at the place where the river tumbled down a stony shore, and saw, dimly through thick curtains of mist, that the mammoths had waded waist-deep into the sea. Several were squirting water over themselves; others grazing on kelp, tugging long slippery strands from a jut of black rocks, munching them like spaghetti.

"The place of the meeting of ice and water," Will Colgate said. "As it once was. By the time I got here, the river was already running, although back then the ice was about where that stone is now."

"Are you really a plumber?"

"Fully certified. Although I've been all kinds of things in my time."

"Including making gravestones?"

"People are mostly cremated now. When they aren't shipped back to the World. Laser engraved brass markers, or modded resin with soulcatcher chips that talk to your phone. It isn't the same," Will Colgate said, and stepped towards the edge of the sea and turned back and called out gleefully. "Isn't that a lovely sight?"

"Yes. Yes, it is."

The mammoths were intruders, creatures from another time and place, but the sight of them at play lifted Mike's heart. While the old man videoed them, walking up and down at the water's edge to get better angles, Mike called the helo crew. They were grounded. Everyone along the coast without IFR was grounded, waiting for the fog to lift. Mike told them it didn't matter. He squatted on coarse black sand rucked by the tread of heavy feet, strangely happy. After a while, Will came back and rummaged in his backpack and set a pan of water on a little hotplate.

"Time for a cuppa, I think."

They drank green tea. Will said that there was a theory that the mammoths bathed in the sea to get rid of parasites. "Another claims that seaweed gives them essential minerals and nutrients they can't find on land. But perhaps they come here to have fun. I mean, that's what it looks like, doesn't it?"

"Are there other people like you?"

Will gave the question serious consideration, said, "Despite the warming, you know, it is still very difficult to live off the land. Not impossible with the right technology, but you can't really go the full primitive. You know, as in stories about feral ecopoets. Stone-tipped spears and such. I suppose it might be possible in a hundred or so years, when it will be warmer and greener, but why would anyone want to do such a foolish thing?"

"Maybe by then the ice will have come back."

"Despite all our heroic efforts, I don't think we will be able to preserve the ice cap. Not all of it. Not as it is. In a thousand years, yes, who knows, the ice may return. But right now we have the beginnings of something new. We've helped it along. Accelerated it. We've lost much along the way, but we've gained much, too. Like the mammoths. Although, of course, they aren't really mammoths, and mammoths never lived in the Antarctic."

"I know," Mike said, but Will was the kind of earnest pedagogue who couldn't be derailed.

"They are mostly elephant, with parts of the mammoth genome added," he said. "The tusks, the shaggy coat, small ears to minimise heat loss, a pad of fat behind the skull to insulate the brain and provide a store of food in winter, altered circadian clocks to cope with permanent darkness in winter, permanent day in summer... Traits clipped from a remnant population of dwarf mammoths that survived on an island in the Siberian Arctic until about four thousand years ago. The species hasn't been reborn, but it has contributed to something new. All of this is new, and precious, and fragile. Which is why we shouldn't try to live out here just yet."

"Who is this 'we'?"

"Oh, you know, people like me," Will said vaguely. "Natural history enthusiasts you might say. We live in cities and settlements, spend as much time as we can in the wild, but we try not to disturb or despoil it with our presence. The mammoths aren't ours, by the way. They're an authority project, like the arctic hares and foxes. Like the reindeer. But smaller things, insects and plants, the mycorrhizal fungi that help plant roots take up essential nutrients, soil microbes, and so on – we try to give a helping hand. Bees are a particular problem. It's too early for them, some say, but there's a species of solitary bee from the Orkneys, in Scotland, that's quite promising..." Will blinked at Mike. "Forgive me. I do rattle on about my work sometimes."

Mike smiled, because the guy really was a little like a pixie from a children's storybook. Kindly and fey, a herder of bees and ants, a friend of magical giants, an embodiment of this time, this place.

"I have trouble accepting all the changes," he said. "I shouldn't really like the mammoths. But I can't help thinking they seem so at home."

And with a kind of click he realised that he felt at home too. Here on the foggy beach, by one of the rivers of Antarctica, with creatures got up from a dream sporting in the iceless sea. In this new land emerging from the deep freeze, where anything could be possible. Mammoths, bees, elves... Life finding new ways to live.

Presently, the mammoths came up from the water, out of the fog, long hair pasted flat, steam rising from the muscular slopes of their backs as they used their trunks to grub at seaweed along the strandline. Will followed them with his camera as they disappeared into the fog again, and Mike stood up and started to undress. Leave on his skinsuit? No, he needed to be naked. The air was chill on his skin, the sand cold underfoot as he walked towards the water. He heard Will call out to him, and then he was running, splashing through icy water, the shock of it when he plunged into the rolling waves almost stopping his heart. He swam out only a little way before he turned back, but it was enough to wash himself clean.

DISPATCHES FROM THE CRADLE: THE HERMIT – FORTY-EIGHT HOURS IN THE SEA OF MASSACHUSETTS

– KEN LIU –

BEFORE SHE BECAME a hermit, Asa <whale>-<tongue>-π had been a managing director with JP Morgan Credit Suisse on Valentina Station, Venus. She would, of course, find this description small-minded and obtuse. *Call a woman a financial engineer or a man an agricultural systems analyst, and the world thinks they know something about them*, she wrote. *But what does the job a person has been channeled into have to do with who they are?*

Nonetheless, I will tell you that she was responsible for United Planet's public offering thirty years ago, at the time the biggest single pooling of resources by any individual or corporate entity in history. She was, in large measure, responsible for convincing a wearied humanity scattered across three planets, a moon, and a dozen asteroid habitats to continue to invest in the Grand Task—the terraforming of both Earth and Mars.

Does telling you what she has done explain who she is? I'm not sure. *From cradle to grave, everything we do is motivated by the need to answer one question: who am I?* she wrote. *But the answer to the question has always been obvious: stop striving; accept.*

37

A few days after she became the youngest chief managing director for JPMCS, on Solar Epoch 22385200, she handed in her resignation, divorced her husbands and wives, liquidated all her assets, placed the bulk of the proceeds into trusts for her children, and then departed for the Old Blue on a one-way ticket.

Once she arrived on Earth, she made her way to the port town of Acton in the Federation of Maritime Provinces and States, where she purchased a survival habitat kit, one identical to the millions used by refugee communities all over the planet, and put the pieces together herself using only two common laborer automata, eschewing offers of aid from other inhabitants of the city. Then she set herself afloat like a piece of driftwood, alone on the seven seas, much to the consternation of her family, friends, and colleagues.

"Given how she was dressed, we thought she was here to buy a vacation villa," said Edgar Baker, the man who sold Asa her habitat. "Plenty of bankers and executives like to come here in winter to dive for treasure and enjoy the sun, but she didn't want me to show her any of the vacant houses, several of which have excellent private beaches."

(Despite the rather transparent ploy, I've decided to leave in Baker's little plug. I can attest that Acton is an excellent vacation spot, with several good restaurants in town serving traditional New England fare—though the lobsters are farmed, not wild. Conservationists are uncertain if the extinct wild lobster will ever make a comeback in the waters off New England as they have never adapted to the warmer seas. The crustaceans that survived global warming were generally smaller in size.)

A consortium of her former spouses sued to have Asa declared mentally incompetent and reverse her financial dispositions.

For a while the case provided juicy gossip that filled the XP-stations, but Asa managed to make the case go away quickly with some undisclosed settlements. "They understand now that I just want to be left alone," she was quoted as saying after the case was dismissed—that was probably true, but I'm sure it didn't hurt that she could afford the best lawyers.

Yesterday I came here to live. With this first entry in her journal, Asa began her seaborne life over the sunken metropolis of Boston on Solar Epoch 22385302, which, if you're familiar with the old Gregorian Calendar, was July 5, 2645.

The words were not original, of course. Henry David Thoreau wrote them first exactly eight hundred years earlier in a suburb of Boston.

But unlike Thoreau, who often sounded misanthropic in his declarations, Asa spent as much time alone as she did among crowds.

EXCERPTED FROM ADRIFT, by Asa <whale>-<tongue>-π:

The legendary island of Singapore is no more. But the idea of Singapore lives on.

The floating family habitats connect to each other in tight clan-strands that weave together into a massive raft-city. From above, the city looks like an algal mat composed of metal and plastic, studded with glistening pearls, dewdrops or air bubbles —the transparent domes and solar collectors for the habitats.

The Singapore Refugee Collective is so extensive that it is possible to walk the hundreds of kilometers from the site of sunken Kuala Lumpur to the surviving isles of Sumatra without ever touching water—though you would never want to do such thing, as the air outside is far too hot for human survival.

When typhoons—a near-constant presence at these latitudes—approach, entire clan-strands detach and sink beneath the waves to ride out the storm. The refugees sometimes speak not of days or nights, but of upside and downside.

The air inside the habitats is redolent with a thousand smells that would overwhelm an inhabitant of the sterile Venus stations and the climate-controlled domes of the upper latitudes. Char kway teow, diesel fumes, bak kut teh, human waste, raja, Katong laksa, mango-flavored perfume, kaya toast, ayam penyet, burnt electric insulation, mee goreng, roti prata, sea-salt-laced reclaimed air, nasi lemak, charsiew—the heady mixture is something the refugees grow up with and outsiders can never get used to.

Life in the Refugee Collective is noisy, cramped, and occasionally violent. Infectious diseases periodically sweep through the population, and life expectancy is short. The fact that the refugees remain stateless, so many generations after the wars that stripped their ancestors of homelands, seems to make it impossible for a solution to be envisioned by anyone from the Developed World—an ancient label whose meaning has evolved over the centuries, but has never been synonymous with moral rectitude. It was the Developed World that had polluted the world the earliest and the most, and yet it was also the Developed World that went to war with India and China for daring to follow in their footsteps.

I was saddened by what I saw. So many people clinging to life tenaciously on the thin interface between water and air. Even in a place like this, unsuitable for human habitation, people hang on, as stubborn as the barnacles on pilings revealed at every low

*tide. What of the refugees in the deserts of interior Asia, who live
like moles in underground warrens? What of the other floating
refugee collectives off the coasts of Africa and Central America?
They have survived by pure strength of will, a miracle.*

*Humanity may have taken to the stars, but we have destroyed
our home planet. Such has been the lament of the Naturalists
for eons.*

*"But why do you think we're a problem that needs solving?"
asked a child who bartered with me. (I gave him a box of
antibiotics, and he served me chicken rice.) "Sunken Singapore
was once a part of the Developed World; we're not. We don't
call ourselves refugees; you do. This is our home. We live here."*

I could not sleep that night.

This is our home. We live here.

THE PROLONGED ECONOMIC depression in much of North America
has led to a decline of the region's once-famous pneumatic tube
transportation networks that connected the climate-controlled
domed cities, so the easiest way to get to the Sea of Massachusetts
these days is by water.

I embarked in balmy Iceland on a cruise ship bound for the
coast of the Federation of Maritime Provinces and States—
November is an excellent time to visit the region, as the summer
months are far too hot—and then, once in Acton, I hired a skiff
to bring me out to visit Asa in her floating habitat.

"Have you been to Mars?" asked Jimmy, my guide. He was a
man in his twenties, stocky, sunburnt, with gaps in his teeth that
showed when he smiled.

"I have," I said.

"Is it warm?" he asked.

"Not quite warm enough to be outside the domes for long," I said, thinking about the last time I visited Watney City on Acidalia Planetia.

"I'd like to go when it's ready," he said.

"You won't miss home?" I asked.

He shrugged. "Home is where the jobs are."

It's well known that the constant bombardment of the Martian surface with comets pulled from the Oort Cloud and the increased radiation from the deployment of solar sails, both grand engineering efforts began centuries ago, had managed to raise the temperature of Mars enough to cause sublimation of much of the red planet's polar dry ice caps and restart the water cycle. The introduction of photosynthesizing plants is slowly turning the atmosphere into something resembling what we could breathe. It's early days yet, but it isn't impossible to imagine that a habitable Mars, long a dream of humanity, would be reality within two or three generations. Jimmy might go there only as a tourist, but his children may settle there.

As our skiff approached the hemisphere bobbling over the waves in the distance, I asked Jimmy what he thought of the world's most well-known hermit, who had recently returned to the Sea of Massachusetts, whence she had started her circumnavigation of the globe.

"She brings the tourists," he said, in a tone that strove to be neutral.

Asa's collected writings about her life drifting over the ruins of the world's ancient sunken cities has been a publishing phenomenon that defies explanation. She eschews the use of XP-capturing or even plain old videography, instead conveying her experiences through impressionistic essays composed in a florid manner that seems at once anachronistic and abiding. Some have called her book bold and original; others said it was affected.

Asa has done little to discourage her critics. *It was said by the Zen masters that the best place for hermits to find the peace they sought was in the crowd*, she wrote. And you could almost hear the disgusted groan of her detractors at this kind of ornate, elusive mysticism.

Many have accused her of encouraging 'refugee-tourism' instead of looking for real solutions, and some claim that she is merely engaging in the timeless practice of intellectuals from privileged societies visiting those less fortunate and purporting to speak for her subjects by 'discovering' romanticized pseudo-wisdom attributed to them.

"Asa Whale is simply trying to soothe the neuroses of the Developed World with a cup of panglossian chicken soup for the soul," declared Emma <CJK-UniHan-Glyph 432371>, the media critic for my own publication. "What would she have us do? Stop all terraforming efforts? Leave the hellish Earth as it stands? The world needs more engineers willing to solve problems and fewer wealthy philosophers who have run out of ways to spend money."

Be that as it may, the Federation of Maritime Provinces and States tourist czar, John <pylon>-<fog>-<cod>, claimed earlier this year that the number of tourists visiting the Sea of Massachusetts has grown fourfold since the publication of Asa's book (such rises in Singapore and Havana are even higher). No doubt the influx of tourist money is welcomed by the locals, however conflicted they may be about Asa's portrayal of them.

Before I could follow up on the complicated look in his eyes,

Jimmy turned his face resolutely away to regard our destination, which was growing bigger by the minute.

Spherical in shape, the floating dwelling was about fifteen meters in diameter, consisting of a thin transparent outer hull to which most of the ship's navigation surfaces were affixed and a thicker metal-alloy inner pressure hull. Most of the sphere floated below the surface, making the transparent bridge-dome appear like the pupil of some sea monster's eye staring into the sky.

On top of the pupil stood a solitary figure, her back as straight as the gnomon of a sundial.

Jimmy nudged the skiff until it bumped gently against the side of the habitat, and I gingerly stepped from one craft to the other. Asa steadied me as her habitat dipped under my added weight; her hand felt dry, cool, and very strong.

I observed, somewhat inanely, that she looked exactly like her last public scan-gram, when she had proclaimed from the large central forum of Valentina Station that United Planets was not only going to terraform Mars, but had also successfully bought a controlling stake in Blue Cradle, the public-private partnership for restoring Earth to a fully habitable state.

"I don't get many visitors," she said, her voice tranquil. "There's not much point to putting on a new face every day."

I had been surprised when she replied to my request to stay with her for a few days with a simple "Yes." She had never so much as granted an interview to anyone since she started her life adrift.

"Why?" I had asked.

"Even a hermit can grow lonely," she had replied. And then, in another message that immediately followed the first, she added, "Sometimes."

Jimmy motored away on his skiff. Asa turned and gestured for me to descend through the transparent and open 'pupil' into the most influential refugee bubble in the Solar System.

THE STARS ARE *invisible from the metal cocoons floating in the heavy atmosphere of Venus; nor do we pay much attention to them from the pressurized domes on Mars. On Earth, the denizens of the climate-controlled cities in habitable zones are preoccupied with scintillating screens and XP implants, the glow of meandering conversation, brightening reputation accounts, and the fading trails left by falling credit scores. They do not look up.*

One night, as I lay in the habitat drifting over the balmy subtropical Pacific, the stars spun over my face in their habitual course, a million diamantine points of crisp, mathematical light. I realized, with a startled understanding reminiscent of the clarity of childhood, that the face of the heavens was a collage.

Some of the photons striking my retinas had emerged from the crease in the rock to which Andromeda is chained when nomadic warriors from the last ice age still roamed Doggerland, which connected Britain to the European mainland; others had left that winking point at the wingtip of Cygnus when bloody Caesar fell at the feet of Pompey's statue; still more had departed the mouth of Aquarius's jar when the decades-long genocidal wars swept through Asia, and aerial drones from Japan and Australia strafed and sank the rafts of refugees fleeing their desertified or flooded homelands; yet others had sparked from the distant hoof of Pegasus when the last glaciers of Greenland and Antarctica disappeared, and Moscow and Ottawa launched the first rockets bound for Venus...

The seas rise and fall, and the surface of the planet is as inconstant as our faces: lands burst forth from the waters and return beneath them; well-armored lobsters scuttle over seafloors that but a geologic eyewink ago had been fought over by armies of wooly mammoths; yesterday's Doggerland may be tomorrow's Sea of Massachusetts. The only witnesses to constant change are the eternal stars, each a separate stream in the ocean of time.

A picture of the welkin is an album of time, as convoluted and intricate as the shell of the nautilus or the arms of the Milky Way.

THE INTERIOR OF the habitat was sparsely furnished. Everything— the molded bunks, the stainless steel table attached to the wall, the boxy navigation console—was functional, plain, stripped of the elaborate 'signature' decorations that seem all the rage these days with personal nanites. Though the space inside was cramped with two people, it seemed larger than it was because Asa did not fill it with conversation.

We ate dinner—fish that Asa had caught herself roasted over an open fire, with the canopy open—and went to bed silently. I fell asleep quickly, my body rocked by the gentle motions of the sea and my face caressed by the bright, warm New England stars that she had devoted so many words to.

After a breakfast of instant coffee and dry biscuits, Asa asked me if I wanted to see Boston.

"Of course," I said. It was an ancient citadel of learning, a legendary metropolis where brave engineers had struggled against the rising sea for two centuries before its massive seawalls finally succumbed, leaving the city inundated overnight in one of the greatest disasters in the history of the Developed World.

While Asa sat in the back of the habitat to steer and to monitor the solar-powered water-jet drive, I knelt on the bottom of the sphere and greedily drank in the sights passing beneath the transparent floor.

As the sun rose, its light gradually revealed a sandy floor studded by massive ruins: monuments erected to long-forgotten victories of the American Empire pointed toward the distant surface like ancient rockets; towers of stone and vitrified concrete that had once housed hundreds of thousands loomed like underwater mountains, their innumerable windows and doors silent, empty caves from which shoals of colorful fish darted like tropical birds; between the buildings, forest of giant kelp swayed in canyons that had once been boulevards and avenues filled with steaming vehicles, the hepatocytes that had once brought life to this metropolis.

And most amazing of all were the rainbow-hued corals that covered every surface of this urban reef: dark crimson, light orange, pearly white, bright neon vermillion...

Before the Second Flood Wars, the sages of Europe and America had thought the corals doomed. Rising sea temperature and acidity; booming algae populations; heavy deposits of mercury, arsenic, lead, and other heavy metals; runaway coastal development as the developed nations built up the machinery of death against waves of refugees from the uninhabitable zones—everything seemed to spell doom for the fragile marine animals and their photosynthesizing symbiotes.

Would the ocean become bleached of color, a black-and-white photograph bearing silent witness to our folly?

But the corals survived and adapted. They migrated to higher latitudes north and south, gained tolerance for stressed

47

environments, and unexpectedly, developed new symbiotic relationships with artificial nanoplate-secreting algae engineered by humans for ocean-mining. I do not think the beauty of the Sea of Massachusetts yields one inch to the fabled Great Barrier Reef or the legends of long-dead Caribbean.

"Such colors…" I murmured.

"The most beautiful patch is in Harvard Yard," Asa said.

We approached the ruins of the famed academy in Cambridge from the south, over a kelp forest that used to be the Charles River. But the looming presence of a cruise ship on the surface blocked our way. Asa stopped the habitat, and I climbed up to gaze out the domed top. Tourists wearing GnuSkin flippers and artificial gills were leaping out of the ship like selkies returning home, their sleek skin temporarily bronzed to endure the scorching November sun.

"Widener Library is a popular tourist spot," said Asa, by way of explanation.

I climbed down, and Asa drove the habitat to dive under the cruise ship. The craft was able to submerge beneath the waves as a way for the refugees in coastal raft-cities to survive typhoons and hurricanes, as well as to avoid the deadly heat of the tropics.

Slowly, we descended toward the coral reef that had grown around the ruined hulk of what had once been the largest university library in the world. Around us, schools of brightly colored fish wove through shafts of sunlight, and tourists gracefully floated down like mermaids, streams of bubbles trailing behind their artificial gills.

Asa guided the habitat in a gentle circle around the kaleidoscopic sea floor in front of the underwater edifice, pointing out various features. The mound covered by the intricate crimson folds of a coral colony that pleated and swirled like the voluminous dress of classical flamenco dancers had once been a lecture hall named after Thoreau's mentor, Emerson; the tall, spear-like column whose surface was tiled by sharp, geometric patches of coral in carmine, cerulean, viridian, and saffron had once been the steeple of Harvard's Memorial Church; the tiny bump in the side of another long reef, a massive brain-shaped coral formation whose gyri and lobes evoked the wisdom of generations of robed scholars who had once strolled through this hallowed temple to knowledge, was in fact the site of the renowned 'Statue of Three Lies'—an ancient monument to John Harvard that failed to depict or identify the benefactor with any accuracy.

Next to me, Asa quietly recited:

The maple wears a gayer scarf,
The field a scarlet gown.
Lest I should be old-fashioned,
I'll put a trinket on.

The classical verses of the Early Republican Era poet Dickinson evoked the vanished beauty of the autumns that had once graced these shores, long before the sea had risen and the winters driven away, seemed oddly appropriate.

"I can't imagine the foliage of the Republican Era could be any more glorious than this," I said.

"None of us would know," Asa said. "Do you know how the corals get their bright colors?"

I shook my head. I knew next to nothing about corals except that they were popular as jewelry on Venus.

"The pigmentation comes from the heavy metals and pollutants that might have once killed their less hardy ancestors," said Asa.

"They're particularly bright here because this area was touched by the hand of mankind the longest. Beautiful as they are, these corals are incredibly fragile. A global cooling by more than a degree or two would kill them. They survived climate change once by a miracle. Can they do it again?"

I looked back toward the great reef that was Widener Library, and saw that tourists had landed on the wide platform in front of the library's entrance or against its sides in small groups. Young tour guides in bright crimson—the color of Harvard achieved either by skin pigmentation or costume—led each group in their day-excursion activities.

Asa wanted to leave—she found the presence of the tourists bothersome—but I explained that I wanted to see what they were interested in. After a moment of hesitation, she nodded and guided the craft closer.

One group, standing on what used to be the steps ascending to the entrance of Widener, stood in a circle and followed their guide, a young woman dressed in a crimson wetsuit, through a series of dance-like movements. They moved slowly, but it was unclear whether they were doing so because the choreography required it or because the water provided too much drag. From time to time, the tourists looked up at the blazing sun far above, blurred and made hazy by a hundred feet of intervening water.

"They think they're doing taiji," said Asa.

"It looks nothing like taiji," I said, unable to connect the languorous, clumsy movements with the quick, staccato motion I was familiar with from sessions in low-gravity gyms.

"It's believed that taiji once was a slow, measured art, quite different from its modern incarnation. But since so few recordings of the pre-Diaspora years are left, the cruise ships just make up whatever they want for the tourists."

"Why do taiji here?" I was utterly baffled.

"Harvard was supposed to have a large population of Chinese scholars before the wars. It was said that the children of many of China's wealthiest and most powerful inhabitants studied here. It didn't save them from the wars."

Asa steered the craft a bit farther away from Widener, and I saw more tourists strolling over the coral-carpeted Yard or lounging about, holding what appeared to be paper books— props provided by the cruise company—and taking scans of each other. A few danced without music, dressed in costumes that were a mix of Early and Late Republican fashions, with an academic gown or two thrown in for good measure. In front of Emerson, two tour guides led two groups of tourists in a mimed version of some debate, with each side presenting their position through ghostly holograms that hovered over their heads like comic thought bubbles. Some tourists saw us but did not pay much attention—probably thinking that the drifting refugee bubble was a prop added by the cruise ship to provide atmosphere. If only they knew they were so close to the celebrity hermit...

I gathered that the tourists were re-enacting imagined scenes from the glory days of this university, when it had nurtured the great philosophers who delivered jeremiads against the development-crazed governments of the world as they heated the planet without cease, until the ice caps had collapsed.

"So many of the world's greatest conservationists and Naturalists had walked through this Yard," I said. In the popular imagination, the Yard is the equal of the Athenian Acropolis or the Roman Forum. I tried to re-envision the particolored reef below me as a grassy lawn covered by bright red and yellow leaves on a cool New England fall day as students and professors debated the fate of the planet.

"Despite my reputation for romanticism," said Asa, "I'm not so sure the Harvard of yesteryear is better than today. That university and others like it once also nurtured the generals and presidents who would eventually deny that mankind could change the climate and lead a people hungry for demagoguery into war against the poorer states in Asia and Africa."

Quietly, we continued to drift around the Yard, watching tourists climb in and out of the empty, barnacle-encrusted windows like hermit crabs darting through the sockets of a many-eyed skull. Some were mostly nude, trailing diaphanous fabrics from their bodies in a manner reminiscent of Classical American Early Republic dresses and suits; others wore wetsuits inspired by American Imperial styles, covered by faux body armor plates and gas mask helmets; still others went with refugee-chic, dragging fake survival breathing kits with artfully applied rust stains.

What were they looking for? Did they find it?

Nostalgia is a wound that we refuse time to heal, Asa once wrote.

AFTER A FEW hours, satiated with their excursions, the tourists headed for the surface like shoals of fish fleeing some unseen predator, and in a way, they were.

The forecast was for a massive storm. The Sea of Massachusetts was rarely tranquil.

As the sea around us emptied of visitors and the massive cloud-island that was the cruise ship departed, Asa grew noticeably calmer. She assured me that we were safe, and brought the submersible craft to the lee of Memorial Church Reef. Here, below the turbulent surface, we would ride out the storm.

The sun set; the sea darkened; a million lights came to life around us. The coral reef at night was hardly a place of slumber. This was when the luminescent creatures of the night—the jellies, the shrimp, the glow-worms and lantern-fish—came out of hiding to enjoy their time in this underwater metropolis that never slept.

While the wind and the waves raged above us, we hardly felt a thing as we drifted in the abyss that was the sea, innumerable living stars around us.

WE DO NOT look.

We do not see.

We travel millions of miles to seek out fresh vistas without even once having glimpsed inside our skulls, a landscape surely as alien and as wondrous as anything the universe has to offer. There is more than enough to occupy our curiosity and restless need for novelty if we but turn our gaze to the ten square meters around us: the unique longitudinal patterns in each tile beneath our feet, the chemical symphony animating each bacterium on our skin, the mysteries of how we can contemplate ourselves contemplating ourselves.

The stars above are as distant—and as close—as the glowing coral-worms outside my portholes. We only have to look to see Beauty steeped in every atom.

Only in solitude it is possible to live as self-contained as a star.
I am content to have this. To have now.

In the distance, against Widener's cliff-like bulk, there was an explosion of light, a nova bursting in the void.

The stars around it streaked away, leaving inky darkness behind, but the nova itself, an indistinct cloud of light, continued to twist and churn.

I woke Asa and pointed. Without speaking, she guided the habitat toward it. As we approached, the light resolved itself into a struggling figure. An octopus? No, a person.

"That must be a tourist stranded behind," said Asa. "If they go up to the surface now, they'll die in the storm."

Asa switched on the bright lights in front of the habitat to get the tourist's attention. The light revealed a disoriented young woman in a wetsuit studded with luminescent patches, shielding her eyes against the sudden glow of the habitat's harsh lights. Her artificial gill slits opened and closed rapidly, showing her confusion and terror.

"She can't tell which way is up," Asa muttered.

Asa waved at her through the porthole, gesturing for her to follow the habitat. There was no airlock in the tiny refuge, and we had to go up to the surface to get her in. The young woman nodded.

Up on the surface, the rain was torrential and the waves so choppy that it was impossible to remain standing. Asa and I clung to the narrow ridge around the entrance dome on our bellies and dragged the young woman onto the craft, which dipped even lower under the added weight. With a great deal of effort and shouting, we managed to get her inside, seal the dome, and dive back underwater.

Twenty minutes later, dry, gills removed, securely wrapped in a warm blanket with a hot mug of tea, Saram <Golden-Gate-Bridge>-<Kyoto> looked back gratefully at us.

"I got lost inside," she said. "The empty stacks went on and on, and they looked the same in every direction. At first, I followed a candy-cane fish through the floors, thinking that it was going to lead me outside, but it must have been going around in circles."

"Did you find what you were looking for?" asked Asa.

She was a student at Harvard Station, Saram explained—the institution of higher learning suspended in the upper atmosphere of Venus that had licensed the old name of the university lying in ruins under us. She had come to see this school of legend for herself, harboring romantic notions of trying to search through the stacks of the dead library in the hopes of finding a forgotten tome.

Asa looked outside the porthole at the looming presence of the empty library. "I doubt there's anything left there now after all these years."

"Maybe," Saram said. "But history doesn't die. The water will recede from here one day. I may live to see when Nature is finally restored to her rightful course."

Sarah was probably a little too optimistic. United Planets' ion-drive ships had just succeeded in pushing six asteroids into near-Earth orbits earlier in the year, and the construction of the space mirrors had not even begun. Even the most optimistic engineering projections suggest that it will be decades, if not centuries, before the mirrors will reduce the amount of sunlight reaching Earth to begin the process of climate cooling and restoring the planet to its ancient state, a temperate Eden with polar ice caps and glaciers on top of mountain peaks. Mars might be fully terraformed before then.

"Is Doggerland any more natural than the Sea of Massachusetts?" Asa asked.

Saram's steady gaze did not waver. "An ice age is hardly comparable to what was made by the hands of mankind."

"Who are we to warm a planet for a dream and to cool it for nostalgia?"

"Mysticism is no balm for the suffering of the refugees enduring the consequences of our ancestors' errors."

"It is further error that I'm trying to prevent!" shouted Asa. She forced herself to calm down. "If the water recedes, everything around you will be gone." She looked outside the porthole, where the reef's night-time denizens had returned to their luminescent activities. "As will the vibrant communities in Singapore, in Havana, in Inner Mongolia. We call them refugee shantytowns and disturbed habitats, but these places are also homes."

"*I* am from Singapore," said Saram. "I spent my life trying to get away from it and only succeeded by winning one of the coveted migration visas to Birmingham. Do not presume to speak for us or to tell me what it is we should want."

"But you have left," said Asa. "You no longer live there."

I thought of the lovely corals outside, colored by poison. I thought of the refugees around the world underground and afloat—still called that after centuries and generations. I thought of a cooling Earth, of the Developed World racing to reclaim their ancestral lands, of the wars to come and the slaughter hinted at when the deck of power is shuffled and redealt. Who should decide? Who pay the price?

As the three of us sat inside the submerged habitat, refugees enveloped by darting trails of light like meteors streaking across the empyrean, none of us could think of anything more to say.

I ONCE REGRETTED that I do not *know the face I was born with.*

We remake our faces as easily as our ancestors once sculpted clay, changing the features and contours of our shells, this microcosm of the soul, to match the moods and fashions of the macrocosm of society. Still unsatisfied with the limits of the flesh, we supplement the results with jewelry that deflect light and project shadows, smoothing over substance with ethereal holograms.

The Naturalists, in their eternal struggle against modernity, proclaim hypocrisy and demand us to stop, telling us that our lives are inauthentic, and we listen, enraptured, as they flash grainy images of our ancestors before us, their imperfections and fixed appearances a series of mute accusations. And we nod and vow to do better, to foreswear artifice, until we go back to our jobs, shake off the spell, and decide upon the new face to wear for the next customer.

But what would the Naturalists have us do? The faces that we were born with were already constructed—when we were only fertilized eggs, a million cellular scalpels had snipped and edited our genes to eliminate diseases, to filter out risky mutations, to build up intelligence and longevity, and before that, millions of years of conquest, of migration, of global cooling and warming, of choices made by our ancestors motivated by beauty or violence or avarice had already shaped us. Our faces at birth were as crafted as the masks worn by the ancient players in Dionysian Athens or Ashikaga's Kyoto, but also as natural as the glacier-sculpted Alps or sea-inundated Massachusetts.

We do not know who we are. But we dare not stop striving to find out.

VENICE DROWNED
– KIM STANLEY ROBINSON –

BY THE TIME Carlo Tafur struggled out of sleep, the baby was squalling, the teapot whistled, the smell of stove smoke filled the air. Wavelets slapped the walls of the floor below. It was just dawn. Reluctantly he untangled himself from the bedsheets and got up. He padded through the other room of his home, ignoring his wife and child, and walked out the door onto the roof.

Venice looked best at dawn, Carlo thought as he pissed into the canal. In the dim mauve light it was possible to imagine that the city was just as it always had been, that hordes of visitors would come flooding down the Grand Canal on this fine summer morning... Of course, one had to ignore the patchwork constructions built on the roofs of the neighborhood to indulge the fancy. Around the church—San Giacomo di Rialto—all the buildings had even their top floors awash, and so it had been necessary to break up the tile roofs, and erect shacks on the roof beams made of materials fished up from below: wood, brick lath, stone, metal, glass. Carlo's home was one of these shacks, made of a crazy combination of wood beams, stained glass from San Giacometta, and drainpipes beaten flat. He looked back at it and sighed. It was best to look off over the Rialto, where the red sun blazed over the bulbous domes of San Marco.

"You have to meet those Japanese today," Carlo's wife, Luisa, said from inside.

"I know." Visitors still came to Venice, that was certain.

"And don't go insulting them and rowing off without your pay," she went on, her voice sounding clearly out of the doorway, "like you did with those Hungarians. It really doesn't matter what they take from under the water, you know. That's the past. That old stuff isn't doing anyone any good under there, anyway."

"Shut up," he said wearily. "I know."

"I have to buy stovewood and vegetables and toilet paper and socks for the baby." she said. "The Japanese are the best customers you've got; you'd better treat them well."

Carlo re-entered the shack and walked into the bedroom to dress. Between putting on one boot and the next he stopped to smoke a cigarette, the last one in the house. While smoking he stared at his pile of books on the floor, his library as Luisa sardonically called the collection; all books about Venice. They were tattered, dog-eared, mildewed, so warped by the damp that none of them would close properly, and each moldy page was as wavy as the Lagoon on a windy day. They were a miserable sight, and Carlo gave the closest stack a light kick with his cold boot as he returned to the other room.

"I'm off," he said, giving his baby and then Luisa a kiss. "I'll be back late—they want to go to Torcello."

"What could they want up there?"

He shrugged. "Maybe just to see it." He ducked out the door.

Below the roof was a small square where the boats of the neighborhood were moored. Carlo slipped off the tile onto the narrow floating dock he and the neighbors had built, and crossed to his boat, a wide-beamed sailboat with a canvas deck. He stepped in, unmoored it, and rowed out of the square onto the Grand Canal.

Once on the Grand Canal he tipped the oars out of the water and let the boat drift downstream. The big canal had always been the natural course of the channel through the mudflats of the Lagoon; for a while it had been tamed, but now it was a river again, its banks made of tile rooftops and stone palaces, with hundreds of tributaries flowing into it. Men were working on roofhouses in the early-morning light; those who knew Carlo waved, hammers or rope in hand, and shouted hello. Carlo wiggled an oar perfunctorily before he was swept past. It was foolish to build so close to the Grand Canal, which now had the strength to knock the old structures down, and often did. But that was their business. In Venice they were all fools, if one thought about it.

Then he was in the Basin of San Marco, and he rowed through, the Piazzetta beside the Doge's Palace, which was still imposing at two stories high, to the Piazza. Traffic was heavy as usual. It was the only place in Venice that still had the crowds of old, and Carlo enjoyed it for that reason, though he shouted curses as loudly as anyone when gondolas streaked in front of him. He jockeyed his way to the Basilica window and rowed in.

Under the brilliant blue and gold of the domes it was noisy. Most of the water in the rooms had been covered with a floating dock. Carlo moored his boat to it, heaved his four scuba tanks on, and clambered up after them. Carrying two tanks in each hand he crossed the dock, on which the fish market was in full swing. Displayed for sale were flats of mullet, lagoon sharks, tunny, skates, and flatfish. Clams were piled in trays, their shells gleaming in the shaft of sunlight from the stained-glass east window; men and women pulled live crabs out of holes in the dock, risking fingers in the crab-jammed traps below; octopuses inked their buckets of water, sponges oozed foam; fishermen bawled out prices, and insulted the freshness of their neighbors' product.

In the middle of the fish market, Ludovico Salerno, one of Carlo's best friends, had his stalls of scuba gear. Carlo's two Japanese customers were there. He greeted them and handed his tanks to Salerno, who began refilling them from his machine. They conversed in quick, slangy Italian while the tanks filled. When they were done, Carlo paid him and led the Japanese back to his boat. They got in and stowed their backpacks under the canvas decking, while Carlo pulled the scuba tanks on board.

"We are ready to voyage at Torcello?" one asked, and the other smiled and repeated the question. Their names were Hamada and Taku. They had made a few jokes concerning the latter name's similarity to Carlo's own, but Taku was the one with less Italian, so the sallies hadn't gone on for long. They had hired him four days before, at Salerno's stall.

"Yes," Carlo said. He rowed out of the Piazza and up back canals past Campo Santa Maria Formosa, which was nearly as crowded as the Piazza. Beyond that the canals were empty, and only an occasional roof-house marred the look of flooded tranquillity.

"That part of city Venice here not many people live," Hamada observed. "Not houses on houses."

"That's true," Carlo replied. As he rowed past San Zanipolo and the hospital, he explained, "It's too close to the hospital here, where many diseases were contained. Sicknesses, you know."

"Ah, the hospital!" Hamada nodded, as did Taku. "We have

swam hospital in our Venice voyage previous to that one here. Salvage many fine statues from lowest rooms."

"Stone lions," Taku added. "Many stone lions with wings in room below 2040 waterline."

"Is that right," Carlo said. Stone lions, he thought, set up in the entryway of some Japanese businessman's expensive home around the world... He tried to divert his thoughts by watching the brilliantly healthy, masklike faces of his two passengers as they laughed over their reminiscences.

Then they were over the Fondamente Nuove, the northern limit of the city, and on the Lagoon. There was a small swell from the north. Carlo rowed out a way and then stepped forward to raise the boat's single sail. The wind was from the east, so they would make good time north to Torcello. Behind them, Venice looked beautiful in the morning light, as if they were miles away, and a watery horizon blocked their full view of it.

The two Japanese had stopped talking and were looking over the side. They were over the cemetery of San Michele, Carlo realized. Below them lay the island that had been the city's chief cemetery for centuries; they sailed over a field of tombs, mausoleums, gravestones, obelisks, that at low tide could be a navigational hazard... Just enough of the bizarre white blocks could be seen to convince one that they were indeed the result of the architectural thinking of fishes. Carlo crossed himself quickly to impress his customers, and sat back down at the tiller. He pulled the sail tight and they heeled over slightly, slapped into the waves.

In no more than twenty minutes they were east of Murano, skirting its edge. Murano, like Venice an island city crossed with canals, had been a quaint little town before the flood.

But it didn't have as many tall buildings as Venice, and it was said that an underwater river had undercut its islands; in any case, it was a wreck. The two Japanese chattered with excitement.

"Can we visit to that city here, Carlo?" asked Hamada.

"It's too dangerous," Carlo answered. "Buildings have fallen into the canals."

They nodded, smiling. "Are people live here?" Taku asked.

"A few, yes. They live in the highest buildings on the floors still above water, and work in Venice. That way they avoid having to build a roof-house in the city."

The faces of his two companions expressed incomprehension.

"They avoid the housing shortage in Venice," Carlo said. "There's a certain housing shortage in Venice, as you may have noticed." His listeners caught the joke this time and laughed uproariously.

"Could live on floors below if owning scuba such as that here," Hamada said, gesturing at Carlo's equipment.

"Yes," he replied. "Or we could grow gills." He bugged his eyes out and waved his fingers at his neck to indicate gills. The Japanese loved it.

Past Murano, the Lagoon was clear for a few miles, a sunbeaten blue covered with choppy waves. The boat tipped up and down, the wind tugged at the sail cord in Carlo's hand. He began to enjoy himself. "Storm coming," he volunteered to the others and pointed at the black line over the horizon to the north. It was a common sight; short, violent storms swept over Brenner Pass from the Austrian Alps, dumping on the Po Valley and the Lagoon before dissipating in the Adriatic... once a week, or more, even in the summer. That was one reason the fish market was held under the domes of San Marco; everyone had gotten sick of trading in the rain.

Even the Japanese recognized the clouds. "Many rain fall soon here," Taku said.

Hamada grinned and said, "Taku and Tafui, weather prophets no doubt, make big company!"

They laughed. "Does he do this in Japan, too?" Carlo asked.

"Yes indeed, surely. In Japan rains every day—Taku says, 'It rains tomorrow for surely.' Weather prophet!"

After the laughter receded, Carlo said, "Hasn't all the rain drowned some of your cities too?"

"What's that here?"

"Don't you have some Venices in Japan?"

But they didn't want to talk about that. "I don't understand... No, no Venice in Japan," Hamada said easily, but neither laughed as they had, before. They sailed on. Venice was out of sight under the horizon, as was Murano. Soon they would reach Burano. Carlo guided the boat over the waves and listened to his companions converse in their improbable language, or mangle Italian in a way that alternately made him want to burst with hilarity or bite the gunwale with frustration.

Gradually, Burano bounced over the horizon, the campanile first, followed by the few buildings still above water. Murano still had inhabitants, a tiny market, even a midsummer festival; Burano was empty. Its campanile stood at a distinct angle, like the mast of a foundered ship. It had been an island town, before 2040; now it had 'canals' between every rooftop. Carlo disliked the town intensely and gave it a wide berth. His companions discussed it quietly in Japanese.

A mile beyond it was Torcello, another island ghost town. The campanile could be seen from Burano, tall and white against the black clouds to the north. They approached in silence. Carlo took down the sail, set Taku in the bow to look for snags, and rowed cautiously to the edge of town. They moved between rooftops and walls that stuck up like reefs or like old foundations out of the earth. Many of the roof tiles and beams had been taken for use in construction back in Venice. This happened to Torcello before; during the Renaissance it had been a little rival of Venice, boasting a population of twenty thousand, but during the sixteenth and seventeenth centuries it had been entirely deserted. Builders from Venice had come looking in the ruins for good marble or a staircase of the right dimensions... Briefly a tiny population had returned, to make lace and host those tourists who wanted to be melancholy; but the waters rose, and Torcello died for good. Carlo pushed off a wall with his oar, and a big section of it tilted over and sank. He tried not to notice.

He rowed them to the open patch of water that had been the Piazza. Around them stood a few intact rooftops, no taller than the mast of their boat; broken walls of stone or rounded brick; the shadowy suggestion of walls just underwater. It was hard to tell what the street plan of the town would have been. On one side of the Piazza was the cathedral of Santa Maria Ascunta, however, still holding fast, still supporting the white campanile that stood square and solid, as if over a living community.

"That here is the church we desire to dive," Hamada said.

Carlo nodded. The amusement he had felt during the sail was entirely gone. He rowed around the Piazza looking for a flat spot where they could stand and put the scuba gear on. The church outbuildings—it had been an extensive structure—were all underwater. At one point the boat's keel scraped the ridge of a roof. They rowed down the length of the barnlike nave, looked in the high windows: floored with water. No surprise. One of the small windows in the side of the campanile had been widened with sledgehammers; directly inside it was the stone staircase and, a few steps up, a stone floor. They hooked the boat to the wall and moved their gear up to the floor. In the dim midday light the stone of the interior was pocked with shadows. It had a rough-hewn look. The citizens of Torcello had built the campanile in a hurry, thinking that the world would end at the millennium, the year 1000. Carlo smiled to think how much longer they had had than that. They climbed the steps of the staircase, up to the sudden sunlight of the bell chamber, to look around; viewed Burano, Venice in the distance… to the north, the shallows of the Lagoon, and the coast of Italy. Beyond that, the black line of clouds was like a wall nearly submerged under the horizon, but it was rising; the storm would come.

They descended, put on the scuba gear, and flopped into the water beside the campanile. They were above the complex of church buildings, and it was dark; Carlo slowly led the two Japanese back into the Piazza and swam down. The ground was silted, and Carlo was careful not to step on it. His charges saw the great stone chair in the center of the Piazza (it had been called the Throne of Attila, Carlo remembered from one of his moldy books, and no one had known why), and waving to each other they swam to it. One of them made ludicrous attempts to stand on the bottom and walk around in his fins; he threw up clouds of silt. The other joined him. They each sat in the stone chair, columns of bubbles rising from them, and snapped pictures of each other with their underwater cameras. The silt would ruin the shots, Carlo thought. While they cavorted, he wondered sourly what they wanted in the church.

Eventually, Hamada swam up to him and gestured at the church. Behind the mask his eyes were excited. Carlo pumped his fins up and down slowly and led them around to the big entrance at the front. The doors were gone. They swam into the church.

Inside it was dark, and all three of them unhooked their big flashlights and turned them on. Cones of murky water turned to crystal as the beams swept about. The interior of the church was undistinguished, the floor thick with mud. Carlo watched his two customers swim about and let his flashlight beam rove the walls. Some of the underwater windows were still intact, an odd sight. Occasionally the beam caught a column of bubbles, transmuting them to silver.

Quickly enough the Japanese went to the picture at the west end of the nave, a tile mosaic. Taku (Carlo guessed) rubbed the slime off the tiles, vastly improving their color. They had gone to the big one first, the one portraying the Crucifixion, the Resurrection of the Dead, and the Day of Judgment: a busy mural. Carlo swam over to have a better look. But no sooner had the Japanese wiped the wall clean than they were off to the other end of the church, where above the stalls of the apse was another mosaic. Carlo followed.

It didn't take long to rub this one clean; and when the water had cleared, the three of them floated there, their flashlight beams converged on the picture revealed.

It was the Teotaca Madonna, the God-bearer. She stood against a dull gold background, holding the Child in her arms, staring out at the world with a sad and knowing gaze. Carlo pumped his legs to get above the Japanese, holding his light steady on the

Madonna's face. She looked as though she could see all of the future, up to this moment and beyond; all of her child's short life, all the terror and calamity after that... There were mosaic tears on her cheeks. At the sight of them, Carlo could barely check tears of his own from joining the general wetness on his face. He felt that he had suddenly been transposed to a church on the deepest floor of the ocean; the pressure of his feelings threatened to implode him, he could scarcely hold them off. The water was freezing, he was shivering, sending up a thick, nearly continuous column of bubbles... and the Madonna watched. With a kick he turned and swam away. Like startled fish his two companions followed him. Carlo led them out of the church into murky light, then up to the surface, to the boat and the window casement.

Fins off, Carlo sat on the staircase and dripped. Taku and Hamada scrambled through the window and joined him. They conversed for a moment in Japanese, clearly excited. Carlo stared at them blackly.

Hamada turned to him. "That here is the picture we desire," he said. "The Madonna with child."

"What?" Carlo cried.

Hamada raised his eyebrows. "We desire taking home that here picture to Japan."

"But it's impossible! The picture is made of little tiles stuck to the wall—there's no way to get them off!"

"Italy government permits—" Taku said, but Hamada silenced him with a gesture.

"Mosaic, yes. We use instruments we take here—water torch. Archaeology method, you understand. Cut blocks out of wall, bricks, number them—construct on new place in Japan. Above

69

water." He flashed his pearly smile.

"You can't do that," Carlo stated, deeply affronted.

"I don't understand?" Hamada said. But he did: "Italian government permits us that."

"This isn't Italy," Carlo said savagely, and in his anger stood up. What good would a Madonna do in Japan, anyway? They weren't even Christian. "Italy is over there," he said, in his excitement mistakenly waving to the southeast, no doubt confusing his listeners even more. "This has never been Italy! This is Venice! The Republic!"

"I don't understand." He had that phrase down pat. "Italian government has giving permit us."

"Christ," Carlo said. After a disgusted pause: "Just how long will this take?"

"Time? We work that afternoon, tomorrow: place the bricks here, go hire Venice barge to carry bricks to Venice—"

"Stay here overnight? I'm not going to stay here overnight, God damn it!"

"We bring sleeping bag for you—"

"No!" Carlo was furious. "I'm not staying, you miserable heathen hyenas—" He pulled off his scuba gear.

"I don't understand."

Carlo dried off, got dressed. "I'll let you keep your scuba tanks, and I'll be back for you tomorrow afternoon, late. Understand?"

"Yes," Hamada said, staring at him steadily, without expression. "Bring barge?"

"What?—yes, yes, I'll bring your barge, you miserable slime-eating catfish. Vultures..." He went on for a while, getting the boat out of the window.

"Storm coming!" Taku said brightly, pointing to the north.

"To hell with you!" Carlo said, pushing off and beginning to row. "Understand?"

He rowed out of Torcello and back into the Lagoon. Indeed, a storm was coming: he would have to hurry. He put up the sail and pulled the canvas decking back until it covered everything but the seat he was sitting on. The wind was from the north now, strong but fitful. It pulled the sail taut: the boat bucked over the choppy waves, leaving behind a wake that was bright white against the black of the sky. The clouds were drawing over the sky like a curtain, covering half of it: half black, half colorless blue, and the line of the edge was solid. It resembled that first great storm of 2040, Carlo guessed, that had pulled over Venice like a black wool blanket and dumped water for forty days. And it had never been the same again, not anywhere in the world...

Now he was beside the wreck of Burano. Against the black sky he could see only the drunken campanile, and suddenly he realized why he hated the sight of this abandoned town: it was a vision of the Venice to come, a cruel model of the future. If the water level rose even three meters, Venice would become nothing but a big Burano. Even if the water didn't rise, more people were leaving Venice every year... One day it would be empty. Once again the sadness he had felt looking at the Teotaca filled him, a sadness become a bottomless despair. "God damn it," he said, staring at the crippled campanile: but that wasn't enough. He didn't know words that were enough. "God *damn* it."

Just beyond Burano the squall hit. It almost blew the sail out of his hand: he had to hold on with a fierce clench, tie it to the stern, tie the tiller in place, and scramble over the pitching canvas deck to lower the sail, cursing all the while. He brought the sail down to its last reefing, which left a handkerchief-sized patch exposed to the wind. Even so, the boat yanked over the waves and the mast creaked as if it would tear loose... The choppy waves had become whitecaps: in the screaming wind their tops were tearing loose and flying through the air, white foam in the blackness...

Best to head for Murano for refuge, Carlo thought. Then the rain started. It was colder than the Lagoon water and fell almost horizontally. The wind was still picking up: his handkerchief sail was going to pull the mast out... "Jesus," he said. He got onto the decking again, slid up to the mast, took down the sail with cold and disobedient fingers. He crawled back to his hole in the deck, hanging on desperately as the boat yawed. It was almost broadside to the waves and hastily he grabbed the tiller and pulled it around, just in time to meet a large wave stern-on. He shuddered with relief. Each wave seemed bigger than the last: they picked up quickly on the Lagoon. Well, he thought, what now? Get out the oars? No, that wouldn't do; he had to keep stern-on to the waves, and besides, he couldn't row effectively in this chop. He had to go where the waves were going, he realized: and if they missed Murano and Venice, that meant the Adriatic.

As the waves lifted and dropped him, he grimly contemplated the thought. His mast alone acted like a sail in a wind of this force; and the wind seemed to be blowing from a bit to the west of north. The waves—the biggest he had ever seen on the Lagoon, perhaps the biggest ever on the Lagoon—pushed in about the same direction as the wind, naturally. Well, that meant he would miss Venice, which was directly south, maybe even a touch west of south. Damn, he thought. And all because he had been angered by those two Japanese and the Teotaca. What did

he care what happened to a sunken mosaic from Torcello? He
had helped foreigners find and cart off the one bronze horse of
San Marco that had fallen... more than one of the stone lions
of Venice, symbol of the city... the entire Bridge of Sighs, for
Christ's sake! What had come over him? Why should he have
cared about a forgotten mosaic?

Well, he had done it; and here he was. No altering it. Each
wave lifted his boat stern first and slid under it until he could
look down in the trough, if he cared to, and see his mast nearly
horizontal, until he rose over the broken, foaming crest, each
one of which seemed to want to break down his little hole in
the decking and swamp him—for a second he was in midair,
the tiller free and useless until he crashed into the next trough.
Every time at the top he thought, this wave will catch us, and
so even though he was wet and the wind and rain were cold,
the repeated spurts of fear adrenaline and his thick wool coat
kept him warm. A hundred waves or so served to convince him
that the next one would probably slide under him as safely as
the last, and he relaxed a bit. Nothing to do but wait it out,
keep the boat exactly stern-on to the swell... and he would
be all right. Sure, he thought, he would just ride these waves
across the Adriatic to Trieste or Rijeka, one of those two tawdry
towns that had replaced Venice as Queen of the Adriatic... the
princesses of the Adriatic, so to speak, and two little sluts they
were, too... Or ride the storm out, turn around, and sail back
in, better yet...

On the other hand, the Lido had become a sort of reef, in most
places, and waves of this size would break over it, capsizing him
for sure. And, to be realistic, the top of the Adriatic was wide;
just one mistake on the top of these waves (and he couldn't go on

73

forever) and he would be broached, capsized, and rolled down to join all the other Venetians who had ended up on the bottom of the Adriatic. And all because of that damn Madonna. Carlo sat crouched in the stern, adjusting the tiller for the particulars of each wave, ignoring all else in the howling, black, horizonless chaos of water and air around him, pleased in a grim way that he was sailing to his death with such perfect seamanship. But he kept the Lido out of mind.

And so he sailed on, losing track of time as one does when there is no spatial referent. Wave after wave after wave. A little water collected at the bottom of his boat, and his spirits sank; that was no way to go, to have the boat sink by degrees under him...

Then the high-pitched, airy howl of the wind was joined by a low booming, a bass roar. He looked behind him in the direction he was being driven and saw a white line, stretching from left to right; his heart jumped, fear exploded through him. This was it. The Lido, now a barrier reef tripping the waves. They were smashing down on it; he could see white sheets bouncing skyward and blowing to nothing. He was terrifically frightened. It would have been so much easier to founder at sea.

But there—among the white breakers, off to the right—a gray finger pointing up at the black—

A campanile. Carlo was forced to look back at the wave he was under, to straighten the boat; but when he looked back it was still there. A campanile, standing there like a dead lighthouse. "Jesus," he said aloud. It looked as if the waves were pushing him a couple hundred meters to the north of it. As each wave lifted him he had a moment when the boat was sliding down the face of the wave as fast as it was moving under him; during these moments he shifted the tiller a bit and the boat turned and surfed across the face, to the south, until the wave rose up under him to the crest, and he had to straighten it out. He repeated the delicate operation time after time, sometimes nearly broaching the boat in his impatience. But that wouldn't do—just take as much from each wave as it will give you, he thought. And pray it will add up to enough.

The Lido got closer, and it looked as if he was directly upwind of the campanile. It was the one at the Lido channel entrance or perhaps the one at Pellestrina, farther south; he had no way of knowing and couldn't have cared less. He was just happy that his ancestors had seen fit to construct such solid bell towers. In between waves he reached under the decking and by touch found his boathook and the length of rope he carried. It was going to be a problem, actually, when he got to the campanile—it would not do to pass it helplessly by a few meters; on the other hand he couldn't smash into it and expect to survive either, not in these waves. In fact the more he considered it, the more exact and difficult he realized the approach would have to be, and fearfully he stopped thinking about it and concentrated on the waves.

The last one was the biggest. As the boat slid down its face, the face got steeper until it seemed they would be swept on by this wave forever. The campanile loomed ahead, big and black. Around it, waves pitched over and broke with sharp, deadly booms; from behind, Carlo could see the water sucked over the breaks, as if over short but infinitely broad waterfalls. The noise was tremendous. At the top of the wave it appeared he could jump in the campanile's top window—he got out the boathook, shifted the tiller a touch, took three deep breaths. Amid the roaring, the wave swept him just past the stone tower, smacking against it and splashing him; he pulled the tiller over hard, the boat shot into the wake of the campanile—he stood and swung the boathook over a window casement above him. It caught, and he held on hard.

He was in the lee of the tower; broken water rose and dropped under the boat, hissing, but without violence, and he held. One handed, he wrapped the end of his rope around the sail cord bolt in the stern, tied the other end to the boathook.

The hook held pretty well; he took a risk and reached down to tie the rope firmly to the bolt. Then another risk: when the boiling soupy water of another broken wave raised the boat, he leaped off his seat, grabbed the stone windowsill, which was too thick to get his fingers over—for a moment he hung by his fingertips. With desperate strength he pulled himself up, reached in with one hand and got a grasp on the inside of the sill, and pulled himself in and over. The stone floor was about four feet below the window. Quickly he pulled the boathook in and put it on the floor, and took up the slack in the rope.

He looked out the window. His boat rose and fell, rose and fell. Well, it would sink or it wouldn't. Meanwhile, he was safe. Realizing this, he breathed deeply, let out a shout. He remembered shooting past the side of the tower, face no more than two meters from it—getting drenched by the wave slapping the front of it—why, he had done it perfectly! He couldn't do it again like that in a million tries. Triumphant laughs burst out of him, short and sharp: "Ha! Ha! Ha! Jesus Christ! Wow!"

"Whoooo's theeeerre?" called a high scratchy voice, floating down the staircase from the floor above. "Whoooooo's there?…"

Carlo froze. He stepped lightly to the base of the stone staircase and peered up; through the hole to the next floor flickered a faint light. To put it better, it was less dark up there than anywhere else. More surprised than fearful (though he was afraid), Carlo opened his eyes as wide as he could—

"Whoooooo's theeeeeerrrrrrrre?..."

Quickly he went to the boathook, untied the rope, felt around on the wet floor until he found a block of stone that would serve as anchor for his boat. He looked out the window: boat still there; on both sides, white breakers crashed over the Lido. Taking up the boathook, Carlo stepped slowly up the stairs, feeling that after what he had been through he could slash any ghost in the ether to ribbons.

It was a candle lantern, flickering in the disturbed air—a room filled with junk—

"Eeek! Eeek!"

"Jesus!"

"Devil! Death, away!" A small black shape rushed at him, brandishing sharp metal points.

"Jesus!" Carlo repeated, holding the boathook out to defend himself. The figure stopped.

"Death comes for me at last," it said. It was an old woman, he saw, holding lace needles in each hand.

"Not at all," Carlo said, feeling his pulse slow back down. "Swear to God, Grandmother, I'm just a sailor, blown here by the storm."

The woman pulled back the hood of her black cape, revealing braided white hair, and squinted at him.

"You've got the scythe," she said suspiciously. A few wrinkles left her face as she unfocused her gaze.

"A boathook only," Carlo said, holding it out for her inspection. She stepped back and raised the lace needles threateningly. "Just a boathook, I swear to God. To God and Mary and Jesus and all the saints, Grandmother. I'm just a sailor, blown here by the storm from Venice." Part of him felt like laughing.

"Aye?" she said. "Aye, well then, you've found shelter. I don't see so well anymore, you know. Come in, sit down, then." She turned around and led him into the room. "I was just doing some lace for penance, you see... though there's scarcely enough light." She lifted a tomboli with the lace pinned to it; Carlo noticed big gaps in the pattern, as in the webs of an injured spider. "A little more light," she said and, picking up a candle, held it to the lit one. When it was fired, she carried it around the chamber and lit three more candles in lanterns that stood on tables, boxes, a wardrobe. She motioned for him to sit in a heavy chair by her table, and he did so.

As she sat down across from him, he looked around the chamber. A bed piled high with blankets, boxes and tables: covered with objects... the stone walls around, and another staircase leading up to the next floor of the campanile. There was a draft. "Take off your coat," the woman said. She arranged the little pillow on the arm of her chair and began to poke a needle in and out of it, pulling the thread slowly.

Carlo sat back and watched her. "Do you live here alone?"

"Always alone," she replied. "I don't want it otherwise." With the candle before her face, she resembled Carlo's mother or someone else he knew. It seemed very peaceful in the room after the storm. The old woman bent in her chair until her face was just above her tomboli; still, Carlo couldn't help noticing that her needle hit far outside the apparent pattern of lace, striking here and there randomly. She might as well have been blind. At regular intervals Carlo shuddered with excitement and tension; it was hard to believe he was out of danger. More infrequently they broke the silence with a short burst of conversation, then sat in the candlelight absorbed in their own thoughts, as if they were old friends.

"How do you get food?" Carlo asked, after one of these silences had stretched out. "Or candles?"

"I trap lobsters down below. And fishermen come by and trade food for lace. They get a good bargain, never fear. I've never given less, despite what he said—" Anguish twisted her face as the squinting had, and she stopped. She needled furiously, and Carlo looked away. Despite the draft, he was warming up (he hadn't removed his coat, which was wool, after all), and he was beginning to feel drowsy...

"He was my spirit's mate, do you comprehend me?"

Carlo jerked upright. The old woman was still looking at her tomboli.

"And—and he left me here, here in this desolation when the floods began, with words that I'll remember forever and ever and ever. Until death comes... I wish you had been death!" she cried. "I wish you had."

Carlo remembered her brandishing the needles. "What is this place?" he asked gently.

"What?"

"Is this Pellestrina? San Lazzaro?"

"This is Venice," she said.

Carlo shivered convulsively, stood up.

"I'm the last of them," the woman said. "The waters rise, the heavens howl, love's pledges crack and lead to misery. I—I live to show what a person can bear and not die. I'll live till the deluge drowns the world as Venice is drowned, I'll live till all else living is dead; I'll live..." Her voice trailed off; she looked up at Carlo curiously. "Who are you, really? Oh. I know. I know. A sailor."

"Are there floors above?" he asked, to change the subject.

She squinted at him. Finally she spoke. "Words are vain. I thought I'd never speak again, not even to my own heart, and here I am, doing it again. Yes, there's a floor above intact; but above that, ruins. Lightning blasted the bell chamber apart, while I lay in that very bed." She pointed at her bed, stood up. "Come on, I'll show you." Under her cape she was tiny.

She picked up the candle lantern beside her, and Carlo followed her up the stairs, stepping carefully in the shifting shadows.

On the floor above, the wind swirled, and through the stairway to the floor above that, he could distinguish black clouds. The woman put the lantern on the floor, started up the stairs. "Come up and see," she said.

Once through the hole they were in the wind, out under the sky. The rain had stopped. Great blocks of stone lay about the floor, and the walls broke off unevenly.

"I thought the whole campanile would fall," she shouted at him over the whistle of the wind. He nodded, and walked over to the west wall, which stood chest high. Looking over it, he could see the waves approaching, rising up, smashing against the stone below, spraying back and up at him. He could feel the blows in his feet. Their force frightened him; it was hard to believe he had survived them and was now out of danger. He shook his head violently. To his right and left, the white lines of crumbled waves marked the Lido, a broad swath of them against the black. The old woman was speaking, he could see; he walked back to her side to listen.

"The waters yet rise," she shouted. "See? And the lightning...

you can see the lightning breaking the Alps to dust. It's the end, child. Every island fled away, and the mountains were not found... the second angel poured out his vial upon the sea, and it became as the blood of a dead man: and every living thing died in the sea." On and on she spoke, her voice mingling with the sound of the gale and the boom of the waves, just carrying over it all... until Carlo, cold and tired, filled with pity and a black anguish like the clouds rolling over them, put his arm around her thin shoulders and turned her around. They descended to the floor below, picked up the extinguished lantern, and descended to her chamber, which was still lit. It seemed warm, a refuge. He could hear her still speaking. He was shivering without pause.

"You must be cold," she said in a practical tone. She pulled a few blankets from her bed. "Here, take these." He sat down in the big heavy chair, put the blankets around his legs, put his head back. He was tired. The old woman sat in her chair and wound thread onto a spool. After a few minutes of silence she began talking again; and as Carlo dozed and shifted position and nodded off again, she talked and talked, of storms, and drownings, and the world's end, and lost love...

In the morning when he woke up, she wasn't there. Her room stood revealed in the dim morning light: shabby, the furniture battered, the blankets worn, the knickknacks of Venetian glass ugly, as Venetian glass always was... but it was clean. Carlo got up and stretched his stiff muscles. He went up to the roof; she wasn't there. It was a sunny morning. Over the east wall he saw that his boat was still there, still floating. He grinned—the first one in a few days; he could feel that in his face.

The woman was not in the floors below, either. The lowest

one served as her boathouse, he could see. In it was a pair of decrepit rowboats and some lobster pots. The biggest 'boatslip' was empty; she was probably out checking pots. Or perhaps she hadn't wanted to talk with him in the light of day.

From the boathouse he could walk around to his craft, through water only knee deep. He sat in the stern, reliving the previous afternoon, and grinned again at being alive.

He took off the decking and bailed out the water on the keel with his bailing can, keeping an eye out for the old woman. Then he remembered the boathook and went back upstairs for it. When he returned there was still no sight of her. He shrugged; he'd come back and say good-bye another time. He rowed around the campanile and off the Lido, pulled up the sail, and headed northwest, where he presumed Venice was.

The Lagoon was as flat as a pond this morning, the sky cloudless, like the blue dome of a great basilica. It was amazing, but Carlo was not surprised. The weather was like that these days. Last night's storm, however, had been something else. There was the mother of all squalls; those were the biggest waves in the Lagoon ever, without a doubt. He began rehearsing his tale in his mind, for wife and friends.

Venice appeared over the horizon right off his bow, just where he thought it would be: first the great campanile, then San Marco and the other spires. The campanile... Thank God his ancestors had wanted to get up there so close to God—or so far off the water—the urge had saved his life. In the rain-washed air, the sea approach to the city was more beautiful than ever, and it didn't even bother him as it usually did that no matter how close you got to it, it still seemed to be over the horizon. That was just the way it was, now. The Serenissima. He was happy to see it.

He was hungry, and still very tired. When he pulled into the Grand Canal and took down the sail, he found he could barely row. The rain was pouring off the land into the Lagoon, and the Grand Canal was running like a mountain river. It was tough going. At the fire station where the canal bent back, some of his friends working on a new roof-house waved at him, looking surprised to see him going upstream so early in the morning. "You're going the wrong way!" one shouted.

Carlo waved an oar weakly before plopping it back in. "Don't I know it!" he replied.

Over the Rialto, back into the little courtyard of San Giacometta. Onto the sturdy dock he and his neighbors had built, staggering a bit—careful there, Carlo.

"Carlo!" his wife shrieked from above. "Carlo, Carlo, Carlo!" She flew down the ladder from the roof.

He stood on the dock. He was home.

"Carlo, Carlo, Carlo!" his wife cried as she ran onto the dock.

"Jesus," he pleaded, "shut up." And pulled her into a rough hug.

"Where have you been, I was so worried about you because of the storm, you said you'd be back yesterday, oh, Carlo, I'm so glad to see you..." She tried to help him up the ladder. The baby was crying. Carlo sat down in the kitchen chair and looked around the little makeshift room with satisfaction. In between chewing down bites of a loaf of bread, he told Luisa of his adventure: the two Japanese and their vandalism, the wild ride across the Lagoon, the madwoman on the campanile. When he had finished the story and the loaf of bread, he began to fall asleep.

"But, Carlo, you have to go back and pick up those Japanese."

"To hell with them," he said slurrily. "Creepy little bastards...

They're tearing the Madonna apart, didn't I tell you? They'll take everything in Venice, every last painting and statue and carving and mosaic and all... I can't stand it."

"Oh, Carlo... it's all right. They take those things all over the world and put them up and say this is from Venice, the greatest city in the world."

"They should be here."

"Here, here, come in and lie down for a few hours. I'll go see if Giuseppe will go to Torcello with you to bring back those bricks." She arranged him on their bed. "Let them have what's under the water, Carlo. Let them have it." He slept.

H<small>E</small> <small>SAT UP</small> struggling, his arm shaken by his wife.

"Wake up, it's late. You've got to go to Torcello to get those men. Besides, they've got your scuba gear."

Carlo groaned.

"Maria says Giuseppe will go with you; he'll meet you with his boat on the Fondamente."

"Damn."

"Come on, Carlo, we need that money."

"All right, all right." The baby was squalling. He collapsed back on the bed. "I'll do it; don't pester me."

He got up and drank her soup. Stiffly he descended the ladder, ignoring Luisa's good-byes and warnings, and got back in his boat. He untied it, pushed off, let it float out of the courtyard to the wall of San Giacometta. He stared at the wall.

Once, he remembered, he had put on his scuba gear and swum down into the church. He had sat down in one of the stone pews in front of the altar, adjusting his weight belts and tank to do so, and had tried to pray through his mouthpiece and the facemask. The silver bubbles of his breath had floated up through the water toward heaven; whether his prayers had gone with them, he had no idea. After a while, feeling somewhat foolish—but not entirely—he had swum out the door. Over it he had noticed an inscription and stopped to read it, facemask centimeters from the stone. *Around this Temple Let the Merchant's Law Be Just, His Weight True, and His Covenants Faithful.* It was an admonition to the old usurers of the Rialto, but he could make it his, he thought; the true weight could refer to the diving belts, not to overload his clients and sink them to the bottom...

The memory passed and he was on the surface again, with a job to do. He took in a deep breath and let it out, put the oars in the oarlocks and started to row.

Let them have what was under the water. What lived in Venice was still afloat.

BROWNSVILLE STATION
– Christopher Rowe –

THE POLITICA DUG through her enormous haversack, complaining nonstop about the amenities on the local she'd taken—been *forced* to take, she said—to the Tampico station so that she could board the *Point a Punto*. Somewhere among the files and newspapers that spilled out of her bag, she claimed, was her ticket for the express.

The Junior Conductor smiled patiently. He would be patient for ninety more seconds, at which point the five minute bell would ring and he would tip a nod to this car's Porter, young Sandra, who, the Junior Conductor was gratified to remember, had proven herself particularly adept at giving the heave to the unticketed.

But no. Here it was, the purple ink of the barcode slightly smudged, but its provenance unmistakable. The Junior Conductor took the politica's ticket and inserted it into the slot on his little silver machine. He turned the crank once, twice, a third time, and the glyphs lit up showing that the woman would be with them all the way through to Key West, the whole rest of the journey.

With that, the politica underwent an alchemical transformation invisible to any observer but of extreme importance to the Junior Conductor. With that, the woman went from being one of the unticketed to being a Passenger.

"This way, ma'am," he said, in the gracious tones of a long-experienced member of the service class. Those tones were a finely distilled draught, containing notes of obsequiousness, superiority, and conspiracy all at once. Oh yes, the Junior Conductor *excelled* at his job.

He had started on the locals, but his ambitions had kept him moving from line to line in the city, so that he was as expert as anyone on the great linear metropolis's innumerable neighborhoods, districts, and regions. Not content to punch commuter tickets on the short run trains, he had worked his way up to the regional expresses, where he served for years, and then was finally recognized and rewarded with the number two position on the *Point a Punto,* the great Gulf-encircling express itself, the finest, fastest means of conveyance in the most magnificent city in the world.

Of course, seas and skies alike were too storm-tossed for any means of long-distance travel other than the protected rails. At least if the travel was to be comfortable, the appointments elegant, and the service gracious. And for the passengers who could afford the *Point a Punto,* such considerations were paramount.

It was possible, it was *theoretically* possible, to travel by rail the whole curving length of the city, from Key West to Cancún, keeping only to locals. One quiet night between the Tampa and New Orleans stops, the Junior Conductor had listened as a trio of Porters discussed this very urban legend. They even got to the point of pulling down schedules and station schematics from the staff car's onboard library, but swiftly overpowered their meager talents at calculation. There were thousands of stations in the linear city, and the Junior Conductor was of the opinion that stories suggesting that there was some Passenger out there who had visited all of them were purest fantasy.

These days, these halcyon days, there were only seven stations that much concerned the Junior Conductor. Those, of course, were the seven served by the *Point a Punto,* with the two great terminals at Cancún and Key West, and the five intermediary stops along the route at Tampa, New Orleans, Brownsville, Tampico, and Coatzacoalcos. The Junior Conductor and his wife kept modest apartments at each of the two terminal cities, as both of them travelled extensively for their work, on the rails in his case and as an engineer in service to the Utilities Directorate in hers.

Thinking of his wife, the Junior Conductor consulted his timepiece. Once the train rolled north out of Tampico he would have his dinner break and, if her duties found her near a telephone, his daily call from his beloved.

But...

"Comms are down, Conductor, sorry." This was a voice crackling over the intercom, carried along hard wires from the radio operator's station in Engine #2 to the lounge in the staff car. The Junior Conductor was briefly distracted by the incongruity of listening to a voice on a communications device tell him that listening to a voice on a communications device was impossible. Currently impossible, at any rate.

"This has been happening more and more often," he said, but he did not hold down the transmit button when he said it. The radio operator on the *Point a Punto* was new, and might take the remark as criticism of *her* when it was not meant as such. Not meant as criticism at all, really, because if he *were* being critical it would have to be of the city's communications infrastructure, which was the responsibility of the engineers of the Utilities Directorate, and the Junior Conductor would never criticize his wife's work, any more than he expected that she would criticize his.

He checked his timepiece again. Given that a conversation with his wife was not in the offing, he was now somewhere between twelve and fifteen minutes ahead of schedule in his break. He could find a seat in the canteen and eat his seaweed salad early, but that might affect his digestion. He wandered to the other side of the empty lounge—the Junior Conductor's habit was to intentionally schedule crew breaks so that he took his alone—and tidied the stack of printouts in the output basket attached to the teletype.

He idly studied the headlines, ignoring national and international events in favor of city news. All the local headlines were about the City Council Session scheduled to take place in Key West at the weekend. He wondered if the politica who had boarded at Tampico was bound for the meeting. She was certainly not a councilor herself, traveling as she was without an entourage, but she might well be an advisor to one, or perhaps a lobbyist for some faction or another bent on influencing policy.

"None of my business," murmured the Junior Conductor, and turned to the sports section.

ON THE APPROACH to Brownsville, while the Junior Conductor was making his habitual final walk through the passenger cars, Porter Sandra found him and told him there was a flash message from Engine #1. He frowned and took the little tightly rolled cylinder of onion-skin paper she handed over.

It read, simply, "SB-JX2-6."

He did not, of course, have to consult the handbook of transportation codes he kept in his breast pocket to know what this meant. An unscheduled six hour stop in Brownsville.

He turned the paper over, but it was blank on the back, and so he called Sandra back from her retreat down the train. "This was all? There wasn't a second message?"

Sandra shook her head. "No, sir. The radio operator brought that back herself by hand, said to give it to you quick, but that was all."

The radio operator had left Engine #2? Even more mysterious than what the message was missing, which was the three-character reason for the unscheduled stop.

Unscheduled stops were troublesome. Unscheduled stops without clear and actionable reasons were *delays*.

The Junior Conductor, of course, remembered the long ago days before he obtained his current position of authority, remembered being like young Sandra there, who would expect no more information than was given on the flash message. There was an unscheduled stop, well, there were protocols for such and they would be followed. The *whys* of such things were no concern of Porters or even Passengers.

But Junior Conductors, now, the *whys* were very much within their areas of concern.

He began making his way toward the Engines.

*   *   *

THE SENIOR CONDUCTOR was standing at the doorway between the first car and Engine #2. A stout old man who rarely left his elevated desk in this forward car except to sound the all aboard in the terminal stations, he, following tradition, left the day-to-day running of the train to the Junior Conductor. Their relationship was good. The Senior Conductor no longer bothered to hide the fact that most of the paperwork he worked at behind his desk consisted of applications for retirement communities in the Antarctic mountains.

"They won't let me in, J.C.," said the old man, his eyes wide. "I've been riding the rails"—*for sixty odd years,* the Junior Conductor filled in mentally—"for sixty odd years, and I've never heard of a Senior Conductor being kept out of the Engines."

The Junior Conductor consulted his timepiece. Seven minutes until deceleration began, then another twenty before full stop in Brownsville Station.

"Perhaps they're under orders, sir," he said, trying to settle his superior down, even though he was deeply worried by what the old man had said. "I'll just see if I can find out what's going on. If you don't mind?"

"No, no not at all, J.C.," said the Senior Conductor and moved back to his desk. "Never heard of such is all."

Three sharp knocks on the intercar door brought no response, so the Junior Conductor plucked the handset off the telephone mounted on the wall and pulled the lever, hard. He heard the ring in the earpiece, yes, but also through the door in Engine #2, where a similar handset was set above the radio operator's station.

No one answered.

He pulled the lever again, twice this time, to similar result.

The code for an intratrain communications failure, the Junior Conductor remembered, was IT-P42-4. He remembered, too, the protocol for such incidents.

He turned the dial on the telephone once to the right, and pulled the lever again.

A voice answered even before the ring completed.

"PtP Engineer, go." The voice was ragged, so much so that the Junior Conductor almost didn't recognize it.

"Sir, this is the Junior Conductor, following procedure in contacting Engine #1 when—"

"J.C.," the Engineer interrupted. "I need to keep this headset clear in case comms come back up from Brownsville." There was a click, and then the hiss of a dead line.

The Junior Conductor had automatically opened his mouth to reply and now let it hang open in shock. Then he became conscious of how foolish he must look and promptly pursed his lips in consideration. The Engineer, of course, was the absolute master of the train and could, as he had just demonstrated, choose to share or not share whatever information he wished. But there was such a thing as protocol. There was such a thing as procedure.

"What did the Old Man say?" asked the Senior Conductor. The Senior Conductor had come up from the Porter Corps and still lapsed into their jargon upon occasion. The Engineer of a train was always "the Old Man," despite gender or age, even when, as was the present case, the Old Man might be decades younger than the speaker.

"Very little," said the Junior Conductor. "I'm afraid I have nothing to report, sir. I'm going to send a Porter up here to act as a runner in case anything... in case anything develops. You'll send them back to find me if it does, yes?"

"Oh, yes, of course, of course," said the Senior Conductor, relaxing back onto his high stool. He seemed much relieved that his number two had taken charge, however precarious the situation and however much in the dark they were about exactly what that situation was.

The car lurched as the train braked hard. The Senior Conductor grabbed for the safety bar set into the wall next to his desk but missed and went tumbling. As for the Junior Conductor, years of instinct and experience served him by allowing him to keep his feet, if barely. He rushed over to his senior and was aghast to see blood flowing freely from the man's scalp.

"Eh, I'm all right," said the Senior Conductor, but his eyes were unfocused and he didn't try to stand when the Junior Conductor offered his arm. "Just going to sit here a moment."

The train was still braking. This was nothing like the scheduled deceleration, this was a full emergency stop, something the Junior Conductor had only experienced in training on an express and only a bare handful of times at that. The Passenger cars would be chaos. He had to get back there, help the Porters.

As he fumbled with the door though, the *Point a Punto* at last came to a screeching, stuttering, shaking halt. For a bare instant, the only thing that prevented full silence from reigning was the sound of steam escaping somewhere out in the tunnel.

Then the overhead speakers whined at an ear-splitting pitch, words lost somewhere in the noise. There was static, and then a voice.

"Attention all passengers. If you are seated, please remain so. If you are not seated, please find the nearest unoccupied seat and take it at once. Do not attempt to return to your assigned seat. Attention all crew. Enact emergency protocol WX-PT9-9."

The running lights in the car flashed off for a fraction of a second, and when they came back up, they were tinted amber.

"I don't know that one," the Senior Conductor mumbled. "I don't know WX-PT... did he say nine? Was it nine? What is that one, J.C.?"

The Junior Conductor shook his head. He, shockingly, did not know the code either. He dug into his breast pocket for the booklet of regulations and codes, cursed as the tiny print seemed to swim before his eyes, and thumbed rapidly through the pages.

He blinked when he found the code, narrowed his eyes, and read it a second time.

"Well, J.C.?" asked the Senior Conductor.

"WX-PT9-9, sir," said the Junior Conductor. "It means, 'flooded tunnel ahead.'"

THE SENIOR TECHNICIAN pushed her way through waist-deep water in the #6 utility access tunnel. Here, the water was rising slowly and steadily, an incredible and unheard of problem, of course, but at least it wasn't the torrential inflow they'd heard about from crews farther east before comms had failed.

She tried to wrap her head around the scope of what was happening and couldn't. The implications were of wide spread, simultaneous systemic failures across at least a half-dozen infrastructural elements, all of which had multiple built-in backups and redundancies. The Senior Technician was 54 years old and had been an employee of the Utilities Directorate for the entire three and half decades of her working life, and she'd never heard of flooding on the scale they were witnessing now.

And it had happened *so fast*.

The railways timepiece her husband had given her on their wedding night vibrated on its chain around her neck. She had set it that morning to remind of her of when he would be arriving in Brownsville aboard the *Point a Punto,* planning to surprise him with a rare mid-week visit. The last information she had indicated that the train had stopped sixty miles short of the station, and for that, she was thankful.

She had little else to be thankful for.

Givens, her apprentice, came wading out of a side tunnel. He was writing as he walked, slashing marks on a whiteboard with a grease pencil and cursing.

"Subsector pumps?" she asked him.

He looked up at her, startled for a moment, then said, "Working at one hundred percent capacity and one hundred twenty percent rated efficiency. Just like all the other pumps we've checked."

This was one of the many maddening things about the situation. The pumping systems were working spectacularly well. There was simply too much water, coming in too fast, for them to keep up with the flows. If there had been breakdowns or blockages, she would have had something to do, something to *fix*.

Fixing things was her way. Early in life, the Senior Technician had realized that social norms and she did not necessarily integrate as smoothly as the toothed wheels in the gearboxes of the toys she habitually took apart and reassembled. This might have proved an insurmountable difficulty had she been interested in politics or the media or any of the other career streams open to someone of her parentage and social class. As things had developed, however, the greatest social difficulty the

Senior Technician had ever faced—prior to meeting her husband
and rather unexpectedly falling in romantic love—was that of
convincing her parents and peers that it did not reflect poorly
on them that she chose the route of trade schools and service
sector employment over what was expected of her.

Her mother, though, a woman not entirely comfortable in her
place but very much someone who had negotiated a peaceful
settlement with life, had ultimately formulated a sort of motto
for the Senior Technician's life which had satisfied everyone.
"The lesser embarrassment is that you excel at something we
don't understand than if you did poorly at something we do."

Her parents had long since retired to the Mountains of the
Moon. The family circulated a round-robin letter to all members
that the Senior Technician dutifully read and added to, careful
to keep her contributions to a series of banalities about married
life and leisure time, and free of any talk of pumps or wiring
bundles or sewage mains, or, her particular speciality, means of
performing stress tests on poured concrete structures.

The Senior Technician blinked. Standing waist deep in water
in a critical access tunnel she had been doing nothing less than
wool gathering. What on earth was wrong with her?

Still, there was something in what she'd just been thinking
about. Concrete. Of course.

"We need to be monitoring the stresses on the load-bearing
buttresses," she said. "Particularly on the seaward side."

Givens was obviously mystified by this seeming change of topic.
"The buttresses?" he asked. "Outside? What about the flooding?"

The Senior Technician began working her away up the tunnel
toward a set of rectangular steel rungs set into the concrete
wall. "There's nothing we can do about that right now," she

said. "Come on. The local structural integrity control center is down on the Matamoros side of the river, but specs call for it to be hardwired to the sub-sector monitors and there's one of those less than a mile away."

She was not ungenerous to her subordinates, especially to those like Givens who trusted her enough to shrug and follow along after just a moment's more hesitation. So once they were above the flooded tunnel and briskly walking northwest, dripping as they went, she told him what she was worried about.

"We've been worrying about the support systems," she said. "We need to be thinking about *what they support*."

Givens nodded, but said nothing. He was used to acting as her sounding board, and knew when to ask questions and when to let her talk.

"The city is more or less tubular, with the flanking buttresses driven down to bedrock on both the seaward and landward sides. Everything we need is inside, and everything we need boils down to two things, power and fluids. Their continued and efficient circulation is our job."

Though she had no particular gifts for biology, the Senior Technician was a diligent student and an admirer of well-built systems. The peculiarities and failings of individual organisms aside, respiration was something to be studied. She had come to the utility of metaphor late in her life—a gift of her husband's—and now saw the city's systems in terms of inhalation and exhalation. Take in (and circulate!) water and air and calories, exhale waste, whether the waste was gases or matter or heat. Her job very rarely directly involved the intakes and the outflows, but all of city life, she knew, was dependent on them. Just like all of city life was dependent on their circulation.

"Their *protected* circulation," said Givens, and she realized she'd been speaking aloud.

"Yes, yes," she said. "Leaks are inevitable, but all this water, all at once, might mean something worse than an unregulated outflow of steam or a release of waste into the Gulf. If the buttresses are undermined, the integrity of the walls themselves could go. A full on breach, exposure to the exterior, who knows what the consequences would be?"

"And we're going to check the old sensor network that monitors the buttresses to try to determine where something like that might occur?"

The Senior Technician shook her head. "I already know where it will occur. At the arcs, where the city bridges local waterways like the Rio Grande here at Brownsville."

Givens let out a low whistle. "How many arcs does the city make? There must be dozens."

They had come to the sub-sector monitoring station. The Senior Technician slashed her identification card through the lock and the bolts released. "Hundreds," she said. "Maybe thousands."

The overhead lighting came on as they entered the unmanned station. It was tinted red, something neither of them had ever seen.

"Wake up the consoles," said the Senior Technician. "I'm going to see if I can get anything on the comms here."

Givens did as he was told, pushing levers and opening valves, while she sat down at communications array and fed it power. There was a hiss of static from the grilled speaker, then a squawk of competing signals as voices in Spanish and English competed with one another and with the hair-raising squeal of raw data given audible form.

She turned the gain with one hand and adjusted the frequency with the other, seeking some kind of clear signal in the tumult. She caught snatches of reports, heard numerous calls for help, and even, somehow, a few seconds of what was clearly a private conversation between two women discussing who they were going to vote for in a local council election.

The chaos of noise subsided slightly and she took the opportunity to press the transmit button and lean into the microphone. "This is Substation"—she glanced at the brass plaque screwed into the table—"TR-549 in Brownsville, calling active crews in the area. Attempting to reach any coordinated response effort to the crisis." Or anyone at all, really, she realized, but did not say.

She waited for a moment before repeating her call. There was a hollow echo of it transmitted back to her, but nothing like a coherent response.

The scents of damp cloth and grease made her realize that Givens was standing right behind her.

"Maybe there is no coordinated response," he said. His voice was as hollow as what had just sounded over the comms.

The Senior Technician frowned at him. "Well, if there wasn't, there is one now, and we're it. Come on, let's see what we've got."

What they had, it turned out, was a limited amount of information, none of it particularly heartening. The buttresses in the Brownsville/ Matamoros sector were under tremendous stress. From what the Senior Technician could make of the data, the seaward buttresses were being undermined, probably by erosion, at a prodigious rate. This left the landward side experiencing torque in directions the buttresses had not been designed to deal with.

"The city"—Givens hesitated—"the city can't actually roll into the sea, can it?"

"I think I'd be more worried about the sea coming to the city than the other way around," murmured the Senior Technician, calmly typing figures into a calculator fished from her toolkit. The numbers didn't take. The calculator had apparently been damaged by water back in Access Tunnel #6.

She set the useless machine aside and closed her eyes, thinking. Evidence indicated that the city was, to use a phrase her husband might have, being assaulted by the Gulf of Mexico. There was nothing she could do about that.

Evidence indicated that locally, the six mile stretch of the city that arced above the Rio Grande delta might come uncoupled at one end or the other and collapse. There might be something she could do about that.

"Look in those cabinets and see what kind of schematics they have for the local city sectors," she told Givens.

"What are we going to do?" he asked, and the Senior Technician suddenly realized that, while she had probably read his birthdate in some personnel file or another at some point, she did not actually know hold Givens was. Looking at him, he seemed impossibly young.

"We're going to use all the creditable information available to us to assess the situation. The assessment will identify various threats and problems to the city's infrastructure and cohesion. We will determine which, if any, of those threats and problems can be countered by the work of two highly trained and skillful technicians. Once that determination is made, we will audit our resources and determine a timeline for actions. Then we will act."

The young man shook his head. "It feels like the world's ending and you want to bail water."

The Senior Technician pointed at the cabinets she had told him to search. "Schematics, now," she said. "Desperation later."

THE PASSENGER CARS, as the Junior Conductor had guessed they would be, were a tumult. Passengers were standing and shouting at the Porters, at each other, at the now-quiet speakers of the intercom system, and when they spotted him, most especially at the Junior Conductor himself.

"Take your seats!" he heard Sandra shouting from the back end of the car he had just entered, but he could not see her through the milling crowd. As he had in each of the previous Passenger cars he'd traversed making his way through the train, the Junior Conductor pulled out his whistle and sounded it long and loud. His luck held, and once again, the crowd calmed.

"Ladies and gentlemen," he said. "The train has stopped short of the station due to an unforeseen emergency. Your safety is our paramount concern. Please take your seats."

But then a young man with incongruously thin black hair combed over the top of his head said, "What is happening? You have to tell us more than that! What *kind* of emergency?"

"An unforeseen one, the Conductor said," said Sandra, suddenly beside the young man and managing somehow to get him seated when he clearly wanted to bluster on.

But the Junior Conductor heard a note in the Porter's voice he'd never heard before. A questioning note, maybe even a *fearful* note. He needed more information, and he needed to share it with the rest of the crew as soon as possible.

But how to get it?

The Engineers were clearly not going to be any more

forthcoming at this point, he could only interpret their actions as panic. The Senior Conductor knew nothing. Thinking hard, he pulled out his rulebook and flipped to the pages in the back that showed the time and distance tables.

Glancing at his watch, thinking back over the past half-hour, he calculated that the train was between forty and fifty miles short of Brownsville Station. The Junior Conductor found himself faced with a complicated choice. He walked to the gangway between two passenger cars and looked out through the window.

The red emergency running lights dimly illuminated the nearby wall. As luck would have it, there was signage at that very spot, the cryptic stenciled letters the track tenders used to communicate among themselves. He couldn't understand any of it, but it reminded him of something. It reminded him of an *option*.

He hustled engine-ward, tapping Sandra on the shoulder and jerking his chin toward the next door. She followed him without question. In moments, they reached the crew lounge, where the Junior Conductor opened a panel and pulled out a large flashlight.

"I have determined," he said, "that my duties to the train demand I leave it."

Sandra looked at him, clearly confused. "There's nothing out there but tracks and tunnel walls," she said. "It would take you—I don't even know how long it would take you to get to Brownsville Station. Days, probably."

The Junior Conductor pulled more supplies out of the emergency kit in the closet: a canteen of water, an extra battery for the flashlight, an oilskin jacket, and, finally, a ring of three large plastic keys. He held these up.

"The tenders caches," he said. "They're spaced evenly between the principal stations, no more than ten miles apart. I'll walk along the tracks toward Brownsville until I find one, then take the tender cart stationed there the rest of the way. They're not as fast as the trains, of course, but they move a sight faster than walking pace. I should be at that station within a few hours."

Sandra said, "Do you know how to operate the carts? That wasn't covered in our training—in fact we were told to never touch any tender equipment at all."

The Junior Conductor considered lying to Sandra to assuage her fears, but then rejected the notion. The whole point of this scheme was to get more and better information about the situation, not to obfuscate with false reassurances. "Conductors are told the same thing," he said. "But at the same time, we're supplied with keys to the stations in event, this is directly from the manual, 'in event of catastrophe.' Whatever is happening, it's clearly catastrophic."

Sandra shook her head. "You didn't answer my question, sir. Do you know how to operate the carts?"

"I'm a fast learner," he said, trying to sound confident and failing to his own hearing.

"I should come with you," said Sandra. She rummaged in the locker and came up with another flashlight.

"No," said the Junior Conductor. "Someone has to keep the passengers calm and you're best suited for that. Better than me, even. And if the train is allowed to continue, someone will have to help the Senior Conductor manage the stop at Brownsville."

"He's helpless without you," protested Sandra. "And I don't have the training to manage a stop."

The Junior Conductor considered that for a moment. He

considered the parameters of his duties and what he knew of Sandra's capabilities. He considered the likely chaos of an emergency full off-loading at Brownsville. Then he pulled his whistle out of the front pocket of his waistcoat and handed it over to the young woman.

"Here," he said. "It's mostly a matter of blowing this as loudly as you can and pointing. I have every confidence in you."

The Porter took the whistle almost reverently, staring at the silver instrument like it was a badge of office. Which, considered the Junior Conductor, it more or less was.

"Now," he said. "Help me open one of the emergency doors. I want to disable the alarm so that the passengers don't have something else to wonder about."

Sandra closed her fist around the whistle and nodded firmly. "Right. You want to prevent the emergency egress alert from sounding, and, I'm guessing, prevent the notification alert from flashing in the engine as well?"

"I hadn't thought of that, but yes. I realize I'm asking you to break at least a half dozen regulations—"

She waved him off. "As it happens, sir, I know how to do both of those things." With that, she stuffed the whistle into her pocket and marched briskly out the break room door, pausing in the passageway only long enough to ensure that the Junior Conductor was following.

At the emergency exit halfway along the car, watching Sandra efficiently unscrew an access panel with a screwdriver hung from her own key ring, he considered asking her exactly how she knew to disable the alarms. But he remembered his early days conducting the locals, and the various extra-regulatory workarounds he'd been taught by older crew members when the pursuit of his duties was hampered instead of helped by following the rulebook. He supposed Porters had their own secrets, just as Conductors did.

The hiss of escaping air told him when Sandra had successfully unsealed the emergency door. The dry, cool, conditioned air of the train was overwhelmed in the passage by a warm, humid, inrushing current that reminded the Junior Conductor of a time his wife had taken him on a tour of the maintenance tunnels in Key West. He brushed the thought aside.

"I'll be back as soon as I can," he said, and stepped down onto the concrete siding.

"Be careful, sir," said Sandra, pausing in closing the door.

"I always am, Porter."

IT WAS IRONIC, thought the Junior Conductor, as he walked along the tracks, that he was both fifty miles from the nearest help and no more than fifty yards from the nearest human habitation. The enormous tube of the linear city had no unpopulated stretches, but the architecture of the express train line, very near the bottommost layer of the city, sealed it off from the local lines, not to mention the neighborhoods and pedestrian passageways above him.

If he could, instead of walking along the tracks, travel straight up through the layers of concrete and steel and plastic that formed the cartilaginous matter of the spinal column of the city, he would find the veins and arteries that carried water and power and air, and also, ultimately, the open spaces where the millions of tightly packed citizens lived.

But he could not. Instead, he was in the express tunnel, which consisted of a rounded-off passageway wide enough for three sets of tracks and the sidings between them. He kept his flashlight switched off as he walked alongside the *Point a Punto*, trailing one hand along the train, imagining that he was scratching the flank of some enormous, sinuous beast. When he reached the engines, he paused.

The hum of the batteries that were keeping the train's systems powered up competed with ticking noises from the cooling engines themselves. The powerful headlamp at the front of Engine #1 was extinguished, probably to save battery power, and this was a relief to the Junior Conductor. If the Engineers saw him out in the tunnel, they would call him back and there was nothing he could say to properly explain the quixotic mission he had set himself. *I have to find out what's happening at Brownsville,* he thought. *I have to bring help.*

Knowing it was foolish, he walked on tiptoe as he passed the Engines. He paused at the prow of Engine #1 and peered into the darkness. Far ahead, he could see the dim red glow of the next set of emergency lights. Perhaps he wouldn't need the flashlight at all. If he kept to the siding, there shouldn't be anything for him to stumble over, even in the darkness.

He walked perhaps a dozen yards before falling flat on his face.

Swallowing a curse, bringing the base of his right thumb to his mouth and tasting blood from a deep scrape, he got to his knees. His feet brushed against whatever it was he'd tripped over.

He looked back toward the *Point a Punto* and found that it was already lost in the darkness. He risked switching on the flashlight and found that his feet had tangled in a coil of thick cable made up of dozens of twisted strands of wire, probably fallen from a tenders cart and no doubt the detritus of some repair job or another. The coil was cleanly cut at one end and frayed at the other, rusted along its whole length, which, were it stretched out, probably came to about six feet.

The Junior Conductor felt dampness at his right ankle, just above the leather of his uniform shoe, and played the flashlight beam over his foot. One of the frayed wires had cut him there, fairly deeply. His sock was soaked with blood already.

When he stood, he found that he could put weight on his right foot, but only with some degree of pain. He supposed he should be worried about infection, but infections were long term, and he had many short term problems to deal with. He hoped the tenders cache was nearby.

BECAUSE HE HAD no sense of how fast he was shambling along, the Junior Conductor could not calculate exactly how far he had progressed towards Brownsville when, some ninety minutes after leaving the train, he came to open-sided shed on the landward side of the tunnel. He had held out a small hope that some representatives of the Tenders Corps would be present, but there was no one to be seen.

The tenders cache consisted of the shed, which provided cover —against what the Junior Conductor could not imagine—for a communication station and a set of track monitoring sensors on a wooden bench, and of carelessly organized piles of rail stock and cross ties. A short spur of track curved off the main lines to a deck on one side of the shed, and it was here that a tenders cart was parked, covered in a tarp.

The Junior Conductor considered pulling off the tarp and going right to work in powering up the cart, but paused. He went over to the shed instead, and turned on the overhead lights, which flickered on and flooded the area with fluorescent white. The communications station was powered down, but the track monitors showed backlit gauges, red arrows pointing to the center, green sections of their readouts. That was good, anyway. Nothing immediately endangering to the *Point a Punto* locally.

He looked at his watch. Two and half hours since the train had stopped.

These comms might be hardwired, he thought, and decided to take the time to power up the unit instead of jumping on the cart. A few minutes of work and some painfully loud squawks from the speakers later, he was slowly turning the frequency dial.

No signals on the standard channels, and the emergency channel seemed to be overloaded to the point that nothing coherent could be made out at all. He caught snatches of words and phrases, but nothing that made any sense. He went to switch off the unit when, for just a moment, a single voice clarified out of the background.

"This is Substation TR-549 in Brownsville, calling active crews in the area. Attempting to reach any coordinated response to the crisis."

It was a calm voice, bespeaking confidence and competence. It was his wife's voice.

HE TRIED FOR exactly ten minutes to raise her on comms. He got no indication that she, or anyone else, could hear his increasingly frantic calls. "This is Tender Cache Beta 81 on the express line—personnel late of the *Point a Punto* calling. The express has stopped short of Brownsville and needs information about the situation there. Can anyone hear me?"

He was aware that there were protocols for radio communications, even in times of crisis—*especially* in times of crisis—but he found that he could not remember them, exactly. He found that he didn't particularly care.

After the ten minutes he had assigned to the task expired to no apparent effect, he turned up the volume on the speakers and moved out onto the little boarding deck next to the tender cart. He pulled off the greasy tarp and was relieved to find that the batteries on the conveyance were fully charged, at least if he was reading their gauges correctly.

The controls seemed simple, but the Junior Conductor was sure that this seeming was a deception. There was a bar set horizontally above the operator's lap that could be moved from left to right, and that was almost certainly what fed power to the motors and accelerated and decelerated the cart. There was a large foot pedal that was probably a brake. There was a lever set into the control panel that seemed too robustly built to be a power switch, and he hoped he wouldn't have to use it at all.

He walked out to where the spur met the main line and threw the switch that would allow the cart access to the seaward tracks, the tracks that led to Brownsville, which was north of him at this point in the arc. He boarded the cart and took a seat at the controls. And realized he was facing the wrong way.

The cart was parked with its prow pointing toward the wall. He would have to back it out.

Experimentally, he moved the horizontal bar a fraction of an inch. The motors whirred to life, but the cart did not move. "Have to engage the drive," he said aloud. He pressed the foot pedal, but nothing happened.

Hash marks on the control panel showed that the mystery

lever had three positions, which the Junior Conductor thought of as top, middle, and bottom. Currently, the lever was in the top position. He took hold of the lever and moved it to the middle. He felt more than heard the drive engage, and when he moved the horizontal bar again, the cart lurched forward, in the wrong direction, and was only stopped from jumping the tracks by a strapped-together bundle of crossties positioned, it now seemed obviously, to prevent that very thing.

Okay, so the bottom position must be reverse.

This proved correct, and the Junior Conductor had soon maneuvered the cart onto the main line. He disengaged the motor, hopped off to throw the siding switch back into its closed position, then boarded again.

If the cart had any running lights or headlights, he could not find them. So he held up his flashlight with one hand, and fed power to the drive with the other. Sliding the horizontal lever less than a third of the way across found him moving down the track at terrific speed, the humid air feeling like a tropical wind.

He found that he was moving so fast that he probably wouldn't have time to decelerate or stop if his flashlight revealed something blocking the track. He thought of his wife's calm voice on the radio. He increased his speed.

THE SENIOR TECHNICIAN ran as fast as she could, but lugging two large fire extinguishers slowed her down considerably. Up ahead, Givens exhausted a third extinguisher's foam and threw it aside in disgust.

"This is pointless!" he shouted over the sound of the flames crackling from the electrical conduit pipe. "The water will be up to this level in another hour or two anyway! Even if we do get this put out we won't have time to rewire this junction before it's flooded."

The Senior Technician wearily handed over one of her extinguishers and waved her hand at the fire, indicating that he should get back to work. There was only room at the access panel for one of them to operate an extinguisher, so she stepped back to give him a little more room and to take a moment to breathe.

The harsh smoke rising from the plastic wrapped cables in the junction caused her to cough. Givens was right. This *was* pointless. But there had to be something she could do, some *good* she could do.

They had encountered two other roving bands of utilities workers as they made their way through the access tunnels in the heart of the city, neither of them in communications with anyone else, neither of them with anyone higher ranked than her among their number. One group had been panicked, rushing from communications station to communications station, desperate for orders. Those she had set to clearing a fouled sump pump before continuing south with Givens. The other group, three very junior technicians, had been grimly monitoring the rising water levels in the transportation tunnels on a panel they'd repurposed with a surprising show of ingenuity. She'd left them to it, telling them to send runners up to the populated levels with news as they saw fit.

"We've been up there a couple of times already, ma'am," one of them had said. "The security patrols are all working to keep people from looting or from rushing the train station, or at least that's what they say they're doing. I don't know how word spread so quickly about the flood with comms down everywhere."

Word of mouth. It was a commonplace bit of accepted wisdom that a rumor born in Cancún at breakfast would be making the rounds in Key West by lunch, all by dint of people whispering to their neighbors. Impossible, of course, but if the flooding was confined to just the sectors around Brownsville then she could believe the locals would hear about it quickly.

Not that she believed the flooding was confined.

Givens tossed aside the extinguisher, turned to her with hands held out to accept their last one. She shook her head. "No, just kick the panel closed. That will keep the worst of the smoke routed inside the conduit anyway. We've still got another mile or more to make it to the arch."

He didn't answer her, but turned and did as she said. He was slump-shouldered and moving with obvious effort, if anything more exhausted than she was despite the difference in their ages. She'd been leaning on him hard for the last few hours.

She found herself trying to remember the procedure for recommending a commendation for an apprentice, then laughed aloud. There was an edge to it, and she clamped her mouth shut.

If Givens wondered why she'd laughed, he didn't bother asking her about it. He leaned against the wall, hands on his knees, head down.

"How many times have you been outside?" he asked, quite unexpectedly.

She considered ignoring him, telling him to get moving, but then said, "I've left the city many times. I've even been overseas. I've visited my parents in Africa twice, and I attended a conference in Paris just last year, you remember that."

"But you took trains and submersibles when you went, right? I mean *outside*. How many times have you seen the sky without a foot-thick matrix of plexiglass between you and it?"

The Senior Technician thought carefully, counting on the fingers of one hand. "I went out in a hurricane eye to help secure a pontoon mooring when I was around your age. When we still thought we could complete the loop with floating sectors secured on Cuba. I went to an observatory near my parents home in the Mountains of the Moon that had a ceiling that could iris open, and they let us see the stars that way for a few minutes, that was, oh, twelve or fifteen years ago. It seems like there was some sort of field trip when I was a little girl to the interior of the Florida peninsula, but I don't remember if we left the vehicles. So, twice, I guess. How about you?"

Givens said, "I've been outside forty-four times."

"What? How is that possible? Why?"

"It's a religious thing. I mean, I'm not religious, but my mother is. And her church teaches that we have to spend time, they say it like this, they say we have to spend time 'between the ground and God.' So they bribe people in our directorate to guide them to exterior exits when the weather's not too bad. It's the whole reason I have this job, really. I was supposed to be an inside man for her congregation."

"Why are you telling me this now?" asked the Senior Technician.

"For two reasons. One to tell you why I'm leaving you now—we're really not doing anybody any good anyway and I would stay if we were, but I'm going to go find my mother and her friends and see what they're planning. The second reason is to tell you that if you can get out, if you can head inland, up the rivers, you can find colonies of people who live outside all the time. If anybody can make it out, I think you can. And I hope you do."

He opened the access door to the stairwell that led up to the populated levels. He paused fractionally as he went through, but did not turn to say goodbye, and neither did she try to stop him.

After a moment, she spoke to herself, alone in the empty corridor. "Okay, okay. That limits my options somewhat," she said. Then she turned and trotted south, toward the endangered arches.

THE JUNIOR CONDUCTOR tried to make sense of what he was seeing. The tracks stopped, ripped apart by some titanic force he couldn't imagine, and there was a crack running below them and the sidings. He could look *down* through that crack to see water. To see *waves*.

This, he believed, was the estuary of the Rio Grande. And he was staring through a tear in the bottom of the city.

A great groaning noise sounded and he felt a tremor that wasn't just his hand. The whole tunnel was vibrating. He thought for a moment that it was a sign that the city was collapsing around him, but then he felt the push of air at his back.

Something was moving up the tunnel behind him. Something large, something moving fast.

The Junior Conductor's jaw dropped open. The *Point a Punto* was approaching. It couldn't be anything else.

Why? he had an instant to wonder before leaping clear of the tenders cart. He landed on his bad foot and stumbled, rolled awkwardly on his right shoulder, and found himself up again, scrambling to get as far from the seaward tracks as possible. He had no idea what would happen when the train reached the breach in the tracks, but he didn't imagine his odds for survival were very high, even if he made it all the way to the wall. This didn't stop him from desperately trying.

The two engines both made it over the crevasse but jumped the tracks. The line of cars suffered from competing shearing forces, gravity drawing them downward while the deceleration and alternating side-to-side motions of the crash juddered back from each coupling, through the superstructure of each car. The train collapsed up against itself like a released spring, filling the tunnel with fire and noise and calamity. It seemed to last for hours, and in fact must have lasted for long minutes, and even when everything was finally still there were aftershocks and explosive noises as parts of the great pile of twisted train collapsed in on itself.

The Junior Conductor, ears ringing, unable to move, unable to see anything but smoke and dust, coughed. He tried to raise his hand to cover his mouth and nose against the fumes and heat, but found that he could not move his arms any more than his legs, could not raise his head or sit up from where he lay flat on his back.

Was he pinned by something, or was he paralyzed? Injured or trapped?

Probably both, he thought.

The ringing in his ears began to subside. He thought he heard the sound of someone crying, and then a cut-off scream. And there was something else, something rhythmic and susurrating. It took him a moment to realize he was hearing the sound of waves. He wondered if this was what an incoming tide sounded like.

He coughed again. His mouth was full of blood. When he turned his head to spit, he thought nothing of it immediately. But then, *Wait, I moved.*

Slowly, tentatively, he curled his hands into fists, then flexed each foot. There was a spike of pain from his previously-injured ankle, and he welcomed it. There didn't seem to be any weight crushing him down, so maybe, maybe…

More long moments passed as the Junior Conductor explored the limits of his mobility, strength slowly returning. The smoke cleared somewhat, the wan light of the crevasse now somewhat stronger as the impact of the train had widened the crack in the sidings.

Finally, he sat up.

He had apparently been thrown some distance up the tracks, because the tear in the city was behind him, the bulk of the debris on the far side. The emergency lights extinguished, and only a few flames and the light from outside showed the extent of the devastation. The Junior Conductor thought he could make out the broken form of a human body in the wreckage, but saw no signs of motion.

JT-XX0-0. All aboard lost.

He patted his pockets and looked around him in the gloom. His flashlight was nowhere to be seen.

He struggled to his feet, took one last hopeless look around, then began limping blindly into the dark toward the station.

THE TRAIN STATION, to the Senior Technician's surprise, was abandoned. There was one train in, a local on the upper tracks, its doors open and the battery-operated flashing signs reading 'now boarding' just beginning to dim. But there was no one to board, and certainly no one to operate the train.

The screens showing in and outbound traffic were black, inoperative. She checked her timepiece. Even if the *Point a*

Punto had made it to the station after its unscheduled stop, it would have long since departed. She had no way of knowing whether or not her husband was still stuck in the tunnel or was instead bound northeast at high speed, toward who knew what danger.

No way of *knowing,* but perhaps some way of *finding out.*

She moved down into the lower levels of the station, its appurtenances growing richer and more luxurious as she approached the platform where the great express made its brief stops in Brownsville. The marble flooring was polished to a high sheen. She sat on the edge of the platform and let her feet dangle above the track sidings. She breathed in, trying to detect some recent sign of smoke and soot. There was none, but, but...

Salt air?

Brownsville Station was near the northern terminus of the arch of city that stretched over the Rio Grande estuary. She had detected no further signs of a collapse in the integrity of the city's superstructure, not unless what she was breathing in could be interpreted as such.

She clicked her flashlight off and on. The beam was strong.

She hopped down onto the sidings, and walked into the express tunnel toward the Matamoros side of the river.

IMPOSSIBLY, THE WOMAN with the flashlight walking resolutely up the tracks turned out to be his wife.

IMPOSSIBLY, THE FILTHY man limping toward her out of the darkness turned out to be her husband.

*   *   *

THE RIOTERS TORE through the station but never entered the tunnels, so they stayed safe, hiding together for several days. The emergency stores from the bridge tenders shack they found kept them from dying of thirst. They ignored their hunger as best they could.

"Do you think the whole city is like this?" he asked her.

She had been thinking about that very thing. "Yes," she said. "Probably the Cuban coastal conurbations, too. And the other islands."

"How could the sea rise so fast? How could there be no sign?"

"I don't think it *was* fast," she said. "I think there probably *were* signs."

ON THE FIFTH day, a series of tremors drove them into the station. She told him that she was afraid the entire arch was going to collapse.

"We can't just stay hidden down here on the tracks," she added.

He had lived most of his life on the tracks, but he nodded. "Where can we go? If the whole city is madness and flooding, where can we go?"

There was only one answer.

"Do you remember my apprentice, Givens?" she asked.

THE ACCESS PANEL fell out and down, landing with a splash of mud that didn't quite reach them. He had thought there would be some hesitation, something said to mark their leaving the city they had served, that had been all they had known. But they heard a shout and the sound of running footsteps behind them.

So they leaped.

WHO DO YOU LOVE?
– KATHLEEN ANN GOONAN –

APHRODITE WAS PERFORMING on a tiny, wooden stage at Sloppy Joe's™ when he walked in. Who Do You Love. Hoodoo, they called him out west, where he had achieved strange, postapocalyptic fame. Sounding the great chords of a dying planet, or some such nonsense. But fame had kept Emile Raphael busy for a good thirty years, the time that had elapsed since he had fled his wife's transformation into this amazement, and before whom he was now deeply humbled. He had stumbled on their shared path. She had persevered.

Knowing the spotlights would blind her, he stood in the doorway, watching. A small sign above her read *Do not touch Aphrodite. She stings.*

Tiny, round purple zoanthid polys, rimmed with waving lime-green tendrils, surrounded her eyes. Her body was a coral garden incorporating many, many species, crowded in a riot of color and shape over her lush, still womanly body. Wilderness, taken into herself in processes they had developed together a half-century ago, before the Great Extinction.

It was a wonder Zoe Raphael-Aphrodite had survived this long. She was a living experiment, a long-running research project, hawking herself as a tawdry sideshow. Probably paid for her life support. Well, his fame, and the money he'd sent back for wife and child, had definitely subsided in the past ten years. He could not even imagine the breadth of all she must have learned since then, what she might contribute to an understanding of marine life. Of all life.

Emile had arrived in Key West™—a self-sealing, completely artificial theme park floating on the now-submerged site of the old, flimsy town—a week earlier, performing on the street, working up the courage to see her.

He shifted the human skull he held from right side to his left. The candle that flickered inside made it uncomfortably hot. He felt the heat through his Burmese python-hide jacket, and through his lionfish-skin gloves, which were quite thin.

His jacket hung open to reveal his ever-changing body-show of extinct life. Hoodoo, of Haitian descent by way of wealthy Palm Beach parents, with his long, white dreads, was tough as his mutant albino crocodile hide top hat after years out in the ruined west, in Asia, and in his favorite city, Paris. Emile Raphael, though, deep inside him, wept at what he saw, at what he'd refused to share, after that first, stinging dose.

He wondered—could she even see?

She reclined, propped on one elbow, in a clear, curved chute down which flowed water. The parts of her above water were enveloped in salt mist that gave the bar's close air the heady scent of sea. He figured it held nutrients, for the thin, long tendrils behind what might pass for her right ear darted in a languid, mesmerizing symphony of hunt. Her chromophores —he did not differentiate between her identity and that of her colonies—were bathed in blue light, and emitted an undulating display of dazzling, fluorescent colors.

Many corals could live without water for intervals of time. Before the Great Extinction, tidal corals might be dry and exposed to sun for several hours a day. He imagined that, over these decades, Aphrodite—Zoe—had further tweaked many of these qualities in the corals she chose to...

To what? To support. To manifest. To merge with. To become.

Small storms of color rushed through her corals, swift as time-lapse clouds. He had, perhaps, come to find out, called by whispers in his mind; a siren enchantment across time and space.

Color was language, on a reef, as was seaborne scent. What was she saying? How could he, now, ever know? The tones assaulted, compelled, and pulled from him unparsed, long-lost, responses. At this moment, he realized they had always fed his art, just below his knowing.

The outline of her old, dear face, with its small, pointed chin, was still apparent, though submerged in blooming, moving crenellation. Her blue eyes, when she lifted them and turned her head to stare with all the others—yes! were hers! and yet—

Of course, she was deeply, irrevocably changed.

Oh, she was stunning. Her head was *Trachyphyllia geoffroyi*, an unfurled brain coral that looked like a tricorner hat, an intense, constantly modulating green in its center, magenta around its rim. Tube corals, azure, gold, and amethyst, undulating like snakes, revealed small living, salmon-hued fan corals dangling below disc anemones.

A rainbow of a woman, a living work of scientific art. A mature tropical reef in the shape of a voluptuous woman, a wild, fluorescing lost world realized, rippling with life. Conscious in

123

every waving polyp. Her mind, if things had gone as they had boldly predicted, if only to themselves, had permeated the sea animals as they had colonized her body.

Her song was alien as the sea.

Just as they had planned.

He almost dropped his skull when he saw her hands. One rested on her stomach, and had two fingers; the other lay open on her forward-turned haunch, and it had three. His own hands throbbed in sympathetic pain. There was the link. Yes, it was surely real. The inserted gene, activated in certain conditions of light... communication with it much as those with prosthetics moved their limbs through thinking...

Jupiter—Joop, their daughter—perched on a tall stool behind her mother, in the shadows. He'd met her in Key West Cemetery™ day before yesterday when she was conducting the Conch Train Tour™.

"Climb aboard the Conch Train™," Jupiter announced, facing the audience in the facsimile of the old tour train, her light-brown, tight-curled hair splendidly long and big, her face nearly as dark as Raphael's mother's, with her strong nose and snapping, pure black eyes. He felt a pang: he had missed much. She'd been ten when he had left.

Of course, she gave the tour the human touch, that extra *soupçon* of Keys Native; Conch. Her voice, when she spoke, was rich and deep. "All of you know about Ernest Hemingway, of course," (a hologram of a young, black-haired Hemingway sitting at a bar stool manifested, turned, smiled, and raised a glass before vanishing) "but Elizabeth Bishop, the Pulitzer

Prize winning poet, lived over on White Street, and Poet Laureate Billy Collins wrote a poem about riding his bike through the cemetery—"

He slipped aboard behind her. "Hoodoo!" yelled one woman at the back. "Love those great tattoos."

Removing his python-skin jacket and draping it over one arm, holding his candlelit skull aloft with his other hand, he said, in his deep gravelly Hoodoo voice, "All that you see are extinct. Sea turtles. Key deer. Bald eagles. Schaus butterflies. Florida panthers. Cowhorn orchids..."

His many tiny scars from skin cancer excisions gave his bodyshow a rough, flickering quality that he thought gave it more depth, so he did not have them removed. "This candle burns in the skull of a member of the most destructive invasive species, humans. We are completely responsible for the destruction of the river of grass, the Everglades, of Florida Bay, of the Great Florida Reef—"

Jupiter turned, and stared at him with a deepening frown. "*Dad?*"

He cleared his throat. "I walk the world doing penance for an ancient wrong we all—"

"Get off my fucking tour!" She pushed him in the chest. He staggered backwards and fell off the Conch Train. He dropped his skull, which bounced against a tombstone. The train glided silently away, floating on its magnetic path. "And stay away from us, you coward," she yelled out the door. "I bet you don't even know you have a grandson!"

* * *

STAY AWAY? NOT possible. Not any longer. He was too old to feel guilty, and he had just found he possessed an unknown, undeserved gift. As he stood in the doorway of Sloppy Joe's™, he could believe his blood had changed to seawater as he absorbed through sight and sound the haunting songs of myriad corals, whose harmonies and rhythms reminded him of the music of many distant cultures.

Then Joop rose from her stool, held one hand over her eyes, and stared straight at him, her face suffused with rage. What a strong woman she'd become! He felt a great deal of pride.

"Who do you love?" he belted out. His and Zoe's old song, back when they started a just-for-fun act with another prof at the University of Miami, and then it was just them, newlyweds, Aphrodite and Who Do You Love, Live! crashing festivals and political speeches with performance art about the death of their beloved sea.

Zoe—no, Aphrodite—turned her head and stared at him, leaning forward, aglow and flashing with intent and love that rushed into his brain. *Who... do you love? Who... do you love? Who... do you love?* Haunting minor tones. Wilderness. Sun-shot depths. Barracuda funnels a full fathom deep; ocean-spanning social networks; creatures that thought in light; plants that fought with color. The long-gone world; the sweet, lost voice of the once-living sea. Well, they both knew her answer to his question. She'd chosen long ago.

Joop was right. He'd lost his nerve. He had let them both down. He didn't deserve to be here. He turned to slip out the door.

"I told you to stay away," Joop hollered as she pushed through the crowd. She grabbed a chair, carried it overhead, reached the door, and brought it down upon her father's head.

APHRODITE

EVEN THOUGH HE had changed, I knew him. Emile Raphael, the handsome, brilliant guy I married when we were doctoral candidates in marine biology. Face sharp and sorrowful. Still tall, but his chest not as broad. More sinewy, perhaps, and the visions flowing over him echoed mine, in more prosaic ways.

I could hear him clearly, now.

He was all my memories of the apocalypse, of when the tragedy unfolding was still fresh, during the years when the data became clear: despite our work, the work of all of us committed to the sea, despite all we'd said and proved and tried to change, the Great Florida Reef was nearly gone.

Miami, having consumed and destroyed the Everglades and Florida Bay, was repentant. Dutch architects were hired to transform the city into the new model, the floating, self-sufficient, scientific wonder that nanotech and brilliant engineering had built along drowned coastlines everywhere; the ones that could afford it. Still, the oil rigs pumped along the coast of Florida; still we sucked fossil fuel to stoke our sickness, our lack of understanding that we were not alone; that we never had been, and that we could not live without those others, however small.

We and our colleagues were not entirely rational during the long time of mourning, back in the thirties when we knew for sure the reef would not recover. Everyone walked the halls with tears in their eyes, but Emile and I had a plan; had done research for five years that we called something else.

We were ready. In the chaos of the changing city, we moved quickly.

We'd talked about it. Lots. When we met as grad students at a heart-wrenching climate change conference in Copenhagen, we got mad drunk and threw desperate ideas at the wall until some stuck. That was in 2026, before the Florida Keys were drowned, back when we still had hope. Our coral gardens, a statewide effort, where accelerated-growth corals were transplanted, looked as if they would succeed. Long-stalled funds to restore the Everglades were finally released, but they came far too late. We were fighting to save the world, of course, not just our little stretch of South Florida, but it's all connected. I used to think everyone was, but I was wrong.

These days, Joop and I sailed down from our compound, about eighty miles to the northeast of Key West, every six weeks or so to make some money, and it was good money. I'd heard about Hoodoo, along with Tall Man, a fire juggler, and Twisted Woman, but I thought the guy in Key West was a copycat, not my ex, who was an international star, 'The Conscience of the Planet.' Ha! No, I didn't give him much thought at all. He was just another performance artist eking out the end-days in the simulacra of Old Key West™. Our beautiful old former state capital was now a state-of-the-art Dutch-designed and Russian-financed floating city that recycled everything and had successfully sealed against hurricanes Christopher, Zena, and Witt. That brought even more tourists, who hoped they would have the chance to ride out the big one for big bucks.

We had Category 3 storms regularly now, and Category 5 storms at least once a year, and one Cat 6, which hit 310 kph.

My Moonies were out in force that night I saw him. They came from everywhere. They loved me. Of course, I wanted all of them to Change, but they didn't know what I was, really, deeply. They simply loved my beauty and my mystery, and were drawn to my song because of their own love of the sea and of nature. The irresistible change was embedded in my genes—as was all the painstaking research I and Emile had done and linked with a wealth of scientific information—but I couldn't reveal it, and dared not use it. That would have been scientifically unethical. Still, I wanted to point to it.

Perhaps you know now: I was, indeed, of two minds. Or more. All right, now: many, and those without the human 'ethics' that were blind to so much. Was I right?

Only Jupiter knew. And my sister Daphne, who had finally accepted the decision I'd made so long ago.

And, of course, Emile.

He left because he couldn't take it; it was too painful to watch me. His excuse for his restlessness, and the growing fame that pulled him away. "Too radical for you?" I remember laughing, incredulous. "After all I've put up with? All Jupiter and I have put up with? Isn't this what we planned?"

He'd pleaded with me not to continue with my transformation, but for more than ten years he hung in there, my partner in crime, my colleague, my intellectual double, my loved one. We spirited equipment and supplies from University labs being replicated in Floating Miami as it neared completion. They would have been thrown away. In the chaos of the transformation, where the vast sums of money being thrown about beggared belief, no one noticed that an old, out-of-date research sloop had gone missing—or maybe the responsible colleague did, and failed to report it. His way of supporting the cause. There was the inevitable storm; it was lost at sea, along with two researchers.

We changed the name to *Mare Liberum*; created a new chain of ownership. There you go.

I know that the injections burned like fire, because I recorded that data, and that I screamed every time, in our boat out on the wide, sparkling, barren Atlantic, for hours. Sometimes days. I just don't remember that pain. I know that Emile nursed me on our ever-rocking sloop for months, frantic. I even looked like a monster; the whites of my eyes swelled, leaving my pupils flat, surrounded by raised, red tissue. My face puffed up. I shook uncontrollably; I had seizures. I refused to go to a hospital, afraid they'd flood me with drugs that would stop the process. A doc Emile found who kind of understood turned out to be Catholic. He just made the sign of the cross and left. Webs of light flowed over dying coral stands below the *Mare Liberum*. The minute rise in water temperature raised waterspouts that spurled erratically across the warmer seas and, more than once, nearly battered us to death. It was always hot. The warmer waters around the Turkey Point Nuclear Plant up near Homestead spawned giant albino sharks that further strained resources. Oil tankers out in the shipping lanes continued their procession, along with ever more gigantic cruise cities that damaged fragile ports.

But I came through. Changed. Joyous! Infused with this new music, this changed sense of time, this mind extending beyond my small, human self, which built hereditary walls between itself and all the rest of the world, and thought itself the pinnacle of evolution. But evolution is, quite simply, change. That's all. I am that change; change in the face of sure death.

In the midst of this, our birth control failed. We were terribly afraid. Emile too, had taken one injection, and it had frightened him. But so far, our girl's good, and she's forty—

strong, beautiful, smart, and understandably grouchy. She has sacrificed too much. My fault; my own guilt.

Genetically, she is a mosaic, with strange genes inherited from Emile and I, chimeras. Amazingly, she has a good marriage! Paul, who works on protecting and increasing our native fish, lives in our family compound with my two sisters, Daphne and India, their spouses, and their kids and grandkids. She has a child, Corey, whom I've never met. This makes me sad; even angry. He needs to know that both his grandparents are ... different.

Our Key West trips on the *Mare Liberum* pay for drone shipments of the drugs and minerals I need.

I'm just hanging on, though. For Joop. The last time she ran the tests, her tragic face crushed me. My lungs are crackly; my organs are failing. One more supermoon spawn, when we release our gametes into the sea, would do it, I think; move me into that Gaia toward which I so deeply yearn. I'd let go.

I'm using all my strength and concentration to remain in human mind, to make this record for you, whoever you might be—perhaps a consciousness more strange than mine. It's the endgame. Stage Four Aphrodite, if you will. I won't miss living above the sea, except for the people. I might miss *me*, if that turns out to be possible; if ocean-distributed me turns out to have the vestige of human memory Emile and I planned for, if ever we might re-emerge to a pristine, recovered world.

All of my research is embedded in the genetic code of every coral I host. They all fight to emerge. I am tired of being a battleground. We all need more room. Joop and I have found four sites that may allow us to survive and thrive, based on analysis of immense data.

Joop knows it all inside out, and much, much more. She has a doctorate in marine biology, like my sisters. Love of the sea has been in our blood for the five generations we've lived in the Keys, and with every generation we've learned more; done more. Daphne pushed Joop off to school before you could say *But what about Mom?* three times fast. They stopped speaking to me for a long time after I became cross-species. But came around; rallied for Joop, to give her her own main chance, and they maintained their crazy sister. I think they were hoping she would make a life elsewhere. I don't think she would take my path, but the heart of another is a dark forest. Hers, particularly, I'm afraid, when I think of her relationship with her father.

Emile's certainly was. Taking off like that. Dirt roads. Barbed wire. Stardom.

It had been all I could do to keep from laughing (it might have sounded like porpoise chirps) when I saw him across that room, over the heads of those faithful Moonies forever trying to spirit me away to their ceremonies. But it would have hurt his feelings.

Ah, true love never dies. I guess.

The Moonies? Sure. I'd gone out to their sacred island—actually an artificial island in Florida Bay; all the real islands are drowned, landless mangrove flats. I'd never go on or around the spring full moon, though, which frustrated them. Jupiter takes me out to sea, to the gardens, and lowers me in a large, lionfish-proof cage so that I can spawn. Before that moon, I'm too tranced to perform, or to even be around people. A few nights following the full moon, my corals release their gametes—at least, the hermaphrodites do.

Language can't show you how that feels, though. Better than the best sex ever? It is sex, of course, and for me, it is absolutely and literally ecstatic. I am out of my body, white spawn broadcast across the sea, swimming toward the light. Ecstasy. Ex-stasis. Rapture. My soul moves from my body into the great currents of life itself.

Jupiter pulls me up, eventually. Sometime during the next few days I come to, human again, but with the memory of that urgency, that animal joy, because I am a million animals, and I share their joy multiplied a millionfold, as they release for their own long journey. They tap into my nerves, my brain. Perhaps my humanity changes them too. I hear their voices, now, multi-fluorescing, for sea creatures communicate with color. Audience members can grab a patch of synth at the door, and see my voice. I'm told it's like diving without the risk. They see things no longer in nature. Of course, they come to see the freak. That's fine. I educate them. By the time I'm done, they are in love with the sea. Some of them become activists.

The process? It's taken decades, obviously. At first, my face stopped people dead if they saw me in the street, abloom with changes that, in nature, would have been the work of centuries, but which, in me, was accelerated. In earlier years, after the long, languid sunset, ever more lurid since the Great Dust Storm, I'd climb the ladder from a good long soak under the pier, and make my way down breezy, atmospheric streets to Sloppy Joe's™.

Jupiter, my protector, my stalwart, my dear heart, usually showed up about that time, having sold whatever lionfish she'd caught during the day. Lionfish, another creature invasive to the fragile Keys ecosystem, eat coral voraciously and have wiped out most native fish species. Fine human food, though.

Now, I'm completely dependent on water. I can barely function out of it.

But—wait—I can *hear* you, you say. There's nothing strange about you. You're speaking. You have language.

Ha! Don't take that too literally. I'm doing this before I do what I need to do, for the record. If you hear this at all, it's in your mind, not in your ears, and I have succeeded. Maybe you're seeing this in pictures. Maybe it's in music. It's not easy to make this leap. But now I'm part of your brain, right? And this is centuries later, perhaps. Maybe light-years. I don't know where you are, who you are, what you are. Maybe you're hanging out in orbit or waking from a light-year of cryogenic sleep and being schooled. Maybe you're a manatee, a parrot, or a child in Chile. Welcome.

But no, I can't really speak. My body and mind are moving away from that. Singing takes place in a different part of the brain, and this is a great novelty, even for me. I can still take in a great breath of water-saturated air, and form word and sound but mostly sound. The sounds of sea creatures. My translation of wavelengths of color, or the clicking, chirping, singing voices of mammal cousins.

Emile didn't really stand out in the Key West crowd. Everyone's trying to outdo the other. But when I saw him, still handsome but oh, so old, shorts held up by a rope, barefoot, and he belted out "Who do you love," every head turned.

Jupiter went ballistic. Poor Emile was curled up on the floor when the cops pulled her off. I was terrified! And mad.

Aphrodite bailed her daughter out of jail, but Zoe spent the night at the ER with her ex-husband while kind nurses doused her with a pail of salt water now and then. I made them believers, at least.

It is hard to be many. But then, it is also pretty hard to be one.

I never was just one. Probably, no one is.

Jupiter got us loaded onto the Magic Penny Water Taxi in Key West Harbor, onto the *Mare Liberum*, and, anger in her every movement—she did not speak, and did not even look at us—out into the Atlantic, solar sails unfurled, and headed northwest, toward home, a trip that would take about 24 hours.

I was below, in my ballast tank of sea water. Emile slept next to me in Jupiter's narrow bunk, his scarred, dream-raddled body twitching.

Neither Emile nor I wanted to see my angry sisters. But Jupiter was pissed, and we were too tired to object.

i am alien

i am you

JUPITER

JUPITER LOVED THIS sail up the Keys in the Atlantic. She could pretend, for a few days, that things were almost like they were when she was a little girl, before the strongest hurricane on record, Victor, washed the thin land layer covering the limestone Keys out into the Gulf of Mexico and gave the *coup de main* to the environmental damage that humans had taken so far down the road.

Well, her cargo had tried. There they were, down there in the *Mare*'s research lab where they'd started it. She hoped Emile was getting a good look at the result of what he'd helped bring about. As far as she was concerned, they were a pair of addicts. No matter how her mother tried to tell her about how amazing it all was, when it came to watching your mother cut off her

135

own fingers because they ached with new growth, because they were ready to be *harvested*, and cut up into tiny chunks to grow, a hundred times more quickly than non-humanized coral, in the chemical bath that accelerated their growth, to plant in one of the coral gardens they'd guarded for years—

Crap. She gave the wheel a vicious twist, and heard something heavy that she hadn't secured crash, below. Her life was hopelessly snarled.

Yes. She'd had it. She was going to live with her family always now. Corey, her seven-year-old son and Paul, her husband, would be out of their minds with joy. She would be too. Let the two down there carry on.

They had never been any good for each other. She'd heard them arguing since birth—arguing, then making love, then working together like a dream for a few months. They'd had a little band, the hopeless hams—Aphrodite and Who Do You Love, wild characters singing eco-songs for tourist change. But they'd always seemed like an act to her. Never like normal people. But how, she asked herself, would she know? What was normal now? Groups of waterfolk living in tight colonies, living the self-sufficiency dream; big university research centers; companies still launching their ships to Mars; cities, sealed from their own pollution, and little in between. Yes, she'd been to the mainland. She'd found Paul there. He was from Minnesota. He always said he was glad he'd chosen this life, and her whole nutty clan, but sometimes she could scarce believe him. He'd put up with a lot. And found it all fascinating, he said. Sweet guy.

She blinked. Pushed autopilot and ran to starboard. Could that have been a sea turtle? They were extinct. Hurricane Victor and subsequent storms, increasingly frequent and harsh, had wiped away their nesting grounds ages ago.

She must have been dreaming.

Below, she grabbed a Green Iguana from the fridge, then made her way from the galley through the lab and aft.

There they were. Mom and dad. Mom sleeping in her ballast-tank, heartbreakingly beautiful, hair-tubes undulating as the *Mare Liberum* plowed through the waves. Her dad—well, he was good-looking. Maybe he'd really been as handsome and talented and smart and all as her mother had always told her. All she knew was that he'd never been around.

She emerged into the sunlight and the vast turquoise sea. She could see right across what had once been Big Pine Key into the Bay, where the water seemed divided into horizontal bands of blue and green. Hardy mangroves still grew in some spots, creating the illusion of tiny islands, but there was no land beneath the roots that sprang like fountains from the trunk, only submerged flats. Still, they provided shade and habitat for sea creatures and for birds.

It was something. But probably not enough.

After some hours, she reached the Seven Mile Bridge. The channel markers were still there, more important than ever since they were all, now, water folk. The sea rushed beneath the *Mare Liberum* as she turned to port, toward the bay.

The bridge rose from water and descended into water. The road on each side was submerged—not deeply; just by a foot or so, but the Keys were once again the isolated islands they had always been, save for a brief century of train and road.

As on all the Keys, the remains of concrete stilt homes were scattered here and there, most empty. The bridge was a brilliant sight, covered with self-sustaining habitats and recycling technology developed via various space programs, festooned with native plants, some growing hydroponically and some in expensive imported soil. It was the hopeful counterpart to Key West™. Real life.

As she swept beneath the bridge, she held steady against the tidal current rushing out through the deep channel, and children leaned against the railing overhead, screaming and waving. A teddy bear landed on the deck next to her. An accident, but she could not stop to return it. She turned and waved her thanks. Corey was seven, probably a little too old for a teddy bear. But maybe not.

He'd never seen Grandma Zoe. She'd thought it would be too scary. Or Grandpa Emile. He was just a legend. Hoodoo. She snorted. Given her own reaction last night, she was realizing that this approach was probably a bad idea. Family dynamics could jump out and bite you, hard.

After sailing in the Bay for several hours, she was almost home. She passed through the cut. An egret hid inside the dark mangrove jungle like a bright white exclamation point. One, where there had once been many. This much was positive: humans were giving up, at last, on South Florida. Though Floating Miami had destroyed an immense amount of habitat despite the care the developers professed to take, no one, up there, lived outside its safe, self-sealing environs in this age of fiercer, more frequent hurricanes. It was against the law here, as there. No one would insure you, and no one enforced the law. You were just on your own.

The rapacious pillage of the Everglades had ceased, and nature—cautiously; gradually—was returning, adapting to the changed salinity and temperature of bay and sea, if it could. But invasive species still ruled, and many niches had emptied. The fragile web of life was torn, and perhaps would not mend. Joop was always reminded that they teetered on the edge of precipitous decline.

Emile emerged from below, clad in his rope-belted shorts. He helped anchor the *Mare Liberum,* then went below. He returned with two cold Green Iguanas. He gazed at their fair colony, about a quarter-mile away.

"Home, sweet home. It's been a long time."

"I'm going to introduce you to Corey. Your grandson."

"Think he'd want to meet the bad guy? The unethical scientist who—well, whatever I did."

"You were not alone, and nobody ever said that."

"Are you telling me my grandson is stupid? Can't pick up on the subtext?"

"I'll bring him out in a few hours, and you can see for yourself."

"You know, you've turned out all right. Kind of weird, but all right."

He'd donned another iteration of his regalia: mutant albino crock hide top hat, secured with a big hat pin, iguanaskin string tie, lionfish cowboy boots. His torso effervesced a changing scenario of a healthy reef, dim in the sun, but hinting at its fluorescing power in the right light.

Jupiter examined her father with a long, careful look, the look of daylight. The first time she'd had a chance.

"Who's weird? I'm the only grownup here." She waved toward the cut. "Remember the Turkey Point nuclear plant up by Homestead? Hot water spawns giant mutant albino crocks. A forty-footer hangs out in the mangroves, so you might not want to swim. Or then, again, you might need a new invasive species hat."

IT WAS SOOTHING to cast off the dinghy. It had drawn a good, full charge from the long sail. The shallow bay was smooth, crystalline green. The bay floor, covered with sea grass when she was a kid, was mostly a lifeless desert, but a mutation that found conditions favorable had put forth scattered, grassy clumps that sheltered tiny, near-transparent fish.

She headed directly toward the colony, where the windowless, roofless concrete stilt homes built to codes developed fifty years earlier, around 2030, were aligned along the watery path of old Route One. Each was the fiercely defended home of old Conch families who thrived in this new environment using cisterns and a hodgepodge of desalinization technologies.

Abba, her niece, had painted a reef mural on the south side of the house, which covered the seam between the original concrete wall and the rebar and concrete-filled block they'd scavenged to rebuild the side of the house. It had been smashed when Victor picked up a cruise boat in the most massive storm surge on record and pushed it across the reef, across four miles of shallow seas, and into Florida Bay, where its remains still rested, taking out a quarter-mile of homes along the way. The Keys had been under order of evacuation, but many Conchs, as was the custom, had stubbornly refused to leave, and their remains had been found as far away as Cape Sable, thirty miles northwest. There had been talk of distributing free nanotech building materials to restore their homes, but in the end it was decided that squatting—which is what it was called, even though they'd owned this property since the 1990s—should not be encouraged.

She reached the edge of the subdivision, where a few large bayfront homes had been made liveable, and her home assumed detail.

Most of Abba's mural was obscured by hanging vegetable gardens. Her extended family—aunts, their husbands, children, and grandchildren who had not lit out for the mainland—occupied several linked, rehabbed houses. In rooftop container gardens, they sowed soybeans for a steady supply, and grew lettuces under a shade lattice on the north side of the house. Nets of farmed clams hung in the shallows in which the houses stood, and orchids flowered in the shade of bean, cucumber, and big-leaved squash vines. The wind farm set up by Keys Electric long ago still produced power, and several houses were covered with solar panels. Potted citrus trees shaded some rooftops. They paid Islamorada, a nearby floating city shaped like a ray that sheltered them in hurricanes, for any fuel they couldn't otherwise produce; it was their biggest expense.

She zipped between unsalvageable houses, over the remains of bayside streets—Heron, Osprey, Cormorant—where she had once skateboarded. Now, their heaved remains shimmered a foot below the dinghy for a few seconds. She crossed submerged lots and deeper canals and tied up at the floating dock lashed to concrete stilts. Across the straight, watery stretch of Route One were more ruined houses, then the green Atlantic, where distant oil rigs labored. Just not for them.

Daphne's flats boat was missing; she'd probably picked up some tourists at Islamorada for an eco-tour of Florida bay.

"Hey!" she yelled, as she climbed the stairs.

"Joop!" Abba, eighteen, ran down the stairs, long black hair streaming behind her, wearing shorts and a halter top. "How's grandma?"

"Okay," said Jupiter, hugging thin Abba tightly for a second. No one but Daphne knew the full scope of Project Aphrodite, and she had always disapproved.

She yelled, "Corey?"

He barreled down the stairs and ran into her so hard that she had to grab the railing.

She hugged him with her free arm. "Hey, kiddo."

"Mom!" He pulled her up the stairs.

"You're pretty strong for seven. Where's your dad? I haven't seen him for weeks."

"Gathering data and calibrating the instruments." Corey was a sturdy, deeply tanned boy with tight brown curls. "He said it was too rough to take me. He won't be back for a few days."

They reached the fourth floor, the living level, open to breezes and spectacular views of the ocean and the bay. Comfortable, cushioned bamboo furniture was scattered here and there. Jupiter took a deep breath. *Home.* She wished there was someone to take the second shift out on the *Mare Liberum.* Couldn't she just leave them there? No. Emile didn't know how to take care of Aphrodite. Each of her corals required a different feeding protocol. Tomorrow they'd be oceanside, and she'd go down in her cage. Some pillar corals were ready to be anchored in Garden #3. Emile could go. He'd be astounded. Maybe she should be proud of them both. She'd consider it, anyway.

"Package here?" she asked Abba.

"Drone's late."

More of the family drifted in, hugged. Then she dropped her bombshell.

"Emile's back."

"What?" India, her mother's youngest sister, sprang out of her chair, grabbed the binoculars, and went over to the bayside railing. "I sure wouldn't recognize him. A top hat? How does he keep it on his head? Where's Zoe?"

"I think I'm going to take Corey out to meet them," said Jupiter.

"Well," said India, giving her a look, "it's up to you. I'll pack you a dinner."

"I'm coming too," said Abba.

"I wish Paul were here," Jupiter said.

Corey ran over to the balcony and yelled, "Grandma and Grandpa, I'm coming to meeeet you!"

"Come here," said Jupiter. "There's something I need to tell you."

"I know all about her."

"Yes. Well. We'll see. Just remember that they both love you."

"They've had a hard life," said India.

When Jupiter bowed her head and started shaking, India said, "Honey, I'm only trying to—"

Jupiter raised her head. Tears streamed down her face, but she was laughing, hard. "You—don't—know—the *half* of it!"

IT WAS LATE by the time the drone brought the necessary supplies, and they headed out to the *Mare Liberum*. They flew toward a splendid sunset, and Jupiter flipped on the running lights.

When she got closer, she noticed Corey staring at the boat.

"Mom..."

He jumped when his mom yelled, "You put out those candles and get rid of that thing right now!" Then she said to Corey, "Look! A cormorant on the channel marker drying his wings. That's amazing!"

They pulled alongside the sloop.

Emile leaned over, holding his hat in one hand, and threw them a line. "Sorry."

"Maybe I should take him back."

"I am sorry. He is too young for all that." He threw Corey a line, holding his hat in one hand.

"Grandpa?" said Corey, staring up. "Is that a manatee on your chest?"

"Uncle Emile?" said Abba.

"Let me help you all up."

"Here's dinner." Zoe handed it up. "India made it."

Emile looked at the basket contemplatively, then smiled. "She was always a great cook." He cleared his throat. "Well, shall we go below? Come on, Abba. Son, I won't bite."

"I might," said Jupiter.

Corey said, "Mom, any juice in the galley?"

Zoe hurried down after them and lit some candles. In the galley, before allowing Corey to go aft, she sat on a bench and took both of Corey's hands. "Honey, your grandmother is—"

He looked at her with an earnest expression. "I know. She's turning into everything wild. Like it used to be. But I know what it was like."

Emile sat on the other bench. "Child, listen."

He leaned his forearms on his legs, clasped his hands, bowed his head for a moment, and then looked up.

"Your grandmother—Zoe Raphael, Aphrodite, Love-of-the-Sea—is all that has died." The candlelight deepened the shadows on his face. "You're just a child. You don't know how it was."

"I do."

"No, you don't."

"I've been in the Islamorada interactive environment—"

Emile shook his head. "That's just nonsense. Yes, it's beautiful, but when they built that, most everything was already gone. They just didn't give people the numbers, so nobody ever did anything about it while it was slipping away. By the time people started to wake up there were ten Florida panthers left. Tourists could see an itsy-bitsy patch of coral when they snorkeled and dove. Once they were back on the boat, they were encouraged to imagine it still stretched from the Dry Tortugas to Elliott Key. But it didn't. No, child. It was gone."

Jupiter saw that he'd found her Scotch while she was gone. He picked up the half-full glass and took another sip. Tears stood in his eyes.

She splashed some in a glass.

COREY

THE OLD MAN, my grandpa, was scary. So was grandma, like clowns are scary, but she smiled and waved at me from inside her glass. Then she closed her eyes and seemed to sleep. I didn't know how she could sleep in the water. Her hair was long, wavy, green tubes of coral. She looked like she was all over strange flowers, all different bright colors and patterns. I thought I saw a skull on the berth next to her, kind of covered with a blanket.

Mom looked really sad. "She's tired, honey," she said. "Maybe you can talk to her tomorrow."

Grandpa was drinking whisky. Abba was poking around. "What a cool lab! You have everything here. Do you know where the coral gardens are?"

"Some old ones. Don't know if they survived."

"Have you ever told anyone where they are?"

He shook his head. "Do you know how many of them were ruined by tourists wanting to see the marvels? We grew the corals in plastic bags and then planted them in rock. But then she got... more strange. Stem cell stuff. We share a large number of genes and proteins with corals. We're ancient animals ourselves. Zoe was brave enough to explore that.

"I woke up one night and saw her injecting herself. Right away I knew what she was doing. I argued. I did my best. I mean, what could I have done? Have her committed? I couldn't guard her day and night from herself. She persuaded me to try it once, but..." he shrugged.

I kept looking at grandma. Aphrodite. That's what grandpa called her. "How come she only has two fingers on that hand?"

"The fingers? Ahhh. They grow back. Fast. She uses a pain patch. Never watch. You'd throw up. I used to cut them up, bag them, hung them. See? There's some over there. No, you don't have to look."

Abba went over and flipped on a little light so she could see them better.

"They grow very quickly in that hormone bath. It's based on work done at the turn of the century, when volunteers planted coral gardens all around the world. It helped, some, but conditions changed so fast. She has a plan, though—"

I asked, "Why isn't she wearing any clothes?"

"Clothing hurts her. She's delicate. And her skin is the organ through which her corals grow. Needs light, but not too much. Too much sun kills corals. Coral is a symbiote. Every little polyp has its own stomach. The zooxanthellae—the algae that produces the color—gets CO_2; the coral gets oxygen. It's like a million little rain forests. If the water temp gets too hot, the algae take off for cooler parts. The corals bleach and then die."

"She's really pretty."

He looked over his shoulder at her. "Her head is turning to brain coral. A complete conceit, of course; brain corals have no brain. It just looks cool, doesn't it? She is her own work of art. Always changing. You should see her when she tethers herself to the sea floor and lets reef fish flock round her. It used to be my job to keep the lion fish away. Maybe she'll let you do that sometime. She doesn't want to scare you, though. Your grandma Zoe is a hermaphrodite—that is, she has male and female coral—and sunset is the best time for some of them. They swim toward the light and mate. Happens every spring. The spawning. Those creatures are called planulae. Some of them swim for weeks or months to find the right place to land and grow."

I kept staring at her, inside the glass tank. I wanted to climb in and hug her, but she looked sharp.

"Grandma," I yelled.

She opened her eyes and looked at me.

"I... she's saying... something. I love you, I think." I pounded it. "Grandma! I love you! Grandma!"

"You do hear her, sometimes? Singing? Speaking? Whispery?

I do. Yes! Don't run away. I won't hurt you. I love you. I'm your grandfather. I wanted to give you a hug. There. That's better. Don't cry. I know. It's hard to take in. We're just trying to take care of her the best we can. I mean, your mom—it's what she does. That's right. I'm crying too. Yes. You may go now. Remember. Just remember. It's all going fast now. Every day we lose more of our own nursery, the world that birthed us.

"Someday you might go away to a university and learn more. I'd be surprised if you don't, child. Bring back something for us. Maybe there's still hope, somewhere, somehow. Remember: you are a part of nature. Not outside of it. Whatever you love, remember: we are all connected."

As COREY, WHO had just turned an uncelebrated thirty, descended near long-dead Conch Reef, the surface of the water billowed above him in a way he always found thrilling. He was entering a different atmosphere, away from the ruined concrete stilt homes on Plantation Key, and his past. First, the *Mare Liberum* had vanished in a storm, along with his mother and grandparents. The rest of his family died soon afterward when Islamorada's seal failed during Hurricane Samantha. He didn't know how he'd survived. He barely remembered those terrible times, and it made him sad to pass the house, where a bunch of drunks lived now. He should know. He'd been one of them for too long. Now he lived on his small boat.

This was a different world than the one he served, Party Isle, a ten-acre floating tourist town. Nothing fancy. After Islamorada was destroyed, there was no interest in building another expensive high-tech place.

He'd grown up hearing tales of the splendor of the Great Florida Reef, once almost two hundred miles long, which had stretched from Miami all the way to the Marquesas, rich with life in the gin-clear shallow sea. Below him now was sea desert, a barren floor.

His winch had broken. It was in the shop. In the meantime, he needed to check on his crates of farmed snapper. He'd fought for the coveted permit that allowed him to call them 'wild' when he sold them at the Fish Market at Party Isle, but in truth, there were no wild snapper. He set aside a few to spawn in his own home setup, and put them out here to grow. Native fish in the Keys had been wiped out long ago by overfishing, pollution, invasive species, and the changing habitat caused by the rising, warming sea.

He wondered if he was in the right place. He looked up. Yeah, there was his float, bobbing above; here was the line, wavering in parallax. It disappeared behind what looked like a wreck. Must be pretty damned old. Wasn't on any charts. When he was ready to set out the crates, a current had seized his boat and swept him along for a good fifteen minutes. He'd figured what the hell; a new spot might be better, let down the crates, and saved the coordinates. No one ever came out here. He often went all day without seeing another boat.

Shafts of sunlight swept the barren seascape, modulated by wind-shifted clouds above. Tropical Storm Figaro had just been named, off Africa's coast, and these storms had a much more statistical likelihood of becoming hurricanes than when he was a child, though the Key West™ Chamber of Commerce and the State of Florida said it was just a normal change in weather patterns, not to worry. He'd been hearing that his whole life.

Hunker down; keblang! The big wind comes, the big surge follows, you're wiped out again. And again. Save your money, water rat. Climb back out of the hole. If you live.

He should have listened to his aunt Daphne. *You have a good mind, Corey. You can only learn so much here, even from us. Do something with your life. Go to the mainland; go to school.*

His mother. Jupiter. He didn't remember her at all. He'd hardly ever seen her.

Ah. There they were. Five crates. Lucky that wreck hadn't sawed off the cable. Another near-mistake: don't take chances. Go with what you know. If he had the winch, he'd pull them up now. The storm might smash them.

He hovered next to one of them, and studied the fish that came near him. No signs of disease. Good. If he had, he'd have to wrap each trap in plastic and infuse the bag with antibiotics, and to do that he'd have to hire help, which he couldn't afford.

Then, about fifteen meters away, something caught his eye. A trick of light? A human skeleton? A skull, at least, and other bones scattered about. Perhaps a long-ago diver trapped in this wreck.

He moved closer, hankering to explore the wreck and irritated that his gloves had been stolen off his boat a few days earlier.

He allowed the current to pull him around the side of the wreck.

Sunlight swept the sea like a great chord.

He held up a hand against a surge of color so powerful that it almost seemed like a blow. He was dizzy. Hearing things. A voice. Wild song.

He closed his eyes and got his breath back into a low, steady pattern, then opened his eyes to a dream.

It was, he realized, a living reef.

He floated above it, seeing fish that, to him, had been only fairy tales. A school of yellow wrasses turned on a dime when he moved his hand. The names came to him easily. A parrotfish grazed on a brilliant pink fan coral, eating algae that might smother it. Elkhorn, staghorn, boulder stars. Sargent majors, sea urchins, damselfish. A large spotted ray flew past him, its great wings flapping into blue distance.

He was pelted with language: names were joy, whispered in his mind. He held back the tears that would fog his mask. He forced himself to keep track of time. Three more minutes... two...

He turned to ascend, and then—in the very center—

A brain coral, surrounded by pink sea fans, waving gently in the current, extending into something so deliberately woman-shaped that he could scarce believe it.

Grandma?

But—much larger than a woman, her outlines bourgeoning as a coral garden that he could not see the end of.

And then it all came back.

A skull. Lit by a candle, held by a man with long white dreads, wearing a top hat. Something a little boy might well put from his mind. His mother, hugging him. "We'll be back soon. Weather might kick up, but it's a supermoon, and Grandma—" she had faltered, and then she squeezed him tight. "Grandma loves you."

He would come back and find, somewhere, the name, *Mare Liberum*. His mother was here somewhere, and his strange old grandfather.

His family.

He reached out and touched what seemed like Aphrodite's outstretched hand, somewhere to the north of what seemed lively, smiling eyes that he knew must be a dream—

A fire ran through him.

The world spoke.

Intimate... immensity...

He streamed into the outer reaches of world and time. The colors were complex, multilayered, stuttering, then smooth, a series of signals that woke him. Images of beautiful sea, and beautiful life, surged through him like a shock. He floated in a cornucopia of astonishing life for he knew not how long, lost in awe.

Go.

No.

Go.

I can't.

Who... do... you... love...

He considered.

The sea. But also the sky. The land. But also the stars.

His life, which now seemed precious. Like all life.

The music he'd run from so hard all his life infused him. He moved to it as he ascended—carefully, slowly—toward light, a thing of the sea rising to what might be the light of the moon, in young, distant seas, in the far-distant time of early life.

MY NAME IS Corey Raphael. I am fifty-five years old at this time, an astronaut-scientist. I am on my way with some of my very close relatives to Kepler 382b, but our ship will adjust course as it receives new information.

We aim to form a planet-spanning reef that communicates with humans, so that humans will care. We're going to try and do it right this time.

Of course, there may be other life there. Or perhaps we can start over. We'll see how it all works out.

These are all stories that my Grandma Zoe saved. They are stories of non-human life, but, as you will see, all life is related. There are millions of stories. Build, tear down, learn, build again. Maybe by the time we get there, we will do better.

Enjoy.

Wake me when it's time.

BECAUSE CHANGE WAS THE OCEAN AND WE LIVED BY HER MERCY

– Charlie Jane Anders –

1. THIS WAS SACRED, THIS WAS STOLEN

WE STOOD NAKED on the shore of Bernal and watched the candles float across the bay, swept by a lazy current off to the north, in the direction of Potrero Island. A dozen or so candles stayed afloat and alight after half a league, their tiny flames bobbing up and down, casting long yellow reflections on the dark water alongside the streaks of moonlight. At times I fancied the candlelight could filter down onto streets and buildings, the old automobiles and houses full of children's toys, all the waterlogged treasures of long-gone people. We held hands, twenty or thirty of us, and watched the little candle-boats we'd made as they floated away. Joconda was humming an old reconstructed song about the wild road, hir beard full of flowers. We all just about held our breath. I felt my bare skin go electric with the intensity of the moment, like this could be the good time we'd all remember in the bad times to come. This was sacred, this was stolen. And then someone—probably Miranda—farted, and then we were all laughing, and the grown-up seriousness was gone. We were all busting up and falling over each other on the rocky ground, in a nude heap, scraping our knees and giggling into each other's limbs. When we got our breath back and looked up, the candles were all gone.

2. I FELT LIKE I HAD ALWAYS BEEN WRONG HEADED

I COULDN'T DEAL with life in Fairbanks any more. I grew up at the same time as the town, watched it go from regular city to megacity as I hit my early twenties. I lived in an old decommissioned solar power station with five other kids, and we tried to make the loudest, most uncomforting music we could, with a beat as relentless and merciless as the tides. We wanted to shake our cinderblock walls and make people dance until their feet bled. But we sucked. We were bad at music, and not quite dumb enough not to know it. We all wore big hoods and spiky shoes and tried to make our own drums out of drycloth and cracked wood, and we read our poetry on Friday nights. There were bookhouses, along with stinktanks where you could drink up and listen to awful poetry about extinct animals. People came from all over, because everybody heard that Fairbanks was becoming the most civilized place on Earth, and that's when I decided to leave town. I had this moment of looking around at my musician friends and my restaurant job and our cool little scene, and feeling like there had to be more to life than this.

I hitched a ride down south and ended up in Olympia, at a house where they were growing their own food and drugs, and doing a way better job with the drugs than the food. We were all staring upwards at the first cloud anybody had seen in weeks, trying to identify what it could mean. When you hardly ever saw them, clouds had to be omens.

We were all complaining about our dumb families, still watching that cloud warp and contort, and I found myself talking about how my parents only liked to listen to that boring boo-pop music with the same three or four major chords and that cruddy AAA/BBB/CDE/CDE rhyme scheme, and how my mother insisted on saving every scrap of organic material we used, and collecting every drop of rainwater. "It's fucking pathetic, is what it is. They act like we're still living in the Great Decimation."

"They're just super traumatized," said this skinny genderfreak named Juya, who stood nearby holding the bong. "It's hard to even imagine. I mean, we're the first generation that just takes it for granted we're going to survive, as like a species. Our parents, our grandparents, and their grandparents, they were all living like every day could be the day the planet finally got done with us. They didn't grow up having moisture condensers and myco-protein rinses and skinsus."

"Yeah, whatever," I said. But what Juya said stuck with me, because I had never thought of my parents as traumatized. I'd always thought they were just tightly wound and judgey. Juya had two cones of dark twisty hair on zir head and a red pajamzoot, and zi was only a year or two older than me but seemed a lot wiser.

"I want to find all the music we used to have," I said. "You know, the weird, noisy shit that made people's clothes fall off and their hair light on fire. The rock 'n roll that just listening to it turned girls into boys, the songs that took away the fear of god. I've read about it, but I've never heard any of it, and I don't even know how to play it."

"Yeah, all the recordings and notations got lost in the Dataclysm," Juya said. "They were in formats that nobody can read, or they got corrupted, or they were printed on disks made from petroleum. Those songs are gone forever."

"I think they're under the ocean," I said. "I think they're down there somewhere."

Something about the way I said that helped Juya reach a decision. "Hey, I'm heading back down to the San Francisco archipelago in the morning. I got room in my car if you wanna come with."

Juya's car was an older solar model that had to stop every couple hours to recharge, and the self-driving module didn't work so great. My legs were resting in a pile of old headmods and biofills, plus those costooms that everybody used a few summers earlier that made your skin turn into snakeskin that you could shed in one piece. So the upshot was, we had a lot of time to talk and hold hands and look at the endless golden landscape stretching off to the east. Juya had these big bright eyes that laughed when the rest of zir face was stone serious, and strong tentative hands to hold me in place as zi tied me to the car seat with fronds of algae. I had never felt as safe and dangerous as when I crossed the wasteland with Juya. We talked for hours about how the world needed new communities, new ways to breathe life back into the ocean, new ways to be people.

By the time we got to Bernal Island and the Wrong Headed community, I was in love with Juya, deeper than I'd ever felt with anyone before.

Juya up and left Bernal a week and a half later, because zi got bored again, and I barely noticed that zi was gone. By then, I was in love with a hundred other people, and they were all in love with me.

Bernal Island was only accessible from one direction, from the big island in the middle, and only at a couple times of day when they let the bridge down and turned off the moat. After a few days on Bernal, I stopped even noticing the other islands on our horizon, let alone paying attention to my friends on social media talking about all the fancy new restaurants Fairbanks was getting. I was constantly having these intense, heartfelt moments with people in the Wrong Headed crew.

"The ocean is our lover, you can hear it laughing at us." Joconda was sort of the leader here. Sie sometimes had a beard and sometimes a smooth round face covered with perfect bright makeup. Hir eyes were as gray as the sea and just as unpredictable. For decades, San Francisco and other places like it had been abandoned, because the combination of seismic instability and a voracious dead ocean made them too scary and risky. But that city down there, under the waves, had been the place everybody came to, from all over the world, to find freedom. That legacy was ours now.

And those people had brought music from their native countries and their own cultures, and all those sounds had crashed together in those streets, night after night. Joconda's own ancestors had come from China and Peru, and hir great-grandparents had played nine-stringed guitars, melodies and rhythms that Joconda barely recalled now. Listening to hir, I almost fancied I could put my ear to the surface of the ocean and hear all the sounds from generations past, still reverberating. We sat all night, Joconda, some of the others and myself, and I got to play on an old-school drum made of cowhide or something. I felt like I had always been Wrong Headed, and I'd just never had the word for it before.

Juya sent me an email a month or two after zi left Bernal: *The moment I met you, I knew you needed to be with the rest of those maniacs. I've never been able to resist delivering lost children to their rightful homes. It's almost the only thing I'm good at, other than the things you already knew about.* I never saw zir again.

3. "I'M SO GLAD I FOUND A GROUP OF PEOPLE I WOULD RISK DROWNING IN DEAD WATER FOR."

BACK IN THE 21st century, everybody had theories about how to make the ocean breathe again. Fill her with quicklime, to neutralize the acid. Split the water molecules into hydrogen and oxygen, and bond the hydrogen with the surplus carbon in the water to create a clean-burning hydrocarbon fuel. Release genetically engineered fish, with special gills. Grow special algae that was designed to commit suicide after a while. Spray billions of nanotech balls into her. And a few other things. Now, we had to clean up the after-effects of all those failed solutions, while also helping the sea to let go of all that CO_2 from before.

The only way was the slow way. We pumped ocean water through our special enzyme store and then through a series of filters, until what came out the other end was clear and oxygen-rich. The waste, we separated out and disposed of. Some of it became raw materials for shoe soles and roof tiles. Some of it, the pure organic residue, we used as fertilizer or food for our mycoprotein.

I got used to staying up all night playing music with some of the other Wrong Headed kids, sometimes on the drum and sometimes on an old stringed instrument that was made of stained wood and had a leering cat face under its fret. Sometimes I thought I could hear something in the way our halting beats and scratchy notes bounced off the walls and the water beyond, like we were really conjuring a lost soundtrack. Sometimes it all just seemed like a waste.

What did it mean to be a real authentic person, in an era when everything great from the past was twenty feet underwater? Would you embrace prefab newness, or try to copy the images you can see from the handful of docs we'd scrounged from the Dataclysm? When we got tired of playing music, an hour before dawn, we would sit around arguing, and inevitably you got to that moment where you were looking straight into someone else's eyes and arguing about the past, and whether the past could ever be on land, or the past was doomed to be deep underwater forever.

I felt like I was just drunk all the time, on that cheap-ass vodka that everybody chugged in Fairbanks, or maybe on nitrous. My head was evaporating, but my heart just got more and more solid. I woke up every day on my bunk, or sometimes tangled up in someone else's arms and legs on the daybed, and felt actually jazzed to get up and go clean the scrubbers or churn the mycoprotein vats.

Every time we put down the bridge to the big island and turned off our moat, I felt everything go sour inside me, and my heart went funnel-shaped. People sometimes just wandered away from the Wrong Headed community without much in the way of goodbye—that was how Juya had gone—but meanwhile, new people showed up and got the exact same welcome that everyone had given to me. I got freaked out thinking of my perfect home being overrun by new selfish loud fuckers. Joconda had to sit me down, at the big table where sie did all the official business, and tell me to get over myself because change was the ocean and we lived on her mercy. "Seriously, Pris. I ever see that look on your face, I'm going to throw you into the myco vat myself." Joconda stared at me until I started laughing and promised to get with the program.

And then one day I was sitting at our big table, overlooking the straits between us and the big island. Staring at Sutro Tower, and the taller buildings poking out of the water here and there. And this obnoxious skinny bitch sat down next to me, chewing in my ear and talking about the impudence of impermanence or some similar. "Miranda," she introduced herself. "I just came up from Anaheim-Diego. Jeez what a mess. They actually think they can build nanomechs and make it scalable. Whatta bunch of poutines."

"Stop chewing in my ear," I muttered. But then I found myself following her around everywhere she went.

Miranda was the one who convinced me to dive into the chasm of Fillmore St. in search of a souvenir from the old Church of John Coltrane, as a present for Joconda. I strapped on some goggles and a big apparatus that fed me oxygen while also helping me to navigate a little bit, and then we went out in a dinghy that looked old enough that someone had actually used it for fishing. Miranda gave me one of her crooked grins and studied a wrinkled old map. "I thinnnnnk it's right around here." She laughed. "Either that or the Korean barbecue restaurant where the mayor got assassinated that one time. Not super clear which is which."

I gave her a murderous look and jumped into the water, letting myself fall into the street at the speed of water resistance. Those sunken buildings turned into doorways and windows facing me, but they stayed blurry as the bilge flowed around them. I could barely find my feet, let alone identify a building on sight. One of these places had been a restaurant, I was pretty sure. Ancient automobiles lurched back and forth, like maybe even their brakes had rusted away. I figured the Church of John Coltrane would have a spire like a saxophone? Maybe? But all of the buildings looked exactly the same. I stumbled down the street, until I saw something that looked like a church, but it was a caved-in old McDonald's restaurant. Then I tripped over something, a downed pole or whatever, and my face mask cracked as I went down. The water was going down my throat, tasting like dirt, and my vision went all pale and wavy.

I almost just went under, but then I thought I could see a light up there, way above the street, and I kicked. I kicked and chopped and made myself float. I churned up there until I broke the surface. My arms were thrashing above the water and then I started to go back down, but Miranda had my neck and one shoulder. She hauled me up and out of the water and threw me into the dinghy. I was gasping and heaving up water, and she just sat and laughed at me.

"You managed to scavenge something after all." She pointed to something I'd clutched at on my way up out of the water: a rusted, barbed old piece of a car. "I'm sure Joconda will love it."

"Ugh," I said. "Fuck Old San Francisco. It's gross and corroded and there's nothing left of whatever used to be cool. But hey. I'm glad I found a group of people I would risk drowning in dead water for."

4. I CHOSE TO SEE THAT AS A SPECIAL STATUS

Miranda had the kind of long-limbed, snaggle-toothed beauty that made you think she was born to make trouble. She loved to rough-house, and usually ended up with her elbow on the back of my neck as she pushed me into the dry dirt. She loved to invent cute insulting nicknames for me, like "Dollypris" or "Pris Ridiculous." She never got tired of reminding me that I might be a ninth level genderfreak, but I had all kinds of privilege, because I grew up in Fairbanks and never had to wonder how we were going to eat.

Miranda had this way of making me laugh even when the news got scary, when the government back in Fairbanks was trying to reestablish control over the whole West Coast, and extinction rose up like the shadows at the bottom of the sea. I would start to feel that scab inside my stomach, like the whole ugly unforgiving world could come down on us and our tiny island sanctuary at any moment, Miranda would suddenly start making up a weird dance or inventing a motto for a team of superhero mosquitos, and then I would be laughing so hard it was like I was squeezing the fear out of my insides. Her hands were a mass of scar tissue but they were as gentle as dried-up blades of grass on my thighs.

Miranda had five other lovers, but I was the only one she made fun of. I chose to see that as a special status.

5. "WHAT ARE YOU PEOPLE EVEN ABOUT"

Falling in love with a community is always going to be more real that any love for a single human being could ever be. People will let you down, shatter your image of them, or try to melt down the wall between your self-image and theirs. People, one at a time, are too messy. Miranda was my hero and the lover I'd pretty much dreamed of since both puberties, but I also saved pieces of my heart for a bunch of other Wrong Headed people. I loved Joconda's totally random inspirations and perversions, like all of the art projects sie started getting me to build out of scraps from the sunken city after I brought back that car piece from Fillmore St. Zell was this hyperactive kid with wild half-braids, who had this whole theory about digging up buried hard drives full of music files from the digital age, so we could reconstruct the actual sounds of Marvin Gaye and the Jenga Priests. Weo used to sit with me and watch the sunset going down over the islands, we didn't talk a lot except that Weo would suddenly whisper some weird beautiful notion about what it would be like to live at sea; one day when the sea was alive again. But it wasn't any individual, it was the whole group, we had gotten in a rhythm together and we all believed the same stuff. The love of the ocean, and her resilience in the face of whatever we had done to her, and the power of silliness to make you believe in abundance again. Openness, and a kind of generosity that is the opposite of monogamy.

But then one day I looked up, and some of the faces were different again. A few of my favorite people in the community had bugged out without saying anything, and one or two of the newcomers started seriously getting on my nerves. One person, Mage, just had a nasty temper, going off at anyone who crossed hir path whenever xie was in one of those moods, and you could usually tell from the unruly condition of Mage's bleach-blond hair and the broke-toothed scowl. Mage became one of Miranda's lovers right off the bat, of course.

I was just sitting on my hands and biting my tongue, reminding myself that I always hated change and then I always got used to it after a little while. This would be fine: change was the ocean and she took care of us.

Then we discovered the spoilage. We had been filtering the ocean water, removing toxic waste, filtering out excess gunk, and putting some of the organic byproducts into our mycoprotein vats as a feedstock. But one day, we opened the biggest vat and the stench was so powerful we all started to cry and retch, and we kept crying even after the puking stopped. Shit, that was half our food supply. It looked like our whole filtration system was off, there were remnants of buckystructures in the residue that we'd been feeding to our fungus, and the fungus was choking on them. Even the fungus that wasn't spoiled would have minimal protein yield. And this also meant that our filtration system wasn't doing anything to help clean the ocean, at all, because it was still letting the dead pieces of buckycrap through.

Joconda just stared at the mess and finally shook hir head and told us to bury it under the big hillside.

We didn't have enough food for the winter after that, so a bunch of us had to make the trip up north to Marin, by boat and on foot, to barter with some gun-crazy farmers in the hills. And they wanted free labor in exchange for food, so we left Weo and a few others behind to work in their fields. Trudging back down the hill pulling the first batch of produce in a cart, I kept looking over my shoulder to see our friends staring after us, as we left them surrounded by old dudes with rifles.

I couldn't look at the community the same way after that. Joconda fell into a depression that made hir unable to speak or look anyone in the eye for days at a time, and we were all staring at the walls of our poorly repaired dormitory buildings, which looked as though a strong wind could bring them down. I kept remembering myself walking away from those farmers, the way I told Weo it would be fine, we'd be back before anyone knew anything, this would be a funny story later. I tried to imagine myself doing something different. Putting my foot down maybe, or saying fuck this, we don't leave our own behind. It didn't seem like something I would ever do, though. I had always been someone who went along with what everybody else wanted. My one big act of rebellion was coming here to Bernal Island, and I wouldn't have ever come if Juya hadn't already been coming.

Miranda saw me coming and walked the other way. That happened a couple of times. She and I were supposed to have a fancy evening together, I was going to give her a bath even if it used up half my water allowance, but she canceled. We were on a tiny island but I kept only seeing her off in the distance, in a group of others, but whenever I got closer she was gone. At last I saw her walking on the big hill, and I followed her up there, until we were almost at eye level with the Trans America Pyramid coming up out of the flat water. She turned and grabbed at the collar of my shirt and part of my collarbone. "You gotta let me have my day," she hissed. "You can't be in my face all the time. Giving me that look. You need to get out of my face."

"You blame me," I said, "for Weo and the others. For what happened."

"I blame you for being a clingy wet blanket. Just leave me alone for a while. Jeez." And then I kept walking behind her, and she turned and either made a gesture that connected with my chest, or else intentionally shoved me. I fell on my butt. I nearly tumbled head over heels down the rocky slope into the water, but then I got a handhold on a dead root.

"Oh fuck. Are you OK?" Miranda reached down to help me up, but I shook her off. I trudged down the hill alone.

I kept replaying that moment in my head, when I wasn't replaying the moment when I walked away with a ton of food and left Weo and the others at gunpoint. I had thought that being here, on this island, meant that the only past that mattered was the grand, mysterious, rebellious history that was down there under the water, in the wreckage of San Francisco. All of the wild music submerged between its walls. I had thought my own personal past no longer mattered at all. Until suddenly, I had no mental energy for anything but replaying those two memories. Uglier each time around.

And then someone came up to me at lunch, as I sat and ate some of the proceeds from Weo's indenture: Kris, or Jamie, I forget which. And he whispered, "I'm on your side." A few other people said the same thing later that day. They had my back, Miranda was a bitch, she had assaulted me. I saw other people hanging around Miranda and staring at me, talking in her ear, telling her that I was a problem and they were with her.

I felt like crying, except that I couldn't find enough moisture inside me. I didn't know what to say to the people who were on my side. I was too scared to speak. I wished Joconda would wake up and tell everybody to quit it, to just get back to work and play and stop fomenting.

The next day, I went to the dining area, sitting at the other end of the long table from Miranda and her group of supporters. Miranda stood up so fast she knocked her own food on the floor, and she shouted at Yozni, "Just leave me the fuck alone.

I don't want you on 'my side,' or anybody else. There are no sides. This is none of your business. You people. You goddamn people. What are you people even about?" She got up and left, kicking the wall on her way out.

After that, everybody was on my side.

6. THE HONEYMOON WAS OVER,
BUT THE MARRIAGE WAS JUST STARTING

I REDISCOVERED SOCIAL media. I'd let my friendships with people back in Fairbanks and elsewhere run to seed, during all of this weird, but now I reconnected with people I hadn't talked to in a year or so. Everybody kept saying that Olympia had gotten really cool since I left, there was a vibrant music scene now and people were publishing zootbooks and having storytelling slams and stuff. And meanwhile, the government in Fairbanks had decided to cool it on trying to make the coast fall into line, though there was talk about some kind of loose articles of confederation at some point. Meanwhile, we'd even made some serious inroads against the warlords of Nevada.

I started looking around the dormitory buildings and kitchens and communal playspaces of Bernal, and at our ocean reclamation machines, as if I was trying to commit them to memory. One minute, I was looking at all of it as if this could be the last time I would see any of it, but then the next minute, I was just making peace with it so I could stay forever. I could just imagine how this moment could be the beginning of a new, more mature relationship with the Wrong Headed crew, where

I wouldn't have any more illusions, but that would make my commitment even stronger.

I sat with Joconda and a few others, on that same stretch of shore where we'd all stood naked and launched candles, and we held hands after a while. Joconda smiled, and I felt like sie was coming back to us, so it was like the heart of our community was restored. "Decay is part of the process. Decay keeps the ocean warm." Today Joconda had wild hair with some bright colors in it, and a single strand of beard. I nodded.

Instead of the guilt or fear or selfish anxiety that I had been so aware of having inside me, I felt a weird feeling of acceptance. We were strong. We would get through this. We were Wrong Headed.

I went out in a dinghy and sailed around the big island, went up towards the ruins of Telegraph. I sailed right past the Newsom Spire, watching its carbon-fiber cladding flake away like shiny confetti. The water looked so opaque, it was like sailing on milk. I sat there in the middle of the city, a few miles from anyone, and felt totally peaceful. I had a kick of guilt at being so selfish, going off on my own when the others could probably use another pair of hands. But then I decided it was okay. I needed this time to myself. It would make me a better member of the community.

When I got back to Bernal, I felt calmer than I had in ages, and I was able to look at all the others—even Mage, who still gave me the murder-eye from time to time—with patience and love. They were all my people. I was lucky to be among them.

I had this beautiful moment, that night, standing by a big bonfire with the rest of the crew, half of us some level of naked, and everybody looked radiant and free. I started to hum to myself, and it turned into a song, one of the old songs that Zell had supposedly brought back from digital extinction. It had this chorus about the wild kids and the wardance, and a bridge that doubled back on itself, and I had this feeling, like maybe the honeymoon is over, but the marriage is just beginning.

Then I found myself next to Miranda, who kicked at some embers with her boot. "I'm glad things calmed down," I whispered. "I didn't mean for everyone to get so crazy. We were all just on edge, and it was a bad time."

"Huh," Miranda said. "I noticed that you never told your peeps to cool it, even after I told the people defending me to shut their faces."

"Oh," I said. "But I actually," and then I didn't know what to say. I felt the feeling of helplessness, trapped in the grip of the past, coming back again. "I mean, I tried. I'm really sorry."

"Whatever," Miranda said. "I'm leaving soon. Probably going back to Anaheim-Diego. I heard they made some progress with the nanomechs after all."

"Oh." I looked into the fire, until my retinas were all blotchy. "I'll miss you."

"Whatever." Miranda slipped away. I tried to mourn her going, but then I realized I was just relieved. I wasn't going to be able to deal with her hanging around, like a bruise, when I was trying to move forward. With Miranda gone, I could maybe get back to feeling happy here.

Joconda came along when we went back up into Marin to get the rest of the food from those farmers, and collect Weo and the two others we had left there. We climbed up the steep path from the water, and Joconda kept needing to rest. Close to the water, everything was the kind of salty and moist that I'd gotten used to, but after a few miles, everything got dry and dusty. By the time we got to the farm, we were thirsty and we'd used up all our water, and the farmers saw us coming and got their rifles out.

Our friends had run away, the farmers said. Weo and the others. A few weeks earlier, and they didn't know where. They just ran off, left the work half done. So, too bad, we weren't going to get all the food we had been promised. Nothing personal, the lead farmer said. He had sunburnt cheeks, even though he wore a big straw hat. I watched Joconda's face pass through shock, anger, misery and resignation, without a single word coming out. The farmers had their guns slung over their shoulders, enough of a threat without even needing to aim. We took the cart, half full of food instead of all the way full, back down the hill to our boat.

We never found out what actually happened to Weo and the others.

7. "THAT'S SUCH AN INAPPROPRIATE LINE OF INQUIRY I DON'T EVEN KNOW HOW TO DEAL"

I SPENT A few weeks pretending I was in it for the long haul on Bernal Island, after we got back from Marin. This was my home, I had formed an identity here that meant the world to me, and these people were my family. Of course I was staying.

Then one day, I realized I was just trying to make up my mind whether to go back to Olympia, or all the way back to Fairbanks. In Fairbanks, they knew how to make thick-cut toast with egg smeared across it, you could go out dancing in half a dozen different speakeasies that stayed open until dawn. I missed being in a real city, kind of. I realized I'd already decided to leave San Francisco a while ago, without ever consciously making the decision.

Everyone I had ever had a crush on, I had hooked up with already. Some of them, I still hooked up with sometimes, but it was nostalgia sex rather than anything else. I was actually happier sleeping alone, I didn't want anybody else's knees cramping my thighs in the middle of the night. I couldn't forgive the people who sided with Miranda against me, and I was even less able to forgive the people who sided with me against Miranda. I didn't like to dwell on stuff, but there were a lot of people I had obscure, unspoken grudges against, all around me. And then occasionally I would stand in a spot where I'd watched Weo sit and build a tiny raft out of sticks, and would feel the anger rise up all over again. At myself, mostly.

I wondered about what Miranda was doing now, and whether we would ever be able to face each other again. I had been so happy to see her go, but now I couldn't stop thinking about her.

The only time I even wondered about my decision was when I looked at the ocean, and the traces of the dead city underneath it, the amazing heritage that we were carrying on here. Sometimes I stared into the waves for hours, trying to hear the soundwaves trapped in them, but then I started to feel like maybe the ocean had told me everything it was ever going to. The ocean always sang the same notes, it always passed over the same streets and came back with the same sad laughter. And staring down at the ocean only reminded me of how we'd thought we could help to heal her, with our enzyme treatments, a little at a time. I couldn't see why I had ever believed in that fairytale. The ocean was going to heal on her own, sooner or later, but in the meantime we were just giving her meaningless therapy, that made us feel better more than it actually helped. I got up every day and did my chores. I helped to repair the walls and tend the gardens and stuff. But I felt like I was just turning wheels to keep a giant machine going, so that I would be able to keep turning the wheels tomorrow.

I looked down at my own body, at the loose kelp-and-hemp garments I'd started wearing since I'd moved here. I looked at my hands and forearms, which were thicker, callused, and more veiny with all the hard work I'd been doing here—but also, the thousands of rhinestones in my fingernails glittered in the sunlight, and I felt like I moved differently than I used to. Even with every shitty thing that had happened, I'd learned something here, and wherever I went from now on, I would always be Wrong Headed.

I left without saying anything to anybody, the same way everyone else had.

A few years later, I had drinks with Miranda on that new floating platform that hovered over the wasteland of North America. Somehow we floated half a mile above the desert and the mountaintops—don't ask me how, but it was carbon neutral and all that good stuff. From up here, the hundreds of miles of parched earth looked like piles of gold.

"It's funny, right?" Miranda seemed to have guessed what I was thinking. "All that time, we were going on about the ocean and how it was our lover and our history and all that jazz. But look at that desert down there. It's all beautiful, too. It's another wounded environment, sure, but it's also a lovely fragment of the past. People sweated and died for that land, and maybe one day it'll come back. You know?" Miranda was, I guess, in her early thirties, and she looked amazing. She'd gotten the snaggle taken out of her teeth, and her hair was a perfect wave. She wore a crisp suit and she seemed powerful and relaxed. She'd become an important person in the world of nanomechs.

I stopped staring at Miranda and looked over the railing, down at the dunes. We'd made some pretty major progress at rooting out the warlords, but still nobody wanted to live there, in the vast majority of the continent. The desert was beautiful from up here, but maybe not so much up close.

"I heard Joconda killed hirself," Miranda said. "A while ago. Not because of anything in particular that had happened. Just the depression, it caught up with hir." She shook her head. "God. Sie was such an amazing leader. But hey, the Wrong Headed community is twice the size it was when you and I lived there, and they expanded onto the big island. I even heard they got a seat at the table of the confederation talks. Sucks that Joconda won't see what sie built get that recognition."

I was still dressed like a Wrong Headed person, even after a few years. I had the loose flowy garments, the smudgy paint on my face that helped obscure my gender rather than serving as a guide to it, the straight-line thin eyebrows and sparkly earrings and nails. I hadn't lived on Bernal in years, but it was still a huge part of who I was. Miranda looked like this whole other person, and I didn't know whether to feel ashamed that I hadn't moved on, or contemptuous of her for selling out, or some combination. I didn't know anybody who dressed the way Miranda was dressed, because I was still in Olympia where we were being radical artists.

I wanted to say something. An apology, or something sentimental about the amazing time we had shared, or I don't even know what. I didn't actually know what I wanted to say, and I had no words to put it into. So after a while I just raised my glass and we toasted to Wrong Headedness. Miranda laughed, that same old wild laugh, as our glasses touched. Then we went back to staring down at the wasteland, trying to imagine how many generations it would take before something green came out of it.

Thanks to Burrito Justice for the map, and Terry Johnson for the biotech insight

THE COMMON TONGUE, THE PRESENT TENSE, THE KNOWN
– NINA ALLAN –

GAIA: You can get the fuck out of my bed, that's what.

GOD: What the hell did I do?

GAIA: You didn't do anything, that's the whole frigging point. Droning on about the life to come all the time, all that dying that they might live sack of shit whilst never a thought for what was going on in your own back yard. You thought there'd always be time to clear up the mess, didn't you? It was always fucking mañana. Well, some of us have work to do. Time is up, big boy. Time to get your sorry ass out of my place so I can do my job.

—From *Mañana,* by Kerry Udomi,
premiered at the Donmar Warehouse, May 12th 2027

THE LAST THING my mother told me before the Severins took me with them to Strasbourg was that she was proud of me. Not that she loved me—words she hardly ever used even by accident— but that she was proud. Pride counted for more than love, in my mother's eyes. "I'm proud of you, Melodie," she said. She held me at arm's length to look at me, then pushed me away. I believe she thrashed out the possibilities in her mind for a long time, but in the end the decision came upon her in less than a second. She didn't abandon me, she relinquished me. I was fourteen.

My mother's name was Bella, which means beautiful. The only time I remember her smiling is in old photographs: ghostly, faded snapshots that she would always snatch away if she caught me looking at them. In the photos, she is with my Aunt Chantal, and later my father. Bella is small and dark, with a slightly upturned nose and short wavy hair. In the photos, she is often laughing. The Bella I knew had a face creased with worry lines, her whole attention bent inwards towards some private or not-so-private anxiety. She cared for me rigorously, devotedly and entirely without sentiment. I never once heard her laugh.

Dad didn't laugh much either but he smiled a lot. He looked the same to me as he did in the photos: well-meaning, rather handsome and vaguely flustered. They're both dead, I suppose. I still have the letter Dad wrote to me after La Palma. I read it once, then put it away. It's like the gateway to another world, that letter. Things aren't good there, but Dad is still alive, still thinking of me, still talking about things I recognise from the world I grew up in. That world is gone now. But thinking about Dad's letter brings it back, at least for a while. I imagine it cupped in my hands like a snow globe. All that glitter.

MY NEW FRIEND Noemi doesn't talk much, she prefers to swim. For a while after I first met her I thought she was mute. Later I realised it was just that she found words difficult to trust.

Noemi's long toes grip the wet rocks as she slopes along the tide line, scavenging for beach finds. For shellfish, mainly, for whelks, which are particularly large close to the inlet, though she finds other things, too: remnants, fragments of history, snapped off like twigs from this particular branch of time. Some of them are even useful.

When I first asked Noemi how old she was, she looked at me as if I had lost my mind.

"I can't remember," she said. "Does it matter?"

"I don't suppose so," I said, then asked her how her name was spelled instead. She took a broken-off piece of birch twig and scratched the five letters into the lower part of the vast mud bank that has formed around the concrete buttresses of the old motorway bridge. N.O.E.M.I., as if her name were an acronym for something. No One Ever Mistakes Irony. Never Overturn Everything Move Instead.

There are deep scars on her shoulders and arms. She doesn't speak about them and I don't dare ask, not yet anyway, perhaps not ever. Noemi is my friend and I don't want to drive her away with unwanted questions. I remember what it was like to have friends, running into school on the first day of term with all the other kids, terrified at not knowing anyone, understanding that by the end of the week I'd know them all, by name anyway, that I'd like some of them and hate the guts of others, and that somewhere seated among them was my friend.

I first met Noemi down by the shore. She was wet from swimming, naked from the waist up, her hair shaved close to her scalp, like a soldier's. I thought at first that she might be a soldier, then realised from the wary way she looked at me that she was no such thing. She is younger than I am, I think, though not by much. She can hold her breath underwater for almost six minutes. I know, because I timed her. When I asked her how she learned to do this, she shrugged and said it was just practice.

"How do you practise something like that?" I asked.

"Fill your lungs slowly. Then think of something else, think of anything except breathing. By the end it's as if you don't need to breathe any more. That's when you know it's time to come up."

Oxygen starvation, which causes hallucinations, then nitrogen narcosis, then death. I worry that Noemi might drown herself accidentally, then tell myself it's stupid to think like that, she knows what she's doing, she's more at home in the water than she is on land.

She makes me realise how much of a land-thing I am, in spite of my training, and always will be. I've been growing potatoes this year, on the patch of waste ground behind the bungalow. The land took months to clear but it was worth it. I keep some of the crop for myself, for eating and for replanting, exchange the rest for eggs and milk at the town market. That we can still call this place a town feels like the highest kind of achievement. There is even a school. I have been there to talk to the children about the La Palma tsunami as part of their summer essay project. They took notes and gawped at me as if I were a living fossil, the same way I once looked at the old man who came into our class to tell us about his grandfather, who had fought in World War Two.

When I tell the children their town was once a busy river port, with a naval base and a canning factory, they gape at that, too.

*　　*　　*

"I FEEL SORRY for the children," Noemi says.

"The schoolkids?"

"No, they'll be all right. I mean the kids who died in the wave. I hate the parents though, every one of them. They made it happen."

"The volcano did that."

"Not really. They knew the way the world was going and they did nothing. They killed their children with their own hands, or they might as well have done."

"Things were more complicated than that. Harder."

"OK, so I'm hard in return."

I have a clockwork radio. It was given to me by the man I called my uncle, Lindsay Ballantine, who had the radio sent to me for my tenth birthday. It is small and light, and I keep it with me always. *I hope you enjoy this,* my uncle wrote in the card that came with it. *The radio works by converting your body's energy into electricity. You don't need wires or batteries. Good for when there's a power cut!* There was something about my uncle's messages that always made me think of secret codes. He was telling me the radio might be useful to me some day.

No matter what else I've had to leave behind, I've held on to the radio.

I scroll through the dial at least once a day, searching for news channels. Sometimes there's music. Once I found a station that was playing old recordings of classical music. I was able to listen to Tchaikovsky's violin concerto all the way to the end, although I had to wind the handle twice to keep the radio going.

The announcer said the soloist was Mehmet Khan. I told Noemi about what I'd heard, just to tell someone. I expected her to give me one of her blank looks. I was surprised when she told me that Khan had been her father's favourite musician.

There was silence between us after she said that, a juddery, hostile substance I didn't dare disturb. Noemi had never mentioned her father before, not even once. Now I know he used to like violin music. Details like this keep people alive, even when they're gone.

"It doesn't matter though, does it?" Noemi said after a while. "Whether you hear something like that again, or not. None of it is relevant. The music, the art, all that stuff—it describes a world that doesn't exist, not any more. Hockney and Van Gogh, all those guys—they might as well have been painting an alien planet. Look at the funny aliens, shopping for clothes and listening to music. Walking around with their umbrellas. It's all gone, it's like it never was. We're dinosaurs."

WE NEED A new language to describe our world, a new set of symbols. In time, they will cease to be new. They will become our common tongue, the present tense, the known. We need new music and new art—Noemi is right. Most of all we need new maps, to see where we are.

A HUNDRED YEARS from now, will someone jerry-rig an old CD player, put on a disc of Tchaikovsky and think: how sad?

I remember our history teacher showing us a film about the Minoans, whose civilisation was overthrown by the Mycenaeans in the wake of a devastating volcanic eruption. I gazed at the image on the screen, a bulbous water jug, painted all over with a swirling blue octopus. How beautiful, I thought, and how sad. Now they're all gone.

I think of the Minoans at night, when the tide comes in. The old motorway flyover stands out sharply against the moonlight, an enormous scaffold, driving into nowhere. I've seen people diving from the snapped-off end, kids mainly, though there's nothing much down there to find except more car corpses.

NOEMI SLEEPS ON the boat most nights, though I've told her that once the weather starts getting dangerous she should come to the bungalow. I keep the camp bed made up for her, just in case. One day a couple of weeks ago I came back from the town and found her here, not sleeping in the camp bed but sitting on the floor beside it. She looked like she'd been crying. The backs of her hands were grazed, from grappling with something in the water, probably, though I don't think that's why she was upset. She once sliced her thigh wide open on a submerged stanchion and was back in diving less than a week later.

THE OCEANS ARE changing. There are more sharks off our coast for a start, not just the usual basking sharks and short-fin mako but warm-water species such as the tiger shark and the bull shark, impossibilities that have nonetheless become possible, easing into reality like the morphed, reformed topography that has become the normal landscape of our daily lives. It is my job to monitor such anomalies, to record any inconsistencies and from them make a reasoned conjecture about what kind of impossibilities might happen next.

Unlike many, I am still being paid. In an isolated community like this one, having a job that is about more than survival feels like an indulgence, a hangover from before, although ICTHA do their best with propaganda. The public rationale is that we're monitoring fish stocks. Sustainable food sources, is the preferred term. The people of Helston call us the boffins on the hill. Mostly they leave us alone, as they did with my uncle. I sometimes think I'm more grateful for that than I am for my salary, although I'm probably kidding myself. A salary means I can do more than just eat. I can buy paper for this diary, unused clothing, other rationed items. I can sometimes buy coffee, which is variable in quality but still coffee.

Coffee always reminds me of my mother.

NOEMI STOWED AWAY on a cargo vessel, a rusty leviathan out of Athens or Istanbul under a private flag. A pirate ship, in other words. The living conditions on board such vessels are known to be desperate, but when I express surprise that the so-called captains are able to find people willing to crew for them, Noemi shrugs off my question as if it were of no account or interest whatsoever.

"At least it's work," she says. "Work, and a place to be. Better than starving on the street. People will kill for less. I've seen it happen."

She tells me that if her hiding place had been discovered she'd have been dumped overboard immediately, no questions asked. I have no doubt she's telling the truth—such stories are commonplace. Before the cargo ship, Noemi lived on one of the floating islands: sprawling, miles-long settlements of wood and steel tethered to what remains of the mainland all along the eastern Mediterranean. Patchwork places—half-ship, half-city—that started out as refugee camps but degenerated rapidly into slave economies as soon as the aid budgets dried up.

NOEMI WAS BORN in a small town in the mountains of Ararat, not far from the city of Van in eastern Turkey. I try to imagine her as a young woman, setting out from her home to study at the University of Ankara. It is like trying to see into another universe.

WHAT I REMEMBER mostly about this place from before is how hot it was. We drove out here one day—Mum, Dad and I—to see my uncle, Lindsay Ballantine. I'd never met him before but from the way my mother behaved in the days leading up to our visit I had already worked out that he wasn't in favour. Helston was landlocked then—the estuary had dried up twenty years before—and the reservoir just beyond the motorway junction had become a lake of nettles and brambles and giant hogweed. My uncle's bungalow was pretty much the same as it is now, except for the vegetable garden.

Uncle Lindsay let me look through his microscope. He brought me lemonade, and was kind to me in a way that surprised me, given that he could barely have known I existed before that day. I understand now that this was because of my Aunt Chantal. I looked very like her as a child, less so now. Lindsay Ballantine had been having an affair with my aunt, which was, as I realised later, the main reason my mother was so against him.

Chantal was very ill for a while, though whether this was directly to do with Lindsay Ballantine I never found out. Chantal moved to Florida when I was ten, on a post-doctoral fellowship. She died in the La Palma tsunami. My mother blamed herself for her sister's death, as she did for everything. She said if she hadn't been so set against Lindsay Ballantine, Chantal might never have gone to America in the first place. Dad said there was no point in thinking like that, we couldn't predict the future, we weren't magicians.

That isn't entirely true though, is it? La Palma was predicted for decades before it happened. And even though the volcanic eruption that sent one side of the island sliding into the ocean was simply the most dramatic among a series of precursors, the changes in weather patterns that led to the remapping had been predicted as long ago as the nineteen-sixties.

The problem is that no one gives much of a shit about the future until it actually happens. In the fable of the grasshopper and the ant, human beings are the most frivolous breed of grasshopper that ever was.

THE REMAPPING IS what they started to call it, on the news and on the forums, back when there were still public forums on the internet, when there was still an internet that wasn't protected by government blocking signals. They preferred to use the word protected, they said, so as not to spread hysteria about censorship, just as they referred to the inundation of one-fifth of the planet's land surface as the remapping.

At least no one insisted we spell it with a capital 'r'.

I have access to a limited-view version of the internet through the ICTHA password, but I don't spend much time on it. It doesn't tell me much that I don't already know.

MY UNCLE, LINDSAY Ballantine, was arrested in 2093, just three months before my sixteenth birthday and a year before La Palma. My mother sent me the news, by email, one of the last I had from her.

When I asked her what he'd done, she said she didn't know.

No one will tell us, she wrote. She said she still hadn't told Chantal because she didn't want to worry her. I didn't know what to say. I was still living with the Severins, in Strasbourg, still trying to pretend that Sara and I were still best friends, although Sara had given up on the self-deception months before.

There was no one thing that broke us apart, unless you count what happened in Aachen, but as La Palma was just one small part of the remapping, so Aachen was just a symptom of what was happening anyway between Sara and me. Friends do grow apart, I understand that. But I never imagined that this could happen with Sara and it broke my heart.

People say that love transcends everything but it doesn't. Not always anyway, not even usually. If the end of our world has taught us anything it is that love is a luxury.

IT WAS MY uncle who made me want to be a marine biologist. That day with the microscope changed me because it made me interested in something outside myself. Not just interested, but obsessed. Glimpsing the single-celled organisms through the magnifying lens made me realise how vast the world was, and how little I knew of it.

My uncle spoke of the paramecia as monsters—perhaps he thought the image would be appealing to a child—but what fascinated me more than anything, even then, was the idea that the world the creatures lived in was different from my world, even though they occupied the same space. How a difference in perspective could transform everything.

It is convenient for us to believe we are the superior animal, the top predator, but it is a fiction. Already there are creatures— whole orders of organisms—more suited for survival in this new environment than we are.

"Killing things does not mean we win," Noemi says. Why is this such a difficult lesson for us to learn?

Noemi won't stay out of the water, even when I tell her the numbers of tiger sharks are increasing to dangerous levels.

"Sharks won't attack you unless you're bleeding," she says. "I would have thought you would know that."

She's right, of course, but I can't help worrying. Noemi seems to have no concept of risk.

THE MAKO SHARK is allergic to captivity. When placed in an aquarium, it becomes disorientated, loses its appetite, and dies within days.

MY UNCLE'S BUNGALOW was uninhabitable when I first arrived here. There was a large hole in the roof, and the kitchen and bathroom had been ripped out, presumably for scrap. I didn't mind that—I can use the municipal—but the state of the place was depressing because of the trash. Someone at the market—a local chicken farmer—told me the bungalow had become an unofficial rubbish dump for the people who lived nearby, which explained the sacks of refuse that were piled almost to the ceiling in two of the three rooms, but did not make it any easier to dispose of them. It took me three months just to get the place clean, all while I was settling into my job with ICTHA and living in the municipal dormitory. The dorms are fine for a while but I knew I needed my own place or I'd go crazy.

The whitewash for the interior walls cost me most of my first pay cheque but I found this was an indulgence I could not forgo, no matter how foolish it seemed.

The wood stove was still in working order, thank goodness, and there was plenty of driftwood. With the walls painted and a fire burning, I had a home.

There were still some things of my uncle's in the bungalow— some dusty crockery in the kitchen pantry and a few pieces of furniture the salvagers had either ignored or else not noticed amidst the trash: two ladder-backed chairs, a metal filing cabinet, a bedside table. Both the filing cabinet and the drawer of the bedside table were locked, but with patience and a bent nail I managed to get them open without inflicting too much damage. The filing cabinet was crammed with papers, so many of them and in no discernible order. It was difficult to know where to start. The bedside cabinet proved less of a challenge. The drawer contained some photographs—a family group including a boy I thought was probably my uncle as a child, one of Chantal, standing outside the bungalow with her hair blowing loose in the wind, another of Chantal with my mother, similar to one of the photos I'd seen amongst my mother's possessions and clearly taken at the same time—and a small pile of letters. I recognised my aunt's writing immediately, from the birthday and Christmas cards that had come to the house during the Florida years.

There was a part of me that insisted that they were private and that I shouldn't touch them. My resolve lasted all of five minutes. What is it about human beings, and their endless hunger for knowledge at any price?

THERE IS A capsized tugboat lodged beneath the motorway bridge, below the tide line, a piece of flotsam wrenched from the harbour by the tsunami's backwash before being swept back upstream by the returning tide. Much of the debris was cleared, after the first incursion anyway, but once the water levels began to rise permanently the cleanups became more sporadic and eventually stopped. Noemi has commandeered the sunken tugboat as her mission control. She has siphoned out the floodwater, constructed some kind of rudimentary airlock so the cabin stays dry, but even so, I can only imagine the interior as depressingly cramped and damp. Dungeon-like. How Noemi manages to sleep there I do not know.

"It must be so dark," I say to her.

"I have a torch," she says. She appears unconcerned. "I found it in the old lifeboat station." Some days later she shows it to me, a solar-powered model and fairly powerful, though I know from experience that they can lose charge suddenly, shut down without warning.

The thought of being trapped underwater without light makes

me queasy with nerves. There is so much hardware down there, so many obstructions.

Noemi is counting fish for me. The boat is her hide.

There has been a significant increase in numbers, these past two years especially, not just of the schooling varieties but across the board.

The sunken motorway intersection is gradually being colonised. Even with the toxic release from the concrete, there is evidence that the natural filtration systems provided by algae and plankton have already begun the process of purification.

Many species are adapting successfully. In time there will be local variants, and ultimately new species.

THE LETTERS FROM the bedside drawer cover a period of about five years, from the time my uncle first moved to the bungalow until Chantal was offered the job in Florida. Whether there were more letters—written before my uncle came to Cornwall or after Chantal flew to America—I do not know. I doubt it, somehow. There are gaps in the correspondence, opening up the possibility that some of the letters may have been destroyed, although again I doubt it. My uncle clearly never intended showing them to anyone, so what would be the point?

I didn't know my aunt very well. She always seemed shy to me, prickly and standoffish and difficult to talk to, though her letters to Lindsay Ballantine reveal an entirely different person: confident, outspoken and directed. I expected the correspondence to be about herself and Ballantine—love letters—but in fact what Chantal mostly wrote about was work. I already knew that my uncle's decision to come to Cornwall was the result of a disagreement with his head of department at the time, a man named Vinson Peshwar. I was surprised to find Peshwar's name cropping up again and again in my aunt's letters. I even wondered if it was a different person, though I soon realised it wasn't.

Peshwar never knew about us, my aunt writes at one point. *I couldn't bear to be around him if he did. He insists it's all in the past, what happened with you two, but I know him well enough to be sure he'd find a way of using you against me, if he found out, which is the last thing I need. He makes life here difficult enough as it is.*

Vinson Peshwar was leading a program of advanced research into cloud seeding. The technology was highly controversial, even then. From what I can make out, Chantal started out siding with Ballantine but later switched her allegiance to Peshwar. It is difficult to imagine she was in love with him: the letters near the end of the sequence express much of the same irritation at Peshwar's arrogance—what Chantal refers to repeatedly as his complete lack of hubris—as those at the start. But she did come to believe in the Rainmaker Program, and it was this change of heart that seems to mark the end of her relationship with my uncle.

Chantal was one of the team that accompanied Peshwar on his trip to the North African People's Republic in 2091. In the worst affected parts of northern Africa, there had been no significant rainfall for almost two years. Peshwar had been granted permission to demonstrate his procedure. The media interest was huge, as you can imagine. You may even have seen the news footage from that time: children dancing in the rainstorm that turned the dust of their refugee camp to a shallow lake within the space of half an hour, the carpets of desert flowers that bloomed in the aftermath. Vinson Peshwar was a hero, for that day at least.

It's what he always wanted, my aunt notes wryly. Not the rain, but the adulation. People telling him he was a genius, that he'd been right all along. His name on the front page of every news site in the world. The rain was just a means towards that end.

And yet a month after her return from Djibouti, my aunt was writing a long, impassioned letter to my uncle, explaining why she'd decided to stay on with the Rainmaker Program. Much of what she wrote concerned the refugee crisis in the NAPR, the increased trafficking of women and children to the Indian subcontinent, the warlords who were using drinking water as a bargaining chip. Chantal had made a friend in the camp near Djibouti, a doctor from Madagascar named Hanny who had worked with victims of the traffickers and the forced labour gangs. *I owe it to women like Hanny*, my aunt writes. *We cannot let this catastrophe continue. Not when we have the power to do something about it.*

Another letter followed three days later, in which she informs Ballantine that if he has heard rumours about her and Vinson Peshwar he should dismiss them immediately.

If anything, I admire him even less now than I ever did, Chantal writes. *Having a brilliant mind is no excuse for the way he behaves, and the man is a bully. I've seen what he can do to people, believe me.*

There is a gap of several months, and then the letters seem to pick up where they left off. Something has changed, though. Chantal informs Ballantine that she is thinking of resigning her position at the university. There are two jobs she is interested in applying for. One is the post in Florida, the other is at the

University of Kerala, as part of a new climate change unit. She seems most excited about the job in Kerala, but then suddenly changes her mind and accepts the Florida post instead. The reason she gives is that the job is more closely connected with the research she's been doing with Peshwar. It seems a shame to let all that go to waste, she writes. It is still a young science.

The first thing that occurs to me is that if my aunt had gone to India, she might still be alive. Of course, Vinson Peshwar went to Florida. How much that had to do with my aunt's decision, I will never know.

"UNDERSTANDING CLIMATE CHANGE: TIMELINE AND ANALYSIS", BY RIMINI PARKS, AGED 16, HELSTON MIDDLE SCHOOL ESSAY COMPETITION "FIRST PRIZE", JUNE 2132

1962   Rachel Carson's The Silent Spring published

1984   Bhopal disaster leads to large scale contamination of water and soil

1990   Radioactive mutations reported near Chernobyl

1995   Greenhouse gas emissions talks in Tokyo end in deadlock

2001   Significant coral die-off reported at Great Barrier Reef

2017 Galilee Basin coalmining expansion greenlighted in
      Queensland

2032 Cuadrilla prosecutions in UK over groundwater
      contamination in Lancashire

2045 Siberian tiger officially declared extinct

2060 'Three typhoons' devastate the Philippines

2074 Five-year drought triggers Kaduna massacre in
      northern Nigeria

2094 La Palma tsunami

2116 Collapse of the Golden Gate Bridge, partial
      inundation of San Francisco

Approximately twenty million people were killed in the La
Palma tsunami, either in the wave itself or in the earthquakes,
building and freeway collapses, wildfires, gas explosions,
spontaneous munitions detonations, air crashes, flooding,
inundation, land slippage and avalanche associated with
the immediate aftermath. This estimate constitutes a minor
proportion of the eventual casualties, those who died in what
has come to be known as the aftershock and throughout
the longer term of the remapping. Over a period of twenty
years, a repeating pattern of severe weather events,
famines and disease pandemics arising from those weather
events, economic collapse and hyper-inflation, breakdowns

in power supply and food distribution, prolonged worldwide telecommunications and internet outages, social upheaval and civil unrest, aerial bombardment and the widespread use of previously banned chemical and biological weapons has led to a decrease in world population roughly equal to if not in excess of that documented during the plague pandemics of the 1300s. As the largest number of casualties occurred in areas of the world where communications and medical facilities have been poor to non-existent, it has been impossible to collate anything approaching an exact number. Although a measure of stability has been restored in some areas, continuing climate inconsistencies and consequent shortages of food and clean drinking water have resulted in uncontrolled levels of civic violence in others. Mass migrations of homeless people in search of better living conditions and adequate food supplies have further exacerbated the ongoing refugee crisis.

Whilst the alterations and fluctuations in climate and pre-existing weather patterns have not been as severe overall as some predicted, there is no doubt that the Earth's human population has been dramatically affected by the climate crisis, mainly because even in the decades before the La Palma disaster, human demands on the planet's ecology were already unsustainable. Factors such as the outsourcing of manufacturing industries far from their main centres of consumption, the forced industrialisation of developing nations using technologies and systems already discredited in more advanced economies, the stripping of assets— both mineral and agricultural—from developing nations at the expense of their home populations, the decimation of natural ecosystems for short-term economic gain have all contributed to our current situation. As we move towards the rebuilding of some kind of workable humanitarian infrastructure, it is generally agreed that our main focus should be upon securing environmentally viable local support systems, as opposed to the re-establishment of the global model. The Earth we now inhabit is an alien world, with new rules and new environments, new pressures upon our ability to adapt. We ignore the needs of our new world at our peril.

One remaining area of controversy is the role played by the controversial Rainmaker Program in triggering the global climate catastrophe that led to the remapping. The Rainmaker Program was a targeted system of cloud seeding, developed in the first instance as a quick-fix response to the widespread droughts and famines that devastated the North African People's Republic during the 2070s and the 2080s. Hailed by its supporters as a universal solution to increasingly unpredictable weather patterns and water shortages, the Rainmaker Program soon drew criticism from environmentalists, who claimed that interference with the weather on such a global scale could have unforeseen and possibly disastrous consequences for the ecological stability of our planet.

Several of the Rainmaker Program's leading scientists suffered a sustained campaign of online harassment and even death threats during the years leading up to La Palma.

The project's co-ordinators, Professor Lyonel Raimond and Professor Vinson Peshwar in particular were targeted. There were rumours that Vinson Peshwar survived at least one serious attempt on his life, although the precise details of the attack remain unknown. Raimond went on to found the New Centre for Climate Studies at the New University of Pittsburgh in 2103. Peshwar died in the La Palma tsunami. Claims about the safety and long term effects of the Rainmaker Program have never been decisively proven either way.

MY UNCLE WASN'T a climate scientist at all, but an entomologist, an expert on ground beetles. He met my Aunt Chantal by chance, in the university canteen. As members of the same faculty, he and Vinson Peshwar started out on friendly terms. They even went hiking together a couple of times, in Snowdonia and in the Peak District. As their attitudes towards the Rainmaker technology began to polarise, the friendship turned to antagonism. In an interview for *Nature* in 2085, Vinson Peshwar referred to Lindsay Ballantine as an amateur busybody. A year later, my uncle resigned his post at the university and moved to the bungalow.

I have never been entirely clear on what he was doing here. I know that at least some of the answers are likely to be found amongst the farrago of papers and letters and press clippings in the filing cabinet, but every time I think about sorting through them a sense of futility descends upon me. My uncle is dead. Everyone he knew is dead. The world he fought to save is dead. What can it possibly matter, what he did, or wrote, or thought?

Every now and then I remove something from the filing cabinet so I can examine it more closely. I make my selections at random, tugging papers or envelopes or photographs from the general chaos without bothering to mark their position or to distinguish them from the rest. One of these documents was part of a letter, a draft that was never sent perhaps, or that was later amended. The top page, the page that presumably would have included the name and address of the intended recipient, seems to be missing. I don't recognise the handwriting—all I know is that it's not my uncle's. Midway down this second page, part of a paragraph has been underlined in red:

Vinson Peshwar is a terrorist. He's like one of those mad doctors in the horror movies—so intent on proving his theories he doesn't care if he kills his patient in the process. He must be stopped.

The last four words have been underlined twice. I am struggling to connect the strident tone of the letter with my uncle, with the dishevelled, otherworldly man who brought me lemonade and opened the world to me through the lens of his microscope.

I want to know what happened here, and at the same time I don't. I'm afraid of what I might discover.

I only knew him for a day, I remind myself. I barely knew him at all.

RADIO RECEPTION IS better at night. I inch the dial slowly around, searching for voices, searching for evidence of a world beyond my own. I find London stations: a channel I've come across before that plays rap-raga, a soap opera centred on the endlessly warring tribes of the refuse collection mafia and the ongoing failure of the city's sewerage system.

When things are bad in London they are very bad, though since the worst of the floodwaters have receded, conditions have stabilised. I hear voices from Germany, a snatch of applause that sounds like static, a woman speaking French. "*Je m'appelle* Soraya Lellouche, coming to you from the city of Algiers," she says. She has someone with her in the studio, or whatever back room or prefab or semi-bankrupt hotel they are broadcasting from. They are speaking too quickly for me to understand much of what they are saying, but there is something about the woman's voice that makes it pleasant to hear.

I try to imagine her life and find I cannot. They say the whole of the NAPR is uninhabitable, desertified, and yet here is this woman, with her bubbling laughter, her argumentative studio companion. One of them puts on a record and the notes shiver up and down the scale, faint but still audible, rippling beneath the barrier of tonality like quicksilver.

Slowly I let out my breath. Large moths thrust themselves against the window glass then veer off again into the darkness. I wonder what species they are. My uncle would know, probably. I feel as if we're becoming closer, my uncle and I. It is often difficult to remember we're not really related.

I DON'T KNOW what happened to Lindsay Ballantine. I don't know if he's dead, or not, though I suppose he must be. I have no idea where he went when they released him from prison.

*   *   *

THE WORLD IS in a state of forgetting. The only way to go on is to forget the way things were before. If you've lost someone it's best not to think of them. It's even better if you can pretend they never existed.

WHEN I MENTION to Noemi about wanting to go online, she asks me why I don't hack in, like everyone else.

"I don't know how," I tell her.

"You should have said." She asks me what I'm looking for. "What kind of information, I mean? Is it restricted?"

"I don't know," I say. "Probably." I tell her about my uncle being arrested. "He was sent to prison, not long before La Palma. I want to know what for."

"How come you don't know already?"

"We lost touch. I mean our families did."

She nods, as if that explains everything, but really she's stopped listening to me. Her whole attention is focussed on the computer. I want to tell her to hurry up, that Magda will be back at any moment, that if my boss finds us in her office we're done for. At the same time I feel exhilarated because for the first time in a long time I'm doing something unauthorised. What's Magda going to do anyway, push me over the bridge?

Noemi's fingers flicker over the keys, like a pianist's, like a drone pilot's, and I can see she's in her element. The revelation is sudden and unexpected.

"How come you know about computers?" I ask.

"I did computer science. At Ankara. That was my major."

"You never said."

"You never asked."

I realise it's true, what she says, that I have never properly imagined Noemi in a world where she was anything, where she did anything other than lope along the shoreline looking for whelks. I have never imagined her sitting at a desk, or sending an email.

Did I imagine her reading, even? The question seems preposterous, but there it is.

"I'm sorry," I say, though I'm not sure what I'm apologising for. Everything, I suppose. All the above. Noemi shakes her head: *forget it*. Pages open and close. She busts through Magda's password and firewall, the barbed wire fence of code that separates the institute from what remains of the outside world, the outer limits of the new internet, the bleak and endlessly unfolding horizons of the spaces beyond.

"Here's something," Noemi mutters, and finally there are images: photos of my uncle, of someone else I don't immediately recognise but who I think may be Vinson Peshwar. The Lindsay Ballantine in the photographs doesn't look much like the man I remember meeting. This man is older, with heavy black glasses and a receding hairline. Yet in spite of his grim expression I know it is him.

... was remanded in custody on a charge of possession of banned substances with intent to cause explosions. The accused, who was previously the subject of a police investigation on grounds of defamation, online harassment and malicious slander, was apprehended close to the home of Professor Peshwar following an anonymous tip-off earlier this morning. Dr Ballantine was previously employed as a senior lecturer in the biology department of the University of East London.

"This was actually on all the news sites, can you believe it?" Noemi says. I know what she means. It is difficult to remember, sometimes, that news was once traded like any other commodity, that news sites used to run conflicting versions of the same story just to get traffic. Not in opposition to the way things were, but out of boredom.

Boredom also has become a luxury. When I think of boredom, I think of something impossible: an endless stream of days exactly the same. Of myself, writing this diary in a world where the future is still a valid possibility. Of buying bread from the market. Of buzzards, dipping and circling like micro-drones above the moor.

I'VE DECIDED NOT to sort through my uncle's papers. They belong to the past. I shall place my journals with them, when the time comes, in the filing cabinet with the rest of the muddle. Good day to you, the person reading this. Whoever you are, I am glad you are reading. It means the future was a possibility, after all.

"HE WAS QUITE some guy, your uncle," Noemi says. "At least he tried."

"He wasn't really my uncle," I reply. "Just a friend of the family."

We are sitting together on the old motorway bridge. I have warned Noemi about diving into the sea from here because of all the cars but she just laughs.

"I've learned where it's safe," she says. "I've learned where it's deep. You should know that by now."

* * *

SOMEONE HAS CREATED a sculpture on the patch of scrubby moorland close to Stithians. It is made from scrap metal—the rusty carcases of cars and broken tumble driers, machines that no longer work and cannot be adapted. These chunks of refuse have been piled up and rammed together to form a strange kind of tree. Corroded padlocks hang from its branches, like petrified fruit. A snapped-off chainsaw points skywards, like a jagged flower. The sculpture is huge, as high as a house. It is infested with weeds: hogweed and brambles and nettles. Spikes of buddleia thrust their way outwards from a smashed car window. The buddleia sways when the wind blows, throbbing with bees.

Someone has spelled out the sculpture's name in pebbles on the ground. Fireweed and dock leaves poke up between the stones without obscuring them. The sculpture's name means Earth, or mother. I have seen people sitting here sometimes, on the ground beside the sculpture, just sitting. The sculpture is not beautiful exactly, but it is striking. The most remarkable thing about it is that it exists.

NOEMI HAS TAMED a tiger shark. That's what she tells me, anyway. "We go fishing together," she says. "Is that so strange?"

I tell her the tiger shark is one of the most ruthless predators in the sea. "It could cut you in half in the water, just like that," I say. She seems not to care.

"They are very intelligent," she says. She is right about that. She tells me the shark's name is Carina.

"Carina?" I say. I can hear myself sounding incredulous, the way the ditzy best friend would, if this were a movie. I miss seeing movies, but only sometimes. They have the quality of dreams.

"Carina is the name of my daughter, who was killed," Noemi says. "She was eight years old when she died," she adds. "The shark reminds me of my daughter, a little. She is a beautiful swimmer."

Her grown-out hair hangs down like seaweed, hiding her face. She traces patterns in the sand with her toes: a hashtag, a noughts and crosses grid, a large letter C.

WHAT IS
– JEFFREY FORD –

ON SEPT. 14TH, 2025, at precisely 6:59AM, an old US Airforce C-17 cargo plane swept down over what was left of Oklahoma City and, staying low, headed due east. Approximately twenty minutes later, by the first light of day, the plane's navigator spotted the skeletal-like remains of an enormous, dead Hackberry tree in the middle of a field, close by a dried out stream bed. The tree coincided with his mission coordinates, and he gave the order to the load master to prepare to make the drop—a 5,000 pound pallet. A few seconds later, the pilot circled back to the location and then a silk white blossom burst open in the sky. The payload drifted down slowly and the plane went round above. The drop was spot on target, so close to the tree that part of its parachute tangled in the branches. After the successful delivery, the aircraft slowly climbed to 28,000 feet and set a course back toward northern Michigan.

An hour and 13 minutes later, the sun, now fully risen, found the pallet sitting, undisturbed where it had landed. The temperature began to rise from the 90 degrees of the previous night toward the 120 it would no doubt reach that coming afternoon. An infernal breeze stirred, lifting the pervasive dust and swirling it over and around the pallet. In no time the atmosphere at ground level was thick with powdered dirt, decreasing visibility with each minute that passed. It was at this time that the radios in the hovels, huts and homes of those still living in Lincoln County crackled with the news that there had been an air drop. The last time such news had come, six months prior, there had been a dozen individuals who'd crawled or leaped out of bed to make ready for the journey. This time there were only five, and each of them noted the chilling final words of the transmission that this would be the last drop.

All five of those who'd been listening every morning for a month and a half for word that relief was on the way had been witness over the past ten years to the onslaught of the drought that at first presented itself as merely a couple of dry years in a row. It seemed the entire mid and southwest suffered it together. Climate change theories were shrilly put forth in the media, delivered with a spirit of desperation. There were scientists who claimed it was already too late. Crops were nominally depleted, but still they were planted (cotton in the case of Lincoln County) and there was an adequate yield at harvest time. Then there intervened a year, 2017, that was quite prosperous, and many of the farmers and the farm communities laughed at the climate change proponents and sided with those politicians who denounced bans on fossil fuels, ridiculed steps to offset the flood of carbon dioxide into the atmosphere. Super storms, increasingly scorching temperatures, tornadoes that leveled cities, floods that redrew coastlines and snow in March were blamed by those in charge at the Oklahoma State House and by other oil company shills across the country on the sins of homosexuals, the result of god's wrath toward abortions and a turning away from the church. Then in 2018, the drought stopped playing games and came on with a vengeance.

A MILE AND a half away from the Hackberry tree where the pallet had landed, Eben Wallis sat in the room he called his 'observatory.' It was an upstairs corner room from which the roof above it and the upper side wall of the house had cracked in an earthquake and fallen off to leave the rest of the floor, the bed and desk and chair open to the sky. After the catastrophe, the room wasn't good for anything else but a sort of perch. He'd enter it from the upstairs hallway through its door, and step out into the morning. There, he'd set up a chair and a telescope. At sunrise, before the day got so hot that the air rippled in the distance, he'd scan the horizon for any signs of activity or change. Most days he saw the same—given the sky was clear enough, although it often wasn't—endless dust, tumbleweeds, no birds. That Sunday he saw the parachute wafting to and fro like a ghost trapped in the Hackberry tree. He noted it down in his journal and then went to dress and prepare himself for the journey.

Although the top corner of his place had suffered a loss the rest of the old farm house was still fairly intact. It was difficult keeping the dust out, and so he had newspaper taped to the windows and weighted snake-like tubes of material at the bottoms of the doors. Most of the windows and exits of the house were sealed up. He lived alone, and had done so for seven years after his wife had died of some strange disease that had turned her green. They'd lost their only son seven years before that. The boy had been killed in Afghanistan fighting the

Taliban. At one time Wallis had been a cotton farmer and had owned all the land for as far as the eye could see around his place. "All the useless land," he said to himself that morning as he loaded a clip into the Ruger and slid the gun into a shoulder holster. He put his straw hat on, pulled the brim down, and went to fetch Jester, his horse. Outside he could feel the breeze rising and predicted a mild stirring of the dust that morning and perhaps a sand storm by afternoon. He tethered Jester to his wagon and started out northwest toward the drop point.

AT THAT VERY moment, Bev Searle turned the key on her 2011 Ford F150, and the beast groaned to life and then sputtered out. She wasn't sure whether it was flooded or just stodgy from lack of use. Running it even for a few minutes to keep it in condition was a waste of gas she could ill afford. It was her desire to always have in reserve at least enough to make it the hour from what remained of Midlothian to what remained of Oklahoma City when the time came for her to finally give up and flee. The trip she'd be embarking on today, to the drop point, would be the longest she'd taken since the last drop. When Midlothian and the surrounding towns were leveled by a series of earthquakes back in 2018 and the federal government sent troops in to rescue whoever was left and move them out of the quake zone that the state had become, Bev stayed behind. Her husband went with the soldiers, promising her that he'd be back with supplies, but after six months went by and he never returned she gave up on him. She didn't blame him for leaving; her grief had been all consuming. There was nothing left in her for him. She refused to go because her three children—four, six, and ten—had died of the mystery illness locals called the green shakes and were buried out back. For years, when the dust covered their graves and tried to obliterate their memory from the earth, she spent an hour or more every morning digging out the headstones.

It was only two years earlier, after having been bitten in the night by centipedes that had infested her bedroom, that she became too sick and too weak to shovel for months in a row. The dust blew over the graves and they were lost to her as if they'd sunk into the ocean. After most people were gone she scavenged around through the fallen and ravaged homes and found the truck with a full tank, a Marlin 60 .22 rifle—18 shot—and an abandoned black dog of indeterminate breed. She could have fled north whenever she wanted to, but the urge never came. She whistled to the dog, Pepper, and it leaped into the bed of the pick up truck. She headed out of her garage and avoided the road, which was nothing but a chaos of crumbled asphalt. Instead she drove around the back of the dangerously tilting two story house and headed out southeast across the waste of blowing dust. She looked at her place in the rear-view mirror and thought about how she'd fret every time the earth started grumbling.

ALTHOUGH THE ENTIRE mid and southwest suffered the devastating drought that depleted the country's food stores and caused mass migration, food riots, water riots, economic collapse, it was only Oklahoma that had succumbed to ever more frequent, ever more powerful earthquakes as well. Back around 2008, the state began to allow fracking as a means of extracting natural gas from the ground. The process involved drilling deep into shale and then injecting powerful streams of water, chemicals and sand into those openings to release the natural gas, which would then flow upward to the wellhead. The waste water and chemicals were trapped in holding wells deep underground. The politicians in the state, primarily the governor, vouched for the safety of the process. Then the earthquakes started. Where there'd been a measly two a year at only 3.0 magnitude, in less than six years that number rose to a thousand, some at magnitudes of 5.0 and even as high as 6.8. You'd think that would have put a halt to the fracking, but no, the governor helped to push through a bill that prevented the fracking companies from being sued, so it was business as usual. As the years went on past 2015, the magnitude and frequency of the quakes increased and left death and destruction in their wake. Eventually the underground wells that held the waste water and chemicals were compromised due to the fierce earthquake activity, and the grim slurry they held infiltrated the ground water. Many believed the chemicals were the cause of the green shakes.

JAMES REBOTH HAD the most successful living set up in what remained of Lincoln County. Also the son of a cotton farmer, he'd prepared for the coming drought and destruction from the very beginning, reinforcing his house, digging deep windmill wells that offered him steady if also contaminated water that needed straining and boiling, and installing a series of solar generators which were effective as long as the dust stayed settled, which was about half the days of the week. Some of the places that remained as habitations still had electricity, but his did not.

There was an outpost of soldiers in Oklahoma City who tried to keep the electrical plant going, but many of the lines that led east had been severed. He made his own. His one goal was to hold onto his land until after the drought passed. He planned then to make a killing planting wheat and corn for a starving nation. The one thing he didn't plan on, though, was how long the drought would last. His wife and grown son were with him and also well versed in the survival techniques necessary to last in the Oklahoma hell. They were, in addition to being well outfitted, well-armed. After the news that morning that the day's drop would be the last, James gathered his wife and son together and explained how they would have to take the entire palette.

"Kill the others?" his wife asked.

"Who'll know?" said his son.

"I'll take the truck. You two take the cart and horse. Larry, you get down and hide in that dried streambed and make your way up behind the drop site. Stay low so no one can see you. Mary, you wait out of sight at the rise of the hill overlooking the spot. We've got to watch carefully cause we don't want to all be shooting at the same person. I'll be a sitting duck out there when they perceive the treachery. We know the woman with the black dog will be there, so you take her out, honey," he said to his wife. "Junior, you go for that troglodyte."

"That reptile guy? Shit, he puts me off anyway. What is that runt?"

"He was taken by the shakes," said the boy's mother. "Only thing is he recovered. When you live through it, not many who do, your skin gets thick as gator skin and you get all kinds of fucked up looking."

"He needs a bullet," said Larry.

"That's for sure," said his father. "Now, I'll get out of the truck and stand behind the open door. After you hear my first shot, start shooting."

"Wait," said Mary. "What about that hippie couple?"

"Oh, fuck them and their stupid homemade horse travois. I don't think they even carry. We can pick them off at our leisure and keep their three horses. Two for the table and one for the stable."

"Meat," said Larry. "We ain't even had jack rabbit in a while."

"OK, let's pack up and move out," said James.

THE FACT WAS, nobody had had jack rabbit lately, although everyone had had an abundance of it not but a month earlier. This drought, like the historic one of the 1930s, the Dust Bowl, saw infestations of certain animals and insects rise in mind-staggering proportions and then suddenly disappear. Just like in the earlier event, this time there were also locusts. 2020 had seen storms of them. The scorpions in 2023. People slept with their boots on, and sometimes when walking across open ground, there was a definitive sound of crunching as if walking on egg shells. They were striped bark scorpions, and their sting was usually not deadly but it hurt like hell. From the spring of 2024 and well into 2025, the jack rabbits swarmed. It was a mystery as to what they even lived on, there being hardly a shred of vegetation as far as the eye could see. Still, they were everywhere, even invading homes. The survivors shot and trapped them, cooked them and ate them. They were fairly tasty if you didn't have to eat them every day.

Their abundance in the drought areas of Oklahoma drew packs

of coydogs from Tennessee through Arkansas where the climate was somewhat better, although still dry. The coydog was a canid hybrid that scientists in the past had predicted would be limited to a few unusual cases in the wild since the dog and the coyote had different mating seasons. Once the drought had come and the temperature had climbed all over the country to remain consistently high, mating seasons were extended and it was noticed by around 2023 that packs of these animals had begun to pop up. They'd not been in Oklahoma before the jackrabbit infestation, but they certainly were after it had struck. These packs didn't bother people when they were well-fed, but like a lot of drought infestations the rabbits seemed suddenly, to a day, just to have disappeared, leaving the dogs hungry. The packs quickly became vicious and wily and looked to other sources of flesh in a land of nothing but dust.

THAT POOR GREEN fellow who James Reboth's son had diagnosed as needing a bullet, was the first one at the drop site, having arrived alone, on foot. He'd known before the others that the plane was coming. He took up a spot 30 yards from the Hackberry tree and sat down in the sand with his legs tucked under him and waited, watching the parachute shift in the breeze. His name was Martin Pell, and he too had grown up in Lincoln County on a cotton farm that had been in his family for generations. Back at the onset of the drought, his mother had succumbed to the shakes and his father to a heart attack. His sister and brother had fled north with the rescue troops, and he had stayed behind with his 95-year-old grandmother who was too weak for the journey. He'd modified their house to withstand the onslaught of dust and dirt, and laid in solar generators and enough gasoline to last for a long haul—not quite as long a haul as it had turned out to be, though. In a reversal of fortune it was Pell's ancient grandmother who nursed him back to health from the green shakes using old farm remedies and Muskogee medicine. In the year it took for him to get back on his feet, 2020, the old woman would sit by his bed at night and tell him tales of her experience living through the 1930s Dust Bowl. "When the black blizzards blew across the fields, I saw Satan's face in their towering clouds," she said.

Pell recovered only for his grandmother to promptly take ill as soon as he was up on his feet and could cook and care for himself. When he thanked her and told her how sorry he was that her effort to save him had made her weak, she commented on her near-demise. "Martin," she said, patting his arm, "to be honest, it'll be a relief." From her deathbed the last thing she told him was that the green cast of his skin and the distortion of his features made him look like Toad of Toad Hall from the book *The Wind in the Willows*. He laughed and remembered that book from his childhood and her reading it to him. He only let himself think of it once, though, seeing as the story he recalled, much of which took place next to a stream, in a lush wood, and between good friends was too much to bear when he woke from that world into the waste of Lincoln County. All through the years of the worsening drought, Pell, who had a degree in electrical engineering from Oklahoma University, used a satellite dish he'd at one time gotten television reception off of to stay tenuously linked with what still existed of the internet. His skill with the computer was how he knew the plane was coming, and why he'd arrived at the site to warn his fellow survivors.

*   *   *

THAT HIPPIE COUPLE mentioned by Reboth's wife, Mary, weren't a hippie couple at all, but a couple of once well-off business professionals who'd lost nearly everything in the Depression that followed the worsening drought. Theo and Susan Shebel were their names. While their money still had any meaning at all, they'd had to gamble on what was the best course of action. Did they get a place out in the country and hunker down, learn to be resourceful until things got better or did they head north in the direction of the great migration and face riots and food lines and the camps set up for the homeless? They chose the former and tried to be smart about it, studying as much about desert survival as possible, storing enough goods and water and gas as possible. They hadn't counted on the earthquakes, one of which had swallowed their truck whole, one that had laid waste to their barn. Luckily their three horses, perhaps the biggest investment they'd made before moving out into the old farm house on the outskirts of the tiny town of Meeker, all survived. Reboth was right that they didn't carry guns, but they did take machetes with them wherever they traveled.

Unfortunately, the machete didn't help Theo that day on their way out toward the drop site. They were riding along on their respective horses. Susan had the extra horse tethered to her own. Each of the animals had a travois attached to it in order to haul back the supplies they could lay claim to. Their place was only about 20 minutes due west of the Hackberry Tree. No more than 10 minutes of the journey had passed when the breeze began to stir and the dust lifted and swirled around them. They lifted their kerchiefs up over their noses and pulled their hats down. Both were already wearing sunglasses for protection against particles flying into their eyes. The horses whinnied and bucked sideways as they sometimes did when the air became thick with dirt. Theo who was trailing a few yards behind Susan heard a sound other than the horses' complaints. It was some kind of high pitched call. Suddenly his horse lifted onto its back legs, whinnying and pawing the air in front. Theo just had enough time to clamp his thighs tight around the animal to keep from falling off.

Something struck him from the side and he could feel the fangs closing on his neck. Another weight leaped onto his back and nails dug into his shoulders. Before the horse landed back on its front hooves, Theo was on the ground. He got out one yelp before his windpipe was crushed by the jaws of the pack leader. With that one cry, Susan Shebel peered back through the drifting dust in time to see Theo's horse go rushing past her.

EBEN WALLIS PULLED up in his cart and parked about the same distance from the tree and pallet as Martin Pell was sitting and twenty yards to his right. The custom was that all those who showed up for a share of the drop formed a semi-circle around the goods and waited until 10 AM before equitably divvying things up. He tipped his hat to his strange looking neighbor, and called, "Remember last week, that unusually clear night when the dust stayed settled and the moon was huge and bright? I couldn't sleep for the beauty of it. "

Martin nodded.

"I thought I saw you through my telescope, creeping across my fields, out toward the back acreage on the way to the sandstone outcropping. Of course, I don't mind, seeing as I'm the emperor of dust now. There's no harm in it. But I'm curious."

Martin laughed. "That was me."

"What were you up to, if you don't mind me asking?"

"Investigating something. Just past the end of your land there's been a wild upheaval of the ground, cracked wide open and part of it lifted by what must have been quite an earthquake. I crept up close to the hole and peered in. There was a shaft going down and light coming up out of it."

"What was it?"

"Something more dangerous to us than the shakes, the drought, the quakes, the dogs, anything."

"I didn't think it could get any worse," said Eben.

"I'll explain once everybody gets here."

At that moment, Bev Searle's F150 came chugging up over the rise to the west of the big tree. She maneuvered the truck into the semi-circle forming around the pallet. When she got out, she brought her rifle and let the dog follow her. She hoisted herself up onto the hood of the truck and sat. "Gentlemen," she called over to Eben and Martin, and then rested back against the glass of the windshield. The dog took up a position, sitting in front of the truck. She tied a kerchief on around the back of her neck and used it as a mask against the slowly rising dust. "Looks like there might be a storm coming," she said.

"Could be," said Eben. "If so, I hope the rest show up on time before it gets bad. I'm desperate to eat something besides rice and canned beans."

"Amen to that, Mr Wallis," she said.

* * *

EACH OF THE three 'neighbors' sitting around the Hackberry tree, waiting for the others to arrive, had wondered numerous times why those who'd stayed behind to scrape a life out of the dust hadn't joined in a community together. There were all manner of ways they could be helpful to each other—sharing the duties of straining fresh water from the deep wells through pillowcases, sharing supplies, offering advice on individual specialties and group protection. It made all kinds of sense. But they never did. They were as shy of each other as a teenager with a secret love. Eben reasoned that they acted that way because that was the nature of the world when they had left it, or it had left them. The days of neighbors sharing, trusting each other had long gone by the turn of the new century. Family units became islands unto themselves, and the people in those families, smaller islands. Bev thought it had to do with possessions. The necessities of survival out in the Oklahoma waste were scarce and one had to protect what one had. Counting on the kindness of others could get you killed. She'd have loved to have had a confidant to talk to over a cup of tea in the late afternoon, but she felt safer with the Marlin .22 and could talk to Pepper the dog if she needed to.

Martin sometimes had daydreams of adventures in the forbidding land with some of the others. Those scenarios really helped him pass the time on the most brutal days of dust, when the sand and dirt blew a mean streak against the siding of his home. But whenever the opportunity came for him to talk to Ms Searle or Mr Wallis, Reboth and his wife and son, Theo and Susan, he was reminded what he had become—Toad of Toad Hall, and forewent conversation. He looked for the community of friends in the stories told in old books he read by candle light—some from the last century, others from the century before. On this day, though, as he waited for the others to arrive, he breathed nervously with excitement, as what he was going to say would leave them no choice but to consider him a friend. He rocked slightly where he sat, smiling.

AT THREE MINUTES to ten, James Reboth's truck could be seen trailing a brown cloud off to the south. He pulled into the semi-circle and took up a spot at the end next to and slightly facing Martin, his back to the rise behind which his wife was hopefully positioned by then. Before turning off his engine and stepping down out of the vehicle, he put on his sunglasses so as the others there couldn't see him searching the streambed for signs of his son. He saw nothing, which could have been good or bad. He lowered the window on the driver's side as he got out, and took up a position behind the open door, hoping his neighbors wouldn't realize he intended to use it as a shield. "Where's Hansel and Gretel?" he said with a smile, meaning Theo and Susan.

"Haven't seen them," said Eben. He didn't like or trust Reboth, who was the main reason he carried his Ruger to the supply drops.

"Well, they've got exactly two minutes to get here before we start divvying the load up. I'm not standing out here all day, waiting on a storm or a troop of coydogs. More for us."

Martin stood and held his arms above his head to draw attention to himself. "Listen to me, folks. Please listen. You don't want to open that palette. You think there's food in there but there isn't."

"What are you talking about?" said Reboth.

"There's a killer in there."

"What kind of killer?" asked Bev.

"Why would they want to kill us?" asked Eben.

"That thing I found on your land, back by the sandstone," Martin said. "It's a missile silo and it's cracked open, anyone can get into it. They know it's been compromised."

"Oh, bullshit," said Reboth and carefully drew his .500 Smith and Wesson from its holster. "You've gone gator crazy, lizard man," he said. Bringing the gun up into the frame of the open window, he pulled off a shot across the semi-circle that blew the edge of Eben Wallis's left shoulder off. Blood and bone shattered and flew, and he was thrown to the ground from his seat on the wagon. The horse bolted and the front right wheel rolled over Wallis's leg.

The others were stunned. Bev wanted to leap off the hood of her truck but she was paralyzed. Martin stood with his eyes wide and his mouth agape. Not for long though, as Reboth's kid popped up from the stream bed thirty yards behind the gathering and squeezed off a shot that struck the green man in the back of his neck and made a hole upon exiting through his throat. He reached up toward his torn windpipe, gasped blood, and went over suddenly, flat on his face in the dust. Mary Reboth was at the top of the rise and she fired on Bev. The bullet smashed through the windshield of the truck. The noise of breaking glass got Bev moving. She jumped down from the truck and hid behind its large back tire. Mary fired the semi-automatic again in rapid succession. Truck metal and glass flew everywhere. Reboth's kid came out of the stream bed and headed for where Bev was hiding. Eben was still alive, though, and from where he lay on the ground, he managed to draw his pistol, aim and shoot out the kid's left eye. A deafening scream went up. Larry Reboth's head literally smoked from within, his socket a smoldering volcano. Wallis fired again and put one through the kid's forehead, which flung him back into the dry stream. Reboth upon seeing the death of his boy, made a target of Eben Wallis and emptied his revolver, filled the gun with a speed loader, and put two more into him. When he stopped shooting, Eben was raw meat, bleeding into the dust.

"Get her," Reboth called over his shoulder to his wife up on the rise and headed for the palette.

Bev had toted that rifle of hers with her everywhere she'd gone since she'd found it under a bed in a dilapidated ranch house four years earlier, but she'd yet to aim it and shoot it at anything but the horizon. More rounds slammed into the truck. One hit the tire she was behind and the air whistled out of it. Bev called for Pepper, hoping the dog hadn't been hit in the hail of lead. She brought the rifle butt up to her shoulder, stood, spun in the direction of her opponent and fired twice. At the same moment, Mary fired and one of her shots hit the forestock of Bev's 22 and shattered the end of the weapon. The barrel bent, leaving the Marlin all but useless. Bev wasn't hit but the shock of the impact brought her to the ground. Mary started down the hill to finish her off.

Meanwhile, James had shot the locking mechanism that held the cables from each corner of the pallet together and attached to the parachute. Once the cables fell away, he stripped the tarpaulin off. He was wary as he approached the plastic blue shrink wrapping with his knife, keeping his pistol at the ready. "Now what kind of killer something or other could they pack in a food pallet?" he wondered. As he sliced away the plastic, he remembered his son was dead, and tears came to his eyes. Inside the pallet there was nothing but cans and boxes of food. Fresh drinking water, medicine, the usual. He knew that lizard fool had gone off his green rocker. Now he and Mary had enough to survive on for more than a year, but the price was steep.

Bev never made it to Eben's gun. Mary stood over her, aiming down the barrel of her rifle between Bev's eyes. Mary thought of her dead son, and Bev thought of her dead children. Before the trigger could be pulled, both women were brought out of their reveries by the sound of galloping hooves, a cacophony of howls and barks. Mary kept her aim on Bev and so never saw the gleam of the machete, or saw Susan Shebel, covered with her husband's blood rushing down off the rise. The blade dug in right at the base of Mary Reboth's skull and severed the spinal column. The rifle went off, but the bullet went wide and kicked the sand up next to Bev's right ear.

"Get up," said Susan. "Quick, get on behind me." She reached out an arm for Bev, who grabbed on, grappled up the side of the horse with her free hand and threw a leg over its back. "Pepper," she cried. The dog barked and followed. Susan spurred the mount now free of its travois and it jerked forward. There was the sound of gun fire and Bev felt the breeze of a passing bullet. She turned as they sped away to see the aiming James Reboth suddenly swarmed by coydogs. His large figure went down beneath the pack. The two women rode hard due northwest, toward Bev's place. In the far distance a dust storm was brewing, a black blizzard that would cover the entire county under yards of dust. They reached the tilting house just in time before the tidal wave of a cloud front overtook them and brought the horse inside to protect it in case the coydogs had followed.

*   *   *

ONCE THEY WERE settled inside, Bev took out a bottle that held the last of her liquor, some forgotten bar back mix of whiskey, cheap bourbon, vodka and gin, and poured two giant glasses. She brought one to Susan who sat in a chair in the living room, head down and long hair veiling her face, weeping over the loss of her husband. The sounds of grief were whispers to the violence of the storm, the racket of sand against the siding. Pepper the dog curled up at Bev's feet when she sat. When Susan finally came around she lifted her glass of liquor and dashed off a quarter of it. "That's it," she said. "I've had it with this shit hole, dust bowl, land of death."

"What happened to Theo?" asked Bev.

"Those creatures took him right off his horse. I tried to help him but he was already dead and they were dragging him off to divvy up by the time I went at them with the machete. There were too many, though. They didn't come for me right away because they were distracted by the fresh kill. I rode for the drop point to get help."

"And it was bloodier there," said Bev. "You came to me like an angel of mercy."

"I read the scene in an instant. Theo warned me today to watch out for Reboth and his crew. He suspected them of something like that. After what happened to my husband I was more than happy to chop a neck," she said and surprised herself by laughing.

"I know," said Bev. "It's all horrible but ridiculous, so nightmarishly ridiculous."

And what they found, in the days that followed was that Bev couldn't have been closer to the truth. Susan moved in with Bev to share tasks and for mutual protection and the two of them took over the Reboths' place, seeing it was the best fortified, was the sturdiest, and had the most equipment. Upon moving in, they discovered that the reason the number of respondents to the food drop had declined so precipitously was that Reboth and his family had been picking them off one at a time and collecting their gear and goods. So between the previous air drop and the recent massacre beneath the Hackberry tree, they'd offed seven individuals and their families. As Susan said to Bev about their discovery, "He thought it was justified because of the conditions. He missed the simplest adage, strength in numbers. I bet he never considered his greed and how it blinded him."

A week or so later it became clear that the coydogs, like the jack rabbits had run their course and simply disappeared. Still the two armed themselves to the teeth and took the horse. They headed for the site of the air drop and had plans to commandeer Reboth's truck full of supplies from the pallet. Once that was accomplished they'd change the flat on Bev's truck and take that as well. Pepper also accompanied them on their journey. They stopped first to look for Theo's remains, but found nearby where the coydogs had jumped him only a half a cracked rib cage picked clean. At the drop site there was no trace of the bodies of James and Mary and Larry or Eben Wallis. The green remains of Martin were intact and had been carried off only a few yards from where he'd dropped. It's where they buried him. It took a few hours to load all of the provisions in the two trucks. Bev told Susan to be wary, and related to her Martin's warnings about death waiting for them in the pallet. They never found anything wrong with the provisions and there were no failed bombs or booby traps. In addition, a few days later they took the horse out across Eben Wallis's land to look for the missile silo, but found nothing of the sort.

In the heat of that afternoon, Susan, Bev, Pepper and the horse hid under an enormous ledge of sand stone from the brutal heat of a rare, clear day. "I'm starting to form a theory, here," said Bev.

Susan laughed and handed her the canteen. "I'm game."

"Everybody, and I mean everybody, myself included, operates not out of a knowledge of what is, but out of a delusion of what they wish. It might be the most powerfully destructive force in the world."

"I follow you," said Susan. "Think of all the players—the oil companies, the fracking outfits, the politicians, the voters, the farmers, the dreamers, oh, and the religious, definitely. Remember when the governor put up the Ten Commandments on the grounds of the capitol. Same one that signed a bill making it impossible to sue the fracking companies. We were all duly warned about the climate, the quakes. The research had been done, and the numbers didn't lie."

"Not just them, though," said Bev. "Not only poor lonely lizard Martin, either. Or Eben Wallis scanning the land through his telescope hoping for a peek at… what? Me, and a fierce belief that if I tended to my children's graves I'd be with them again. As chaotic in its delusion as a black blizzard rolling across the bone dry fields and equally empty of meaning."

"True. Well, Theo and I had led ourselves to believe that our degrees from good schools and money were all we needed to survive the drought."

"And your showing up to save me in the nick of time. If I was to tell that story to most anyone, they'd think, 'Oh, now that's surely a miracle.' 'Or don't give me that hand of God business. That never happens.' When what it was was just a spot where random moments met—not fraught with meaning, not fraught with luck too good to be true, or anything at all."

"You know, Pepper might be the only one out here that bears no responsibility for this clusterfuck of a disaster." The two women laughed, and in that moment could feel they'd drawn the closest they might ever had gotten to what actually is.

DESTROYED BY THE WATERS
– RACHEL SWIRSKY –

THE OCEAN IS warm enough to dive without a wetsuit. Derek wears swimwear like everyone else. Zack is the lone holdout, bulky in three millimeters of Neoprene. To Derek's eyes, it shows all the beloved-but-bittersweet changes in Zack's body, the sags, the knobs, the lumps. At twenty, he was a muscular god. Now: mortal.

Derek's body has changed too, heaven knows. But he didn't have as far to fall.

Zack remains tall, thick-haired, athletic. He comes to stand behind Derek. His body is warm and solid. Gently, he asks, "What are you thinking?"

From this angle, the ocean is utterly blue. The water is mildly restive, an insistent pitch and yaw beneath their feet.

Derek says, "You can't even tell anything was here."

Zack points to a few darker spots. "I think those are the tops of houses."

They're only a brush darker than the rest of the water.

*   *   *

They'd honeymooned in New Orleans. They were so young then, pockets full of no money and potentials full of question marks. One of the groomsmen had an aunt who needed a house sitter so they flew standby and scrounged enough cash for meals and cheap drinks.

Jackson Square: a five dollar palm reading that turned into a two-hour-long conversation about Katrina. (He said, "The city will come back. There's too much will to live here to keep it down." He was right until he wasn't.)

Decatur Street: ten p.m. on a Monday, a tiny Italian restaurant hung with large, dark portraits of the proprietor's family. The bored sommelier taking a shine to the newlyweds, sneaking them sips from bottles of fancy wine.

Canal Street: storefronts plumed with masks and shiny with souvenirs. Four drunk guys, a beer bottle thrown, taunts about Derick's manicured nails and coral-colored shirt.

Endless bus loops: sitting or standing, sweating against each other's skin. Ignoring the windows to watch the passengers—tourists complaining about the humidity frizzing their hair, sway-hipped women in sundresses, men with moist tank tops slicked to their chests.

Everywhere: grief, anger, exhaustion, work. Some were silent, but others talked, trauma honing words into catharsis, stories that took strangers by the collar and refused to let them go.

Derek and Zack: dropping the next day's meal budget into a charity box, but prevailingly, overwhelmingly were elated by each other. Floating in a bubble like the ones that rose through the expensive champagne which the sommelier had given them in a flute, holding her fingers to her lips and saying, "Shhh."

* * *

It's a small boat: eight divers and the dive master. They gather to listen to the site debriefing. Derek sits furthest back, watching the others. From this angle, the ocean's surface is sporadically broken by ruins.

The dive master is a tiny woman who compensates with a loud voice and broad gestures. "Enclosed dives are dangerous. Before you even think about exploring, get out your line." She mimes unwinding the spool at her hip. "Think of it like diving a wreck. Even if it's just an old apartment building, even if you think it will be easy to find the bedroom window you came in through again—"

Zack listens, nodding. Derek can see the almost imperceptible movement of Zack's lips as he compares what she's saying to his research on the site. He is the kind of man who watches safety guidelines every single time.

The dive master jabs her finger into the side of her head. "Remember your map! Land use says you can swim anywhere within this radius. This is for *your* safety. Outside this zone, the ruins have not been cleared of debris and other hazards. Your LCDC will flash if you get near the boundary. Don't make me come get you."

The other divers are so *young*. Derek watches one smooth face after another. Even the dive master's complexion is cherubic. One of the bare-chested boys left his dampening Yale shirt on the bench, in range of spray. A girl wears dark eyeliner and pink lipstick which will raccoon and wash off respectively as soon as they meet the water. She stands aside, glancing occasionally at the boys her age, body exclaiming nervousness as she cups her elbows and rocks foot to foot.

Have these kids ever known a world where New Orleans *wasn't* flooded or underwater? Twenty-something tourists should have been here throwing beads or throwing up. They should have been stumbling over uneven pavement, and going to historically important bars they didn't recognize, and throwing bottles at gay couples, or whatever it was kids did these days. They should have been bothering the locals, and there should have *been* locals, giving readings in Jackson Square and talking about how New Orleans would always make it through. These kids didn't deserve a world that let everything *flood*, let everyone *drown*. Did they know *anything* about Charleston, Bangladesh, Baltimore—?

Derek's breath starts to go. He knows the whirlpool will suck him down into a panic attack if he lets it.

He forces the thoughts away before it's too late, but Zack must have heard the quickening of his breath, because he wraps his arms around Derek and whispers urgently, "Everybody got out. They got everybody out."

Here. They got everybody out here. The omitted word stings.

Derek pushes Zack away. "I'm fine."

The girl in pink lipstick glances in their direction, but no one else does. They're watching the sky, the water, each other—not the old couple in back.

THREE WEEKS AGO: Zack had woken late, the arid morning already pressing close, Derek gone on morning errands. An icon lingered in the upper right-hand corner of his vision—Derek had left a note. When he opened it, all it showed was the purchase of two fares to Louisiana and a few associated bookings.

Derek came home later with groceries. He still liked to choose produce by hand.

"I don't understand," Zack said. "We haven't gone diving in ten years."

Derek said nothing as he transferred stone fruit into an apple-patterned Franciscan bowl. He ran his thumb over the soft spot on a peach and frowned.

Zack flipped through the bookings, as if they might display something different this time. "And New Orleans—we haven't been back since our honeymoon—"

Zack gave Derek a sober look. He could tell his husband was nervous by the way he turned the peach over and over in his hands.

"Derek," Zack said, as gently as he could. "Is this about Noah?"

Derek's whole body flinched. They usually avoided their son's name. He closed his eyes and steadied himself before setting the fruit in the bowl.

He turned to open the refrigerator. "They're not refundable."

Zack said, "You can't tear your heart out again. I can't go through it. *You* can't go through it."

Derek said nothing. The refrigerator exhaled a cold breath.

Arguments queued up in Zack's brain. He'd spent most of his career in hospital administration, and he was trained to come at things from multiple angles. He tried a goal-oriented approach: What do you want from this? How do you think it will help? He tried emotional pleas: I'm worried—it hurts to see you set yourself up for so much pain. He tried guilt: Why didn't you talk to me first so we could set a plan together? He tried pragmatism: It's been too long since our last dive. We should take time to train back up before making decisions.

He tried intransigence. "You can't make me participate in this. I can't stop you, but I won't go with you."

(They both knew this was a lie.)

Finally, when minutes had become hours, in desperation and exhaustion, Zack lost his temper. "Why play around? Why not go straight to Baltimore?"

Derek went small and still.

Zack said, "I can't believe I said that."

Derek's voice was a composed, weary monotone. "It doesn't matter."

After that, there was nothing left to say.

They went to bed. They brushed their teeth and put on pajamas and spoke politely in the bathroom. They laid down. Derek cuddled into Zack's side, and Zack wrapped him in his arms.

DEREK DIGS IN his dive bag so he doesn't have to talk to Zack, or look at the girl with pink lipstick. He feels Zack's stare, and he knows his husband is trying to figure out whether he is okay or not, and what to do if he isn't. Zack's constant solicitous vigilance makes Derek feel more self-conscious, not less, but after everything they've been through, he can't blame Zack for watching.

Derek is grateful for the distraction when the kid from Yale tries to strike up a conversation with the other college-age divers. "Anyone else doing a night dive? I'm going on a ghost tour tonight."

A boy with blond dreads is, and they fall to talking about ghost stories they've heard from other divers. The kid from Yale wants to go see Madame LaLaurie and her tortured slaves, but the blond boy wants to go past the Superdome because he's read that's where the best ghosts are.

"And there's the ghosts who died in the flood," the blond boy says. "They must be really pissed."

Zack moves protectively in front of Derek. He repeats his mantra, ostensibly for the kids, but Derek knows it's really meant for him. "Everyone got out. There was an evacuation."

The blond boy gives him a condescending look. "You know *someone* didn't."

Zack's tone doesn't change, but Derek can hear anger sharpening his syllables. "*Real* people died in American floods. Show some respect."

Before things can escalate, the boat's engine changes pitch. It slows. The dive master calls for everyone to gear up.

Zack shakes his head and makes a noise of self-remonstration. He worries the zipper at his collar. "They're just stupid kids," he mumbles.

In a calming tone, Derek says, "I know."

"They don't understand they can *hurt* people, talking like that."

Derek soothes. "I know."

THERE'S AN OLD story in Zack's family about how, when he was six years old, Zack walked up to his uncle who had fought in Vietnam and asked, "How do you protect someone from a bullet?"

Zack didn't remember doing it, and he didn't remember the reply. He did remember his mother telling the story over and over again: her Zack, the protector.

That night three weeks ago, after learning about Derek's plans for New Orleans, Zack had lain awake. He watched the predawn, then the dawn, then the light of morning. Over fifty years, he'd grown to know Derek's gestures and expressions, his beliefs, his preoccupations, the thoughts he spoke aloud and the ones he signaled with a tightened lower lip and the dark ones he'd later try to laugh off.

Memories lapped at his ankles, of the first eighteen months after Noah's death when Derek had lost all the extra weight he'd been carrying since they met, all the roundness in his cheeks and softness in his arms, shriveling into himself. He remembered how Derek had slumped, hobbies and friendships wearing away, as he stared for days out of windows at Tucson's thunderheads. It's been a long, arduous journey back from that, one that still isn't done after four years. Zack imagines crashing all the way back down again, imagines how waterlogged years would accumulate, pieces of their lives rotting like wet wood, until they were bloated nothings.

When the restless clock finally turned nine, Zack called their therapist. At their emergency session, she only said, "Derek has made a lot of progress. If he says he's ready to do this, we should support him."

Against them both, Zack had no recourse. Over fifty years, he'd also learned that sometimes one's beloved sets his heart on a path of pain and will not be deterred. Sometimes all one can do is be there and be ready to help afterward.

His voice was heavy as he murmured to himself, "New Orleans. Another good memory gone." Like Oakland where they raised Noah, and New York City where he sang with his choir at St. Patrick's, and Houston where he spent two weeks with his grandparents every year, and Minneapolis where he went to college.

Zack sat in their den and began researching the dive.

*   *   *

IN THE OLD days, the dive master would have had to take them in a single group she could keep an eye on. Instead, she passes through, making sure she's connected to each diver's Lens-Compatible Dive Computer.

Zack and Derek rented LCDCs onshore with the rest of their gear, but a Scandinavian brother and sister don't have them. The brother coughs up for a cheap, wrist-mounted spare; the sister shrugs and says she'll just go down with the dive master.

Derek connects the tank to his air hose, and then double-checks Zack's while Zack double-checks his. He cleans his mask, and feels grateful for the seals they have these days that don't flood. Sometimes it's nice living in the future, when it isn't horrible. Equipment that didn't feel heavy twenty years ago now drags on Derek's shoulders. He snaps together a dozen buckles and clips.

While they work, Zack frets. "Try not to get too close to anything. They say they cleared the most dangerous debris before opening the site, but three divers were hospitalized in the past year."

Zack found this news early in his research on the New Orleans site, and has been repeating some variation of it almost every day since. He does this when he's worried, fixates on details. As far as Derek can tell, Zack is completely oblivious to it.

"The judge ruled they were being reckless," Derek says without enthusiasm.

Zack gives his consistent answer. "It proves there's still dangerous stuff down there."

Sometimes, Derek privately marvels that a man like Zack who is brilliant and incisive in any other circumstance can't tell that his subtext is running away with his tongue.

At the edge of the boat, masks on and regulators in, Zack gives Derek a last, entreating look. His eyes are full of the question *Are you sure?* But he has the courtesy not to say it.

NOAH: DELIVERED TO their arms as a white infant with a mop of dark hair, startled eyes, and a strangely authoritative cry. They'd wanted to name him Devon, but his birth mother had only given him this one thing. It seemed petty to refuse. Noah was the most popular boy's name the year he was born. Eighty-thousand Noahs entering one prediluvian world.

DEREK'S EARS FILL with the sound of his own breathing.

Gravity pulls them down a few feet before their inflated vests draw them back to the surface. They signal the boat they're okay, clasp hands, and orient themselves for descent.

A message from Zack flashes across Derek's lens. <<*Remember, I love you.*>> Zack squeezes his hand. Derek squeezes back.

They pause every few feet to clear their ears. Derek could swear he feels a thrum throughout his body from the signal the LCDC uses to repel large predators, but Zack would say that's his imagination. Underwater, the neoprene that made Zack so awkward on land sleeks to his muscular contours. Derek could almost mistake him for the boy he'd been at twenty.

They're somewhere in the French Quarter, but the changed environment makes it almost unrecognizable. Underwater, light disperses reds and distends blues, blotting any vestiges of vividness. Neon markers indicate unsafe areas within the cleared zone. Visibility is poor, clouding into nothing a few body-lengths away.

It's easy to see why the kids think there are ghosts here. It's not only stories and history; it's a quality of the place. Even before it was swallowed by the ocean, Derek has to admit New Orleans felt haunted to him. Life went by in disjunctive vignettes, with emotions and scenery that seemed to fracture moment by moment. It was because of alcohol and giddiness and too much nighttime wandering, but his memories of the city flashed like strobes, from glaring brights to intermittent fluorescents and pink-washed neons and shop windows coughing orange glow onto the asphalt.

Derek and Zack stop, hovering six feet over the drowned street. Their bodies sway with the breath of the ocean as they linger, looking.

Zack taps Derek's shoulder to get his attention. <<*Are you okay?*>>

Derek starts his reply, then stops.

Is he okay?

Strangely, impossibly, he is.

It's shock, isn't it? It must be shock. For the first eighteen months after Noah's death, he'd stood at the threshold of hospitalization. How can he feel *nothing?*

Polar ice sheets. Methane gas pockets. He couldn't escape the terms that ricocheted like bullets through the news. Worst case scenario. Experts failed to predict.

He and Zack hadn't even visited Noah's apartment in Baltimore before he died. They were busy with their friends and their lives so they sent money for him to fly home instead. He was just renting; they figured they'd go see his place once he'd really settled.

Derek had nothing to imagine when the news came. No way to viscerally understand what had happened. Photographs were no substitute. He needed to know how the city air had smelled when it mixed with oncoming water. He needed to see the place where his son had died, what the color of the carpets was, the color of the walls, the color of the windowsills. After Noah's death, he'd done nothing but try to imagine the drowning of Baltimore. What he ate was salt, what he heard was roaring, and what he saw was bleach and bones.

Derek spikes himself with thoughts he's learned not to let through because they always arrow into panic attacks. The worst: *Maybe if he'd stayed with his mother, he wouldn't have died.*

Maybe they should have looked at the blue-eyed bundle of him, and seen his grasping hands and brooding eyebrows, and known to send him back where he'd come from. He could have had another forty, fifty years. What could they possibly have given him to make up for that?

The thoughts race their customary track, but his anxiety is only an echo. He's as still as water eight meters deep.

<<*I'm fine.*>> Derek tells Zack, but his husband doesn't seem convinced.

They scull through the water above a side street. Derek doesn't know which, but Zack might. There's room for them to swim side-by-side, fins arcing smoothly through the water. The windows have been carefully stripped, but many stores hold furniture, even some goods.

Derek glimpses something shiny, and dives the last couple of meters to street level. Zack follows. It's a mask, surprisingly well-preserved for being at the bottom of the ocean, still sequined and decorated with brittle, stripped quills.

The store must have been one of those cheap souvenir places. If Derek digs through the junk, will he find key chains and plastic shot glasses? Divers aren't supposed to go inside the buildings, but the mask has fallen out. Derek shakes it loose from the layer of silt that pins it to the street.

He holds it up for Zack to look at. His husband frowns. Zack points at the mask. The stream of bubbles coming from his regulator moves faster. In confusion, Derek peers at his find.

Zack's gestures become more urgent. <<*Get back!*>>

Derek instantly withdraws. The mask drops from his gloved fingers. Sequins shine as they fall.

Zack swims between Derek and the storefront. Derek follows his line of sight to a long, skeletal hand.

ZACK WAS ALWAYS one of the best school athletes growing up. He liked sports—as a relatively quiet boy without much else in common with his peers, it gave him something to do and a way to fit in. His build didn't lend itself to any sport particularly, but it left him with plenty of options. His favorites were solo— swimming, biking, running—letting his muscles go while he spent time in his head.

Being both quiet and an athlete also kept anyone from noticing that Zack was gay. That meant he could keep people from picking on weaker kids—including the gay ones—sometimes, if he got there at the right time. People knew Zack didn't like it when they made fun of the disabled class, or the fat cheerleader it was easy to make cry. So they didn't do it if he was around.

Probably, no one from his high school would have remembered much about Zack, if it hadn't been for the day two months before graduation when he came back late from an after-school run. As he circled back onto campus, he saw a guy with a handgun crossing the parking lot.

Zack ran him down.

The kid got off a shot by accident. It grazed Zack's shoulder, but otherwise, he was fine.

Later, it turned out the kid had found out he was failing biology and wouldn't be able to graduate. He'd gone home, gotten high, and grabbed his grandpa's gun. On his way back to his teacher's classroom, he'd stopped to make sure her car was still in the faculty lot, which was when Zack saw him.

At his graduation party, Zack's mother urged him to tell the story to his uncle, the Vietnam vet. Zack felt both embarrassed and proud of himself as he stood beside his uncle's chair, leaning down a bit because he didn't hear well from his left ear.

"I guess I figured out how to protect someone from a bullet," Zack said.

"Good job," muttered his uncle, reaching for a handful of pretzels as he watched the muted football game on TV.

Zack was nonplussed by the reaction. "You know, my mother always tells that story? How I asked you how to protect someone from a bullet?"

His uncle looked up, eyes suspicious under heavy brows. "Stop a bullet?" He grunted, a heavy, humorless sound that didn't seem to be meant for Zack or anyone else. He shoved a pretzel into his mouth. "Want to protect someone, stop the goddamn war."

*   *   *

In the cloudy water, Zack's body almost forms a wall between Derek and the shop window. Derek can hardly see past him to the trailing, bony fingers in the mud.

Zack pulls his flashlight from its loop on his vest and shines it down to get a better look. <<*There must have been an accident. I'm calling the dive master. We shouldn't disturb*>>—

Zack's text ends as a mass of mud shifts, throwing more dirt into their faces. His flashlight beam swings loosely for a moment, illuminating flashes of grit and dark water.

It stabilizes as Zack grabs hold again, showing the skeletal hand. It rises up from the ocean floor like a living thing, trailing forearm and elbow. The bones are uncannily articulated. The flashlight suffuses them with a weird, greenish glow.

Something bulky shifts overhead. Zack's light, shining upward, catches the jut of ribs. Zack reaches for them with his free hand, and the bones fall on him as if attacking.

A glow catches Derek's attention from below. It's the skeletal arm, pinned to the street by a clot of debris. The hand waves free, still stretching upward.

Derek had assumed the flashlight was giving the bones an illusory illumination, but in fact, they *are* glowing. Derek pulls on the hand. With a tug, it disconnects from the wrist. It starts to float upward, but Derek tightens his grip.

Up close, the bones aren't even fully distinguished from each other. Finger joints are painted on, and the back of the hand is a single piece. He prods the palm. One finger flickers off before lighting again.

<<*They're fake.*>> Derek tells Zack. <<*You can tell the dive master not to come. It's a toy filled with glow sticks. Whatever kids use these days for glow sticks.*>>Derek releases the hand. It floats upward, its own lamp.

<<*It's the ghost tours.*>> Derek surmises. <<*Glowing skeletons in masks.*>>

He looks up. Zack hovers above him, holding the bulk of the fake skeleton—its ribs and spine and trailing femurs. The skull is missing. Zack looks as if he might change attitude in the water and begin a grim waltz.

DEREK WAS THE one who got sick, but Zack had the nightmares. They began with the smell of brine—at first a faint whiff, not unpleasant, but soon thickening into a miasma of rotting fish and beached animals. Zack would slowly come into a sense of his body. Floating: arms outstretched, hands and fingers extended, feet moving instinctively to keep him upright. The back of his neck broke the surface. Heat prickled on his face. His nostrils drew humid, salty air into his lungs.

A stillness so potent he could hear it. A silence like buzzing.

Like a stirring alligator that breaks the illusion of a log, the water would change. It would sling its mighty weight against him: walls of water, rocks, and silt. Human-made wreckage bruised and bloodied him—a doorknob punching into his stomach, the uniquely painful shape of an iron on his thigh.

Inexorably, the water rose, one silty inch after another. Zack would flail, rocks and metal slashing his hands. Brine filled his mouth, his nostrils, his sinuses, his throat. He woke choking.

Zack's doctor diagnosed him with sleep apnea, but the

nightmares never fully resolved. He never told Derek what they were about.

ZACK'S SCREAM ISN'T a sound. His regulator remains in his mouth; he is too well-trained an athlete to remove it. He screams with his whole body, twisting and tearing at the skeleton, trying to crack its deceitful bones.

<<*It's fake, Zack.*>> Derek repeats, but he can see the frantic quality of Zack's movements. Each of his husband's fists is wrapped around one of the skeleton's ribs as he tries to crack it in half. Its legs trail beneath it as if treading water.

Part of a rib breaks off. It snags Zack's sleeve, and Derek murmurs thanks for the wetsuit. If Zack doesn't stop, something much worse could happen. A hose could get severed.

Bracing himself against shrapnel, Derek swims around his husband, coming in from behind to comfort and restrain him. He repeats himself as he moves, a gentle, steady flood of <<*Zack, they aren't real.*>>

Zack's hands open. The broken skeleton moves upward through the water.

<<*I know.*>>

THREE AND A half weeks ago, Derek had been having breakfast with a friend when the name "New Orleans" caught his ear. He'd looked over at the next table where a fit, young straight couple were discussing travel plans.

"New Orleans?" he asked.

The boy nodded. His blond ponytail trailed down his back,

bright in the sun. "They cleared it out maybe a year, two years ago? You didn't hear?"

Derek navigated the following conversation automatically. They haven't dived in ten years; Derek learned how to dive when he was twenty-three; yes, the Great Barrier Reef has changed a lot since then; no, they hadn't invented warmsuits back when he and Zack dived in Alaska.

New Orleans.

It had been both the first city to go under, and the only one to get everybody out. New Orleans was used to worst case scenarios. Without their foresight and infrastructure, things would have been much worse.

The other flooded cities weren't under enough water for diving. It would be a long time before they were opened to visitors, if they ever were.

On the train home, Derek sat with his head leaning against the window, watching the desert pass. With work and therapy, things had been getting better, but most days, Derek still felt his life orbiting around the absence at its center. Sometimes he felt the whole middle of him was gone. If this was the closest he'd ever get to his son's grave, then he had to go—he had to prove to himself that he could.

Two and a half weeks ago, Zack had come home from therapy in angry silence. Their therapist had seen Derek at his worst. How were they supposed to go through that again? How could they take it? New Orleans. A whole city killed by the ocean. His heart would break.

When news had come about Baltimore, Zack had left work immediately, even though the hospital could have fired him. He didn't care; he knew that Derek would need him. Derek was tender, nurturing, fragile. He needed someone to take care of him.

Zack sat in the den on the old smoke-grey couch and set his head between his knees. He couldn't do anything about his frustration, so he had to let it go. He took a deep breath, let it out, then sat straight as he sent his lens an inquiry about diving in New Orleans.

Derek asks Zack: <<*How much air do you have?*>>

He knows the answer. He checked their LCDC link before doing anything else. Zack used a lot of air with his exertion, but he's not in danger.

Derek had hoped the act of checking would help call Zack back to himself. Stiffly, Zack shifts, checking his physical gauges before reporting. <<*I have enough air. We can keep going.*>>

Derek has no intention of letting Zack push himself any further than he already has. <<*I already messaged the dive master.*>> he says. <<*I told her we're surfacing early.*>>

She'd also confirmed Derek's guess. She hadn't seen any of the skeletons herself, but she said other dive masters had come back with stories. The ghost tour companies got fined if they were caught, but it was hard to prove which ones were responsible.

<<*I love you so much.*>> Zack says.

Without tone, it's hard to tell, but over fifty years, Derek has gotten to know Zack well enough to understand his subtleties. Zack is apologizing. He thinks he's failed Derek, which breaks Derek's heart.

<<*I love you, too.*>> Derek answers.

Derek takes Zack's hand and runs his thumb over the torn fabric of his husband's gloves. With his other hand, he reaches upward, making sure their path is clear for ascent.

Their fingers twine. The waters lighten around them as they rise. One day, one of them will say Noah's name and smile.

THE NEW VENUSIANS
– Sean Williams –

TODAY I APOLOGIZED in person to a Tuvaluan. Now I'm on Venus with my grandfather, who I haven't seen in ten years. To top it all off I'm suddenly unsure about my prepositions.

On? Over? In?

It's entirely my fault. You don't make puns while visiting a monument to the first country swallowed by rising oceans—because people live a long time and they're still sore about it. Even really good puns like *I don't sea what the fuss is all about* or *They didn't do it on porpoise!* I get that now.

Still, that place was a real dive.

God, I can't help myself! Anyway, the damage is done. Someone saw the log and complained about my poor taste, so I had to d-mat back to the monument (basically a deck stranded in the middle of an ocean where the low-lying archipelago used to be) in order to express my regret and sorrow directly to a representative of the Tuvaluan diaspora. Afi Tekena looked old enough to be my grandmother's grandmother, all thick gray hair and wrinkles and constellations of age spots making up her own personal Zodiac. My sign was Teenage Girl Needs To

Learn About Respect, and you know, fair enough. I did bad, which I admitted, and she accepted it with solemn grace. Maybe she thought the public shaming was lesson enough.

My parents disagreed.

"Just because you can d-mat anywhere now," Mom scolded me, "doesn't mean you should treat everywhere like home."

"You have to learn to observe other people's boundaries, Tash," said Dad. "You can't do what you want and stroll away from the consequences."

"I didn't stroll anywhere," I said. "Ten feet in any direction and you're in the water."

They exchanged a look and I knew I'd made a tactical error.

"We're tailoring the punishment to fit the crime," Mom said. "We're sending you to Grandpa."

"But isn't he—?"

"Yes."

"Does that mean I—?"

"The permits have already been organized." Mom works for OneEarth, so surprise surprise, she pulled strings. "You have one hour to pack."

"One hour!" The complete unreasonableness of this demand momentarily overwhelmed the crazy nature of what they were doing to me. No counselor this time. No talking therapy. No lectures, which frankly I would've preferred, even the ones I'd heard dozens of times before. Just sixty minutes to pack everything I might want to take to another planet?

Holy shit. *Venus.* And I still don't know if I'm on, over or in it.

When I look out the grimy yellow porthole, all I see is cloud.

*   *   *

THE TRIP TOOK eleven minutes at the speed of light, which means I'm now that much younger than I would've been if I'd stayed behind. I'm orbiting a lot closer to the sun too, and therefore ageing more slowly. I can't decide if that's a good or bad thing.

It's all moot when I'm face to face with Grandpa, Hudson Sixsmith, who looks like Afi Tekena dried a shark, stood it on its tail, and painted a human face on its chin. Thin, dry, and wrinkled. And wearing a tuxedo, oddly.

"Birdie has always had terrible timing," is the first thing he says to me.

He's talking about Mom. She hates her real name.

"You can send me back if you want," I tell him, thinking *please please please*.

"Nonsense. That would be rude." His withered mask shifts into a new shape, one of consternation, or perhaps resignation. "I'm forgetting my manners. Please, come in."

He steps back and waves me out of the booth and into his home. It's an aerostat called *Hieronymus* floating high above the hellish surface of Venus. I imagined something like a modern laboratory crossed with an old man's den from a video drama, a mixture of brushed aluminum and stuffed leather, but what I see is nothing like that. Light filters through stained portholes along both sides of a cigar-shaped central cabin with hatches leading above and below. The ceiling is high but it's adorned with hooks and racks from which hang a motley assortment of pipes, cables, wires, ropes, vines and dirty clothes. It's a jungle. It's a frat-boy's bedroom. It's a mess.

It *smells*.

"Been here on your own a long time, have you?"

"Twenty-two years," he says, brushing off a faded deckchair and inviting me to sit. "Few people visit."

I stay standing, looking around me in horror. "I wonder why."

He bristles. "Not for lack of invitation. I have been attempting to raise interest in what I found here, but will anyone listen? Not at all. Instead they distort my data and question my qualifications. They—" He catches himself on the verge of indignation with a deep breath. "They send me their unruly students, but you're not one of those. You are an unruly granddaughter. What did you do, again? I'll make some tea while you tell me. Sit, sit."

It takes me longer to overcome my feelings about the filthy chair than to elucidate my crimes. Why dwell on those when Mom has no doubt given him a blow-by-blow account?

"I remember Tuvalu," he says, coming back from a corner of the aerostat where a fabber has been working hard, making tea, cups, saucer, milk, sugar and a silver tray from random atoms and energy. It all looks preposterously shiny, like the tuxedo, and I realize then that he's making an effort to be hospitable. If he hadn't skipped basic cleanliness and gone straight to Five-Star Service, I would've noticed sooner.

"I visited the islands just before they went under," he's saying while he pours. "Took some samples, but they are gone now, lost in the Water Wars. This was back before we scanned everything as a matter of course, so there are no patterns archived. Whatever species lived on those scattered rocks either drowned or adapted to the wider ocean."

"Afi Tekena looked plenty lively to me."

"I'm not talking about people, Natasha. I'm talking about bacteria, the real rulers of the Earth."

Right. Okay. I concentrate on the cup of tea he's handing me. It's fragrant and hot, and I breathe deeply of it to mask the smell of sulfur and old socks.

"What is it you do here, exactly?" I ask him, keen to put some more distance between us and the topic of my transgressions.

"Much the same as I did back then." He leans into his deck chair, looking marginally human now he's sitting down. I hadn't noticed the beard before: it's sparse and white and really needs to go. "Sample. Analyze. Speculate. Preserve where possible. At this altitude in the Venusian atmosphere the conditions are very hospitable for biological processes. There's even water vapor! Why anyone would willingly waste their time sifting through Martian dust or stirring Galilean slush is a mystery beyond my comprehension—particularly when what I have found here overturns the history of life in our solar system."

My stomach sinks. Please don't make me be the audience for a madman. "Is that my punishment, then? To help you panhandle for microbes from inside a rusty old balloon?"

"Goodness me, no," he says. "We have to go outside to do that."

"Bit of a long way to fall, isn't it?"

"Fifty kilometers. Into hurricane winds, acid, and temperatures high enough to melt lead."

"There you go. That would be cruel and unusual, even for Mom and Dad."

"I will provide protective garb. And a very strong rope."

He winks and I breathe a huge sigh of relief. He's messing with me. Old people: it's so hard to read them sometimes. Their faces are non-Euclidean and complicated, and they can be crafty when they think they have the upper hand. Never let them believe that for too long: that's my motto.

"So let's get started. I'm game."

"Tell me something first," he says, leaning forward to look me in the eyes. The intensity of his gaze is startling. "What are you doing with your lenses? What is that activity I see?"

"Life-logging," I say, feeling the usual disorientation that comes from talking about life-logging while I'm life-logging (and now I'm life-logging about life-logging about life-logging—*argh*).

"But there is no Air here," he says, pointing out the obvious. "There's just the local network in *Hieronymus*."

"That's okay. What doesn't trickle through now I can upload later." I watch him closely for signs of disapproval. Some old people are weird about me chronicling our intersections—as though anything I think or say can make the slightest difference to them. "Sample. Analyze. Speculate. Preserve. That's what you said, right? You do it with bugs, I do it with my life. Are you cool with that?"

"I am very cool with that, Natasha." Grandpa nods, tapping the fingers of his right hand against his leg. "Birdie did the right thing, sending you here."

Great, I think, expecting a lecture. His house, his rules. I have to lump it before I'm allowed to go home et cetera. "Call me, Tash. Everyone does."

"Everyone is wrong, then. Drink your tea. There is time for a tour, I think, before the end of the world."

"The what?"

"I will explain."

"IMAGINE TWO MEN," he tells me as he leads me through *Hieronymus*' cramped chambers and tunnels and assigns me a berth the size of my suitcase. Does that mean I'm spending the night here? I hope not. The toilet is unspeakable. Unloggable. I've deleted the images to spare the innocent.

"Two men utterly at odds…"

One deck is entirely devoted to tanks of nutrient fluids in which samples from the Venusian clouds are growing. I see misty tendrils of green and blue, waving in gentle currents.

"The first man stands outside nature, content to monitor and record without intervention: *do no harm* is his motto. The second seeks understanding through probing and experiment, believing that he is part of nature. *Life cannot harm life,* he believes. *All things transform.*"

Hieronymus' underside is a hangar full of junk designed to dangle, scoop, swing, and occasionally fly through the Venusian atmosphere. Here, the sulfuric smell is strongest. And here Grandpa displays his fastidious side. Everything is efficiently cleaned and stowed. As he walks me around the space, his hands lightly tap the surfaces and edges of random things. I'm left with the impression that he could navigate this space blind, if he had to. Probably he has entrusted his life to some of these odd-looking machines, just as he trusts his life to the aerostat every minute of every day. Landing for repairs is not an option.

"When two men of opposing principles engage over the same territory, conflict is inevitable."

"Jeez, enough already, Grandpa. If you think only men disagree with each other, come back to Earth and meet my friends."

He huffs and ascends a ladder right up to the top of the aerostat. I put aside my quite reasonable objection to follow. He can move quickly when he wants to.

The uppermost level, where the gondola at its widest point meets the underside of the air sac, is an observation deck. All of the windows are real, those that aren't switched to virtual. Grandpa doesn't use lenses. He says they itch.

"My aerie," he says, holding out his arms, and I obediently look around.

The view is pretty cool. It's afternoon on Venus, which lasts a full Earth day when you're following the air currents at this altitude. From where I'm standing I can see clouds through a gap in the clouds, and clouds below, clouds above, and clouds on all the virtual windows surrounding us. Clouds of every shape and shade of white imaginable, some stretched into thin, straight lines, some bunched up into vast arcs and columns. When I read 'clouds' in a description of Venus before coming here I pictured the ones at home, but this is something else entirely. On cloud-world, there are clouds to spare. It's clouds all the way down.

There's one exception: a dark hole in some of the windows, marring the otherwise perfect view.

"What's that?" I ask, pointing.

"That," he says, "is the Eye."

"Of the storm?" I shift uneasily away from the nearest image. The thought of a Venusian tornado is slightly terrifying. Also, it seems to be looking back at me.

"In a sense." Grandpa takes a seat in front of an old-fashioned ship's wheel and folds his arms. "What you see is the work of my worst enemy."

"The other dude from your quaint little parable, I presume. The one who likes to get his hands dirty?"

"In a manner of speaking, yes. You might appreciate his sense of humor. There is a thing called the Bosch reaction—"

"As in Hieronymus Bosch, of this place?"

"No, Carl Bosch, but therein lies the pun. The Bosch reaction pits hydrogen against carbon dioxide, producing elemental carbon and water. Do you see where this is going?"

"Not really. Oh, wait, isn't the atmosphere of Venus mostly carbon dioxide, which is why it's so hot?"

"Largely so, yes. The greenhouse effect gone wild is the usual analogy. Get rid of the carbon dioxide, and things would be very different."

"Huh. You'd need lots of hydrogen, I bet."

"Indeed. Vast amounts. You would have to harvest a gas giant or electrolyze an ocean to come remotely close."

"That's a lot of balloons." I process a mental image of every kids' party I'd ever been to, times a zillion. Which prompts another thought: "Wait, couldn't you just fab it?"

"If you had a fabber big enough, or enough of them, and enough power to run them. Yes, a grandiose fool might think so."

I look at the image then back at my grandfather. A zillion parties worth of hydrogen spewing forth into a largely carbon dioxide atmosphere, causing a rain of water and... Would that look something like this?

"You're kidding."

"I wish I was."

"All to turn Venus into a big swimming pool?"

Grandpa shrugs.

"And what about your bugs? Where will they live if the clouds go away?"

He shrugs again. "You are not asking the most pertinent question."

"Oh, yeah, okay." The bugs aren't the only things floating in this atmosphere. "What happens to us?"

"We crash, I guess."

I've gotta say, Grandpa seems pretty relaxed about it all. Me, not so much.

THE END OF the world. It's a big deal. I should be worried about that, I suppose, but mainly I just don't want to die.

"Send me home."

"Are you certain this is what you want?"

"Of course! This goes way beyond cruel and unusual. It's practically homicidal."

I climb, march, and stomp my way back to the booth, where Grandpa obediently keys in the codes required to override the usual block on interplanetary d-matting. I take a deep breath as the mirrored door closes and I brace myself for losing another eleven minutes of the universe's usual programming.

But nothing happens. There's no flash of light as scanning starts, no slight bump as my atoms start moving again at the other end. The door simply opens and there's Grandpa waiting for me with a hangdog expression.

"Lines are cut," he explains. "We are quarantined until it's over."

I'm furious, but not with him. "Completely cut?"

"Yes. We can't even call your parents."

Serves them right, I think. They'll be worried sick. "What does OneEarth think this is, a disease?"

"It is a contagion of sorts. Moral. Ideological. Hubristic. When some madman changes a world simply because he can, one must draw a line."

I brush past him, feeling weak in my knees, and drop into the now-welcoming deckchair. "Can he really do this? Is it even possible?"

"My enemy has seeded a section of the Venusian atmosphere with a custom-made Bosch reactor that is designed to replicate itself, which it has been doing faithfully ever since activation. The result, the Eye is limited now only by the amount of air it can suck in. At any moment I expect it to reproduce."

"Two eyes?"

"Then four, then eight."

"Ah, man." I know the story about the rice grains and the chessboard. We are so stuffed.

"Who is this guy, anyway? Doesn't he believe in asking *permission*?"

Grandpa looks tired, as if he's been grappling with these very questions himself. "I think he is making a point about capacity and culpability... After all, we nearly destroyed the Earth. What's to stop us destroying another world? This is a pretty good place for a demonstration. Venus, population one."

"Normally." I feel a bilious sinking in my gut, like the aerostat is already dropping out of the sky. "I don't want to die. I don't want to die full-stop, but I definitely don't want to die here."

"Nor shall you, Natasha, if I have anything to say about it. Don't cry." He reaches out and takes my hands. It's like touching old snake skin, soft with oil and crisscrossed with irregular diamonds. The fact that he has lived long enough to have hands like these makes me feel somewhat reassured. "*Hieronymus* has endured the atmosphere of Venus longer than any other vessel. It will weather this final storm."

"Are you sure?"

"Together, we can make it perfectly ship-shape."

Ship-shape? That's an odd phrase, until I remember the details of the Bosch reaction. Hydrogen plus carbon dioxide equals carbon plus aitch-two-oh—

"We're not going to crash land. We're going to splash down."

"You're a smart girl, Natasha. You and I, we're going to be the first people to sail on Venus."

IF WE DON'T drown first.

That's my mantra as we meticulously check *Hieronymus* for leaks, starting at the stern and making our way slowly to the fore. (Are they the right terms? I can't look them up. Curse you, Air-less Venus!) We have plenty of time. For all the horrific power of the Eye, which is growing in magnitude every minute, its effects take time to spread. One of the virtual screens on the upper deck shows thick rivers of carbon dioxide being sucked into the center of the storm and waves of water vapor radiating outwards. I slave my lenses to it, giving me a window into the death of an old world. It looks like a wound.

Grandpa whistles while he works, and why not? Our circumstances are perfectly surreal. To get into the spirit, I paint a skull-and-crossbones over the ship's wheel on the upper deck. When (not *if*, I tell myself) this log is uploaded, everyone will know that I went down in style.

Storm winds strike *Hieronymus*, setting it rocking from side to side. Atmospheric pressure is already falling—by a tiny amount where we are, but falling nonetheless. I imagine us diving with increasing speed into a brand-new ocean, only there's no ocean yet, just the first hints of rain falling in the Eye's boiling heart.

Rain. On Venus. When it hits the superheated rock it blasts immediately back into steam. How long until everything cools down enough to support liquid water is anyone's guess.

We have time to rest, anyway. I curl my legs up in my tiny berth with a sleep-mask on and concentrate on not throwing up, or screaming, or wishing I could go back in time and take back my stupid jokes, or whatever madness is gripping me that particular moment. I can hear Grandpa whistling again. Is that *The Pirates of Penzance*? Maybe he's not so bad, now I've had time to reflect.

Eventually I nod off and dream about being at a birthday party where someone's making cake in a fabber as fast as I can eat it. And I can eat it pretty fast. Zap! Cream sponge. Zap! Custard tart. Zap! Chocolate meringue. Down my gullet it all goes, barely touching the sides.

I sneeze awake feeling nauseous and hungry at the same time. Somewhere, I can smell toast.

It's Grandpa. He's upstairs munching on a Vegemite and cheese sandwich, staring at the virtual screens. There are three Eyes now, the one at the night-side equator and now one at each pole. Night has fallen for us. There are no visible stars.

"We've descended a kilometer," he says without looking around. "I could try bringing us up, but what's the point? Eventually we'll run out of air."

The dream stirs in my mind. "Can't we fight this? I mean, seed anti-Eyes turning everything back the way it was. Could that work?"

He turns to face me, and I try not to dwell on the fact that he appears to have doubled in age overnight.

"Maybe," he says. "If we had time to design and field test prototypes..."

I sag. "Stop right there. I know what 'maybe' means. I have parents."

"Do not despair, Natasha. I promised that you would come to no harm."

"But this isn't—"

"Natural? Fair? Right?" He shrugs. "These concepts do not apply where monsters are concerned. What if this is more than just a cautionary tale about the power of our technology? Molding nature in our image is what we humans do, after all. Perhaps my enemy believes that he is acting for the greater good by creating another world for humanity. Don't our needs trump those of mere bugs?"

"A back-up planet... seriously?"

He shrugs. "By my calculations, if the Bosch reaction continues unchecked, some three quarters of this world will be covered in water. Not as deeply as Earth, but covered nonetheless. A new biosphere will form, one that humanity can seed if it chooses to. In a generation or two, people might live here. The long day will take some getting used to, and it's possible that extreme weather might continue to put paid to my enemy's long-term plans—but if you can change an atmosphere wholesale, why not a planet's rotation? Where does it end? Once it has begun, who can stop it?"

Hieronymus lurches like my mood. I sit cross-legged on the floor and gnaw at my fingernails.

"Is he still here?" I say. "Your enemy?"

"Why do you ask?"

"You said earlier: 'population one'. He should at least stick around to watch."

"That would be the admirable thing, would it not?" Grandpa

sighs. "When people set themselves above nature, they put their very humanity at risk. Perhaps my enemy has fallen victim to his own critique."

I think of all my friends. They'll jump at the chance to swim in a brand new ocean, no matter what it cost.

"If we don't fight him, he's going to win, you know. Once it's done, no one's going to want to change it back."

"Maybe not. And soon it will seem perfectly natural that Earth has a watery twin, just as we once imagined it to be. Maybe in the distant future, when we have no need of worlds or water, some brave soul will mount a cause to restore its original nature. They will uncover my patterns and introduce them to new clouds. What has been done will be undone... and I will be vindicated."

His attention wanders off into fantasy-land, I think at first.

"Four," he says. "There are now four Eyes."

I turn to look at the screens, hollowness spreading through my chest. A new hole has opened up not far from us. That explains the rising turbulence.

It's happening fast now.

"Come," he says, "let me show you how to operate this old boat. You might as well learn something while we move to a safer vantage point."

Hieronymus steers like a sack of eels. I tell myself it'll handle better in water, but who am I kidding? Going from aerostat to hydrostat (is that even a real word?) is unlikely to improve its mood.

From afar we watch what looks like a black, volcanic cone rise up from the center of the first Eye. It's the graphite byproduct of the Bosch reactors, piling up *en masse*. Thunderheads gather about its waist, shooting out blue sheets of lightning. Fearing what might happen if another Eye opens below us, we decide to strive for greater altitude, first by expanding the air sac and then by reducing the weight of the gondola. To do that, Grandpa enlists my help to chuck things out of the hangar into the roiling clouds below.

That means donning a pressure suit, black with bright yellow highlights, which makes me feel like a proper spacegirl.

"Are you sure you won't need this stuff again?"

My voice is loud behind the faceplate. His crackles in my ears. "No."

"I suppose you can fab it again anyway, if you do."

An inactive drone spins downward into mist, scooting suddenly to the left as wind takes it. Then it is gone as though it never existed.

"Every mountain deserves a name," I tell Grandpa. "If we name it after you, that'll really stick it to the bad guy."

"There is already a Mount Hudson in Chile."

"Chile's a long way from here."

"Nonetheless."

"Hmmmm. 'Mount Sixsmith,' then. That doesn't sound so bad. And this way we can have Mount Onesmith, Twosmith, Threesmith, and so on, depending on how many of these things we end up with."

"The 'six' in 'Sixsmith' is not a number, Natasha," he says. "It refers to sickles."

"Whatever. It can mean anything we want, here. We're the first official inhabitants of New Venus. What we say goes."

"Perhaps. Language is, after all, no exception to the rule *All things transform*."

"As your enemy says? Well, maybe he isn't a complete idiot."

I maneuver a heavy engine closer to the open hatch, grunting with every heave. Grandpa watches through the sealed inner door. He's the brain of this operation, I'm the brawn. The suit is doing a great job of evaporating my sweat, but I'm still hot. I haven't wrestled like this since Saxon Vargas took me out on our last date. I bare my teeth, wishing I could've dumped him like this.

Kick. The engine goes over. I don't follow its descent, just fold up with hands on my knees, gasping for breath.

"Are we done yet?"

"I believe that is sufficient."

I stagger back in relief as the hatch slides closed and seals. The hangar looks pretty empty now, like a stage waiting for the set to be built. But I'm not an actor. I'm the audience, and I didn't ask for this fully immersive theater experience. I didn't choose it.

Mind you, who has ever seen anything like this? When my log uploads I'm going to be popping like nobody's business.

And then there's Grandpa. How he would have coped without me I don't know. Not just clearing the hangar. Clearing his head. Sometimes I catch him staring out the window and I know he's absorbing everything while he can, before it's gone forever.

How would I feel if someone walked into my home of twenty-two years and shat all over it?

Yeah, yeah. Lesson learned. Consider me older—minus the eleven minutes d-mat still owes me—and immeasurably wiser.

All I have to do is avoid dying so my parents can say "I told you so."

* * *

"ARE YOU PERMITTED to drink?" Grandpa asks as the clouds slowly lighten around us. It's dawn, and we've reached the absolute upper limit of the aerostat's buoyancy, barely clinging to fifty-one klicks above the planet's surface. On Earth, that would put us halfway into space. Here, it's positively tropical.

We both know it's not going to stay that way for long.

"If I say 'yes, totally', will you believe me?"

"Good enough." Grandpa fabs a bottle of fancy-looking champagne and two crystal flutes. He pops the cork on the upper deck, pours, and we clink a toast without words. The bubbles tickling my nose are transient, bittersweet, and pure gold. A last hurrah before the end.

"Grandma Sixsmith should be here with you," I say. "Big moment like this. What happened to her, anyway?"

"Who, Alice?" The question seems to take him off guard. His face works for a moment, as though testing unfamiliar expressions for best fit. "Alice and I did not see eye to eye... on anything, it turns out."

"Oh, I see! Is *she* your enemy?"

"No, no. This is not some lovers' tiff writ large. Our tiffs were small, numerous, and eventually too tiring. We parted well."

"That you hid out at—around? near?—the Planet of Love suggests otherwise, Grandpa."

"Honestly, it does not. You will understand when you're older. Look!"

He points out through a non-virtual window, and I crane to see what has caught his attention.

It's the sky. The clouds have parted for the first time in... how long?

The sky is orange, like blowtorched sugar.

This is happening much faster than I thought possible.

"It's dangerous to know things too well, or to think that you do," Grandpa says, raising his glass to the tatty sliver of light that is widening as we speak. He could be talking about Grandma or his home or something else entirely. "You grow bored. It changes. Maybe you discover that you were wrong all along."

Hieronymus dips beneath us. I feel the nose angle downward, dragging the deck with it. The bottle of champagne overbalances and froth spills everywhere.

I drain my glass in one compulsive motion, even though I feel sick to the stomach.

"We have passed the tipping point," Grandpa says, waving me to a seat. I have no role to play in what's to come, except to cling tight as the atmosphere implodes and look on the bright side. What's the worst that could happen?

There are so many answers to that question I don't even know where to begin.

"Grandpa?"

"Yes, Natasha." He is standing at the wheel, gripping it with both knobbly hands.

"Don't tell Mom about the champagne. You'll get us both in trouble."

"That is the least of our concerns at this moment."

"I needed to tell you anyway, looking ahead." Really I want to ask him if we're going to die, but feel as though voicing the possibility would make it real. He keeps promising that I'll be all right. Let's leave it at that. "What's your plan, exactly?"

"I am going to aim for Mount Sixsmith," he says, pointing at the first and biggest of the Eyes. "Don't worry. We won't smash into it. I have chosen this destination because that is where the reactors have been drawing energy out of the atmosphere for the longest. There will still be turbulence, but my calculations suggest that the ocean forming at the base of the mountain will be tepid at most. It would be terrible to ditch in a boiling sea."

It sure would be. I hadn't considered that particular outcome before and now wish I could get it out of my mind.

"I mean for after. What are you going to do about the guy who did this?"

"That's surely up to the Peacekeepers. Has he broken any laws? It's not as if Venus belonged to anyone, except, in the most diffuse way, the entire human race. If his actions result in a net benefit, maybe he should be rewarded, not punished."

Hieronymus judders as its rate of descent increases. The clouds close around us again.

"Seriously?" I ask him, trying not to grip the sides of my chair too hard too early. Save it for later, for when things get really rough. "You'd be happy if he got off scot-free?"

"I didn't say that." He spins the wheel, guiding the aerostat around a gushing column of thick, black cloud. Beneath the skull and crossbones I painted earlier, he does look a little like a pirate, with scrappy white beard and shirt (remnant of the tux) rolled up to his elbows, revealing an honest-to-god tattoo of the Venus de Milo. "I merely acknowledge that people will have different perspectives to me. We have never seen eye to eye before. Why change now?"

Faster and faster we fall. I have to keep talking or go crazy with impotent fear.

"Why doesn't anyone believe you about what you found here? Surely you sent back patterns of your bugs..."

"Oh, the discovery of life is not the issue. My survey was the most thorough possible, and my samples the most complete, confirming the theory that life evolved here as it did on Earth and elsewhere. It was what I found next that caused the controversy."

When I close my eyes I can still see the window onto Mount Sixsmith, gaping hungrily like a lamprey's mouth. A churning stain surrounds it, the first ocean on Venus in a geological age. It's spreading like blood across uneven lava plains, hissing and bubbling at the edges.

"Would you tell me about that, Grandpa, in great detail? Please?"

His silence stretches so long I fear he's not going to oblige me—and then how am I going to drive out my anxiety? By babbling about my nonexistent love life?

Finally he says, "I'm not sure what I fear most: that you would fail to understand, or that you would not."

I wrestle gratefully with the double negative as our descent becomes ever more precipitous.

"Try me."

"Very well. You need to understand, Natasha, that no one fully knows how Venus came to be this way. 'Greenhouse effect gone wild' be damned. The universe does not obediently bend to fit our best theories, even for a convenient narrative that helps us put what we did on Earth behind us.

"Climate change had a profound effect on all the world, not just Tuvalu. Millions died. But we avoided the grand catastrophe of our sister planet by being clever and building powerful machines. Bravo for us. We know better now."

"*Sibling* planet," I correct him automatically.

"Complacency is a dangerous thing," he says, ignoring me. "What I discovered in rock and gas samples were anomalous chiral and isotopic signatures that suggest an entirely different explanation for Venus' present condition. Once I fully comprehended their import, I knew that we were far from safe—from ourselves, and from our machines."

"I'll be frank with you, Grandpa. Not understanding much so far."

"To put it simply, I do not believe that conditions on Venus are an accident—or at least not a natural one. It is the end result of a technological process—a war maybe, or a contaminant that destroyed an entire biosphere, sending what life remained here to the very fringes, where it clung on against all odds in a much reduced form."

"You mean your bugs... they did this to themselves?"

"That is what I believe."

I picture the fuzzy fronds in Grandpa's tanks. "Ouch."

"Precisely, if something of an understatement."

There's a hearty boom from outside. I open my eyes a crack to see that we're dropping through a forest of lightning strikes, which dance around us like the bars of an electric cage.

I slam my eyes shut again and fold my legs and arms around me. *Much safer in here* my lizard brain advises me.

"So... wait... let me get this straight. If Venus wasn't always this way, what does that mean for the bad guy in this scenario? Is he still a bad guy for turning the world back to the way it was?"

"What do you think, Natasha?"

"I don't know. I'm confused."

"I do not blame you. If someone destroys your house, and you discover in the process that it was in fact built on the ruin of another house, doesn't that fundamentally changes your perspective?"

"But Venus is no one's house any more, not really."

"All right, then. Look at it another way. What if a man has dedicated his life to standing outside nature, preserving everything he found—only to discover that it was never natural at all?"

That's Grandpa, I assume. "He'd be pretty pissed off, I expect."

GRANDPA SAYS NOTHING.

Which gives me time to think. And make some connections. And approach a conclusion that seems inescapable and maddening.

"Grandpa, tell me you didn't."

"I cannot until you tell me what you think I did."

Smart-ass. "*You* built the reactors? *You* destroyed Venus? *Why?*"

"To send a message to those fools who wouldn't listen! Thanks to d-mat and fabricators, we have the power to subvert, even destroy nature. What's more, we can't assume that we won't, because it happened right here. Whoever's hand pulled the trigger the first time, and it might have been very much like yours, perhaps they too thought themselves outside the law: *All things transform.*"

What else did he say my first day on Venus? *Life cannot harm life.* "I don't think that's going to hold up in court."

"I don't care. They can't ignore me now!"

Hieronymus jolts violently. For a moment I had completely forgotten where we were, but my ignorance had not been blissful.

"If you knew all along that this was going to happen," I say, unable to prevent a hurt tone, "why did you let me aboard?"

"Birdie wanted to give you a shock. I believe you have received one."

"You know she's not going to buy that. Particularly if we die here."

He sighs. "It was not my intention to subject you to this... I mean it sincerely, Natasha... I was going to wait until you left. But then I saw your lenses and I knew why I had been holding off, the one thing my plan lacked..."

Lenses. Life-logging.

"A witness," I say. "For your confession?"

"For Venus. For this poor world and all that intelligent beings have wrought upon it, as their natures dictated. For all those whose lives might be lost if we blunder on unchecked."

Dammit. I have been an audience for a madman after all: my grandfather, his own worst enemy, who would destroy a world to make a moral point and might kill us on the way.

"Open your eyes, Natasha."

I am angry with him in a way that transcends any irritation I've ever felt for my parents.

"No. I'm not going to! I don't care if you think that makes me like everyone else, sticking my head in the sand because the world scares us sometimes. I'm scared right now, and I'm not afraid to admit it. Why shouldn't I be? I'm trapped in here with you and your mad scheme. And what's worse, nothing I can do will make a difference. I could try to fight you for control of the wheel—and probably win, by the way—but would that help bring Venus back? Or Tuvalu? Or anywhere else?"

"Please, Natasha. You have to see this."

"Why?"

"You'll regret it if you don't."

His tone saps the fight out of me. Grandpa sounds old and sad, not foolish or monstrous or any of the other things he called himself earlier. Maybe the real reason he kept me around was so he wouldn't be alone.

I steel myself to do as he says, and when my eyelids separate I see him at the wheel, first, then the skies beyond him, second. We are falling down a vast chimney lit by sunlight from far above. The view is neither of Earth nor of Venus. There are colors and shapes here that never existed before, except maybe on Jupiter and even then no human has ever seen anything like them, not with naked eyes. This is real, and at the same time palpably transient. The reactors are still working. The entire atmosphere is collapsing in on itself, dragging us down with it. In time everything will reach a new equilibrium, and long before then all this will be gone.

It's astonishingly beautiful.

Trailing tattered clouds in our wake, we fall headlong towards the face of Venus.

An ocean the color of tears rises up to meet us.

WITH A SPLASH that sends water dozens of yards into the air, *Hieronymus* comes to the end of its journey and, to my amazement, doesn't immediately sink. It bobs on restless waves in the shadow of Mount Sixsmith, which is just as black and menacing as it looked from above. The lightning has passed now the Bosch reactors in our vicinity have run out of ready fuel. Elsewhere, twenty-three others are still working hard.

The air sac deflates, detaches, and drifts away in the grip of a powerful current. A loud gurgle comes from the deck below, and

I make haste to see what's going on, still wearing my pressure suit just in case. Going down with the ship is not on my agenda.

The sample tanks are emptying.

"Is this supposed to be happening?" I call up to Grandpa.

He appears behind me on the ladder, but doesn't linger.

"Yes. They will drown or adapt, like us."

He's heading below, and I follow him, at least until he starts taking off his clothes.

"Woah, Grandpa. Don't you think I've seen enough scary shit for one day?"

"You are perfectly safe, Natasha." I don't think he's talking about his nudity. Behind my turned back, I hear him rummaging through the mostly empty hangar. "The controls of *Hieronymus* are locked, but they will release in an hour. It is programmed to follow the tide away from the mountain. I suggest you stick to this course. When the flanks collapse, there will be tsunamis."

I risk a glance over my shoulder. He's pulling on a pressure suit with bright pink highlights.

"Where do you think you're going?"

"It is time for all good Venusians to return home. And Earthlings too. The d-mat booth and the channel to Earth will also unlock shortly."

Naturally, I already suspect that he is behind the blockade. What's the point of having a witness if she flees at the first opportunity?

Any anger I feel, though, is swamped by concern as he opens the hatch. We both pull on our masks, even though air pressure keeps the seething water at bay. The atmosphere is a ferocious mix of chemicals that smells very bad. I look down into the water, seeking the fuzzy fronds, but there's no sign of them.

"You're not a Venusian, Grandpa."

"Not yet."

He jumps into the water so suddenly I'm taken by surprise. I thought I'd have longer to make him see reason. "Grandpa! What are you doing? Don't you know it's bad manners to leave without saying goodbye? Grandpa!"

I find myself jumping in after him. The water is thick and full of bubbles, like warm soda. My mad ancestor is a shadow receding along the underside of *Hieronymus*, swimming with slow but steady strokes. He doesn't look back. The current is strong. I cling to the edge of the hatch with one hand, torn between security and letting him go.

Then he's disappeared into the murk, and it's too late to do anything.

I pull myself inside and hurry back up top. There's no sign of him in the water, anywhere I look. The boat won't turn so I can search for him, and I have a little frustrated cry, feeling alone and betrayed by everyone. Then the Air reconnects and my ears fill with voices. There's a world of people eleven minutes away and they all want to know what just happened.

I don't need to say anything to them yet. My log is already uploading, and they'll work it out when they watch it. What Grandpa did. No doubt they'll argue about it forever. Was he deluded or a visionary? Did he make his case, and if so, what was that case, exactly?

Mom and Dad are in the mix, fairly babbling with fear and relief. "Tash Sixsmith, tell me you had nothing to do with this!" Blah blah. I should go home and face the music, but I hesitate. It doesn't seem right to leave just yet, not until I have an opinion, at least. Yes, I was a victim of Grandpa's mad plan, but that doesn't mean I'm powerless. As the one and only temporary Venusian left, probably, it would be helpful to have something to say. Something more meaningful, or at least useful, than *Sorry*.

As *Hieronymus* glides away from the black cone of Mount Sixsmith, I send a message to Afi Tekena.

"Hey, I found you some new islands."

INSELBERG
– NALO HOPKINSON –

Yam, feed me now.
Yam, when I am dead,
I shall feed you.

—A Nigerian grace

EVERYBODY GATHER ROUND the bus, now! Thank you please. Sir, beg you, don't try to pick the trumpet flowers. You might cause damage. Yes, sir; me know say you paid for an all-inclusive tropical vacation here on the little nipple of mountain top that is all left of my country, but trust me. Some things you don't want all-included. Not since the sea uprise and change everything. Things like trumpet flower bushes.

How many of you coming on the wondrous, watery tour? Gather in, everybody, so I could count heads. You in for a treat this morning, mek I tell you. Submerged cities, underwater skyscrapers, and an audience with the Wise Old Fish of the Mountaintop. If you ask him nice, maybe 'im will let us come back down from the peak. But be polite, you hear me? The tour last week had some from foreign ladies who feel say they were too tourist to mind them manners when tendering the requisite offering to the Wise Old Fish of the Mountain.

Sir, what you carrying on like that for? Didn't I tell you not to pick the trumpet flowers? Stop with all the screaming, please. I warned you you might cause damage. Is all right, though. The trumpet flower plant is fair-minded. Even though you kill two of her future possible generations, she only take from you the same number of orchids you take from her. What, you didn't realize that "orchid" is Latin for "testicles"? Chuh. Just give thanks is only two flowers you pick. I don't know what woulda happen if you had pick three, or four.

Try and lie still, sir. Our friendly resort staff soon come and fix you up good-good. Just remember, gratuities not included in your bill. Our workers rely on your extra generosity as a reward for their good service, ascording to how seeing to your needs is the only industry ya-so nowadays. Here; you can use my scarf to stanch the bleeding. You don't want the smell of blood to bring the mongooses out from their holes.

But stop; the rest of oonuh not on the bus yet? Get on, get on! Can't keep the Perspicacious Mister Fish waiting! Yes, find yourselves a seat. We provide every luxury on dis-ya bus. We oxygenate and filter the air for your comfort, no extra charge. You can even take off your helmets; no air-borne irritants in here! In your seat pockets, you will find your inflatables. You each get seven hundred. Don't fret; they indexed to the American dollar. In case of sudden tropical depression, you will find they remain relatively stable. Can't promise the same about Mister Fish, though!

Now, before we can set out on today's marvellous and malleable tour of our once prosperous nation, oonuh haffee tell me if the password change.

Well?

No, lady, is not game me playing. What? You think I already know the password, only I not saying? But seeyah! After is you people from foreign who come up with the new passwords! You know, a code phrase you always want us to say to you at irregular intervals? Time was, it was "Yahman." No? Is the same one? Yahman, then; yahman.

All right, driver. We ready.

Guests of this beautiful resort, don't mind the lurching of the bus. This is one of the ones that wake up one morning with legs instead of wheels. Even the bus-them and all had to come to them senses and swim for dear life when that last duppy tide come through! Never mind, though. Here in the islands—or the mountains—we could do worse than have sentient buses. Biggest problem is when them take it into them head to hold our pickney-them to ransom in order to get more fuel.

Pickney? That mean child.

No, Ma'am; is no problem that you bring your nine year-old on the trip with us. It will be educational for her, yahman.

By the way; if anybody see a pig deh-bout while we following the camino, him name Malky. If you see him, call him for me, do. Thank you please.

Over on your left, you can see the trembling waters of the island's former nuclear plant. You know what they say: "If my swamp a-rock, you best don't knock."

Mister, I mean don't get it into your head to go for no sea bath over there. You might come out again as pretty as me. You think I didn't notice you staring at me? If you tell me your room number, you and me could spend a little sweetness later. Ten percent surcharge, of course, and you haffe provide certification you had three clean blood tests in the past six months.

The extra eyes give me 360 degree vision, and at least me never have to worry with combing my hair any more. To tell the truth, I think I was happy to lose it all and get more vision instead. Papa Fish tell me I must count my blessings.

If you cast your gaze just beyond the shivering bay... see that scrim on the other side of it? Forming what look like an edging between the mountain and the sea? Yes, Sir; like a frill. Well, that frill stretch all the way around the foot of the whole mountain, except for the places where the cruise ships dock at the resorts. You can guess what that frill is? Any of you ever read a book name *The Goats Look Up*? No, my mistake; *Stand on Zanzibar*. Ask not for whom the bell tolleth. That's all me a-say.

The bridge we crossing on right now is taking us over some famous ruins of former industry. This new body of water, we call it Sugar Lake. No, you can't get out the bus to take pictures. I know it smell nice, like boiled sugar sweeties. Funny thing about that duppy tide; time was, the biggest you would get is a king tide, and that was plenty big. All that melted ice from way up and down yonder. Hey you, little nine year-old pickney; you could tell me some of the effects of rising seas, of swollen oceans pushing an island like this one down under the sea? You look like a smart girl who pay mind to her lessons.

Yes, floods. What else? Rivers running backwards, sewage rising up into the water table, crops deading because the soil get salinated. Very good! You forget one, though. For a long time, we didn't have beaches no more. People like you and your mummy stopped visiting us. Things did bad them there days. Not enough jobs, food crops doing poorly. But is all right; oonuh coming back again, both the tourists and the things that drowned. Why? Nuh this-yah duppy tide, this new thing? Nowadays, is like nothing that get drowned is really gone.

Duppy? How you mean, what it mean? Now that I think about it, oonuh been worrying out my soul case from the beginning, asking me what words mean. Aha. I see most of you never drink your phrasebooks this morning. You have to take a dose every day, for your protection. The water here not safe for oonuh to drink. You don't have resistance built up.

But I was saying: when the long time ago sugar plantations get submerge, is like that event leave a residue. A big sugar plantation duppy. It just sit down there below and a-brood. It make of every plantation the island ever had. All of them. All those boiling houses where people who look like me—but with fewer eyes—get forced to feed long poles of sugar cane they cut from the fields into the grinders, to squeeze out the sweet juice. Then they had to pour the juice into some rahtid big cauldrons to render it down to molasses, and then to sugar. Every so often, one of the people who looked like me (except; eyes) would nod off from fatigue and get a hand caught in a grinder. Fine. So all those duppy hands, they sitting down below, too.

Beg pardon, Ma'am. I don't mean to upset your little girl, and she so clever. But I have this tour guide script to follow, you see? Koo here, see how the script get tattooed on the inside of my bottom lip, in peeny little letters? The whole script fix deh-yah in my mouth, so you understand I don't have no choice but to speak it. Is Master Fish make it to be so, yahman.

I could continue? Thank you please.

Oonuh sure you don't spy a pig out there in the murk? I hope
he not lost. He's such a little guy, only standing as high as my
shoulder. I prefer to have him with us on these rides. He help to
keep the mongooses away.

Long and short of it is, that swamp below make of molten
sugar. True we call it Sugar Lake, but is more like Syrup Swamp.
Now we have to move along. If the bus stop here too long, the
heat of the bridge will burn her poor feet. The pain give her the
belly runnings, and we inside that self-same belly at the moment.

The facilities? Absolutely, sir. The water reclammation unit
is at the back of the bus. Any other bodily fluids you care to
donate while you in there are gratefully appreciated. Or any
bodily solids. You don't even have to remove any bones first.
And sir? Don't fret if what you see coming out of you don't look
exactly like what you expect. If, for example, your pee turn into
hundreds of little frogs and hop away to hide in the dark corners.
Is how you folks say it? "Change is good." Right? Yahman.

Next stop is the Twinkling City. See all the rainbow colours as
the light catch the oil slick? Pretty, nah true? Pickney-child, you
too smart for me. You right. No light not in the sky to make
refractions in the oil slick.

The actual city, of course, is down below the surface. Oonuh
want to see? All right, I will open up one window. You gwine
haffe peer out one at a time. Don't worry; I will stand by and
make sure the murk don't reach long fingers in and pull you out
for the mongooses. Oh! Out he gone! Why he open the window
before I was ready? Never mind. I ready now. Who else want to
look? Yes, lady. Lean out. I will grab your waist. If you screw
up your y'eye-them and gaze hard, you might see thousands
and thousands of lights flickering down below. We nah know

where the electricity coming from to power the city, but there underneath the oil, it still going. Traffic lights still clicking from red to green and back again. Factories still a-run. I bet you anything the university still full up of scholars, experimenting on the wonders they find in the uprisen sea, and studying the results, and making discoveries, and arguing, and publishing.

Now, as I was saying to the rest of oonuh; the oil slick have a circumference of approximately 325 square miles, and is about 29 feet deep. I say, "oil slick" because is that it was at the beginning of the duppy tide, but like everything here, it change up. It have a way nowadays to rise up all of a sudden and grab sea gulls from out the air. At night, it will sometimes whisper to us in our dreams. Those who can't hear it have a way to die screaming before they wake up. Perhaps you already beginning to hear it when you sleeping? Show of hands? All of oonuh hearing it except that man in the noisy shirt? Maybe the shirt drowning out the sound of things you need to hear. Sir, when we get back to the resort, they will have a ticket waiting for you, for a flight home. You will have to leave right away, before night come. Your choice, though. Only try don't doze off between now and when we get back.

Come back in now, lady. My arms don't get tired, exactly, but put a tender life in my hands like this, and after a while, I start to get certain impulses. To let go, or to hold too tight. Quick, close the window!

Yes, of course I was here when the duppy tide make landfall. Is the reason I still here. On our TV stations, we had meteorologists telling us for days to get out, get out. Local weather website had a live feed. I would watch it on my phone during breaks at work, and on my computer when I was home in the evenings.

What? You think say "tropics" mean "backward?" Chuh.

The feed didn't look so bad, though. Long shots of dark sea and a dark sky. Screech of the wind whistling past the fixed camera. Camera view little bit unsteady from the wind making it vibrate. Nothing we never see before. Until I look at it good and realize the camera image not split into the usual two equal horizontal bars of slate sky on top of midnight sea. Up at the top of the image, a shallow bar of lighter grey. That was all the camera could see of the sky. The lower bar, the one taking up more than seven-eighths of the computer screen? That was the duppy tide rising up. I wait too long to leave. Most people did evacuate long since, but I couldn't find Malky. You sure you don't see him out there in the dark? Sometimes I think I spot him, but I can't really tell in the murk.

I couldn't leave him all alone.

We have to speed up. Time getting short. Over here in this boiling bay, all the fights we ever fight, for freedom, for independence, revolts against hunger, protests for wages.

That laughing waterfall? This land had stewards before us. Rush, driver, rush past all of them. All the zombis. How many of oonuh know is this part of the world zombis come from? No hands. Well, you know now.

Finally. Last stop. I will let you out the bus just now, but don't get too close to the whirlpool. You haffe koo 'pon it from a distance. This island have a bedrock of ancient limestone, so we get sinkholes. Some terrible things get push down into sinkholes over the centuries; lost, and then forgotten. But that thing outside? That is all the sinkholes, with all their cargo. That is sinkhole papa. And yet, all the ocean it swallow, the levels only rising, not going down. Massa Fish the—well. I was going to say, "The Unflappable," but a fish had best be able to flap, you don't find? So. Massa Fish the Intensely Flappable. You feel him now? That vibration rumbling up through you, that sound too low to hear, but so deep it make your insides shiver? My generous guests, what you looking at is the open maw of Massa Fish. He shouting. He been shouting since the duppy tide beach him up here on the mountain. And me think say him finally getting an answer. Check the skyline. Dark. Seven-eighths black, with a little grey line of sky on top. Duppy tide a-come down again, even vaster! Massa Fish a-call out for him mama! I so excited to see what changes she will bring this time, I could turn myself inside out! Any last questions, fish food?

How to escape the tide? Me sorry, friends; me don't have the answer.

I never did escape.Yahman.

ONLY TEN MORE SHOPPING DAYS LEFT TILL RAGNARÖK
– James Morrow –

For many years my wife and I resisted the craze that had captivated so many of our fellow bored professionals, a fad scornfully dubbed 'egotourism' by the *Wall Street Journal*. When the Chomolungma Corporation installed a cable-car line whose final stop lay two kilometers from the summit of Mount Everest—*Tell your grandchildren you climbed to the highest point on the planet!*—we were not remotely tempted. When Challenges Unlimited designed and built a commercial submarine sturdy enough to negotiate the Marianas Trench without imploding—*Are you ready to brave the deepest depth on Earth?*—Lucretia and I remained unmoved. When Daredevil Enterprises strung a zip-line from one end of Borneo to the other— *You haven't lived till you've snatched a fig from an orangutan's grasp!*—we elected to stay home. But then along came EEI, Extreme Excursions International, offering its customers, *The transcendent experience of traveling to the Arctic and standing at the top of the world*, and we simply couldn't resist.

Apart from the thrill of it all, Lucretia speculated that the North Pole might get her "creative juices flowing again," an appropriate metaphor, I thought, given the rapid rate at which the ice pack was melting. She hadn't yet abandoned her dream of ditching her career as an NYU film studies professor and writing fiction full time, but after composing the first half of an autobiographical novel (an alternately hilarious and poignant narrative spun from her youth as an army brat), she was beset by a chronic case of writer's block. As for me, Simon Ramsey, having spent the past decade as a video journalist specializing in urban motifs—the bizarrely ethical protocols followed by street gangs, the dazzlingly complex art of running the New York subway system, the grand innovation whereby Brooklyn adolescents were turning their schoolyards into vegetable gardens—I decided it was time to expand my horizons. I would bring along my Sony Vistaview and shoot some polar bear and musk ox footage with an eye to making a depressing documentary about endangered Arctic species.

Per the itinerary detailed in the glossy, full-color brochure put out by EEI, the members of our tourist group converged on the Aéroport de Montréal-Trudeau. In addition to Simon and Lucretia Ramsey of Manhattan, our party included Claude and Janet Houghton of Baltimore plus Bernie and Mimi Seltzer of Miami. The six of us flew by chartered cargo plane to Iqaluit Airport in the Canadian territory of Nunavut, where we met up with our intrepid guides. Although this was only the third Polar expedition organized by EEI, we seemed to be in competent hands, nine adroit digits belonging to Jackson Milford, a rugged, grey-bearded, sun-wrinkled salvage master turned entrepreneur (he had lost a forefinger to a winch), plus the ten additional digits of his assistant, Golly Harbison, a boulder of a man who might have easily found employment playing a golem on TV.

Later that afternoon we boarded the icebreaker *Proteus*, which took the eight of us on a three-day cruise up the Davis Strait along the western shore of Greenland, then across Baffin Bay to Etah, a deserted village sitting at the foot of Brother John's Glacier. No sooner had we disembarked than two more EEI personnel—jovial Inuit sisters named Estuuya and Tapeesa—appeared and directed us into a Quonset hut facetiously labeled the Admiral Peary Hotel. The place was poorly heated and stank of kerosene, but we all slept soundly.

The following morning Jackson and Golly pointed us toward a sleek and peculiar three-coach vehicle, a combination limousine and snow caterpillar, dotted with one-way portholes and painted bright blue with gold trim. After scrambling aboard this luxurious train, we discovered that (just as the brochure had promised) each coach boasted a twin bed, a hot shower, a microwave oven, a coffee maker, and a large supply of gourmet frozen meals. At 11.30 hours, Jackson assumed the driver's seat and put the caterpillar in gear. The quadruple set of tank-treads began their rotations, carrying us inexorably toward our destination and leaving behind twin paths of glacial rubble and pulverized permafrost. By midnight we were free of the tundra, grinding and growling our way across the boundless, sterile, eternally rotating ice pack.

Three days later, at 15.30 hours, the caterpillar lurched to a halt, and Golly passed among us bearing welcome news. The enchanted coordinate called 90°N lay a mere three miles ahead. Everybody should exit the vehicle and start walking north "until we realize we're actually walking south."

I gulped down my coffee and grabbed my camera. Chattering like kids at a pajama party, we six adventurers armored ourselves in down parkas, pulled on our mukluks, snapped our snow goggles into place, and, abandoning the caterpillar, collected in the shadow of an ice hummock. The temperature stood at -50° centigrade. We straightaway began our trek, Jackson at the head of the parade, his GPS set to flash and whine the instant we reached, as he put it, "the apex of God's creation and the peak experience of your lives." Straight ahead the never-setting sun nuzzled the horizon, its glow so pallid I fancied myself on the outermost planet of an alien solar system, even as the red and blue streamers of the aurora borealis twisted and shimmered on all sides.

We had gone barely three hundred paces when the most unnerving noises I'd ever heard filled the featureless terrain, a series of percussive reports suggesting cannonballs falling on a glass prairie. The ground trembled violently, and an instant later a fissure came zagging across the ice pack like a terrestrial lightning bolt, the stark and ominous stroke dividing us into two groups—Jackson, the Houghtons, and the Seltzers on one side, Golly, Lucretia, and I on the other. The fissure widened, becoming a kind of German Expressionist canal, its retreating banks carrying the two components of our fractured party farther and farther away from each other.

"Shit, it's a lead!" cried Jackson.

"Never seen one this far north before!" shouted Golly.

"A what?" I screamed.

"A lead!" Jackson replied. "A lane of open water!"

"They form without warning!" Golly explained. "One of 'em nearly doomed Peary!"

"Make it stop!" wailed Bernie Seltzer.

"We didn't sign up for this!" cried Janet Houghton.

"I want my money back!" yelled her husband.

"To the caterpillar!" shouted Jackson.

"What about us?" screamed Golly.

"We'll send a rescue team!"

Now came a second tremor, as ferocious as the first, rattling the air with brittle thunder. An instant later a floe calved off from Jackson's side of the channel, leaving him, the Houghtons, and the Seltzers adrift on a raft of ice. Destabilized by its hapless and shrieking passengers—even Jackson was in a panic—the floe suddenly capsized, dumping the explorers into the black water, whereupon the swift current imprisoned them beneath the shelf.

"Jesus Christ!" shrieked Golly.

"Holy living fuck!" cried Lucretia.

Instinctively I rushed to the edge of the lead and flung myself facedown on the ice. The strap holding my Sony Vistaview slid from my shoulder, whereupon the camera skated to the lip of the channel and plopped into the water, but this was the least of my worries. Now Lucretia and Golly appeared beside me, likewise prone. We stretched out our arms as far they could reach. The water's surface remained unbroken; no wet hands rose from the frigid depths. Slowly, lugubriously, we three survivors regained our feet. We whimpered and wept, the tears freezing on our cheeks, then gradually composed ourselves and wondered aloud what else could go wrong.

Our question was answered sooner than we would have wished. Glancing toward the snow caterpillar, we watched in horror as the ever expanding fissure coursed between the tank-treads. The pack opened its maw and, bellowing like an immense Arctic dragon, swallowed the caterpillar whole, leaving us stranded and alone at the top of the world.

* * *

ALTHOUGH HE WAS the only experienced North Pole explorer among us, Golly had no idea what we should do next. One obvious option, he noted, was to remain where we were and wait for some EEI employee back in the U.S.A. to realize that an awful fate must have befallen the Milford-Harbison expedition. "But we'll probably die of dehydration before a rescue plane finds us, the ice pack being no less a desert than the Gobi." Alternatively, we could start hiking in the general direction of Greenland and hope to encounter an indigenous hunting party that, having failed to find any caribou, seals, or walruses at the usual latitudes, was now venturing into zones where no Inuit—or very few Inuit—had gone before. "Of course, that plan, too, is less likely to end in salvation than dehydration. All things considered, I vote for getting out of here. We might be wandering to our doom, but at least we'd be doing *something*."

Golly's strategy (if that's what it was) sounded reasonable to Lucretia and me, and so we three began our journey, hiking along the banks of the newly formed channel. For eight hours we moved south beneath the pale eye of the never-setting sun, eventually reaching a cluster of hummocks configured in a natural lean-to. Acting on an unspoken consensus, we entered the shelter, lay down, and began following a regimen of cat naps alternating with prattle, actual conversation being too dangerous, for once we started discussing happy memories and home fires, there would be no end to it.

Shortly after first light—a dawn by the clock, not by the quixotic sun—we abandoned the lean-to and resumed our white odyssey. We had gone barely three miles when a distant and astonishing tableau emerged. At first we thought it a mirage, a phenomenon as common at the North Pole as in any other flatland, but then the blessed truth presented itself. We had stumbled upon an Inuit village, a ring of dome-shaped dwellings covered with animal hides, each hut fronting a plaza where perhaps twenty indigenes, half of them children, warmed themselves around a communal cooking fire. Apprehending our scent, a cadre of guard dogs began barking, ribbons of steam pouring from their jaws.

"It's a miracle!" I exclaimed.

"A thousand miracles!" added Lucretia.

"Jesus always bats last!" declared Golly.

Galvanized by the dogs, a delegation of three Inuit women came toward us. Their intentions, we soon realized, were benevolent, for they bore a kettle of boiled walrus meat—or so the shortest among them, speaking in English, identified the offering—plus a sealskin canteen filled with potable water. We feasted greedily and drank eagerly.

"I wonder what they use for fuel," said Lucretia.

"Good question," said Golly.

"Permafrost peat," said the tall woman. "Thanks to the greenhouse effect, we find flammable chips all over the pack these days."

"It's an ill apocalypse that blows nobody good," said the stout woman.

"The peat also serves for making lager beer," said the short woman. "Would you like to try some aputi?"

"No, thank you," I said.

An instant later two robust men approached. At their request we furnished our names, and then the elder indigene introduced himself as "Chief Yakone of the Inuit nation called the Pikatti," his companion as "Prince Ugalik, my learned firstborn son."

"I have attended Reykjavík University," Ugalik explained.

"Where you studied the history of your people?" Lucretia asked.

"Western philosophy, actually," said the prince, "with an emphasis on the pre-Socratics. I'm going for a doctorate."

"The Pikatti—I confess that your tribe is unknown to me," said Golly.

"That is as it should be," said Prince Ugalik. "There are but eighty-five of us on the planet, including our children, and we all live right here."

"Eighty-five?" said Golly. "That's a pretty minimal nation."

"A nation nevertheless," said Ugalik. "In any event, it's best for humankind that we remain a lost tribe. I hope you aren't anthropologists, because then we would be obliged to kill and eat you in the venerable ceremony of Amaruk."

"What's an anthropologist?" said Golly quickly.

"There are no anthropologists for miles around," said Lucretia.

"We're merely tourists," I said. "I'm a video journalist, and Dr. Ramsey is a film studies professor."

"Truth to tell, there is no Amaruk ceremony," said Chief Yakone. "That was my son's idea of a joke. But it is imperative that our tribe remains free of anthropological scrutiny. For twelve centuries we have performed a sacred mission on behalf of the Earth and all its lifeforms. Should our benevolence come to light—this is admittedly a peculiar thing to say—the cosmos would be thrown off kilter."

"Our lips are forever sealed," I said, beating back a smirk.

"Your sacred mission is our eternal secret," said Lucretia with a pained smile.

"Lunatic indigenes, just our luck," Golly whispered to me.

"We live in cataclysmic times," said Ugalik. "Wounds are opening in the ice. The demon-god Qaumaniq arises. But at the moment we are filled with hope, for two stalwart strangers have come among us, Sivuugun and Luava, just as the Pikatti legend foretells."

Yakone touched my shoulder. "We rejoice in your advent, Sivuugun, Lord of Lenses." The chief squeezed Lucretia's right-hand mitten. "We welcome you to our tribe, Luava, the Tenured One. You and your husband will together save our people and the rest of the world from catastrophe."

"Sivuugun, Luava—and who am I?" asked Golly.

"From the logo on your parka, I infer you are either Jackson Milford or Golly Harbison," said Ugalik. "I have read your brochure."

"'The demon-god Qaumaniq,' is that another one of your jokes?" I asked the prince.

"There is nothing—or almost nothing—amusing about the end of the world," said Ugalik.

"I'm pleased you're so impressed with me, but I'm not the savior you've been expecting," I said.

"I'm out of my depth, too," said Lucretia.

"Do you have a CB radio, sir?" I asked Yakone. "We would like to get home as soon as possible."

"Haven't you been listening, Sivuugun, Lord of Lenses?" said the chief. "You and the Tenured One have come to slay Qaumaniq."

"Slaying isn't my forte," I said.

"Nor mine," said Lucretia.

"How demonic a demon is Qaumaniq?" asked Golly.

"Follow me," said Ugalik, "and all will become clear."

*   *   *

FOR THE BETTER part of an hour we followed the Pikatti prince as he marched past his village along the newborn water lane, then across the ice field beyond, a tract as immense and forbidding as the frozen lake where, according to Dante, an immobilized Satan presides over the Ninth Circle of Hell.

"So how are the cubs doing?" asked Ugalik.

"The polar bear cubs?" I replied. "You would know better than I."

"The Chicago Cubs."

"They won the pennant last year, but they lost the series to New York."

"Fucking Mets," said Ugalik.

At last we drew within view of our destination, a lozenge-shaped mass of what appeared to be crimson aspic, perhaps three feet high and twenty long, the whole amoeboid anomaly held fast in the ice field like an imprisoned whale. Armed with bows and arrows, a dozen Pikatti had formed a circle around the thing, keeping a steady watch, as if at any moment it might burst out of the ice and go rampaging across the pack. Ugalik urged us forward. Although it stank prolifically (imagine rotten eggs blended with dead fish), the amoeba was alive and breathing, or so I interpreted the gelatinous waves rippling across its protoplasmic flesh, likewise the sounds it made, a rhythmic, rasping cadence suggesting the exhalations of a blacksmith's forge.

A brawny but agile middle-aged man dressed in caribou pelts swooped and glided gracefully among the archers, chanting what Golly called "Inuktitut locutions beyond my comprehension." Catching sight of his visitors, the furry man stopped dancing and sauntered toward us, a gorget of walrus tusks swaying from his neck. The prince presented him as "Tikasuk, our shaman," then introduced us as "noble Sivuugun and valiant Luava, heroes of the legend, plus Mr. Harbison, along for the ride."

"I shall do my best to facilitate your hallowed task," said Tikasuk in low, rumbling tones, the voice of an articulate sea lion. He pointed toward the anomaly. "Behold the demon-god Qaumaniq, ancient avatar of cynicism."

"Of what?" I asked.

"Cynicism," said Tikasuk.

"I don't understand."

"You've never heard of cynicism?" said Tikasuk.

Ugalik said, "If Satan is the wellspring of mendacity— if Beelzebub is sovereign over the flies—then Qaumaniq is misanthropy incarnate."

"I must say, it doesn't look like a demon," noted Golly. "More like a meatloaf."

"The Greek Cynics of antiquity," said Ugalik, "Antisthenes and his followers, were honorable men, pretentious perhaps, but sincere in their contempt for ease and pleasure. By contrast, for those who worship Qaumaniq, ease and pleasure are the point of existence, as long as those fruits are distributed exclusively to their benefit."

Naturally it occurred to me that the prince and the shaman were playing a game with our heads, and the demon-god would prove to be an innocuous and perhaps even artificial component of some tribal ritual or other. And yet the indigenes' palpable sincerity persuaded me to take their story—for the moment— at face value.

"But aren't most Pikatti deities invisible?" asked Lucretia. "Isn't intangibility the primary attribute of a god, regardless of latitude?"

"*Mutatis mutandis*, Qaumaniq is much like your King Kong," Ugalik replied. "My dear film studies professor, was the god of Skull Island invisible? Was intangibility his primary attribute?"

"King Kong?" said Golly. "Do you mean this thing is a movie prop?"

Ugalik rolled his eyes and groaned.

"How did your amoeba get locked in the ice?" I asked.

"Over the centuries many nations have claimed credit for the binding of Qaumaniq," said Ugalik. "Viking lore speaks of a formless devil hunted down and chained by Eric the Red. An Aleut legend tells of the hero Chikuk, who caught a white seal as big as the moon and trapped it in a glacier. True, the Aleuts live thousands of miles from here, but the pack is always turning, fitfully but forever clockwise, which means their seal and our demon could be one and the same. Personally, I believe it was our indomitable Pikatti ancestors who found and fought and immured the beast."

"We have an epic poem about it," noted Tikasuk.

"Then there's *The Blob*, a cinematic narrative once celebrated in the West," said my wife. "The space monster's reign of terror ends only after the protagonists freeze it with fire extinguishers, load it onto a cargo plane, and deposit it in the Arctic."

"Let's not play Ugalik's game," I muttered in Lucretia's ear.

"Next he'll be taking us to meet Santa Claus," mumbled Golly.

Suddenly Qaumaniq's phlegmatic demeanor changed, and the thing began quivering from end to end. As the archers nocked their arrows, a globule of protoplasm, twice the size of a soccer ball, detached itself from the amoeba's surface like a matured scab, then sprouted a pair of appendages resembling hot-water bottles. Flapping these uncanny wings, the creature ascended.

"What the hell?" said Golly.

A bowman fired. The arrow flew true, piercing its target. The globule plummeted and struck the ice, where it lay twitching like a shot goose before expiring.

"Obviously we have much to learn about Arctic metaphysics," said Lucretia.

Now Qaumaniq spewed forth a second winged globule, then a third, then a fourth, but in each case an archer felled the excrescence before it could soar away.

"Those are tulugaqs, red ravens," Tikasuk explained. "An eruption of this sort occurs almost every day. Alas, our archers rarely—"

Before he could finish his sentence, a large flock of tulugaqs, twenty at least, emerged from Qaumaniq. The archers fired, bringing down half the hellish squadron, but the other ten globules escaped the volley and flapped off in the general direction of Greenland.

"Our archers rarely kill all the ejecta," said Tikasuk. "The fugitive tulugaqs fly across the Arctic Circle and keep on going in search of suitable habitations."

"Each globule seeks out and fuses with a human being of similar temperament," said Ugalik. "The relationship is the epitome of symbiosis. The tulugaq enhances its host's cynicism quotient, and the host provides the tulugaq with a congenial place to live."

"So without Qaumaniq, there would be no cynicism in the world?" asked Lucretia.

"There has always been cynicism, O Tenured One," said Ugalik. "There will always be cynicism. But owing to Qaumaniq, the scourge has reached epidemic proportions. The crisis became especially acute when the northern ice cap began to melt, as this allowed the demon to launch unprecedented numbers of tulugaqs from its increasingly exposed flesh."

Lucretia said, "If I were to believe you—which, by the way, I don't—then the greenhouse effect is enhancing the cynicism of those who already take a cynical view of the greenhouse effect. I cannot imagine a vicious cycle more... well, vicious."

"A very astute analysis, Dr. Ramsey," said Ugalik. "In the years to come the effects of this dreadful feedback loop will grow ever more dire. Eventually Qaumaniq will break free of its prison, and then there will *really* be hell to pay."

"Drip, drip, drip," said Tikasuk.

"Can't you simply kill the damn thing?" asked Golly. "What if your archers attacked it?"

"Arrows and harpoons can kill the children of Qaumaniq, but such missiles are powerless against Qaumaniq itself," said Tikasuk.

"Your blob is immortal?" asked Lucretia.

"Hardly," said Ugalik. "That's why we celebrate the coming of Sivuugun and Luava. Tomorrow we shall refloat the *Nuliajuk*— the state canoe of the Pikatti nation—and then we shall sail away in quest of the weapon with which you and your husband will destroy Qaumaniq."

"What sort of weapon might that be?" I asked.

"Have we not filled your brain with enough improbabilities for one day?" asked Ugalik.

"True enough," I said.

"Since I don't have a part to play in your legend," said Golly, "I'm hoping that, after you've launched your canoe, you might you drop me off at the Admiral Peary Hotel in Etah."

"But you *do* have a part to play, Mr. Harbison," said Tikasuk. "To free the canoe, we shall need your broad back and trollish strength."

"I assume that around these parts 'trollish' is a flattering term," said Golly.

"Not really, no," said Ugalik. "But if you refuse to play ball with us, you might find yourself cast adrift on an ice floe without food, water, or a good book. May we count on your assistance?"

SUCH WAS THE high caliber of Pikatti hospitality that Lucretia, Golly, and I were accorded the most desirable accommodations in the village, the hut where the guard dogs slept. Thanks to the evening's promiscuous consumption of peat lager (the brewing of which was surely the least impressive of the tribe's arts), we entered our lodge in a deliciously drowsy condition. While Golly pressed my wife for details about *The Blob*, which was evidently to good movies as aputi was to actual beer, I nuzzled into the soothing mountain of canine fur and allowed the dogs and the lager and my love for Lucretia to salve my fear that I would not leave the Arctic alive.

Shortly after dawn, Prince Ugalik roused us. For breakfast the Pikatti cooks had prepared a locavore chowder that they served from a cauldron in which pollock eyes and capelin fins bobbed about like croutons. As the morning progressed, we learned that Chief Yakone was requiring a majority of the tribe's adults to join him in refloating the state canoe. The work team would depart at noon. Ugalik would serve as captain of the *Nuliajuk*.

"Tell me about the weapon," I asked the prince.

"Our legends speak of a mystic narwhal, Atuqtuaq, large as an iceberg, golden as the sun."

"I was afraid it would be something like that," I said.

"Golden?" said Golly.

"Some sort of benign bacterium," said Ugalik.

"The tusk of Atuqtuaq is longer than seven harpoons," added Tikasuk. "According to the legend, Sivuugun and Luava will summon the narwhal from the depths of the vast sea that white men call Baffin Bay. They will command him to pierce the heart of Qaumaniq."

"As you might imagine, Simon and I know nothing about summoning narwhals," said Lucretia.

"Once the *Nuliajuk* is underway, I shall teach you the chant," said Tikasuk.

Three hours later, my wife, Golly, and I joined a party comprising the chief, the prince, the shaman, and forty other Inuit, the lot of us tromping eastward across the pack. The strongest men hauled sledges loaded with provisions, including blankets, oil lanterns, victuals, and kegs of peat lager. To my eye our procession suggested some epic athletic competition whose devotees were always trying, without success, to have their venerable sport recognized by the International Winter Olympics Committee.

At last the *Nuliajuk* rose before us. With its stately mainmast bisecting the horizon and its palisades of upright oars, the vessel more closely resembled a Viking longship than a canoe. After much heaving and hoeing, grunting and groaning, straining and—yes—sweating, we succeeded in pushing the *Nuliajuk* to the edge of an emergent lead. No further effort was required, for the canoe proceeded to launch itself, the keel incising the ice so deeply that a segment of the shelf snapped off and the hull entered the channel with a resounding swoosh.

Ugalik now selected his company, eighteen burly men capable of, in the prince's words, "rowing a two-ton longship through ice-choked waters for hours at a time on minimal rations." With resolute faces and swaggering gaits, the crew of the *Nuliajuk* followed Ugalik and Tikasuk up the gangway, and then came (with fearful faces and diffident gaits) Lucretia, Golly, and I. On the prince's orders, four men unfurled the sail, a patchwork of scraped animal hides. The crazy quilt caught the breeze, flapping like a battle flag—for was this not the banner beneath which Sivuugun and Luava would defeat Qaumaniq and its children? The rowers found their benches, unshipped their oars, and began to pull. The *Nuliajuk* glided forward, and we were off on the ultimate extreme excursion. Come to the top of the world and test your mettle against a demon. Journey to the Arctic and toss quoits of ice onto a narwhal's tusk.

FOR FIVE DAYS and five nights we coursed down the liquid groove, the wind keening all around us. As if seeking to heal the lacerated pack, the banks of the channel continually lurched toward each other, fusing in our wake and threatening to crush our stern, "for such is the way of leads," Ugalik informed us. Aboard the *Nuliajuk* anxiety reigned. We were not a happy ship.

Transcending our fear, ignoring the -40° centigrade winds, Lucretia, Tikasuk, and I managed to convene an anthropological seminar in the prow. Repeatedly the shaman sang the chant by which Atuqtuaq might be summoned, while his dullard

American students struggled to learn it by heart. The syllables left a strange and pungent taste in my mouth, as if I'd eaten ambrosia and washed it down with peat lager. Lucretia reported a similar sensation. Travel to the North Pole and imbibe the sap of the mythic world-tree. Dare to visit 90°N and drink of Yggdrasill, whose limbs reach far into the heavens.

On the morning of the sixth day, owing to a felicitous conjunction of wind and muscle and luck, the *Nuliajuk* sailed into the Kane Basin, watery portal to Baffin Bay. The surrounding sea was a treacherous gazpacho clotted with bergs, clogged with floes, and veiled in fog, but at least we were free of the pack. By late afternoon we had pulled within sight of the torn and bleached shores of Greenland, borne by currents that, the shaman informed us, the golden narwhal was known to ply.

But before Lucretia and I could began the chant, another vessel, much larger than the *Nuliajuk*, loomed out of the mist, a palatial cabin cruiser with the name *Expedience* painted on its stern, followed by *Virginia Beach*. Glistening mounds of ice and snow rose from the multiple decks, giving the cruiser the appearance of a colossal ocean-going layer cake. A distress flag fluttered from the radar antenna. Ugalik dutifully brought the canoe within hailing distance. Leaning over their respective gunwales, Ugalik and his fellow skipper, one Walter Paycock, entered into a loud conversation. The *Expedience,* it seemed, had run short of beverages. Might the *Nuliajuk* supply the yacht with bourbon, vodka, sherry, or champagne?

"We have only peat lager," said Ugalik. "You know—aputi?"

"Never heard of it," said Walter Paycock.

"It's pretty awful, but we can spare a keg."

"Bring it on board, and we'll tell you all the latest news from below the Arctic Circle. Just lash your dinghy to our stern. My bosun will drop a transom ladder."

And that is how an Inuit prince, an Inuit shaman, and three displaced Americans ended up lounging in a sumptuous, carpeted, steam-heated drawing-room on the salon deck of an opulent yacht. Among the well-shod consumers of our dubious beer were a half-dozen U.S. politicians (four men and two women), three male lobbyists, of which Walter Paycock was one (his speciality being pollution control abatement), and a celebrated D.C. radio talk-show host, Whip Hemsoth, who credited himself with a theological innovation he termed "Christian nihilism." Although I was happy to share our aputi with the company of the *Expedience*, the attendant discourse brought me to the brink of despair.

"We didn't expect to run into any Eskimos on this trip, but I want you to know I have no problem with you people," said Senator Bart Grimsby of Colorado, sipping his lager. "I'm not prejudiced."

"How fortunate for you," said Ugalik.

"What brings you to this neck of the woods?" asked Golly.

"Well, you might call it a nature cruise, but it's also a kind of therapy voyage," replied Alabama Governor Jeremy Brisket.

"'Therapy voyage,' that's good, Jeremy," said Walter Paycock.

"Back in D.C.," Governor Brisket continued, "we all have to pretend we detest tax increases, regulatory zealots, environmental fanatics, government overreach, creeping socialism, the budget deficit, the fetus deficit, faggots wearing engagement rings, and scientists telling ordinary folks what to do, when in fact we don't give a flying fuck about any of those things. God, it feels good to leave all those crocodile tears at home. Here we can be ourselves. On Walter's boat a man can look his buds in the eye, raise a glass of bourbon, and say, 'Dear friends, we have poleaxed the planet, and that makes our peckers twiddle.'"

"Not my pecker," said Carlotta Frostig, the junior senator from West Virginia, and the yacht's company laughed in unison.

"You blubber lovers make damn good beer," said Senator Lawrence Duggery of Kentucky, gulping his aputi.

"Our poleaxed planet—is that where the nature part of your journey comes in?" asked Lucretia.

"Yup," said Leonard Colander, a lobbyist for Exxon. "Earlier this year we navigated the coast of Nigeria. Lagos is now mostly under water. God, that sight gave me a woody."

"You're the last honest man, Lenny," said Whip Hemsoth.

"Yes siree, a mighty fine brew," said Senator Duggery.

"Then we cruised through the Panama Canal and kept heading west," Mr. Colander continued. "Most of Australia's beaches are drowned, did you know that?"

"Praised be Qaumaniq," said Lucretia evenly.

"What?"

"Never mind."

"Wish I could go back in time and thank all those dinosaurs who laid down their lives so we could have fossil fuels," said Senator Frostig.

"New Guinea is now a swamp," said Governor Ethan Walloper of Mississippi. "Sumatra is flooded to the gills. Singapore has became ducktopia. Bangkok looks like fucking Venice. If you think we lost any sleep over this, you don't know how the world works."

"I've never imagined I knew how the world works," said Ugalik.

306

"What about your witch doctor?" asked Governor Walloper. "Does he know?"

"I skipped witch doctor school that day," said Tikasuk.

"Love Jesus, embrace your inner storm trooper, and leave the planet a more miserable place than you found it—that's Christian nihilism in a nutshell," said Whip Hemsoth. "If there's a better path to fulfilling your purpose and engorging your wedding member, I haven't found it."

"I'm afraid I can't hold up my end of this particular conversation," said Ugalik. "It's time we returned to our canoe."

"We're truly grateful for the lager," said Senator Grimsby. "How can we repay you?"

"By getting the hell out of Baffin Bay and never coming back," said Ugalik.

MOVING AT A brisk pace, our departure being more of an escape than an exit, we left the salon deck, descended to the main deck, and headed aft. The fog had lifted. The aurora borealis glinted to port like celestial tinsel. Before we could climb down the transom ladder to the moored canoe, the sky above the bay grew suddenly dark. We glanced heavenward. A massive formation of birds glided across the face of the sun, blotting out its radiance and casting an enormous mobile shadow on the sea.

No, not birds.

Something else.

"Tulugaqs!" cried Ugalik. "A thousand tulugaqs!"

As the sunlight returned, a throng of thirty globules peeled off from the flock and dived toward the *Expedience*. The alpha tulugaq smashed through a salon deck porthole, creating an aperture through which the entire squadron abruptly disappeared, winged bears on the scent of honey.

"Now comes the habitation phase," said Ugalik, and even as he spoke a sensuous commotion filled the air, moans of ecstasy, orgasmic gasps, *a capella* choruses of erotic satisfaction.

"Look to starboard!" yelled Tikasuk, pointing. "There! There!"

A hundred yards beyond the *Expedient*'s stern, a subaquatic phenomenon carved a great trough in the sea, the implacable event hurtling toward us with mad vehemence, as if Captain Nemo had made it his mission to sink the yacht.

"It breaches!" cried Ugalik.

With a volcanic gush of floes, rollers, and spindrift, an unbound Qaumaniq lurched to the surface, sinewaves of seawater cascading down its crimson flanks. In the full majesty of its liberation, the odiferous monster proved as long and cylindrical as a zeppelin. Wriggling frantically to sustain its momentum, shedding shards of frozen slime, Qaumaniq launched globules in all directions. Abruptly the great red amoeba altered course and began circling the *Expedient* in a gavotte of infinite gratitude. Finally, after centuries of captivity, the demon-god had found a congregation.

"Ascend!" Ugalik commanded me, clamping a mitten on the sleeve of my parka.

"Now!" cried Tikasuk. "Climb!"

I knew immediately what the prince and the shaman meant. The closer to the heavens we positioned ourselves, the farther our invocation would travel.

Together Lucretia and I mounted the ice-glazed interior stairways, tread by treacherous tread, until we reached the apex of the ship, a flying bridge ornately fretted with snow crystals.

We wasted no time. Stretching to full height, we pressed our frigid tonsils toward our sacred obligation.

"Tukkuyummavuvungga Atuqtuaq itigaituk Qaumaniq!" Lucretia and I trilled in unison. "Uukkarnit piggaluyungmik Qaumaniq umiaktovvik Atuqtuaq!"

Below, the huge pulsing slug continued its courtship dance, swimming impassioned rings around the *Expedient*.

"Tukkuyummavuvungga Atuqtuaq itigaituk Qaumaniq!" chanted Sivuugun and Luava. "Uukkarnit piggaluyungmik Qaumaniq umiaktovvik Atuqtuaq!"

From the salon deck the clamor of concupiscence continued to rise, but we ignored it and kept on singing.

"Tukkuyummavuvungga Atuqtuaq itigaituk Qaumaniq! Uukkarnit piggaluyungmik Qaumaniq umiaktovvik Atuqtuaq!"

Suddenly, off the port bow, Baffin Bay yawned open. The tremendous mouth began to rotate, transmuting into a furious maelstrom that cast forth ragged ice floes, sheet after sheet, like pieces of a gigantic and insoluble jigsaw puzzle.

Now came the narwhal, lurching upward from the core of the vortex. The beast was indeed golden, or rather a bright copper, as if clothed in chain-mail wrought from new pennies. As thick and long as a cedar of Lebanon, his tusk was truly magnificent, a lance wielded by a cetacean Galahad. Overwhelmed by his magnificence, I nearly swooned. Lucretia grasped the bridge rail. Atuqtuaq was among us, and we had fallen irretrievably in love with him.

Sensing his prey, the narwhal deployed himself amidships. He waited. Dancing all the while, the amoeba rounded the *Expedient*'s stern and headed toward the prow. Atuqtuaq struck, running his enameled javelin athwart Qaumaniq. The impaled demon bellowed. The air resounded with exhilaration: Ugalik's crew cheering, whooping, hurrahing, and clapping. Atuqtuaq withdrew his tusk. From the demon's wound rushed a sudden pulpy torrent, slicking the sea and turning the waters bright red. Qaumaniq, now a cadaver, remained briefly in view, its humps and knolls riding the rollers, an archipelago of protoplasm, and an instant later the thing was gone, drifting soundlessly toward the bottom of the bay.

Cautiously Lucretia and I descended to the main deck and made our way to the stern, where we joined a jubilant Ugalik, a gleeful Tikasuk, and a begrudgingly admiring Golly. The five of us scrambled down the ladder and boarded the canoe. On Ugalik's orders two sailors untied the mooring lines, and shortly thereafter the oarsmen pulled us free of the *Expedient*.

Naturally I assumed that the golden narwhal, his task complete, would return to the swirling funnel whence he came. But Atuqtuaq had a further boon in mind. Fanning the waves with his mighty flukes, the creature swam south, passed the *Expedient*'s stern, and continued for some thirty meters. Swerving abruptly, Atuqtuaq charged the yacht, ripping the rudder from its hinges. He attacked a second time, diving beneath the keel and turning the twin propellers into ineffectual masses of metal. Now came the third attack, Atuqtuaq impaling the *Expedient* itself, becoming the cabin cruiser's replacement rudder, substitute screws, and operative engine. Working his flukes furiously, the narwhal abducted the helpless yacht, pushing it away from the Greenland shore toward the open sea.

"I wouldn't want to be on the *Expedient* right now," said Golly.

"I wonder where he's taking them?" mused Ugalik.

"I need a tankard of aputi," I said.

"So do I," said Lucretia.

"Noble Sivuugun, valiant Luava," said Ugalik, "we shall now turn our state canoe into a mead hall and drink a thousand toasts to you."

MY TALE HAS run its course. Little of it is credible, and all of it is true. Times are better now, would you not agree? While far from extinct, cynicism is on the wane. Though still alive and hungry, the cult of expedience is losing ground.

Ever since the shattered remains of Walter Paycock's yacht washed up on the beaches of Labrador—and especially since the bodies of its jaded passengers were reportedly seen decorating the tusk of a roving narwhal like chunks of beef on a shish kebab—certain previously intractable politicians and financiers have acquired an uncharacteristic affection for reality. Thanks to the initiatives of these movers and shakers, the gossamer continents of carbon dioxide that enswathe the Earth have been shrinking, slowly but steadily. My wife and I remain guardedly optimistic, a cautious Cunégonde and an equally mistrustful Candide, planting our garden in good faith and hoping that the weeds and rodents will take only their fair share.

Although I never succeeded in making a depressing documentary about endangered species, I recently acquired, on the strength of a speculative screenplay, enough backers to enter the precarious world of indie dramatic filmmaking. My first feature will be called *Shadows on the Ice*, a biopic about Matthew Henson, the African-American explorer who accompanied Admiral Peary to the Arctic and was in fact the first expedition member to stride across the Pole. As for Lucretia, I am pleased to report that she escaped academe as planned. Last year she published *Nirliq and the Frozen Ghosts*, a critically acclaimed and marginally successful fantasy novel rooted in Inuit mythology. She has made a good start on the sequel.

Almost every night, after crawling into bed, my wife and I embrace, make love, and softly serenade each other to sleep. "Tukkuyummavuvungga Atuqtuaq itigaituk Qaumaniq," sings Lucretia. "Uukkarnit piggaluyungmik Qaumaniq umiaktovvik Atuqtuaq," I sing back.

We are duty-bound never to forget those words. Any day now, another ontologically ambiguous and ecologically undesirable amoeba could manifest itself. But Atuqtuaq is out there. The golden narwhal continues to bide his time. He cruises the seven seas—making maelstroms, feasting on cuttlefish, sporting with lesser members of his kind—even as he anticipates the day when noble Sivuugun and valiant Luava will again rouse him from his vortex and, marveling at his beauty, savoring his preternatural presence, send him forth in fealty to the future.

LAST GODS
– SAM J. MILLER –

THE GODS WERE circling when the sun rose, nine long patches of black that did not brighten with the sea as the sky lit up. I watched Them, Their knife-blade fins like polished onyx slicing the surface, formation shifting but the huge old matriarch always at the head. They swam between the sunken buildings, dwarfing the concrete bunkers, sketching intricate patterns that only They—and the Watcher in the tower—and I, slinking away on the ragged hill behind the town—could comprehend.

I saw my Gods, and my gut went sour.

It's fine. It's not your responsibility. You asked another Watcher to take your shift.

But she was a drunk, and everyone knew it. And if the warning didn't sound—if boats were boarded while They were in the water—people would die. And it would be on me. And the village that had taken me in, sheltered and fed me in spite of my missing arms, would cast me out.

I watched my Gods, and I could taste the bell rope between my teeth. Plastic and bracken and the sweat of the other Watchers, men and women with hands. My head jerked, acting out the signal even though I was shirking my duty. Two tolls, then three, repeating: the signal that said *They are here, Their formation indicates They mean us no harm, but no boats may be boarded.* My neck ached. My jaw burned. And my face went red and hot, because I wasn't in the tower, because I was skulking from the town like an outcast unbeliever. I watched the Gods, the beauty of Them, Their black implacable bulk, the white patch above and behind the eyes, and my whole body tingled with joy. And with shame.

The bell would sound. It had to. The village would come awake. Fishermen would scrape away ice and mutter prayers, and fling offerings to the Gods. Fires would be kindled, voices and laughter unleashed. This was a day like any other.

Except... not.

Because Kelb had come to my cabin last night. Knocked at my window. Told me to meet him at sunrise outside of town. Told me he was going... somewhere.

I told him yes. Even though everyone knew there was no Somewhere. Nowhere left on land to go. No animals still living, no cities away from the water still inhabited, nothing but icy poisoned wind and scorched rock. I told him yes, even though I knew I risked losing everything. I told him yes because I could not tell him no, not ever, and that had been true when I was eight and he was ten, my maimed foster brother's only friend. I told him yes because everything Kelb did was rough, brutish, beautiful. Every morning I watched from the tower as he stumbled from his cabin, peeled off his shirt, scooped cold salt water over his black-furred torso. Kelb was oblivious to the cruelty of it, this display of fine muscled flesh and limber arms, oblivious to the hunger in my eyes, oblivious to me as anything other than the sad armless little sixteen-year-old sister of his dead best friend.

Our town looked so tiny, standing outside of it. I hurried, into the landscape of snow and sharp black rocks and bent sticks that people said had once been trees. I wanted to be out of earshot, so that if I didn't hear the bells it might have been because I was too far away. And not because my replacement had failed miserably, and my life was over. My stomach tightened with the same old empty lonely feeling that always followed the ecstasy of a visit from our Gods.

But this time the emptiness did not go as deep as it could have. Because strapped to my back, cold and sharp and heavy, was the cymbal of Summoning. Burdening me down and buoying me up. An egregious sin, and a source of salvation. I had taken it on mad reckless reasonless suicidal impulse, lifting it off the wall with one expert foot and placing it on the floor atop my torso wrap and lying on top of it and tying it tight with my feet, but feeling it there I was glad I had.

Over the hill, in a down-swoop of land that could have been the cresting of a wave, was Kelb. A dark blur at first, swelling into a man as I approached. Squatting, his bare red hands assembling from snow something forbidden. Hearing me, not looking up.

"Stop that," I said. I kicked the little house apart and he laughed.

"Oh Adze. There's no ocean in sight. Your precious Gods can't see what we do."

"They see everything," I whispered. His blasphemy never failed to redden my cheeks with a mingling of fear and desire.

He hugged me hello, then stepped back. Put his hands on my shoulders, and then on my stumps. A gesture somewhere between brotherly and... not. And it occurred to me, for the first time, that maybe he *did* know how I felt about him. Maybe he counted on it.

"Eat," he said, pressing a square of bladderwrack jerky into my mouth.

Around his neck he wore a thick plait of braided seaweed, studded with shards of broken glass. Not the worn-down, safe, pretty sea-glass that most of us used as jewelry. This was jagged stuff, cruel and dangerous, salvaged from the factory wrecks to the south. Only thick, strong skin and superhuman confidence kept it from cutting him.

"If I ever needed any more proof that the Gods hate us, bladderwrack jerky would do the trick," he said.

"Shh," I said. "You shouldn't say things like that. Where are we going, anyway?

"To see someone," he said, stepping faster to keep pace with me. Armless as I was, no man had legs to match mine.

"No one lives on land," I said. "And anyway what do you need me for?"

"Does it ever get frustrating?" Kelb asked, after putting another square into my mouth. "Having to depend on other people?"

"What do you mean?"

"You know. No arms. Not being able to do anything for yourself."

I laughed. "No. That's what it means, to be part of a community."

"But they landlocked you. Stuck you in the tower—"

"They took me in," I said. "A crippled orphan—they gave me a place. A role. And I'm not stuck. I rotate shifts with three other women. And anyway they're considering me for the Priesthood."

Or they were. Before this.

"Pssh," he said, and I didn't know if he was scoffing at the idea that they'd ever extend such an honor to crippled unworthy me, or at the idea that anyone would want to be part of the Priesthood in the first place.

Of course he didn't understand. Kelb's weirdness was part of why I liked him so much. He thought like most of my neighbors think, only more so. He was hungrier. His dad had been different too. The Gods killed him, for making a net. Nets are one of the many things men are not allowed to build. Cages are another. We still see birds, sometimes—scrawny, sickly things, flying lost from some faraway place where there still might be insects or seedplants—but the last time someone succeeded in catching and caging one, the Gods destroyed her home before the day was done.

I was lucky, in a way. My maiming marked me as forever outside, locked me away from their greed and their blasphemy. I could not share their constant, crippling hunger for more.

"Who is this supposed someone we're going to see?" I asked, when the bladderwrack was done and Kelb seemed to have nothing else to say.

"A trader."

Two days before, out on the ocean, our fishing party met another village's. I had heard the Priesthood whispering about it. Different towns had different Priesthoods, different customs, and contact frequently spread crazy ideas. I wondered if this fictional trader was one of them.

"Look," he said, scooping up a fistful of snow. He held it out to me, palm up. Poked it with a finger of his other hand, showed me the scraps and flakes of colored plastic. One was larger than the others, showed what might have been a hand. "Snow is different on land. It keeps things."

"That's why we shouldn't be here," I said, giving his hand a swift kick to spill the snow back to the ground.

"I always forget what a devil you can be with those legs," he said.

We walked faster.

Travel over land wasn't explicitly forbidden, but the Gods frowned upon it. The inland cities were swallowed when the seas began to rise; all that was left was high frozen barren land poisoned by war and waste. The coastal cities still stood, huge buildings rising rusting from the sea, home to humans so barbaric the Gods would not allow them even the smallest of boats.

"I'm surprised you came," he said. "And happy. Always held out hope that Schoon's sister would have a little of his rebel spirit."

Schoon's rebel spirit got him killed, I did not say, because the name still hurt in my mouth.

We walked between high drifts of snow. We crossed smooth patches of ice, and treacherous stretches of sharp slippery stones. I shivered and prayed, thinking back to that last glimpse of my village. How the smoke rising from our homes looked thinner, flimsier, like our fires could not keep out the cold for long. The bunkers had been built back when men still thought they could outsmart the sea, find a safe place to carry on the sinful lives that had displeased the Gods so much that They made the sea swallow up all that we had. Those men never finished their safe place. They vanished like sand under the waves, fighting and clawing for the last little bit of land. Only a handful learned that the only way to survive was to make peace with the sea. And with the Gods. And that meant a Priesthood to learn what behavior angered Them, and keep each settlement in line. Because Gods never gave warnings. If we displeased Them, we died.

"Used to be the land was as rich as the sea," Kelb said, as we entered a wide snowless space, pointing out to the blasted ash-colored hills.

"That's what they say," I said.

"You don't believe it?"

I shrugged. "It's one of those things where even if it's true, there doesn't seem to be much point in mooning over it."

"Still. It's nice to think that once there was food other than fish and seaweed. You know they used to call this place New Jersey."

Shushing his blasphemies got tiresome after a while, so I said nothing. But naming things implied ownership, conquest, and it made me shiver. He turned to take in the landscape, and for the first time I noticed the sealskin bag he carried on his back, so full it bulged.

"What's in there?" I asked.

"You might have been born out here," he said. "One of the land settlements."

"There's no such thing."

They say I was four when I came, the cauterization scars on my arm stumps still raw and weeping. I had no memory of my life before the village took me in, handed off from another people that met ours at sea, on the hunt—people with no fixed village, who traveled with the ice by canoe and slept in temporary homes. They hadn't spoken what we speak, but they offered goods to reward the family who took me in. My father was good-hearted and hungry, and had taken in Schoon the same way. He said I wasn't one of the people who had handed me off—the skin tone didn't match—and I wondered for the millionth time who my people were, whether they were holier than we, what they did with my arms when they chopped them off, how strict and wise their Priesthood, whether my deep love for the Gods and my lack of thing-hunger came from them.

"There's a man," Kelb said, yielding to the pressure of my resentful silence, "who lives out this way. He has something I want."

"What?"

Kelb kept walking.

"How does he live?" I asked. "On land. What does he eat?"

"People bring him food. They want what he has."

"Is it something forbidden?"

"Let's just say the Gods wouldn't like it."

A net, a cage, a metal blade? Kelb saw my face, and laughed. "Wake up, little sister. There are plenty of people who think like me. Who think the Gods are just a bunch of dumb animals, and that if we ever want to have a shot at a real life for our people, we have to get over this fear of Them."

I shut my eyes and prayed. I prayed that the Gods would forgive his blasphemy, and I prayed that he was wrong. I knew not everyone shared my reverence, but could people seriously think they could act in opposition to the will of the Gods? That kind of craziness could anger Them enough to wipe us all out.

I prayed for strength, too. Because somehow his blasphemy made him more beautiful, and echoed inside my head, seductively.

I should have cared more, about who this man was we were visiting and what he had. But I didn't. Because I didn't ever want us to get there.

We passed buildings, bare wood against the earth. Some in shambles, some still standing.

"Sorry you're too big for me to carry on my shoulders," he said, slowing down at my thousandth stumble.

"Like you were so good at it," I said. "You weren't that much older than me."

"True, true. If Schoon had lived—"

Kelb didn't finish the sentence. I didn't ask. I could imagine dozens of ways it could have ended, some wonderful. As long as he left it unfinished I could hope it would have been one of the wonderful ones. I was almost startled to see that some small part of me really believed we could be together. That he wanted me the way I wanted him.

Eventually we reached a wide flat swath of ice. Black and clear of snow. The going here was easier, although I could see Kelb was uncomfortable. His head darted around like a minnow, watching for cracks and soft spots and sudden eruptions of divine vengeance from beneath.

Sunset surprised me. Had we really been walking so long? We left the ice, crossed sand. I whispered the twilight prayer and let the dark come upon me, enter me, take away my sight and return me to the primal union of all with all.

"I can't navigate without the sun," Kelb said. "We need to stop and get some sleep."

We found a cabin quickly enough, one of the empty and decrepit ones. The familiar freezing wind sliced through where a wall had been, but we had furs for warmth, and we were both exhausted.

But once we were laid out on the floor Kelb fell instantly asleep, and I found I could not follow. My mind swam dolphin-fast, circling truths I didn't want to arrive at. What he was—what he *really* was, this boy I loved, this strange and twisted man. What I was—the kind of person who would steal the cymbal of Summoning, the kind of person that saw Kelb for who he was and wanted him anyway.

Carrying that kind of hate inside, he would not last long. Nothing in his life could ever eclipse his anger at the Gods. Not love, not me, not ever. And still, I wanted him. Even though I knew he was doomed, knew he was out of balance with the world, still I hungered for him.

"Kelb," I whispered, wanting hands more than I had ever wanted them before. There was no end to the places I could have put them. People did so many things with their hands, to the people they desired. Instead I snuggled under his fur blanket, spooned my body in behind his. "Kelb," I said again, lips against his ear. He turned, awake and alert and erect. My beautiful, damned boy. He did not need me. How could he know need, with hands like that? They moved up and down me, insatiably hungry. He was separate, savage, alone. And as my mouth gnawed desperately at his chest and stomach, arms and hands, I saw, for the first time, how my own hunger exceeded his.

In the morning he kissed my forehead, helped me dress. Kelb showed none of the shame and contempt that I knew men often had, after showing someone such a secret part of themselves... but he still avoided eye contact, and said little.

"What's up with that?" he said, tapping the cymbal strapped to my back. "Gonna summon your Gods to come make everything better? Gonna hold an impromptu solstice ceremony?"

"Just felt like having it," I said. "You never know. Doesn't the sound of the cymbal cheer you up?"

"Risky business," he said, covering his goosepimpled torso with a shirt. "Get caught taking that out of the village and they'll kick you out for sure. Maybe offer you up to Them for good measure."

I tried to think of something to say that would be remotely true and at least a little funny, but since I still didn't know what my reasons were for bringing it I said nothing.

"Must be nice," he said, gruffly, but also tenderly, wincing as he shouldered his bag. "Not to ever have to carry things. Not to be burdened down."

"It is nice," I said. He waited for the follow-up, where I complained about how hard it was, but I had no complaints. Having hands made you put your faith and love in what you could hold to yourself and whisper *Mine*. And I was different. Or that's what I had been telling myself. Until last night. Until I saw how deep my own wanting went.

"What's in the bag?" I asked, mostly just to shake loose a train of thought that was taking me nowhere nice.

"Trade goods," he said. "He's not going to just *give* me what I want."

By the time we got to the cabin with smoke curling up from it, the sun was high above us. An old man sat outside, in a bright ridiculous purple plastic chair. The sea-scroungers sometimes came back to the village with that kind of plastic absurdity—long pink birds and green pigs and giant balls—but representations were forbidden and we'd shred them in the gear wheels and melt the flakes in a vat to make waterproof sheeting and crude work clothes.

"Greetings, travelers," he said.

"Are you Zimm?"

"I am," he said, and stood, and bowed. "And you must be Kelb. The one who frowns all the time, and wears glass shards like an idiot, and wants to kill the Gods."

Of course it was all bluff and bluster, standard man-talk to make himself seem strong. But how could such ugliness be mistaken for strength? The Gods swept fat seals and whole schools of fish into the reach of our hunters; They kept us safe from storms and kept our Shore clear of toxic animals. Perhaps I was spoiled, having been spared the society of men.

Zimm asked "You come to trade?"

"I do."

He ushered us in. The cabin was packed with hundreds of boxes, different sizes and shapes and colors. At a table, he set a small metal cylinder. Then he stabbed at it with a queer sort of knife, until the top lay raggedly open. A sweet, funny smell filled the room.

"Corn," he said, tilting the top to show us. Small triangles, the brightest shade of yellow I had ever seen. Bright like the sun was supposed to be, behind the toxic forever-clouds.

"Cans," Kelb said, picking up a cylinder from the stack. "I've never seen them like this."

I marveled at it too. The rusted husks of cans were everywhere; I had never imagined them in any other state.

"I've got a lot of things you've never seen before."

The man made me nervous. He ate in front of us, right from the can. Gave me a spoonful; smiled lewdly as he slid it into my mouth; enjoyed the squirmy look on my face as I bit down on the bright yellow wrong-tasting triangles. They were crunchy like kelp polyps, but the sea-taste that made food *food* was missing.

"Girl doesn't have a name?" he asked.

Something protective flexed in Kelb. He tightened, the way a man in a canoe might when a meat-whale breached.

"I'm Adze," I said.

"You two brother and sister?"

"No," Kelb said curtly, but said no more. He leaned slightly across the table, and his face was stormy and I loved him so much my body hurt. Zimm shrugged, and we kept eating.

Squares of thin fabric hung on his walls, covered in lines and colors. Kelb saw it, and stood. "Is that... it?"

"That's it," the man said. "What you heard about. Why you came."

"What's *it*?" I asked.

"Paper," Kelb said, and stood. "Can I touch it?"

"Touch away."

"*That's* paper?" I asked.

It looked so flimsy, so harmless. I had imagined some drug or weapon, some magic tool of long-dead gods.

What I knew about paper: that the old world had run on it, that it had helped men make the planet a living hell and finally destroy it. That people clung to it, even after everything. Carried pieces of it with them; wept over it, drew strength from it. With paper, somehow, men could make things even the Gods feared. And only the settlements whose Priesthoods banned paper altogether survived.

But this—this stuff could not have kept my nose warm. How could it harm a God, or destroy a planet?

"So what are you looking for?" Zimm said. "Books? Photographs? Words? Pictures?"

"I want something that will prove what I already know. That the Gods are nothing but animals. No different from anything else in the sea."

"You're an idiot," I whispered, but he was too focused on Zimm's smiling nodding head.

From one of his hundreds of boxes, the old man pulled a small square. When he set it down on the table, I saw that the square was made of many many pieces of paper, stacked together. "Something like this?" he said, and handed one piece to Kelb.

This was a smile I had never seen before. The smile I knew lurked somewhere inside of my scowling handsome friend. The one I dreamed that someday I would lure to the surface. A smile of pure and mighty happiness. I shivered inside, seeing it now. Maybe paper *was* magic. How else could something sit in a box for ages, yet emerge and make men feel things?

"Is this what I think it is?"

Zimm nodded. "The Gods, as our prisoners."

Kelb held it up for me. The square showed a God. But wrong, somehow. Flat and tiny, as though seen from far away. Captured. Caught inside this fearsome paper stuff.

"Orca," Zimm said, tracing his finger along four strange symbols in a corner. An old name for the Gods, one that made me quiver with the intimacy it implied. The hubris, to limit them to one word.

In the paper, a God leapt from water bluer than any sea or sky had ever been. It leapt through a giant circle, held by two humans. More humans surrounded it, seated in high chairs. They looked down on it. They smiled. They cheered. It belonged to them; their pet, like the seal pups we sometimes raised when the weather was good and the sea was bountiful.

"No," I said, sick to my stomach, turning away.

"Get enough of these and it'll be easy to get the whole village on your side," Zimm told Kelb, handing him more. "I even got some that show Gods getting killed, cut up, tortured, you name it. Show these around and everybody will start sharpening their spears."

Kelb turned from paper to paper. I shut my eyes, to hide from what his face was doing.

Eventually, abruptly, Zimm snatched the stack of papers back. Looked at Kelb, then at me. His eyes hurt like harpoons must hurt. "What have you got for it?"

Kelb said nothing. Looked at the floor. Looked at his hands. And in his silence, I knew. Finally. Why I was there. Why he had asked me.

"I'll give you all the pictures you want," Zimm said. "For her."

He didn't flinch. The proposition didn't shock him. It had been his plan all along.

"Kelb," I said, or tried to say, but fear had left my mouth waterless.

"You could have corn every day," Zimm said, reaching out to touch me. I kicked his leg, hard. He cried out in pain, then laughed. Not pleasantly. Took a step closer.

"Stop," Kelb said, and unbuckled his sack, dumped its contents on the table. Seal meat, cured and smoked. Dried fish. An unspeakable sum. More than Kelb could ever have stockpiled. Some of it had to be stolen. That much meat meant people would starve.

"I get that much food for the spoonful of corn I fed her," Zimm said. "Richer settlements to the North pay me plenty. I want her."

Kelb counted out three cards. "That much food for these," he said, his voice a child's. "Or no deal." He stood up straighter, made his face hard.

"Fine," Zimm said, making a great show of undisappointment. "Never was one for damaged goods anyway."

And then Kelb's hand on my shoulder, steering me towards the exit. "We're leaving."

The cold had never been so cold. My mouth hurt from the metal sweetness of the 'corn,' and from how hard I fought to keep from screaming obscenities at Kelb. The Shore glittered, at the bottom of a steep hill to our right. Black dots circled. I wondered if the Gods could see us from there; know who we were and where we lived and what we had done. What was in Kelb's heart.

"What changed your mind?" I asked, starting down the hill. "You brought me to sell to him. Didn't you?"

Kelb said nothing.

"Was it the sex? Would you have handed me over if last night hadn't happened?"

I kept my head down and blundered forward, into bitter wind. We reached the flat expanse of ice after an hour or many of walking.

"Adze," he said.

"No!" I called, stepping onto the ice.

"Adze," he said, and I ran. He followed, repeating my name with every breath. Finally I let him overtake me. His hands grasped my shoulders. His hands were so big, so strong. "I'm sorry," he said. "Okay. I'm sorry. I never—I didn't..."

"You're a liar," I said. I tried to wriggle free, but he would not let me. "You're insane. I was stupid not to see it. I saw you how I *wanted* to see you. How I *used* to see you, when you were the only one who would be nice to Schoon and me, because we were orphans, we were damaged."

Kelb pulled me tighter. He hugged me. He wept. He never wept when Schoon died. "I'm sorry," he said, over and over, until it wasn't about Zimm and his horrible paper or his plan to sell me anymore.

It would have been easy to kick him in the crotch or knees, incapacitate him, take the cards from his bag, chew them up and spit them out, flee back to the village. I told myself the reason I didn't was because I couldn't make it back alone, but I knew that was half the truth or less. The whole truth was that I still loved him, wanted him, couldn't bear the hurt of him hating me. And the whole truth was that we were the same.

The sweet kind child-Kelb was real, but so was the savage monster. Kelb was both. A gentle boy who loved me fiercely, and a wicked murderer who would sell me into slavery. An idealist who loved humanity and wanted us to be free of backwards superstition... who didn't care who died in the pursuit of his ideals.

Kelb was both, and so was I. A devout believer and a wicked sinner.

We were the same. We were animals who wished we were more than that.

The gods were just animals.

I shook free of him. I shut my eyes. If he brought those cards back, he'd endanger everyone. "Go," I said, knowing what needed to be done to save my village, and wanting desperately not to know. "I'll catch up. I want some space."

He nodded, kissed my forehead, went. I squatted, and sat. We were out where the ice was thinnest, a skin of blue-green above unthinkable depths. I prayed, but felt nothing. I waited until he had gone too far to come back and stop me. With my teeth I tore off my sealskin boots, unwrapped my footwrappings. My toes deftly opened my jacket, burrowed deep to unwrap my torso. I shimmied until the cymbal came loose. I lifted it, flipped it over so the smooth bottom was flush with the ice. So the ice would act as an amplifier.

I lay on my back and rested my ankle on the cymbal. I lifted my leg and brought it down as hard as I could, striking the cymbal with a force no other human could match.

"Adze!" Kelb cried, stopped short by the hollow ring, which wobbled in the air but would sound clear as singing through the water under the ice.

I stood up. I lifted my leg to point accusingly in his direction. He ran towards me, towards land, but he was very far away from both.

I thought about shouting *I'm sorry*, but what was the point? What did it matter what I was?

A black shape passed beneath me, majestic and immense. I shut my eyes and kept my leg extended. I was not afraid. I was the bearer of the cymbal. They would trust me.

A crack split the air. A sharp black head broke the ice between us, then dove. The God spiraled her body beneath the water, shoving her tail out of the water and bringing it down hard against the broken edges of the ice. Cracks fanned out.

"Adze, please!" Kelb called. More loud cracks; the snouts of two more Gods shattering through the ice in front of me. I stood my ground, standing over my warm clothes, shivering.

He stopped running. He stared at me, close enough now that I could see the pain on his face. See the fear—and then, something worse than fear. Something he'd never felt before: belief. Final, fatal, too-late belief. *What cruelty,* I thought, *that he should find his in in the moment that I lose mine.*

Kelb sobbed, once, then turned and ran again.

He ran even though he knew it was folly, because it might buy him a few more minutes of life. A thousand times we had seen seals behave the same way, when the Gods separated them from their rookeries, trapped them out on the ice and then tipped the ice to spill them into their mouths.

In a matter of moments he stood on a massive separate sheet. Raw ocean roiled all around him. I counted twenty fins, circling.

I expected Kelb to scream, kick, curse, fight. Die flailing at the Gods the way he had lived his whole life. But Kelb merely walked to the edge of the ice and knelt. His eyes shut. His lips moved. Praying or apologizing or promising. I wouldn't let myself look away. I watched them slap the water with their tails, in great synchronized sweeps, one after the other, until the churning water destabilized the ice and Kelb spilled into the sea. One came up from beneath him, held him in its jaws almost delicately. Kelb did not fight. He turned to look at me one last time, his mouth a sideways squiggle, either smile or frown, before the matriarch grabbed hold of the upper half of him and pulled.

Some villages believe that if a God drags you down, you become one of them. And maybe that's true for them. But for us, when they pull us under, we die.

The way back to land was long, and riddled with broken ice. If they wanted to kill me I was going to die.

I stood up, walked to the pink-frothing edge of the ice. I showed my puny armless self to the Gods. The matriarch rose and held position, exposing her entire gorgeous head. Blood still stained her teeth. If I had hands, I could have reached out and touched her.

For forty seconds, she stared at me. Her eye pierced through to what I had somehow failed to see before this day. She was an animal, and so was I. She was not a God, and I had not been chosen for divine protection. I wasn't better or purer or more full of faith than anyone else. I was a wicked, sinful creature, born out of balance and bound there, like all my accursed kind. Hungry even when full. Wanting, always. Defined by the wanting and damned by it. Inventing Gods to give meaning to our lives, and shape to our hungers, but they could not stop us from destroying everything, including ourselves, including them. My armlessness, my inability to ever hurt them, was the only reason to let me live.

She withdrew, then. Slid back through the ice. Cried out underwater to her brothers and sisters. I stood there, shivering and wet beneath a useless sun, and watched my Gods abandon me.

DROWNED

– Lavie Tidhar –

THIS IS A story my father told me, from the time before we came to live on the Land. In that time there were many wonders and magical things in the world. The world was very small then, unlike now. My father says the world was very large in the old days and then it grew smaller, and smaller still, until a person could cross from one side of the Earth to another in the time that it takes the sun to rise and set over the Land. "Imagine that," old Grandma Toffle says and laughs with all her good white teeth, "Imagine that, little Mai!"

Old Grandma Toffle claims to remember many wonders, but her mind flits and darts like a dragonfly on water. She says she remembers going up in the air, for instance. This is the story old Grandma Toffle tells, especially when she's in her cups:

"One day, little Mai, when I was a small girl, smaller even than you, on an early morning that was cool and bright, with the droplets of last night's rain still shining on the needles of the pine trees, I heard a noise. My father was in the yard, mending cloth, and my mother was working beside him, picking tomatoes in the garden, for they were red and sweet then, a good harvest—oh!

You have never tasted such tomatoes as the ones I tasted then. I stood between them, and I looked up, for I had never heard such a sound, and I saw a dark bird fly slowly across the sky. It emitted a strange sound, and its wings did not move, and as it came closer I saw it was a contraption like a bicycle with wings, and a woman was sitting in a harness. She looked down and she smiled and—oh! It was such a smile as to catch the cruellest heart and make it soft and malleable. My father looked up, and my mother also, and I knew all in our Land looked up too, for we had never seen a flying woman, or a man, at that.

"'Is it a plane?' I asked my mother, trying out the word, but she shook her head and said, 'No, no, there are no more planes.' At that I was a little sad, for I had always dreamed of going up in a plane and looking down on all the people and the Land."

"You always did look down on all the people," says old Grandma Mosh, who lives beyond the stream, and old Grandma Toffle shoots her an angry look, for it is known that the two have fought all their lives and will continue to fight even from beyond the grave.

"The curious contraption circled overhead," old Grandma Toffle says, "then drifted low, and lower still, and I ran after it, and all the others came out of their gardens and yards and ran after it too—"

"I remember," old Grandma Mosh says.

"You don't remember what you had for lunch a week ago!" shoots back old Grandma Toffle, and old Grandma Mosh grins with the teeth that she still has.

"But I was the fastest," old Grandma Toffle says, "and I reached the pilot first, just as she landed. Her long hair was tied back, and she wore large aviator glasses over her eyes, which she removed on landing. She landed in the small field this side of the brook, as the field lay fallow that year. She looked at me running towards her and she smiled.

"'Hello, little girl,' she said. She spoke Language, but with an accent that was different to ours. At that I got shy and I said nothing, at first. The other children, who ran behind me, all came to a stop, and together we stood and stared at her. We waited and shortly our parents came, walking a little slower, but no less excited, I think, than we were.

"'Hello,' said the pilot—a little shy herself, I think now. Mr Gideon the Bellwether—you don't know him, of course, little Mai, for he died many years ago now, in the time the storm came—"

"The second storm," old Grandma Mosh says.

"First or second or third, it was not the storm that got him," old Grandpa Win interjects. "It was his wife, who had enough at last of his ways—"

"He fell and broke his leg in the ditch over the hill," old Grandma Mosh says.

"But how did he get there and why?" old Grandma Win says, darkly, and old Grandma Toffle scowls at them both.

"Who is telling this story?' she says.

This is a problem I sometimes have, I find. The stories and their tellers all become confused, for to grow up and grow old is to carry more and more stories, and who can truly say how Mr Gideon, who was the great grandfather of our current Mr Gideon, or so I think at any rate, really died, or why, and during which storm? But it's important to know these things, and carry the tale forward. But suffice it to say that Mr Gideon was Bellwether that year, and so it was he—

But let old Grandma Toffle tell the story.

"'Hallo!' Mr Gideon said, and puffed out his chest, quite self-importantly.

"And, 'Hallo,' said the pilot, pleasantly enough.

"'Have you come from afar?' said Mr Gideon, speaking for all.

"'From beyond the plains of Suf,' said the pilot. 'And before that I was in Tyr for a time.'

"'What news do you bring?'

"The pilot shrugged. 'll is as it was,' she said. 'In Tyr they sing still of the old days, and water, and in Suf the sun harvest is plentiful. I myself was hoping to beg your hospitality for a day or three, and for sunlight, if you'd spare it, for my aircraft.'

"At that I could not supress a cry of delight—" said old Grandma Toffle—

"A squeal!" said old Grandma Mosh.

"For it really *was* an aircraft, it was a sort of plane!"

"It was not."

"It was too!'

"'Be welcome here,' said the Bellwether, ceremoniously, as was and is the custom, 'share of our bread and story with us small, and tell us of the Land and of the Sea.'"

"The pilot inclined her head in gratitude. 'The sky is clear and the winds are quiet, for it is early yet,' she said. 'And I have light enough to lift again, and take a person with me.' Her eyes reflected sunlight and her smile was warm. The adults cast uncertain looks at each other, and we in our eagerness all raised our hands and vied for her attention. 'Pick me! Pick me!'

"'I can only take one."

"'Please,' I said. 'Please, take me.'"

"Shameless," huffed old Grandma Mosh. "You were always shameless, Esme!'

"Oh, leave it be, Nettle Mosh!'

"Tell me, tell me," I would say, each time, even though I knew the story.

"She sat me at the back of her machine," said old Grandma Toffle, "and gave me my own eye goggles to wear, and strapped me in, and she sat in front at her controls. The engine turned and hummed and then we were speeding along the fallow field, slow at first but then growing faster, though not very fast, I don't think, and yet somehow the wing—it was a single, fixed wing, you see, pointing forward, like the feather on an arrow I think—somehow the wind lifted us up and we were in the air. I screamed with the exhilaration—"

"She was terrified!" cackled old Grandma Mosh.

"And then we were high above the houses and the fields, moving as slow as a bee, and the wind whipped at my face. I remember how beautiful I thought the pilot was, up there. She was a being of Sky and not of Land at all. I saw the mountains all round us, and the brook winding its way across the Land until it disappeared amidst the greenery. The sun shone over us and everything was clear and fresh and new."

Old Grandma Toffle falls quiet at this point, and so does her great rival, old Grandma Mosh. Both sigh, almost in unison. The memory, polished like a diamond, shines in both their minds. One on the Land and one in the air.

"Then we came down and the ground rushed towards us and we stopped, and we were back on the Land," old Grandma Toffle says, matter-of-factly. "And that was that."

"I would never go in the air," says old Grandma Mosh. "A woman must have both her feet firmly on the ground."

But old Grandma Toffle doesn't respond, and she sighs again, and then her head begins to droop and, before too long, she starts snoring. And so I must reconstruct that moment for myself, imagining it, what it would feel like to be in flight; for no flyer has come again since that time, though I hope still to meet one, one day.

But this is not at all the story I was going to tell, which my father told me, from the time before we came to live on the Land.

In that time there were many miracles and wonders in the world, such as giant ships that crossed the sea from one side of it to another, endlessly back and forth, back and forth, and carrying inside them mountains of things that were made by no human hand. For example, I once saw a picture of thousands and thousands of tiny little plastic spacemen, all lime-green and white, with purple stripes, and grinning, thousands and thousands of little grinning spacemen all thrown in a heap. It was a time the Roads had not been abandoned and people went everywhere by private pods, and all food came from giant temples and people went praying in them all of the days and there was everything in the temples that they could want and more, but it was never enough for them. In that time too much of the land was lost, gradually at first but then more and more violently, and many people and things drowned.

This is how my father claims our ancestors came to the Land, but I do not think he is telling the truth, in all likelihood he is lying: but then he would just argue that it isn't lying it's telling stories, and stories have a logic of their own.

Be that as it may, the story he likes to tell concerns Flora and Deuteronomy, who were young, and husband and wife. They lived on the edge of a great city on the shore of the ocean—

"Like the drowned cities of the coast?" I ask, and father says, "Yes, but much farther away, and lost now, Little Mai."

Old Grandma Mosh waves me to silence and so I sit by the fire and listen to the story.

"Deuteronomy was tall and handsome," my father says—

"Like you, Daddy!'

He smiles. "Exactly," he agrees. "He was tall and handsome, and Flora was very beautiful too, and she—"

"Was she a princess? "

"No," he says. "The monarchic system had mostly been abolished at that time... but there is a sort of princess in this story."

"Does she live happily ever after?" Old Grandma Toffle says, waking up abruptly with a loud snort.

"No," father says. "She dies."

"Shhh!' says Old Grandma Mosh. "Do you want to hear it or not?"

"I suppose..." I say. I don't much like the idea of a dead princess in this story. But then lots and lots of people died during that time.

"Flora was a marine biologist," father says, "and her husband was a current hunter, he would go out into the storms with a fishing net and catch electricity. It was dangerous work but it paid very well, because the haul you could get in the middle of a storm was very great indeed. At that time the city, which was called Puerto Soledad, was still a hungry and lumbering beast; alone on the skeletal coast, it withstood the ravages of the storms, and even thrived, for a time. Some of the most exciting art of the last decade of that century came from that city, and its people were proud and stubborn at once.

"Flora herself—she would be your great-great-great-great—well, I'm not honestly sure how many—grandmother, loved the sea, for all that it was rough and treacherous. She'd called it a ruthless killer, and yet said that she felt it was a tortured thing, that it was lashing out against those who had wounded it. She had a fanciful side to her, but she loved the sea just as her husband loved the storms, and they were never happy when they came here. People seldom are, you know, when forced to leave the place they'd known and become exiles."

"So why did they do it? Why did they leave? "

"For you," my father says. "For us. That is, they'd had a baby, and—"

"Ah," says old Grandma Mosh, dreamily.

"*Ah,*" says old Grandma Toffle, knowingly.

"And they wanted the baby to have a future, and grow up, and be happy. And though they loved the violence of the sea and the violence of the storm, they feared for the life of their child. Do you know, Mai, people will go a very long way to protect their children, even at the cost of their own lives."

"And then they leave you," says old Grandma Toffle, whose son, Oful Toffle, fell in love with a man from Tyr and went to live with him, beyond the blasted plains.

And Old Grandma Win nods sagely, and puffs on her pipe, and the aromatic smell of her home-grown cannabis fills the air and makes me sleepy.

"That they do, the little bastards," she says and chuckles, quite happily.

"Ungrateful sods," old Grandma Mosh says. I've known them for as long as I have been alive—and how to account for the fact that I am living, that I had not existed and yet now exist, that there is a little Mai in this Land where there had never been a Mai before? I love father and I love mother (who is a salvager and away again, en route to the lost cities of the coast), and I love this Land, for how can I not? But my mind wanders; it is late, outside the stars are shining bright down on fields and houses. And father says:

"One day, Flora went out into the sea. The sea was calm that day, and the endless white clouds of the hurricane storms had parted and the sun shone down on a water as flat and taut as blue cloth; and Flora came to the rock pools that she loved, where sea anemones beautiful beyond recall preyed on tiny fish. She wore her dry suit and her goggles and she carried her spears and her ropes and her nets and traps, for her work involved charting the twisting and meandering paths of migrating fish swarms which the people of that land depended on for food.

"The rock pools were far from habitation and secluded and people seldom came there, and Flora liked to go there by herself, suspended for a time between water and land.

"This time, however, she discovered she was not alone."

"Ahhh..." old Grandma Win whispers, ominously. They'd all heard the story. So had I, of course. It's a frustrating one, like most of my father's stories. It's fanciful with its tales of massive cities and great storms and mass death and fleeing refugees, and his refusal to *conclude* anything—the mystery unsolved, the questions unanswered. I've read many of the great writers of the past—Adaf, the Strugatskys, Pak Kyongni—and some had the same tendency, as slippery as fish in the stream, as elusive as a sunbeam—this tendency to *evade*. But perhaps all stories are like that. They aren't neat at all.

"The corpse," my father says, "floated serenely in the water. She had been cut and, cut, she'd bled. Around her body tiny creatures fastened onto open wounds, and the water was murky with a curious, opaque quality, strangely green."

He says, "It was the corpse of a young woman."

"How awful," says old Grandma Mosh.

"Terrible..." whispers old Grandma Win around her pipe.

Old Grandma Toffle is fast asleep. She lets out a contented fart that we all do our best to ignore. The wood in the fireplace bursts in a shower of sparks. Outside a dog howls.

"How did she die? "

"It was thought that she was murdered."

"Who was she?"

"Flora was used to the dead. She was used to the drowned. And she thought, what is one drowned person amongst so many? When she turned the corpse over, carefully, with her gloves, she saw the face, and she recognised it, vaguely. It was a girl called Cassandra and she was a member of one of the climate-clans, those families that had grown powerful in those last decades of the old world: they were a ruthless peoples as befitted that age, their dryland fortresses funded by the lucrative exploitation of energy harvesting and refugee smuggling, genetic manipulation and production of food crops, anything and everything. Remember there were no more princesses? Not by title, perhaps, but in practice this Cassandra was as close as one could get.

"It was not that the climate clans saw themselves as bad persons. They argued that they were practical, and hard because the world was hard. In their way they fought for the preservation of the human race, but at a cost that meant the majority must suffer for the ones with the power. This is a principle that has guided much of human history, Mai. You must remember that."

"This is boring," I say. I snuggle into his arms. It is warm and I am drowsy. "This is boring, who murdered her? Who killed Cassandra?"

"No one did. At least..."

"A suicide?"

"This is what Flora thought, at first. There were wounds on the woman's body but they were shallow, even, and there were no signs of defensive wounds. A lot of people chose suicide at that time. But why would the daughter of the most powerful of climate clans choose to come here, to these distant rock pools, and kill herself?

"Flora was uneasy. She took a sample of the water, which was teeming with tiny organisms. She always did that. She loved the rock pools habitat. Then she notified the Sentinels and they came quickly, and sealed the scene. She knew their captain, Minos.

"'You knew her, didn't you?' he said. He was not unfriendly. He stood staring at the pool moodily, smoking a tobacco cigarette.

"'A little.'

"'How so?' He didn't seem surprised; Flora reasoned that he already knew.

"'Adjacent fields,' she said. 'She was a bio diversity researcher, wasn't she? I must have ran into her at a conference or two. I only ever saw her from a distance, though.'

"'She was meant to assist in the family business,' Minos said. He tapped his foot on the ground. Overhead the grey-white cloud cover returned, obliterating the sky. 'She was a disappointment to her father and the clan.'

"'We were always envious of her, because she must have had access to all the best equipment,' Flora said. 'While we make do with hand-me-downs, with equipment patched together, unreliable half the time.'

"Minos nodded; but he did not seem overly interested. The Sentinels brought out the corpse, gently. For a moment the woman hung there, over the water, her long hair streaming down. Flora saw that the wounds had closed. The woman seemed very pale. She had lost a lot of blood. Flora worried for the creatures in the rock pools, but they seemed much as ever. With the coming of the tide the pools filled up and the water floated out to sea and the pools were replenished."

"I know how this ends," I said. "I do, I remember now, there is a lesson in there somewhere..."

"Maybe you should go to sleep," my father says, "it's late, and tomorrow—"

But I do not want to think about tomorrow. I know the story, I have heard it a hundred times already before. We place much store, in stories. We tell them to each other and to strangers, and they tell us their tales in exchange. And this is not, after all, the story of Cassandra, one drowned among so many. This is the story of Flora and Deuteronomy and how they came to the Land, the story, in a way, of how I came to be.

It was late when Flora returned home. Deuteronomy was already there, preparing their supper. They sat down, to spicy fish soup and rice from the plantations up on the high mountains, and afterwards they went to bed, and Flora felt a little tiny being kick inside her.

And in the morning, very early, the Sentinels came knocking on the door; Deuteronomy answered it, and saw Minos, who looked like he hadn't slept at all, and Minos said, "I am here for Flora."

Deuteronomy was about to protest (despite the armed Sentinels standing in a semi-circle behind Minos) but Flora pacified him; and she went with Minos and his troops.

They rode in a large armoured vehicle. I saw pictures of it once and it looked like an armadillo. Wars were frequent at that time and the climate clans' armies often fought with each other; and so Minos and his troops travelled in convoy, armoured and armed and prepared.

But this was their turf, their manor. They rose high into the mountains, and Flora could see far ahead, over the whole of the sprawling chaos of Puerto Soledad, the ramshackle houses piled disorderly on top of one another, and the great sea wall that held the storms at bay, and the great white ocean-going ships which were like miniature towns on the waters, and the dome of grey-white hurricane weather clouds, and a lone bird in the sky, diving. And she was afraid.

Then they passed through the gates to the fortress of the clan and drove farther and higher, to the peaks where the lords of that part of the world ruled from their eyries. The fortress was built of hewn volcanic stone and steel and was impregnable. And this is where this Cassandra had lived.

And Flora was led into this hall of stone and there she met the Lord Piyama. He was a tall and stooped man with short cropped grey hair and impeccable manners and a gun and a knife on his belt. And he said, "You are the one who found my daughter."

"Yes."

"I would like to know who murdered my daughter."

"Lord," Flora said. "I am merely a biologist. A diver. You need forensics, detectives, I don't—"

He looked at her witheringly. "They tell me they do not know. The records have been erased or altered. No one saw her go. They tell me that she bled to death, slowly, in the water. Why?"

"Lord, I do not know. It is—"

She wanted to say suicide, I know she did. It was a popular, relatively painless way to do it, in an age when people often welcomed death as a relief. To bleed in water. When Flora dove at sea she often came across fresh corpses. At least, she thought, it fed the fish.

"At least tell me what she did, before she died."

And Flora realised how much in need this ruthless man was, how desperate and hurting, that he—*he!*—would ask her that. They had no kings by title in that vanished age, but they had lords and masters by greed and power.

She bowed her head. They both knew there was no refusing.

"Why me?"

"You knew her. At least..." He looked at her, his face impassive, the hurt was only in his eyes. "I guess I never did."

Flora was tired, and irritable, and scared. She said, "And in return?"

It was how they spoke back then. Everything had a price, nothing was freely given, not even stories. Imagine getting paid for telling stories!

He nodded, approving. "Anything in my power to grant," he said, "is yours to take."

"I want to go from here," she said, though it broke her apart to say it, for she loved this land, her home, and she loved the sea. "I want to go where it is safe to live."

"Nowhere is safe." He looked at her, surprised at the suggestion.

"Then give me passage," she said, "to wherever it is in this world I would go."

"If you find my daughter's killer," he said.

Implied in the words, the consequences of her failure. She swallowed bile. She felt quite sick, the thing inside her growing, kicking. She nodded.

This isn't really the story my father tells. My father tells that Flora and Deuteronomy came here in a storm: a great hurricane which sucked them up into the air, twirling and twirling them about like ragdolls, and it carried them across the sea, a raging storm with an eye at its heart, one of the last great storms of the old age: the storm had torn every stone and every tree from out of Port Soledad and flattened the coast clean, and it ripped the black volcanic rock from the Lord Piyama's fortress, and his army, and their guns, and tore them all to shreds and never stopped. And the storm howled with mad exhilaration across the sea from land to Land, and placed my ancestors gently on the ground.

But my father is given to strange flights of fancy, and one should seldom take him at his word; a bad habit perhaps inherited from his ancient great-great-great-to-whatever-number grandmother.

"'So?' Minos said. He looked at Flora without expression. She shrugged. 'Can I see her laboratory?' she said.

"He escorted her, down endless corridors, past whispering servants and priceless paintings and sculptures made by the finest artists of that time, filled with violence and passion, with the rage of the Earth. And they came at last to Cassandra's quarters.

"They were set into the side of the mountain, and the view truly was breathtaking, from the reinforced glass windows Flora could see the storms forming in the sea so far away. She saw the islands of humanity rise from the deeps. She saw the sea, the sea she loved. And she wondered what she has gotten herself into, and what she could do. And she touched her belly protectively.

"Mai? Are you asleep?" father says.

"No," I murmur. I can see it so clearly, that vanished world, its players re-enacting this ancient drama. Minos, impassive. Flora, pacing, calibrating instruments, filling beakers. She felt as though Cassandra had left her a clue, a scientific puzzle for Flora alone to solve. What had she been working on? Was that the reason that she was killed?

In his throne room the old lord paced, back and forth, back and forth, brooding. In the rooms the servants came and went on silent feet. What had Cassandra been working on when she died? Her area of speciality was genetic manipulation, she had access to the best science the world had to offer, patents and secrets long lost to us in the flood, things only the climate clans knew. But the equipment told Flora nothing, the notes were cryptic, it was all nonsense, she thought: murder was usually simple, a matter of money or love.

She interviewed the servants. Cassandra was secretive, she had ways in and out of her apartments no one could access. The whole citadel was riddled with secret tunnels. Flora returned home, and she lay in Deuteronomy's arms. His hand was on her tummy, open palmed, and he said, in wonder, "I felt him kick."

"Him!" Flora said, laughing. "You don't know that."

"I would like a little girl."

"Girls," Flora said, "are more trouble."

She did not tell Deuteronomy about the conditions of her bail; she didn't need to. She lay there long into the night, brooding, as Deuteronomy slept beside her. An earthquake rattled the house, but neither of them much noticed.

"Hush, little Mai," father says. All is quiet in the house, and he lifts me in his arms and I snuggle against his chest. He smells of earth and harvest, of fresh water and olive trees.

"But you don't understand," I say, or try to. "I know what really happened, I know what Cassandra was doing."

"Hush, now," he says, and he tucks me in. All is quiet, the house is warm with the slow heat of embers. You see, in my dream, Flora returns to her own, makeshift lab; and she studies the sample of water she'd taken from the rock pools, and what she sees is something strange, something she does not understand. Tiny life forms, unlike any she'd seen: and living, still, in the sample, multiplying.

This is the story as it is sometimes told, you see. How Flora discovered the truth of Cassandra's own child bearing, the creatures which lived in her blood. What they were, we still don't know. A new form of life, a new seed for a dying Earth. Something innocent, and new, like a baby.

And she went into the rock pools and floated there, serene against the hurricane sky; and she carefully and deliberately cut herself, low shallow cuts, and let her blood flow into the water, and her children to emerge into the waiting ocean just beyond the rocks.

This is the story we sometimes tell in my family, as fanciful as it is. Cassandra's body as an incubator, her blood a conduit to future dreams: something twisted and violent, emblematic of those last days of the world as it was.

"But where was the knife?" I mumble; I turn in my bed. "There was no knife, was there, in the rock pools? None that Flora saw. None that the Sentinels found. So how did she cut herself?"

And this is the story of how we came to the Land. It is a story of violence and blood and lies, a story of make believe, as all stories are.

"Well?" demanded the Lord Piyama.

Flora stood before him, her hand on her belly. If she failed, she and her unborn child would become parts, harvested for organs, the rest made into compost. No one was very sentimental, in that bygone age.

"It was Minos," she said. "It was Minos, the Sentinel."

There was a shocked silence in the hall of the Lord. Minos stood like a statue. Flora had grown quite fond of his quiet presence, his efficiency, his lack of unnecessary speech. She almost liked him.

But he was not a good man. Remember that. None of them were, back then: they could not afford to be.

"Minos?" the Lord Piyama said. "That's absurd."

Flora shrugged. She had learned from Minos, and her face, like his, was without expression. "He helped your daughter, he hid her passing to and from the citadel. He deleted or falsified the records. I see it in the way he doesn't talk, the way his eyes are still. He loved her. What happened, Lord, I do not truly know. How they came to be at that place at that time. But someone carried the knife away, when it was done. Someone watched as she bled. There wasn't much pain, I don't think. She was spared that, at least. But it was him, I am sure of it."

She had pieced together a story. It could have been right. Cassandra's quarters were too clean, her records too sparse, personal information missing in odd places. No one else could have had that kind of access. It was possible, it was even plausible. But was Cassandra murdered, or did she kill herself?

Did he help? Did he cry? He doesn't strike me, in my version of this story, as a man who cried often, or well. But I think he did love her.

The Lord Piyama turned his azure eyes on his Sentinel. "Is it true, Minos? Can it be true?"

Flora tensed, expecting any moment a bullet in the head, a knife in the back. But Minos was as impassive as always, and he looked at his lord with calm. "Does it matter?" he said. "You have already decided."

And the Lord Piyama nodded.

And Flora knew, then, that she was right.

Later, as Minos' corpse was carried away from the hall, she did not avert her gaze. He was guilty, she was sure of that: he was guilty of *something*.

And so was she, but she felt she could live with the guilt. She touched her belly again, she couldn't help it. She loved the little creature growing inside here so much. She could live with a little guilt.

... And so it was that we came to the Land.

I don't know who really killed Cassandra, if anyone did. I don't know if Minos and her were lovers. I do not even know, in truth, if they really did exist. This all happened so long ago and in another world, almost. Puerto Soledad lies under the waves, and Lord Piyama's skull had long been picked clean by the gulls. The world is quieter now, and an ancient headstone in our cemetery is all that's left of Flora and Deuteronomy.

... Yet sometimes I like to think of those tiny little creatures released into the ocean, and I wonder where they are now, and what they had evolved into.

"It's a ridiculous story," old Grandma Win says, and old Grandma Mosh nods vigorously in reply. And perhaps it's true. But my mother had seen the ocean; and one day I will, too.

THE FUTURE IS BLUE
– CATHERYNNE M. VALENTE –

1. NIHILIST

MY NAME IS Tetley Abednego and I am the most hated girl in Garbagetown. I am nineteen years old. I live alone in Candle Hole, where I was born, and have no friends except for a deformed gannet bird I've named Grape Crush and a motherless elephant seal cub I've named Big Bargains, and also the hibiscus flower that has recently decided to grow out of my roof, but I haven't named it anything yet. I love encyclopedias, a cassette I found when I was eight that says *Madeleine Brix's Superboss Mixtape '97* on it in very nice handwriting, plays by Mr. Shakespeare or Mr. Webster or Mr. Beckett, lipstick, Garbagetown, and my twin brother Maruchan. Maruchan is the only thing that loves me back, but he's my twin, so it doesn't really count. We couldn't stop loving each other any more than the sea could stop being so greedy and give us back China or drive time radio or polar bears.

But he doesn't visit anymore.

When we were little, Maruchan and I always asked each other the same question before bed. Every night, we crawled

353

into the Us-Fort together—an impregnable stronghold of a bed which we had nailed up ourselves out of the carcasses of several hacked apart bassinets, prams, and cradles. It took up the whole of our bedroom. No one could see us in there, once we closed the porthole (a manhole cover I swiped from Scrapmetal Abbey stamped with stars, a crescent moon, and the magic words *New Orleans Water Meter*), and we felt certain no one could hear us either. We lay together under our canopy of moldy green lace and shredded buggy-hoods and mobiles with only one shattered fairy fish remaining. Sometimes I asked first and sometimes he did, but we never gave the same answer twice.

"Maruchan, what do you want to be when you grow up?"

He would give it a serious think. Once, I remember, he whispered:

"When I grow up I want to be the Thames!"

"Whatever for?" I giggled.

"Because the Thames got so big and so bossy and so strong that it ate London all up in one go! Nobody tells a Thames what to do or who to eat. A Thames tells *you*. Imagine having a whole city to eat, and not having to share any! Also there were millions of eels in the Thames and I only get to eat eels at Easter which isn't fair when I want to eat them all the time."

And he pretended to bite me and eat me all up. "Very well, you shall be the Thames and I shall be the Mississippi and together we shall eat up the whole world."

Then we'd go to sleep and dream the same dream. We always dreamed the same dreams, which was like living twice.

After that, whenever we were hungry, which was always all the time and forever, we'd say *we're bound for London-town!*

until we drove our parents so mad that they forbade the word London in the house, but you can't forbid a word, so there.

EVERY MORNING I wake up to find words painted on my door like toadstools popping up in the night.

Today it says NIHILIST in big black letters. That's not so bad! It's almost sweet! Big Bargains flumps toward me on her fat seal-belly while I light the wicks on my beeswax door and we watch them burn together until the word melts away.

"I don't think I'm a nihilist, Big Bargains. Do you?"

She rolled over onto my matchbox stash so that I would rub her stomach. Rubbing a seal's stomach is the opposite of nihilism.

Yesterday, an old man hobbled up over a ridge of rusted bicycles and punched me so hard he broke my nose. By law, I had to let him. I had to say: *Thank you, Grandfather, for my instruction.* I had to stand there and wait in case he wanted to do something else to me. Anything but kill me, those were his rights. But he didn't want more, he just wanted to cry and ask me why I did it and the law doesn't say I have to answer that, so I just stared at him until he went away. Once a gang of schoolgirls shaved off all my hair and wrote CUNT in blue marker on the back of my skull. *Thank you, sisters, for my instruction.* The schoolboys do worse. After graduation they come round and eat my food and hold me down and try to make me cry, which I never do. It's their rite of passage. *Thank you, brothers, for my instruction.*

But other than that, I'm really a very happy person! I'm awfully lucky when you think about it. Garbagetown is the most wonderful place anybody has ever lived in the history of the world, even if you count the Pyramids and New York City and Camelot. I have Grape Crush and Big Bargains and my hibiscus flower and I can fish like I've got bait for a heart so I hardly ever go hungry and once I found a ruby ring *and* a New Mexico license plate inside a bluefin tuna. Everyone says they only hate me because I annihilated hope and butchered our future, but I know better, and anyway, it's a lie. Some people are just born to be despised. The Loathing of Tetley began small and grew bigger and bigger, like the Thames, until it swallowed me whole.

Maruchan and I were born fifty years after the Great Sorting, which is another lucky thing that's happened to me. After all, I could have been born a Fuckwit and gotten drowned with all the rest of them, or I could have grown up on a Misery Boat, sailing around hopelessly looking for land, or one of the first to realize people could live on a patch of garbage in the Pacific Ocean the size of the place that used to be called Texas, or I could have been a Sorter and spent my whole life moving rubbish from one end of the patch to the other so that a pile of crap could turn into a country and babies could be born in places like Candle Hole or Scrapmetal Abbey or Pill Hill or Toyside or Teagate.

Candle Hole is the most beautiful place in Garbagetown, which is the most beautiful place in the world. All the stubs of candles the Fuckwits threw out piled up into hills and mountains and caverns and dells, votive candles and taper candles and tea lights and birthday candles and big fat colorful pillar candles, stacked and somewhat melted into a great crumbling gorgeous warren of wicks and wax. All the houses are little cozy honeycombs melted into the hillside, with smooth round windows and low golden ceilings. At night, from far away, Candle Hole looks like a firefly palace. When the wind blows, it smells like cinnamon, and freesia, and cranberries, and lavender, and Fresh Linen Scent and New Car Smell.

2. THE TERRIBLE POWER OF FUCKWIT CAKE

OUR PARENTS' NAMES are Life and Time. Time lay down on her Fresh Linen Scent wax bed and I came out of her first, then Maruchan. But even though I got here first, I came out blue as the ocean, not breathing, with the umbilical cord wrapped round my neck and Maruchan wailing, still squeezing onto my noose with his tiny fist, like he was trying to get me free. Doctor Pimms unstrangled and unblued me and put me in a Hawaiian Fantasies-scented wax hollow in our living room. I lay there alone, too startled by living to cry, until the sun came up and Life and Time remembered I had survived. Maruchan was so healthy and sweet natured and strong and, even though Garbagetown is the most beautiful place in the world, many children don't live past a year or two. We don't even get names until we turn ten. (Before that, we answer happily to Girl or Boy or Child or Darling.) Better to focus on the one that will grow up rather than get attached to the sickly poor beast who hasn't got a chance.

I was born already a ghost. But I was a very noisy ghost. I screamed and wept at all hours while Life and Time waited for me to die. I only nursed when my brother was full, I only played with toys he forgot, I only spoke after he had spoken. Maruchan said his first word at the supper table: *please*. What a lovely, polite word for a lovely, polite child! After they finished cooing over him, I very calmly turned to my mother and said: *Mama, may I have a scoop of mackerel roe? It is my favorite.* I thought they would be so proud! After all, I made twelve more words than my brother. This was my moment, the wonderful moment when they would realize that they did love me and I wasn't going to die and I was special and good. But everyone got very quiet. They were not happy that the ghost could talk. I had been able to for ages, but everything in my world said to wait for my brother before I could do anything at all. *No, you may not have mackerel roe, because you are a deceitful wicked little show-off child.*

When we turned ten, we went to fetch our names. This is just the most terribly exciting thing for a Garbagetown kid. At ten, you are a real person. At ten, people want to know you. At ten, you will probably live for a good while yet. This is how you catch a name: wake up to the fabulous new world of being ten and greet your birthday Frankencake (a hodgepodge of well-preserved Fuckwit snack cakes filled with various cremes and jellies). Choose a slice, with much fanfare. Inside, your adoring and/or neglectful mother will have hidden various small objects—an aluminum pull tab, a medicine bottle cap, a broken earring, a coffee bean, a wee striped capacitor, a tiny plastic rocking horse, maybe a postage stamp. Remove item from your mouth without cutting yourself or eating it. Now, walk in the direction of your prize. Toward Aluminumopolis or Pill Hill or Spanglestoke or Teagate or Electric City or Toyside or Lost Post Gulch. Walk and walk and walk. Never once brush yourself off or wash in the ocean, even after camping on a pile of magazines or wishbones or pregnancy tests or wrapping paper with glitter reindeer on it. Walk until nobody knows you. When, finally, a stranger hollers at you to get out of the way or go back where you came from or stop stealing the good rubbish, they will, without even realizing, call you by your true name, and you can begin to pick and stumble your way home.

My brother grabbed a chocolate snack cake with a curlicue of white icing on it. I chose a pink and red tigery striped hunk of cake filled with gooshy creme de something. The sugar hit our brains like twin tsunamis. He spat out a little gold earring with the post broken off. I felt a smooth, hard gelcap lozenge in my mouth. Pill Hill it was then, and the great mountain of Fuckwit anxiety medication. But when I carefully pulled the thing out, it was a little beige capacitor with red stripes instead. Electric City! I'd never been half so far. Richies lived in Electric City. Richies and brightboys and dazzlegirls and kerosene kings. My brother was off in the opposite direction, toward Spanglestoke and the desert of engagement rings.

Maybe none of it would have happened if I'd gone to Spanglestoke for my name instead. If I'd never seen the gasoline gardens of Engine Row. If I'd gone home straightaway after finding my name. If I'd never met Goodnight Moon in the brambles of Hazmat Heath with all the garbage stars rotting gorgeously overhead. Such is the terrible power of Fuckwit Cake.

I walked cheerfully out of Candle Hole with my St. Oscar backpack strapped on tight and didn't look back once. Why should I? St. Oscar had my back. I'm not really that religious nowadays. But everyone's religious when they're ten. St. Oscar was a fuzzy green Fuckwit man who lived in a garbage can just like me, and frowned a lot just like me. He understood me and loved me and knew how to bring civilization out of trash and I loved him back even though he was a Fuckwit. Nobody chooses how they get born. Not even Oscar.

So I scrambled up over the wax ridges of my home and into the world with Oscar on my back. The Matchbox Forest rose up around me: towers of EZ Strike matchbooks and boxes from impossible, magical places like the Coronado Hotel, Becky's Diner, the Fox and Hound Pub. Garbagetowners picked through heaps and cairns of blackened, used matchsticks looking for the precious ones that still had their red and blue heads intact. But I knew all those pickers. They couldn't give me a name. I waved at the hotheads. I climbed up Flintwheel Hill, my feet slipping and sliding on the mountain of spent butane lighters, until I could see out over all of Garbagetown just as the broiling cough-drop red sun was setting over Far Boozeaway, hitting the crystal bluffs of stockpiled whiskey and gin bottles and exploding into a billion billion rubies tumbling down into the hungry sea.

I sang a song from school to the sun and the matchsticks. It's an ask-and-answer song, so I had to sing both parts myself, which feels very odd when you have always had a twin to do the asking or the answering, but I didn't mind.

Who liked it hot and hated snow?
The Fuckwits did! The Fuckwits did!
Who ate up every thing that grows?
The Fuckwits did! The Fuckwits did!
Who drowned the world in oceans blue?
The Fuckwits did! The Fuckwits did!
Who took the land from me and you?
The Fuckwits did, we know it's true!
Are you Fuckwits, children dear?
We're GARBAGETOWNERS, free and clear!

But who made the garbage, rich and rank?
The Fuckwits did, and we give thanks.

The Lawn stretched out below me, full of the grass clippings and autumn leaves and fallen branches and banana peels and weeds and gnawed bones and eggshells of the fertile Fuckwit world, slowly turning into the gold of Garbagetown: soil. Real earth. Terra bloody firma. We can already grow rice in the dells. And here and there, big, blowsy flowers bang up out of the rot: hibiscus, African tulips, bitter gourds, a couple of purple lotuses floating in the damp mucky bits. I slept next to a blue-and-white orchid that looked like my brother's face.

"Orchid, what do you want to be when you grow up?" I whispered to it. In real life, it didn't say anything back. It just fluttered a little in the moonlight and the seawind. But when I got around to dreaming, I dreamed about the orchid, and it said: *a farm.*

3. MURDERCUNT

IN GARBAGETOWN, YOU think real hard about what you're gonna eat next, where the fresh water's at, and where you're gonna sleep. Once all that's settled you can whack your mind on nicer stuff, like gannets and elephant seals and what to write next on the Bitch of Candle Hole's door. (This morning I melted MURDERCUNT off the back wall of my house. Big Bargains flopped down next to me and watched the blocky red painted letters swirl and fade into the Buttercream Birthday Cake wax. Maybe I'll name my hibiscus flower Murdercunt. It has a nice big sound.)

When I remember hunting my name, I mostly remember the places I slept. It's a real dog to find good spots. Someplace sheltered from the wind, without too much seawater seep, where no-one'll yell at you for wastreling on their patch or try to stick it in you in the middle of the night just because you're all alone and it looks like you probably don't have a knife.

I always have a knife.

So I slept with St. Oscar the Grouch for my pillow, in the shadow of a mountain of black chess pieces in Gamegrange, under a thicket of tabloids and *Wall Street Journals* and remaindered novels with their covers torn off in Bookbury, snuggled into a spaghetti-pile of unspooled cassette ribbon on the outskirts of the Sound Downs, on the lee side of a little soggy Earl Grey hillock in Teagate. In the morning I sucked on a few of the teabags and the dew on them tasted like the loveliest cuppa any Fuckwit ever poured his stupid self. I said my prayers on beds of old microwaves and moldy photographs of girls with perfect hair kissing at the camera. *St. Oscar, keep your mighty lid closed over me. Look grouchily but kindly upon me and protect me as I travel through the infinite trashcan of your world. Show me the beautiful usefulness of your Blessed Rubbish. Let me not be Taken Out before I find my destiny.*

But my destiny didn't seem to want to find me. As far as I walked, I still saw people I knew. Mr. Zhu raking his mushroom garden, nestled in a windbreak of broken milk bottles. Miss Amancharia gave me one of the coconut crabs out of her nets, which was very nice of her, but hardly a name. Even as far away as Teagate, I saw Tropicana Sita welding a refrigerator door to a hull-metal shack. She flipped up her mask and waved at me.

Dammit! She was Allsorts Sita's cousin, and Allsorts drank with my mother every Thursday at the Black Wick.

By the time I walked out of Teagate I'd been gone eight days. I was getting pretty ripe. Bits and pieces of Garbagetown were stuck all over my clothes, but no tidying up. Them's the rules. I could see the blue crackle of Electric City sparkling up out of the richie-rich Coffee Bean 'Burbs. Teetering towers of batteries rose up like desert hoodoo spires—AA, AAA, 12 Volt, DD, car, solar, lithium, anything you like. Parrots and pelicans screamed down the battery canyons, their talons kicking off sprays of AAAs that tumbled down the heights like rockslides. Sleepy banks of generators rumbled pleasantly along a river of wires and extension cords and HDMI cables. Fields of delicate lightbulbs windchimed in the breeze. Anything that had a working engine lived here. Anything that still had *juice*. If Garbagetown had a heart, it was Electric City. Electric City pumped power. Power and privilege.

In Electric City, the lights of the Fuckwit world were still on.

4. GOODNIGHT GARBAGETOWN

"OI, TETLEY! FUCK off back home to your darkhole! We're full up on little cunts here!"

And that's how I got my name. Barely past the battery spires of Electric City, a fat gas-huffing fucksack voltage jockey called me a little cunt. But he also called me Tetley. He brayed it down from a pyramid of telephones and his friends all laughed and drank homebrew out of a glass jug and went back to not working. I looked down—among the many scraps of rubbish clinging to my shirt and pants and backpack and hair was a bright blue teabag wrapper with TETLEY CLASSIC BLEND BLACK TEA written on it in cheerful white letters, clinging to my chest.

I tried to feel the power of my new name. The *me*-ness of it. I tried to imagine my mother and father when they were young, waking up with some torn out page of *Life* or *Time* magazine stuck to their rears, not even noticing until someone barked out their whole lives for a laugh. But I couldn't feel anything while the volt-humpers kept on staring at me like I was nothing but a used-up potato battery. I didn't even know then that the worst swear word in Electric City was *dark*. I didn't know they were waiting to see how mad I'd get 'cause they called my home a darkhole. I didn't care. They were wrong and stupid. Except for the hole part. Candle Hole never met a dark it couldn't burn down.

Maybe I should have gone home right then. I had my name! Time to hoof it back over the river and through the woods, girl. But I'd never seen Electric City and it was morning and if I stayed gone awhile longer maybe they'd miss me. Maybe they'd worry. And maybe now they'd love me, now that I was a person with a name. Maybe I could even filch a couple of batteries or a cup of gasoline and turn up at my parents' door in turbo-powered triumph. I'd tell my brother all my adventures and he'd look at me like I was magic on a stick and everything would be good forever and ever amen.

So I wandered. I gawped. It was like being in school and learning the Fuckwit song only I was walking around *inside* the Fuckwit song and it was all still happening right now everywhere. Electric City burbled and bubbled and clanged and belched and smoked just like the bad old world before it all turned blue. Everyone had such fine things! I saw a girl wearing a ballgown out of a fairy book, green and glitter and miles of ruffles and she wasn't even *going* anywhere. She was just tending her gasoline garden out the back of her little cottage, which wasn't made out of candles or picturebooks or cat food cans, but real cottage parts! Mostly doors and shutters and really rather a lot of windows, but they fit together like they never even needed the other parts of a house in the first place. And the girl in her greenglitter dress carried a big red watering can around her garden, sprinkling fuel stabilizer into her tidy rows of petrol barrels and gas cans with their graceful spouts pointed toward the sun. Why not wear that dress all the time? Just a wineglass full of what she was growing in her garden would buy almost anything else in Garbagetown. She smiled shyly at me. I hated her. And I wanted to be her.

By afternoon I was bound for London-town, so hungry I could've slurped up every eel the Thames ever had. There's no food lying around in Electric City. In Candle Hole I could've grabbed candy or a rice ball or jerky off any old midden heap. But here everybody owned their piece and kept it real neat, *mercilessly* neat, and they didn't share. I sat down on a rusty Toyota transmission and fished around in my backpack for crumbs. My engine sat on one side of a huge cyclone fence. I'd never seen one all put together before. Sure, you find torn-off shreds of wire fences, but this one was all grown up, with proper locks and chain wire all over it. It meant to Keep You Out. Inside, like hungry dogs, endless barrels and freezers and cylinders and vats went on and on, with angry writing on them that said HAZMAT or BIOHAZARD or RADIOACTIVE or WARNING or DANGER or CLASSIFIED.

"Got anything good in there?" said a boy's voice. I looked round and saw a kid my own age, with wavy black hair and big brown eyes and three little moles on his forehead. He was wearing the nicest clothes I ever saw on a boy—a blue suit that almost, *almost* fit him. With a *tie*.

"Naw," I answered. "Just a dry sweater, an empty can of Cheez Whiz, and *Madeline Brix's Superboss Mixtape '97*. It's my good luck charm." I showed him my beloved mixtape. Madeline Brix made all the dots on her *i*'s into hearts. It was a totally Fuckwit thing to do and I loved her for it even though she was dead and didn't care if I loved her or not.

"*Cool*," the boy said, and I could tell he meant it. He didn't even call me a little cunt or anything. He pushed his thick hair out of his face. "Listen, you really shouldn't be here. No one's gonna say anything because you're not Electrified, but it's so completely dangerous. They put all that stuff in one place so it couldn't get out and hurt anyone."

"Electrified?"

"One of us. Local." He had the decency to look embarrassed. "Anyway, I saw you and I thought that if some crazy darkgirl is gonna have a picnic on Hazmat Heath, I could at least help her not die while she's doing it."

The boy held out his hand. He was holding a gas mask. He showed me how to fasten it under my hair. The sun started to set rosily behind a tangled briar of motherboards. Everything turned pink and gold and slow and sleepy. I climbed down from my engine tuffet and lay under the fence next to the boy in the suit. He'd brought a mask for himself too. We looked at each other through the eye holes.

"My name's Goodnight Moon," he said.

"Mine's..." And I did feel my new name swirling up inside me then, like good tea, like cream and sugar cubes, like the most essential me. "Tetley."

"I'm sorry I called you a darkgirl, Tetley."

"Why?"

"It's not a nice thing to call someone."

"I like it. It sounds pretty."

"It isn't. I promise. Do you forgive me?"

I tugged on the hose of my gas mask. The air coming through tasted like nickels. "Sure. I'm aces at forgiving. Been practicing all my life. Besides..." My turn to go red in the face. "At the Black Wick they'd probably call you a brightboy and that's not as pretty as it sounds, either."

Goodnight Moon's brown eyes stared out at me from behind thick glass. It was the closest I'd ever been to a boy who wasn't my twin. Goodnight Moon didn't feel like a twin. He felt like the opposite of a twin. We never shared a womb, but on the other end of it all, we might still share a grave. His tie was burgundy with green swirls in it. He hadn't tied it very well, so I could see the skin of his throat, which was very clean and probably very soft.

"Hey," he said, "do you want to hear your tape?"

"What do you mean *hear* it? It's not for hearing, it's for luck."

Goodnight Moon laughed. His laugh burst all over me like butterfly bombs. He reached into his suit jacket and pulled out a thick black rectangle. I handed him *Madeline Brix's Superboss Mixtape '97* and he hit a button on the side of the rectangle. It popped open; Goodnight Moon slotted in my tape and handed me one end of a long wire.

"Put it in your ear," he said, and I did.

A man's voice filled up my head from my jawbone up to the plates of my skull. The most beautiful and saddest voice that ever was. A voice like Candle Hole all lit up at twilight. A voice like the whole old world calling up from the bottom of the sea. The man on Madeline Brix's tape was saying he was happy, and he hoped I was happy, too.

Goodnight Moon reached out to hold my hand just as the sky went black and starry. I was crying. He was, too. Our tears dripped out of our gas masks onto the rusty road of Electric City.

When the tape ended, I dug in my backpack for a match and a stump of candle: dark red, Holiday Memories scent. I lit it at the same moment that Goodnight Moon pulled a little flashlight out of his pocket and turned it on. We held our glowings between us. We were the same.

5. BRIGHTBITCH

ALLSORTS SITA CAME to visit me today. Clicked my knocker early in the morning, early enough that I could be sure she'd never slept in the first place. I opened for her, as I am required to do. She looked up at me with eyes like bullet holes, leaning on my waxy hinges, against the T in BRIGHTBITCH, thoughtfully scrawled in what appeared to be human shit across the front of my hut. BRIGHTBITCH smelled, but Allsorts Sita smelled worse. Her breath punched me in the nose before she did. I got a lungful of what Diet Sprite down at the Black Wick optimistically called "cognac": the thick pinkish booze you could get by extracting the fragrance oil and preservatives out of candles and mixing it with wood alcohol the kids over in

Furnitureford boiled out of dining sets and china cabinets. Smells like flowers vomited all over a New Car and then killed a badger in the backseat. Allsorts Sita looked like she'd drunk so much cognac you could light one strand of her hair and she'd burn for eight days.

"You fucking whore," she slurred.

"Thank you, Auntie, for my instruction," I answered quietly.

I have a place I go to in my mind when I have visitors who aren't seals or gannet birds or hibiscus flowers. A little house made all of doors and windows, where I wear a greenglitter dress every day and water my gascan garden and read by electric light.

"I hate you. I hate you. How could you do it? We raised you and fed you and this is how you repay it all. You ungrateful bitch."

"Thank you, Auntie, for my instruction."

In my head I ran my fingers along a cyclone fence and all the barrels on the other side read LIFE and LOVE and FORGIVENESS and UNDERSTANDING.

"You've killed us all," Allsorts Sita moaned. She puked up magenta cognac on my stoop. When she was done puking she hit me over and over with closed fists. It didn't hurt too much. Allsorts is a small woman. But it hurt when she clawed my face and my breasts with her fingernails. Blood came up like wax spilling and when she finished she passed out cold, halfway in my house, halfway out.

"Thank you, Auntie, for my instruction," I said to her sleeping body. My blood dripped onto her, but in my head I was lying on my roof made of two big church doors in a gas mask listening to a man sing to me that he's never done bad things and he hopes I'm happy, he hopes I'm happy, he hopes I'm happy.

Big Bargains moaned mournfully and the lovely roof melted away like words on a door. My elephant seal friend flopped and fretted. When they've gone for my face she can't quite recognize me and it troubles her seal-soul something awful. Grape Crush, my gannet bird, never worries about silly things like facial wounds. He just brings me fish and pretty rocks. When I found him, he had a plastic six-pack round his neck with one can still stuck in the thing, dragging along behind him like a ball and chain. Big Bargains was choking on an ad insert. She'd probably smelled some ancient fish and chips grease lurking in the headlines. They only love me because I saved them. That doesn't always work. I saved everyone else, too, and all I got back was blood and shit and loneliness.

6. REVLON SUPER LUSTROUS 919: RED RUIN

I WENT HOME with my new name fastened on tight. Darkgirls can't stay in Electric City. Can't live there unless you're born there and I was only ten anyway. Goodnight Moon kissed me before I left. He still had his gas mask on so mainly our breathing hoses wound around each other like gentle elephants but I still call it a kiss. He smelled like scorched ozone and metal and paraffin and hope.

A few months later, Electric City put up a fence around the whole place. Hung up an old rusty shop sign that said EXCUSE OUR MESS WHILE WE RENOVATE. No one could go in or out except to trade and that had to get itself done on the dark side of the fence.

My mother and father didn't start loving me when I got back even though I brought six AA batteries out of the back of

Goodnight Moon's tape player. My brother had got a ramen flavor packet stuck in his hair somewhere outside the Grocery Isle and was every inch of him Maruchan. A few years later I heard Life and Time telling some cousin how their marvelous and industrious and thoughtful boy had gone out in search of a name and brought back six silver batteries, enough to power anything they could dream of. What a child! What a son! So fuck them, I guess.

But Maruchan did bring something back. It just wasn't for our parents. When we crawled into the Us-Fort that first night back, we lay uncomfortably against each other. We were the same, but we weren't. We'd had separate adventures for the first time, and Maruchan could never understand why I wanted to sleep with a gas mask on now.

"Tetley, what do you want to be when you grow up?" Maruchan whispered in the dark of our pram-maze.

"Electrified," I whispered back. "What do you want to be?"

"Safe," he said. Things had happened to Maruchan, too, and I couldn't share them anymore than he could hear Madeline Brix's songs.

My twin pulled something out of his pocket and pushed it into my hand till my fingers closed round it reflexively. It was hard and plastic and warm.

"I love you, Tetley. Happy Birthday."

I opened my fist. Maruchan had stolen lipstick for me. Revlon Super Lustrous 919: Red Ruin, worn almost all the way down to the nub by some dead woman's lips.

After that, a lot of years went by but they weren't anything special.

7. IF GOD TURNED UP FOR SUPPER

I WAS SEVENTEEN years old when Brighton Pier came to Garbagetown. I was tall and my hair was the color of an oil spill; I sang pretty good and did figures in my head and I could make a candle out of damn near anything. People wanted to marry me here and there but I didn't want to marry them back so they thought I was stuck up. Who wouldn't want to get hitched to handsome Candyland Ocampo and ditch Candle Hole for a clean, fresh life in Soapthorpe where bubbles popped all day long like diamonds in your hair? Well, I didn't, because he had never kissed me with a gas mask on and he smelled like pine fresh cleaning solutions and not like scorched ozone at all.

Life and Time turned into little kids right in front of us. They giggled and whispered and Mum washed her hair in the sea about nine times and then soaked it in oil until it shone. Papa tucked a candle stump that had melted just right and looked like a perfect rose into her big no fancy hairdo and then, like it was a completely normal thing to do, put on a cloak sewn out of about a hundred different neckties. They looked like a prince and a princess.

"Brighton Pier came last when I was a girl, before I even had my name," Time told us, still giggling and blushing like she wasn't anyone's mother. "It's the most wonderful thing that can ever happen in the world."

"If God turned up for supper and brought all the dry land back for dessert, it wouldn't be half as good as one day on Brighton Pier," Life crowed. He picked me up in his arms and twirled me around in the air. He'd never done that before, not once, and he had his heart strapped on so tight he didn't even stop and realize what he'd done and go vacant-eyed and find something else to look at for a long while. He just squeezed me and kissed me like I came from somewhere and I didn't know what the hell a Brighton Pier was but I loved it already.

"What is it? What is it?" Maruchan and I squealed, because you can catch happiness like a plague.

"It's better the first time if you don't know," Mum assured us. "It's meant to dock in Electric City on Friday."

"So it's a ship, then?" Maruchan said. But Papa just twinkled his eyes at us and put his finger over his lips to keep the secret in.

The Pier meant to dock in Electric City. My heart fell into my stomach, got all digested up, and sizzled out into the rest of me all at once. Of course, of course it would, Electric City had the best docks, the sturdiest, the prettiest. But it seemed to me like life was happening to me on purpose, and Electric City couldn't keep a darkgirl out anymore. They had to share like the rest of us.

"What do you want to be when you grow up, Maruchan?" I said to my twin in the dark the night before we set off to see what was better than God. Maruchan's eyes gleamed with the Christmas thrill of it all.

"Brighton Pier," he whispered.

"Me, too," I sighed, and we both dreamed we were beautiful Fuckwits running through a forest of real pines, laughing and stopping to eat apples and running again and only right before we woke up did we notice that something was chasing us, something huge and electric and bound for London-town.

8. CITIZENS OF MUTATION NATION

I LOOKED FOR Goodnight Moon everywhere from the moment we crossed into Electric City. The fence had gone and Garbagetown poured in and nothing was different than it had been when I got my name off the battery spires, even though the sign had said for so long that Electric City was renovating. I played a terrible game with every person that shoved past, every face in a window, every shadow juddering down an alley and the game was: *are you him?* But I lost all the hands. The only time I stopped playing was when I first saw Brighton Pier.

I couldn't get my eyes around it. It was a terrible, gorgeous whale of light and colors and music and otherness. All along a boardwalk jugglers danced and singers sang and horns horned and accordions squeezed and under it all some demonic engine screamed and wheezed. Great glass domes and towers and flags and tents glowed in the sunset but Brighton Pier made the sunset look plain-faced and unloveable. A huge wheel full of pink and emerald electric lights turned slowly in the warm wind but went nowhere. People leapt and turned somersaults and stood on each other's shoulders and they all wore such soft, vivid costumes, like they'd all been cut out of a picturebook too fine for anyone like me to read. The tumblers lashed the pier to the Electric City docks and cut the engines and after that it was nothing but music so thick and good you could eat it out of the air.

Life and Time hugged Maruchan and cheered with the rest of Garbagetown. Tears ran down their faces. Everyone's faces.

"When the ice melted and the rivers revolted and the Fuckwit world went under the seas," Papa whispered through his weeping, "a great mob hacked Brighton Pier off of Brighton and strapped engines to it and set sail across the blue. They've been going ever since. They go around the world and around again, to the places where there's still people, and trade their beauty for food and fuel. There's a place on Brighton Pier where if you look just right, it's like nothing ever drowned."

A beautiful man wearing a hat of every color and several bells stepped up on a pedestal and held a long pale cone to his mouth. The mayor of Electric City embraced him with two meaty arms and asked his terrible, stupid, unforgivable question: "Have you seen dry land?"

And the beautiful man answered him: "With my own eyes."

A roar went up like angels dying. I covered my ears. The mayor covered his mouth with his hands, speechless, weeping. The beautiful man patted him awkwardly on the back. Then he turned to us.

"Hello, Garbagetown!" he cried out and his voice sounded like everyone's most secret heart.

We screamed so loud every bird in Garbagetown fled to the heavens and we clapped like mad and some people fell onto the ground and buried their face in old batteries.

"My name is Emperor William Shakespeare the Eleventh and I am the Master of Brighton Pier! We will be performing *Twelfth Night* in the great stage tonight at seven o'clock, followed by *The Duchess of Malfi* at ten (which has werewolves) and a midnight acrobatic display! Come one, come all! Let Madame Limelight tell your FORTUNE! TEST your strength with the Hammer of the Witches! SEE the wonders of the Fuckwit World in our Memory Palace! Get letters and news from the LAST HUMAN OUTPOSTS around the globe! GASP at the citizens of Mutation Nation in the Freak Tent! Sample a FULL MINUTE of real television, still high definition after all these years! Concerts begin in the Crystal Courtyard in fifteen minutes! Our Peep Shows feature only the FINEST actresses reading aloud from GENUINE Fuckwit historical records! Garbagetown, we are here to DAZZLE you!"

A groan went up from the crowds like each Garbagetowner was just then bedding their own great lost love and they heaved toward the lights, the colors, the horns and the voices, the silk and the electricity and the life floating down there, knotted to the edge of our little pile of trash.

Someone grabbed my hand and held me back while my parents, my twin, my world streamed away from me down to the Pier. No one looked back.

"Are you her?" said Goodnight Moon. He looked longer and leaner but not really older. He had on his tie.

"Yes," I said, and nothing was different than it had been when I got my name except now neither of us had masks and our kisses weren't like gentle elephants but like a boy and a girl and I forgot all about my strength and my fortune and the wonderful wheel of light turning around and around and going nowhere.

9. TERRORWHORE

ACTORS ARE LIARS. Writers, too. The whole lot of them, even the horn players and the fortune tellers and the freaks and the strongmen. Even the ladies with rings in their noses and high heels on their feet playing violins all along the pier and the lie they are all singing and dancing and saying is: *we can get the old world back again.*

My door said TERRORWHORE this morning. I looked after my potato plants and my hibiscus and thought about whether or not I would ever get to have sex again. Seemed unlikely. Big Bargains concurred.

Goodnight Moon and I lost our virginities in the Peep Show tent while a lady in green fishnet stockings and a lavender garter read to us from the dinner menu of the Dorchester Hotel circa 2005.

"Whole Berkshire roasted chicken stuffed with black truffles, walnuts, duck confit, and dauphinoise potatoes," the lady purred. Goodnight Moon devoured my throat with kisses, bites, need. "Drizzled with a balsamic reduction and rosemary honey."

"What's honey?" I gasped. We could see her but she couldn't see us, which was for the best. The glass in the window only went one way.

"Beats me, kid," she shrugged, re-crossing her legs the other way. "Something you drizzle." She went on. "Sticky toffee pudding with lashings of cream and salted caramel, passionfruit soufflé topped with orbs of pistachio ice cream..."

Goodnight Moon smelled just as I remembered. Scorched ozone and metal and paraffin and hope and when he was inside me it was like hearing my name for the first time. I couldn't escape the *me*-ness of it, the *us*-ness of it, the sound and the shape of ourselves turning into our future.

"I can't believe you're here," he whispered into my breast. "I can't believe this is us."

The lady's voice drifted over my head. "Lamb cutlets on a bed of spiced butternut squash, wilted greens, and delicate hand-harvested mushrooms served with goat cheese in clouds of pastry..."

Goodnight Moon kissed my hair, my ears, my eyelids. "And now that the land's come back Electric City's gonna save us all. We can go home together, you and me, and build a house and we'll have a candle in every window so you always feel at home…"

The Dorchester dinner menu stopped abruptly. The lady dropped to her fishnetted knees and peered at us through the glass, her brilliant glossy red hair tumbling down, her spangled eyes searching for us beyond the glass.

"Whoa, sweetie, slow down," she said. "You're liable to scare a girl off that way."

All I could see in the world was Goodnight Moon's brown eyes and the sweat drying on his brown chest. Brown like the earth and all its promises. "I don't care," he said. "You scared, Tetley?" I shook my head. "Nothing can scare us now. Emperor Shakespeare said he's seen land, real dry land, and we have a plan and we're gonna get everything back again and be fat happy Fuckwits like we were always supposed to be."

The Peep Show girl's glittering eyes filled up with tears. She put her hand on the glass. "Oh… oh, baby… that's just something we say. We always say it. To everyone. It's our best show. Gives people hope, you know? But there's nothing out there, sugar. Nothing but ocean and more ocean and a handful of drifty lifeboat cities like yours circling the world like horses on a broken-down carousel. Nothing but blue."

10. WE ARE SO LUCKY

IT WOULD BE nice for me if you could just say you understand. I want to hear that just once. Goodnight Moon didn't. He didn't believe her and he didn't believe me and he sold me out in the end in spite of gas masks and kissing and Madeline Brix and the man crooning in our ears that he was happy because all he could hear was Emperor William Shakespeare the Eleventh singing out his big lie. RESURRECTION! REDEMPTION! REVIVIFICATION! LAND HO!

"No, because, see," my sweetheart wept on the boardwalk while the wheel spun dizzily behind his head like an electric candy crown, "we have a plan. We've worked so hard. It *has* to happen. The mayor said as soon as we had news of dry land, the minute we knew, we'd turn it on and we'd get there first and the continents would be ours, Garbagetowners, we'd inherit the Earth. He's gonna tell everyone when the Pier leaves. At the farewell party."

"Turn what on?"

Resurrection. Redemption. Renovation. All those years behind the fence Electric City had been so busy. Disassembling all those engines they hoarded so they could make a bigger one, the biggest one. Pooling fuel in great vast stills. Practicing ignition sequences. Carving up a countryside they'd never even seen between the brightboys and brightgirls and we could have some, too, if we were good.

"You want to turn Garbagetown into a Misery Boat," I told him. "So we can just steam on ahead into nothing and go mad and use up all the gas and batteries that could keep us happy in mixtapes for another century here in one hot minute."

"The Emperor said..."

"He said his name was Duke Orsino of Illyria, too. And then Roderigo when they did the werewolf play. Do you believe that? If they'd found land, don't you think they'd have stayed there?"

But he couldn't hear me. Neither could Maruchan when I tried to tell him the truth in the Peep Show. All they could see was green. Green leafy trees and green grass and green ivy in some park that was lying at the bottom of the sea. We dreamed different dreams now, my brother and I, and all my dreams were burning.

Say you understand. I had to. I'm not a nihilist or a murdercunt or a terrorwhore. They were gonna use up every last drop of Garbagetown's power to go nowhere and do nothing and instead of measuring out teaspoons of good, honest gas, so that it lasts and we last all together, no single thing on the patch would ever turn on again, and we'd go dark, *really* dark, forever. Dark like the bottom of a hole. They had no right. *They* don't understand. This is *it*. This is the future. Garbagetown and the sea. We can't go back, not ever, not even for a minute. We are so lucky. Life is so good. We're going on and being alive and being shitty sometimes and lovely sometimes just the same as we always have, and only a Fuckwit couldn't see that.

I waited until Brighton Pier cast off, headed to the next rickety harbor of floating foolboats, filled with players and horns and glittering wheels and Dorchester menus and fresh mountains of letters we wouldn't read the answers to for another twenty years. I waited until everyone was sleeping so nobody would get hurt except the awful engine growling and panting to deliver us into the dark salt nothing of an empty hellpromise.

It isn't hard to build a bomb in Electric City. It's all just laying around behind that fence where a boy held my hand for the first time. All you need is a match.

11. WHAT YOU CAME FOR

IT'S SUCH A beautiful day out. My hibiscus is just gigantic, red as the hair on a peep show dancer. If you want to wait, Big Bargains will be round later for her afternoon nap. Grape Crush usually brings a herring by in the evening. But I understand if you've got other places to be.

It's okay. You can hit me now. If you want to. It's what you came for. I barely feel it anymore.

Thank you for my instruction.

ABOUT THE AUTHORS

· NINA ALLAN ·

Nina Allan's (www.ninaallan.co.uk) fiction has appeared in a wide variety of venues, including *The Year's Best SF and Fantasy 2014*, *The Year's Top Ten Tales of Science Fiction 7*, and *Solaris Rising 3*. Her first novel *The Race*, set in an alternate future Britain, has issues of environmental degradation running through its heart. It was shortlisted for the BSFA Award, the John W. Campbell Memorial Award and the Kitschies Red Tentacle. "The Common Tongue, the Present Tense, The Known" is a loose sequel to the story 'Microcosmos', which originally appeared in *Interzone* in 2009. Nina lives and works in rural North Devon. Her second novel *The Rift* is due in 2017.

· CHARLIE JANE ANDERS ·

Charlie Jane Anders (allthebirdsinthesky.tumblr.com) is the author of *All the Birds in the Sky*, which was an *L.A. Times* Bestseller. Her stories have appeared in *Asimov's Science Fiction*, *The Magazine of Fantasy & Science Fiction*, *Tor.com*,

Lightspeed, TinHouse, ZYZZYVA, McSweeney's Internet Tendency and several anthologies. She's won a Hugo Award, a Lambda Literary Award, and the Emperor Norton Award for "extraordinary invention and creativity unhindered by the constraints of paltry reason."

· JEFFREY FORD ·

Jeffrey Ford (www.well-builtcity.com) is the author of the novels *The Shadow Year, The Physiognomy, The Girl in the Glass* and *The Portrait of Mrs. Charbuque.* His story collections are *The Fantasy Writer's Assistant, The Empire of Ice Cream, The Drowned Life,* and *Crackpot Palace.* His new collection, *A Natural History of Hell* will be released by Small Beer Press in July 2016.

· KATHLEEN ANN GOONAN ·

Kathleen Ann Goonan (www.goonan.com) lives on a tiny subtropical island a foot above sea level in a thrice-flooded house, where she occasionally, and ever more rarely, glimpses endangered creatures of the sea, land, and air. Three times a Nebula finalist, her first novel, *Queen City Jazz,* was a *New York Times* notable book, and *In War Times,* her sixth, was the American Library Association's Best Science Fiction Novel of 2008 and won the John W. Campbell Memorial Award. *This Shared Dream,* her latest novel will be released as a mass market paperback in October 2016. She recently completed an *Evoke* game narrative focusing on international literacy, is a Professor of the Practice of Science Fiction and Creative Writing at Georgia Institute of Technology Atlanta, and has published over fifty short works of science fiction. She is presently working on two novels, a film script, and assembling her second short fiction collection.

· NALO HOPKINSON ·

Nalo Hopkinson (www.nalohopkinson.com), born in Jamaica, has lived in Jamaica, Trinidad, Guyana, and now teaches creative writing at the University of California Riverside in the United States. She is the author of six novels, two short story collections, and a chapbook including *Brown Girl in the Ring*, *Midnight Robber*, *The Salt Roads*, *The New Moon's Arms*, *The Chaos*, and *Sister Mine*. She edited anthologies *Whispers from the Cotton Tree Root: Caribbean Fabulist Fiction*, and *Mojo: Conjure Stories*. She is a recipient of the John W. Campbell Award for Best New Writer, the Locus Award for Best New Writer, the World Fantasy Award, the Sunburst Award (twice), the Aurora Award, the Gaylactic Spectrum Award, and the Norton Award. Her most recent book is collection, *Falling in Love with Hominids*.

· KEN LIU ·

Ken Liu (http://kenliu.name) is an author and translator of speculative fiction, as well as a lawyer and programmer. A winner of the Nebula, Hugo, and World Fantasy Awards, he has been published in *The Magazine of Fantasy & Science Fiction*, *Asimov's*, *Analog*, *Clarkesworld*, *Lightspeed*, and *Strange Horizons*, among other places. He also translated the Hugo-winning novel, *The Three-Body Problem*, by Liu Cixin. Ken's debut novel, *The Grace of Kings*, the first in a silkpunk epic fantasy, is a finalist for the Nebula Award. Sequel *The Wall of Storms* is due later this year. His debut short story collection in English, *The Paper Menagerie and Other Stories*, was published in March 2016. He lives with his family near Boston, Massachusetts.

· PAUL MCAULEY ·

Paul McAuley (unlikelyworlds.blogspot.com) is the author of more than twenty novels, several collections of short stories, and a BFI Film Classic monograph on Terry Gilliam's film *Brazil*. His fiction has won the Philip K. Dick Memorial Award, the Arthur C. Clarke Award, the John W Campbell Memorial Award, the Sidewise Award, the British Fantasy Award and the Theodore Sturgeon Memorial Award. His most recent book is novel *Into Everywhere*. He is currently working on a novel, *Austral*, set in the forests and fjords of the Antarctic Peninsula, and lives in North London, just 46 metres above sea level.

· SAM J. MILLER ·

Sam J. Miller is a writer and a community organizer. His fiction is in *Lightspeed, Asimov's, Clarkesworld*, and *The Minnesota Review*, among others. He is a nominee for the Nebula and Theodore Sturgeon Awards, a winner of the Shirley Jackson Award, and a graduate of the Clarion Writer's Workshop. His debut novel *The Art of Starving* is forthcoming from HarperCollins. He lives in New York City, and at www.samjmiller.com

· JAMES MORROW ·

Born in 1947, **James Morrow** (jamesmorrow.info) has been writing fiction ever since, as a seven-year-old living in the Philadelphia suburbs, he dictated "The Story of the Dog Family" to his mother, who dutifully typed it up and bound the pages with yarn. This three-page, six-chapter fantasy is still in the author's private archives. Upon reaching adulthood, Morrow continued making fiction, eventually producing ten novels, most of them in theological-satirical mode. He has won the World Fantasy Award twice (for *Only Begotten Daughter* and *Towing Jehovah*), the Nebula Award twice (for "The Deluge" and the novella *City of Truth*), and the Theodore Sturgeon Memorial Award once (for the novella *Shambling Towards Hiroshima*). In recent years Morrow has taken to writing historical fiction informed by a fantastika sensibility, including *The Last Witchfinder* (dramatizing the birth of the Enlightenment), *Galápagos Regained* (about the coming of the Darwinian worldview), and a novel-in-progress centered on the A.D. 325 Council of Nicaea. A story collection, *Reality by Other Means: the Best Short Fiction of James Morrow*, appeared last year from Wesleyan University Press. He makes his home in State College, Pennsylvania, with his wife, an enigmatic sheepdog, and a loopy beagle.

· KIM STANLEY ROBINSON ·

Kim Stanley Robinson is a winner of the Hugo, Nebula, and Locus Awards. He is the author of seventeen novels and five collections of short fiction. His books include the bestselling Mars trilogy and the critically acclaimed *Forty Signs of Rain, Fifty Degrees Below, Sixty Days and Counting, The Years of Rice and Salt, Antarctica*, and *2312*. In 2008, he was named a 'Hero of the Environment' by *Time* magazine, and he recently joined in the Sequoia Parks Foundation's Artists in the Back Country program. His most recent books are major new novel

Aurora and *Green Earth*, a revised omnibus of the 'Science in the Capital' books. He lives in Davis, California with his wife of more than 30 years, environmental chemist Lisa Howland Nowell, and their two sons.

· CHRISTOPHER ROWE ·

Christopher Rowe (www.christopherowe.net) has published more than twenty short stories, and has been a finalist for the Hugo, Nebula, World Fantasy, and Theodore Sturgeon Awards. Frequently reprinted, his work has been translated into a half-dozen languages around the world, and has been praised by the *New York Times Book Review*. His story "Another Word For Map is Faith" made the long list in the 2007 Best American Short Stories volume, and his early fiction was collected in a chapbook, *Bittersweet Creek and Other Stories*, by Small Beer Press. His Forgotten Realms novel, *Sandstorm*, was published in 2010 by Wizards of the Coast. He holds an MFA in writing at the Bluegrass Writers Studio of Eastern Kentucky University and is hard at work on *Sarah Across America*, a new novel about maps, megafauna, and other obsessions. His first short story collection is due from Small Beer Press next year. He lives in a hundred-year-old house in Lexington, Kentucky, with his wife, novelist Gwenda Bond, and their pets.

· RACHEL SWIRSKY ·

Rachel Swirsky (www.rachelswirsky.com) holds an MFA from the Iowa Writers Workshop. Her short fiction has been published in numerous magazines and anthologies including *Tor.com*, *Subterranean Online*, and *Clarkesworld Magazine*. It has also been nominated for the Hugo Award, the World Fantasy Award, and the Locus Award, and won the Nebula Award twice. Her second collection, *How the World Became Quiet: Myths of the Past, Present and Future*, came out from Subterranean Press in 2013. She had a book of illustrated ballet stories as a child from which she learned about Coppelia, but alas her attempts to perform ballet were stymied by her lack of grace.

· LAVIE TIDHAR ·

Lavie Tidhar (lavietidhar.wordpress.com) grew up on a kibbutz in Israel and has since lived in South Africa, the UK, Vanuatu and Laos. He is the author of six novels including World Fantasy Award winner *Osama*, *Martian Sands*, *The Bookman Trilogy*, and *The Violent Century*. Tidhar has published more than 130 short stories, including linked short story collection *Hebrewpunk*, and edited *The Apex Book of World SF* anthologies. His most recent books are novel *A Man Lies Dreaming* and the collection *Central Station*.

· CATHERYNNE M. VALENTE ·

Catherynne M. Valente (www.catherynnemvalente.com) is the *New York Times* bestselling author of over two dozen works of fiction and poetry, including *Palimpsest*, the Orphan's Tales series, *Deathless*, *Radiance*, and the crowdfunded phenomenon *The Girl Who Circumnavigated Fairyland in a Ship of Her Own Making*. She is the winner of the Andre Norton, Tiptree, Mythopoeic, Rhysling, Lambda, Locus, and Hugo Awards. She has been a finalist for the Nebula and World Fantasy Awards. She lives on an island off the coast of Maine with a small but growing menagerie of beasts, some of which are human.

· SEAN WILLIAMS ·

Sean Williams (www.seanwilliams.com) is an award-winning, #1 *New York Times*-bestselling author of over forty novels and one hundred stories, including some set in the *Star Wars* and *Doctor Who* universes, and some written with Garth Nix. His latest is *Hollowgirl*, the concluding volume of his Twinmaker trilogy. He lives up the road from Australia's finest chocolate factory with his family and a pet plastic fish.

"ONE OF THE MOST RESPECTED EDITORS IN THE GENRE."
NEW YORK TIMES BEST-SELLING AUTHOR SEAN WILLIAMS

FOURTEEN NEW
STORIES BY:
CHARLES STROSS
GWYNETH JONES
JOHN BARNES
PETER WATTS
KRISTINE KATHRYN RUSCH
KARL SCHROEDER
STEPHEN BAXTER
ROBERT REED
HANNU RAJANIEMI
KATHLEEN ANN GOONAN
GREGORY BENFORD
DAMIEN BRODERICK
& BARBARA LAMAR
JOHN C. WRIGHT
DAVID MOLES

ENGINEERING INFINITY

EDITED BY JONATHAN STRAHAN

The universe shifts and changes: suddenly you understand, you get it, and are filled with wonder. That moment of understanding drives the greatest science-fiction stories and lies at the heart of Engineering Infinity. Whether it's coming up hard against the speed of light – and, with it, the enormity of the universe – realising that terraforming a distant world is harder and more dangerous than you'd ever thought, or simply realizing that a hitchhiker on a starship consumes fuel and oxygen with tragic results, it's hard science-fiction where a sense of discovery is most often found and where science-fiction's true heart lies.

This exciting and innovative science-fiction anthology collects together stories by some of the biggest names in the field, including Gwyneth Jones, Stephen Baxter and Charles Stross.

"Engineering Infinity is a brilliant concept from the title onwards, and brings the good old sense of wonder back to SF." - *Eric Brown*

US ISBN: 978-1-907519-52-9 // UK ISBN: 978-1-907519-51-2

FEATURING STORIES BY **KEN MACLEOD** • **PAT CADIGAN** • **ELLEN KLAGES**
ALASTAIR REYNOLDS • **KAREN LORD** • **GREG EGAN** • **LINDA NAGATA**
ADAM ROBERTS • **HANNU RAJANIEMI** • **ALIETTE DE BODARD** AND MORE

REACH FOR INFINITY

EDITED BY **JONATHAN STRAHAN**

"One of the most respected editors in the genre."

What happens when we reach out into the vastness of space?

What hope for us amongst the stars?

Multi-award winning editor Jonathan Strahan brings us fourteen new tales of the future, from some of the finest science fiction writers in the field.

The fourteen startling stories in this anthology feature the work of Greg Egan, Aliette de Bodard, Ian McDonald, Karl Schroeder, Pat Cadigan, Karen Lord, Ellen Klages, Adam Roberts, Linda Nagata, Hannu Rajaniemi, Kathleen Ann Goonan, Ken MacLeod, Alastair Reynolds and Peter Watts.

"A strong collection of stories that readers of science fiction will certainly enjoy."
Locus Magazine on Engineering Infinity

US ISBN: 978-1-78108-203-4 // UK ISBN: 978-1-78108-202-7

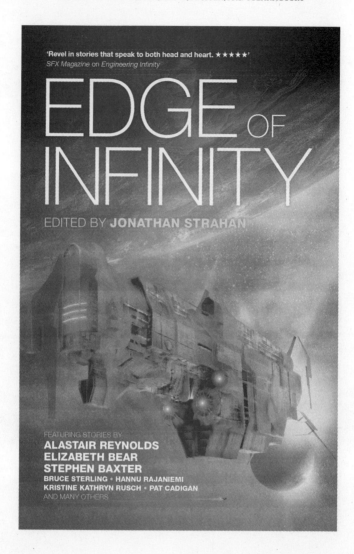

'Revel in stories that speak to both head and heart. ★★★★★'
SFX Magazine on Engineering Infinity

EDGE OF INFINITY

EDITED BY JONATHAN STRAHAN

FEATURING STORIES BY
ALASTAIR REYNOLDS
ELIZABETH BEAR
STEPHEN BAXTER
BRUCE STERLING • HANNU RAJANIEMI
KRISTINE KATHRYN RUSCH • PAT CADIGAN
AND MANY OTHERS

Those were Neil Armstrong's immortal words when he became the first human being to step onto another world. All at once, the horizon expanded; the human race was no longer Earthbound.

Edge of Infinity is an exhilarating new SF anthology that looks at the next giant leap for humankind: the leap from our home world out into the Solar System. From the eerie transformations in Pat Cadigan's "The Girl-Thing Who Went Out for Sushi" to the frontier spirit of Sandra McDonald and Stephen D. Covey's "The Road to NPS," and from the grandiose vision of Alastair Reynolds' "Vainglory" to the workaday familiarity of Kristine Kathryn Rusch's "Safety Tests," the thirteen stories in this anthology span the whole of the human condition in their race to colonise Earth's nearest neighbours.

Featuring stories by Hannu Rajaniemi, Alastair Reynolds, James S. A. Corey, John Barnes, Stephen Baxter, Kristine Kathryn Rusch, Elizabeth Bear, Pat Cadigan, Gwyneth Jones, Paul McAuley, Sandra McDonald, Stephen D. Covey, An Owomoyela, and Bruce Sterling, Edge of Infinity is hard SF adventure at its best and most exhilarating.

US ISBN: 978-1-78108-056-6 // UK ISBN: 978-1-78108-055-9

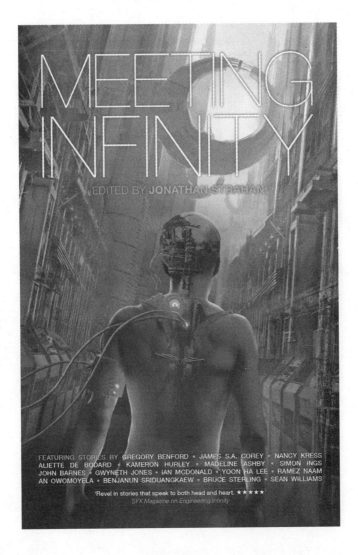

The world is rapidly changing. We surf future-shock every day, as the progress of technology races ever on. Increasingly we are asking: how do we change to live in the world to come? Whether it's climate change, inundated coastlines and drowned cities; the cramped confines of a tin can hurtling through space to the outer reaches of our Solar System; or the rush of being uploaded into cyberspace, our minds and bodies are going to have to drastically alter.

Multi-award winning editor Jonathan Strahan brings us another incredible volume in his much praised science-fiction anthology series, featuring stories by Madeline Ashby, John Barnes, James S.A. Corey, Gregory Benford, Benjanun Sriduangkaew, Simon Ings, Kameron Hurley, Nancy Kress, Gwyneth Jones, Yoon Ha Lee, Bruce Sterling, Sean Williams, Aliette de Bodard, Ramez Naam, An Owomoyela and Ian McDonald.

"One of the year's most exciting anthologies." *io9 on Edge of Infinity*

US ISBN: 978-1-78108-380-2 // UK ISBN: 978-1-78108-379-6

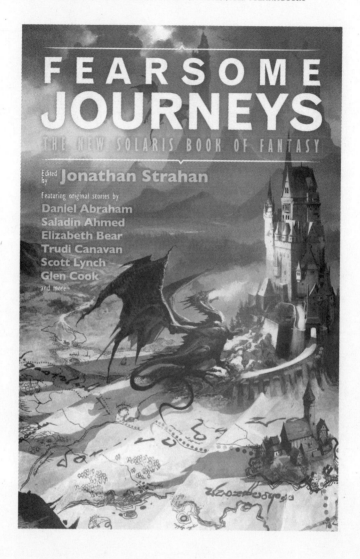

How do you encompass all the worlds of the imagination? Within fantasy's scope lies every possible impossibility, from dragons to spirits, from magic to gods, and from the unliving to the undying.

In Fearsome Journeys, master anthologist Jonathan Strahan sets out on a quest to find the very limits of the unlimited, collecting twelve brand new stories by some of the most popular and exciting names in epic fantasy from around the world.

With original fiction from Scott Lynch, Saladin Ahmed, Trudi Canavan, K J Parker, Kate Elliott, Jeffrey Ford, Robert V S Redick, Ellen Klages, Glen Cook, Elizabeth Bear, Ellen Kushner, Ysabeau S. Wilce and Daniel Abraham Fearsome Journeys explores the whole range of the fantastic.

US ISBN: 978-1-78108-118-1 // UK ISBN: 978-1-78108-119-8

From sorcerous bridges that link worlds to the simple traditions of country folk; from the mysterious natures of twins to the dangerous powers of obligation and contract. Laden with perils for both the adventurous and the unsuspecting, magic is ultimately a contradiction: endlessly powerful but never without consequence, and rigidly defined by rules of its own making. Award-winning Jonathan Strahan brings together some of the most exciting and popular writers working in fantasy today to dig into that contradiction, and present you with the strange, the daunting, the mathematical, the unpredictable, the deceptive and above all the fearsome world of magic.

Includes stories by Garth Nix, K J Parker, Tony Ballantyne, James Bradley, Isobelle Carmody, Frances Hardinge, Nina Kiriki Hoffman, Ellen Klages, Justina Robson, Christopher Rowe, Robert Shearman, Karin Tidbeck, Genevieve Valentine and Kaaron Warren.

US ISBN: 978-1-78108-213-3 // UK ISBN: 978-1-78108-212-6

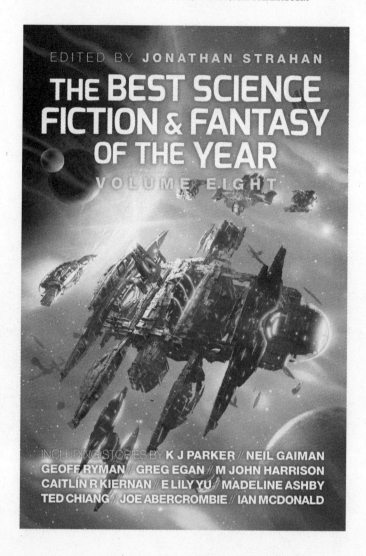

EDITED BY JONATHAN STRAHAN

THE BEST SCIENCE FICTION & FANTASY OF THE YEAR

VOLUME EIGHT

INCLUDING STORIES BY K J PARKER // NEIL GAIMAN
GEOFF RYMAN // GREG EGAN // M JOHN HARRISON
CAITLÍN R KIERNAN // E LILY YU // MADELINE ASHBY
TED CHIANG // JOE ABERCROMBIE // IAN MCDONALD

From the inner realms of humanity to the far reaches of space, these are the science fiction and fantasy tales that are shaping the genre and the way we think about the future. Multi-award winning editor Jonathan Strahan continues to shine a light on the very best writing, featuring both established authors and exciting new talents.

Within you will find twenty-eight incredible tales, showing the ever growing depth and diversity that science fiction and fantasy continues to enjoy. These are the brightest stars in our firmament, lighting the way to a future filled with astonishing stories about the way we are, and the way we could be.

US ISBN: 978-1-78108-216-4 // UK ISBN: 978-1-78108-215-7

EDITED BY **JONATHAN STRAHAN**

THE BEST SCIENCE FICTION & FANTASY OF THE YEAR

VOLUME NINE

FEATURING STORIES BY
**LAUREN BEUKES
PAOLO BACIGALUPI
JOE ABERCROMBIE
K. J. PARKER
KEN LIU
GARTH NIX
ELIZABETH BEAR
KAI ASHANTE WILSON
RACHEL SWIRSKY
CAITLÍN R. KIERNAN
GENEVIEVE VALENTINE**
AND MANY MORE

Science fiction and fantasy has never been more diverse or vibrant, and 2014 has provided a bountiful crop of extraordinary stories. These stories are about the future, worlds beyond our own, the realms of our imaginations and dreams but, more importantly, they are the stories of ourselves. Featuring best-selling writers and emerging talents, here are some of the most exciting genre writers working today.

Multi-award winning editor Jonathan Strahan once again brings you the best stories from the past year. Within you will find twenty-eight amazing tales from authors across the globe, displaying why science fiction and fantasy are genres increasingly relevant to our turbulent world.

US ISBN: 978-1-78108-309-3 // UK ISBN: 978-1-78108-308-6

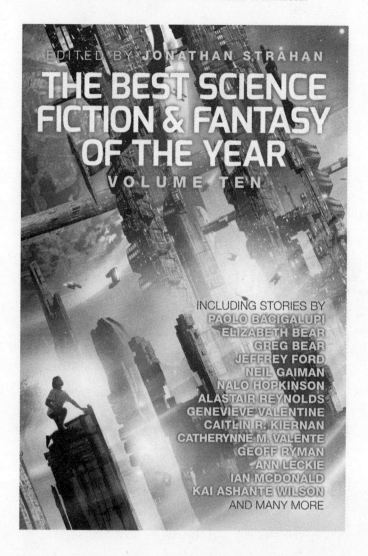

Jonathan Strahan, the award-winning and much lauded editor of many of genre's best known anthologies, is back with his tenth volume in this fascinating series, featuring the best science fiction and fantasy from 2015. With established names and new talent, this diverse and ground-breaking collection will take the reader to the outer reaches of space and the inner realms of humanity with stories of fantastical worlds and worlds that may still come to pass.

FEATURING: Neil Gaiman // Elizabeth Bear // Greg Bear // Geoff Ryman // Ann Leckie // Jeffrey Ford Nalo Hopkinson // Nisi Shawl // Ian McDonald // Paolo Bacigalupi // Alyssa Wong // Kelly Link // Alastair Reynolds Tamsyn Muir // Simon Ings Gwyneth Jones // Usman T. MaLik // Nike Sulway // Caitlín R. Kiernan // Robert Reed Kelly Robson // Catherynne M. Valente // Kim Stanley Robinson // Genevieve Valentine // Vonda N. McIntrye Sam J. Miller // Kai Ashante Wilson

US ISBN: 978-1-78108-437-3 // UK ISBN: 978-1-78108-436-6